"I'll show won't forge

"Don't." Natali avoiding Demit. .... Please don't touch me. I have to face people when I leave here, and—"

"You don't want to go back there obviously aroused?" he challenged, needing to hear it—to see it in the helpless flush and the disconcerted casting of her gaze around the room before she brought it back to his, her eyes deeply shadowed with painful desire.

He pressed his hand flat to the door beside her head, leaning close enough to smell the warm peach scent of her skin, aching for the graze of her rising breasts against his chest. Below his belt, a heavy rush of blood pulled him tight.

Flustered and anxious, she still managed to send a coy glance south. Her body arched ever so slightly and she brushed against him. She released a powerless whimper on a sobbing, "Yes…"

"I want you very badly, Natalie. Not after five o'clock. Now," he told her, willing her to fall in with his demands. To let him bend her over the desk and take both of them where they were screaming with agony to go.

Canadian **Dani Collins** knew in high school that she wanted to write romance for a living. Twenty-five years later, after marrying her high school sweetheart, having two kids with him, working several generic office jobs and submitting countless manuscripts, she got 'The Call'. Her first Mills & Boon® Modern™ Romance won the Reviewers' Choice Award for Best First In Series from *RT Book Reviews*. She now works in her own office, writing romance.

Books by Dani Collins

Mills & Boon® Modern™ Romance

The Russian's Acquisition
An Heir to Bind Them
A Debt Paid in Passion
More than a Convenient Marriage?
No Longer Forbidden?

Seven Sexy Sins

The Sheikh's Sinful Seduction

The 21st Century Gentleman's Club

The Ultimate Seduction

One Night With Consequences

Proof of Their Sin

**Visit the author profile page at
www.millsandboon.co.uk for more titles**

SEDUCED
INTO THE
GREEK'S WORLD

BY
DANI COLLINS

Published in Great Britain 2015
by Mills & Boon, an imprint of Harlequin (UK) Limited,
Eton House, 18-24 Paradise Road, Richmond, Surrey, TW9 1SR

© 2015 Dani Collins

ISBN: 978-0-263-25066-4

SEDUCED
INTO THE
GREEK'S WORLD

To Cobe and Madison, who aren't with me
nearly enough, but were when I was writing this book.
xoxo Dani

CHAPTER ONE

HER LAUGH WAS so pure and spontaneous it caused Demitri Makricosta to look away from the Italian beauty flirting with him and seek out the source of the sound. As a connoisseur of fake laughter, often given to offering imitations himself, he found the naturalness of the woman's chuckle utterly engaging. It was feminine without being girlish or giggly, warm and sexy without being a put-on.

For a moment he didn't take in anything else but her. Short blond hair swung and fell as she tipped the precision cut backward. Her skin held a pale, translucent quality that made him think her cheek would feel cool but downy soft against his lips. He wondered how her skin smelled. Like summer fruit, maybe. Her profile was feminine and cute, right up to the tilt of her nose, while the rest of her was a study in mouthwatering curves.

Encased in a Makricosta uniform.

Damn, damn and damn.

The disappointment that flooded through him was surprisingly acute.

He took a more thorough tour of her uniform, wishing he didn't recognize it. It wasn't the pencil skirt and wispy red jacket over a bowed white top that the French staff wore here in Paris, which gave him a beat of hope. But if she'd been corporate, she'd have only a scarf or tie in company colors as part of her business ensemble.

Unfortunately, those long pants and the warm blazer

belonged to one of the Canadian outfits. The Makricosta Elite in Montreal, if he wasn't mistaken—and he shouldn't have any doubt because he had final say on every marketing decision in the family hotel chain right down to the front-line image of the staff.

He didn't *want* to recognize it. That was the problem. His male interest was seriously piqued by the woman wearing it.

Which wasn't like him. Women were fairly interchangeable for him. He never wondered, "Who is she? What's her story?" Especially when he already had a female hand resting on his cuff and a voice murmuring, "*Bello?* What is it?"

"I thought I recognized someone," he prevaricated, sending his companion a placating smile before glancing once more at the laughing woman—his employee—across the lobby.

She was nodding at someone, tucking her hair coquettishly behind her ear, saying something about email that he read on her lips as noise from different sources echoed across the foyer's marble floor and pillars.

Curious what kind of man was keeping that bright look on her face, Demitri leaned back on the velvet settee, losing the touch of his prospective afternoon delight as he did.

Gideon.

Shock went through him as he recognized his brother-in-law. Not that Gideon looked as though he was encouraging the woman, but Demitri still rose to his feet in brotherly indignation. His sister had been through a lot, especially a few years ago when Gideon's PA had intimated to Adara that she and Gideon were having an affair. Demitri wasn't going to sit here while some fresh tart made a play for Adara's husband.

"I do recognize him," he stated grimly. "Excuse me."

But Gideon and the blonde were already parting ways by the time he rounded the colonnade and approached.

The woman swung away with a brisk walk toward the front desk while Gideon glanced up in time to catch sight of Demitri. His expression hardened with determination.

That was when Demitri remembered he was avoiding the man.

"Good," Gideon stated as he approached. "I was going to find you before I left. Adara's birthday. You'll be there."

The eye to eye, man-to-man directive was annoying, but vaguely reassuring. Demitri liked seeing that Gideon was determined to make his wife happy. When that PA had set her sights on Gideon, Demitri had been on the verge of taking her for a tour himself to keep his sister's marriage intact. In the end, Gideon had salvaged his own marriage. He'd fired the woman before anything more than a few false and snarky claims had been made. Despite Adara's worries that Gideon was straying, in reality his devotion to her had never wavered and still appeared rock solid.

Which was good, Demitri supposed. He didn't wish any more strife on his sister than she'd already weathered, but she was so *annoyingly* happy. So determined to bring him into the fold of happily-ever-after she'd created for herself. The whole situation with his brothers and all their kids, the number of secrets kept from him… It grated in a way Demitri didn't like to dig into, so he slid his attention back to the blonde threatening his sister's happiness and latched on to ensuring she didn't try anything further with Gideon.

Better that than dealing with Gideon's demands.

"The date is in my calendar. I'll try to make it." Demitri dismissed him lightly.

Gideon folded his arms. His roots as a dock-rat sailor were visible in the piercing glint of his eyes. "Is there a reason you won't make it a priority?"

Given that Gideon had been part of the family for several years, Demitri didn't think he had to explain why these reunions Adara kept trying to organize were about as appealing to him as an impacted wisdom tooth.

"I'll do my best," he lied.

"Would you?" Gideon said flatly. The words *just for once* were silently tacked onto the end, loud and clear.

And here came Reason One why he had no desire to be around his family. *What are you doing with your life? Hold the baby. Isn't he adorable? When are you going to quit chasing skirts and settle down?*

Demitri mentally projected two words back at his brother-in-law, punctuated them with a tight smile before he walked away. Wasn't it enough that he had stepped up when Adara was pregnant? Hell, the only reason he'd gone into the family business was for her and Theo. Maybe he'd kept his own hours in the early years, but these days he showed up all the time, and kicked ass, if none of them had noticed. They could all play white picket fences with their new babies if they wanted to. He had zero interest in becoming a family man—and would make a terrible one—so they could all back the hell off.

Irritated, he glanced toward the Italian starlet watching him like a spaniel that had heard the car keys. As much as he would welcome the diversion of sex right now—lovemaking was his go-to coping strategy for any sort of tension—he was oddly disinterested in taking her upstairs. The blonde filled a bigger space in his mind, niggling at him.

Maybe she hadn't meant to cause this brief altercation with Gideon, but animosity toward her still bled into him like adrenaline. He wasn't so immature he couldn't figure out that he was blame shifting. Every time familial obligations tugged at him lately a wave of anger and rebellion came over him. Dark, miasmic thoughts sent him in search of self-destruction on one level or another.

Usually he subscribed to being a lover, not a fighter.

Forced himself to stay on the sane side of violence, too aware of the streak of it in his father. But nameless rage sat in him whenever he confronted the fact that his only real family, his brother and sister, the two people he trusted unequivocally, had kept him out of the loop on the existence of their eldest brother.

Had they not trusted him? Why had they cut him out like that? The betrayal sliced down the center of connection he felt toward them and pushed him out in the cold. If he didn't keep a lid on his emotions, his temper would mushroom out like a radiation cloud. It made for a lot of pressure. A cold, hard, dark feeling deep in his core that he refused to deconstruct, afraid of what he might find.

Instead, he channeled it into a wave of icy energy that carried him past the curious looks from the registration desk through to the administration offices, where he found the blonde Canadian in a chair cozily nudged up against the hotel manager's. The guy wasn't looking at where she pointed on the computer monitor. He was gazing down to where her breasts strained against the fabric of her shirt.

"I need to speak to you," Demitri said.

Natalie glanced up and felt the full impact of Demitri Makricosta, the youngest brother of the family that employed her. The one with the scandalously disreputable reputation. She'd seen him in person before, but always from a distance. Never like this, with his dark brown eyes pushing her back into her chair and then making a proprietary inspection of her buttons.

He was incredibly attractive. That fact was legendary across the hotel chain and impossible to ignore when he was barely ten feet away.

She tried comparing him to his older brother, Theo, who bore a resemblance but was more polished, kept a low profile and remembered every name and number he came across.

But there was no minimizing this man. All she could think was how Demitri was known for the wicked streak that was evident in his winged eyebrows and distant smile. Also for the women he picked up effortlessly, not to mention his utter disregard for little things like policies and procedures. Greek by birth but raised in America, he had a Mediterranean warmth to his skin tone under a shadow of stubble. He dressed like a citizen of the world in tailored pants and a suit vest buttoned over his shirt that accented his very fine shoulders and trim waist. He looked like the hottest of the 1920s gangsters.

Bad. He looked very, very bad. Full to the brim with sin.

She glanced up from taking him in and her gaze tangled with his. One of his superior brows went up in challenge of her checking him out. This was definitely a different kind of man from any she'd ever known. Sharp and far too knowing. How mortifying to be so obvious.

Decorum, Natalie. You're a mom.

Swallowing her discomfiture, she glanced at Monsieur Renault as she rose. A blush stung her cheeks.

"I'll go back to my office and you can call me when you're done. It's nice to meet you, Mr. Makricosta," she said as she approached the door, expecting him to move aside and give her a dismissive nod.

"It's you I want to talk to, Miss...?" He held out a hand.

Shock made her hesitate before she placed her hand in his and was jolted by the warm grip that enclosed hers. "Adams," she provided in a jagged, baffled voice. "Me? Are you sure?" Who did he think she was?

"I'm sure. Show me to your office." He released her and waved her into the hall.

Brushing past him and cooking in self-conscious warmth, she walked ahead of him down the narrow hall to her shared office. Her coworkers were away from their desks. That had been perfect at lunch when she'd connected with her daughter on one of her daily webcam calls. Zoey was having the time of her life with Grandma, not missing Natalie at all, which was a relief, but it still broke Natalie's heart. She'd shed a couple of tears after she'd disconnected, missing her girl dreadfully, and thankful for the privacy to do so. Now, however, her office mates' absence left an isolated mood in the small, musty-smelling room with its rain-blurred windows.

When he closed the door behind them, she felt as though all the oxygen was pulled out. "I'm not sure—?"

"Leave my brother-in-law alone," he said flatly.

"I— What?" The accusation was such a missile from the blue, she could only stare, insides flash-freezing. "Gideon? I mean, Mr. Vozaras?" she stammered.

"Gideon," he confirmed, but there was an underlying stealth to the word. As though he thought she was overstepping by using the man's name.

"What makes you think there's something going on between us?" She was so shocked she couldn't process how appalling the accusation was.

"I don't think there is. I know him and I know my sister, but I saw you flirting with him in the lobby, asking for his email. Back off or I'll have you fired."

"He showed me a photo of his son! The email is about work." Affront arrived, pushing into her face as a hot flush, straining her tone with the strident notes of the wrongly accused. "I don't go after married men! That's a disgusting thing to suggest. Especially when his wife was kind enough to give me this opportunity. That's the only reason he spoke to me at all. She asked him to pass along a message about a report she wants me to write. I said I hoped their son had got over his cold, and he showed me a photo of the boy after he'd found his way into the refrigerator."

The flicker of disdain that ticked in one of Demitri's

cheeks only infuriated her further, fueling her need to bring him down from his high horse.

"Who the hell are you to pass judgment anyway? Everything I've ever heard about your moral standards leaves me stunned and incredulous that you'd question mine."

That got his attention. His death glare gave her pause, but she was too outraged to stop.

"Oh, was that out of line? You don't think someone you only met seconds ago has the right to call you out? I thought rash personal comments were our special thing."

Okay, that did go too far. A hot blush flooded upward while she clenched her mouth shut. And folded her arms. And set her chin as she screwed up her courage to ask through her teeth, "*Are* you going to fire me?"

"For?" he prompted with a pithy look.

"Exactly," she shot out, unable to catch back the haughty response even though she was dying inside. She was so mad and embarrassed she couldn't even look at him. She liked this job. Needed it. The whole point in coming away on this assignment was to better her position in the organization. More compensation and responsibility translated to more stability and security for Zoey.

Yet here she was risking everything. What had possessed her to go off like that? Guilt? Because she'd secretly coveted Adara's doting husband, who so obviously loved his wife and child and supported them both in every possible way? Of course any woman would secretly wish she had that, but Natalie wasn't about to steal it to get it.

"What's your first name?" he asked.

"Natalie. Why?" She eyed him while keeping her face averted, half expecting him to pick up the phone to HR. Man, he was good-looking. And not the least bit ruffled. In fact, he almost looked as though he was laughing at her, which was so incensing she had to look away again.

"What are you doing here, Natalie? In Paris, I mean. What has Adara got you on? What's the special report?"

A chance to show off. Something she had imagined would help her take a step up the corporate ladder. So much for that. "I'm part of the software upgrade." It was hard to keep her voice steady as defensiveness and contrition pecked her. She kept it short. "I'm training the staff and working out the bugs. I've done Toulouse. I'm here in Paris for the week. Then I go to Lyon."

"You're an IT nerd?" His skepticism as he gave her another top-to-toe once-over was almost as irritating as the label.

"I wouldn't have guessed you're a marketing genius," she shot back, blithely matching his dismissive tone, thinking, *Stop it.* But he was so *infuriating.*

"A highly creative one," he assured smoothly. "Ask around. Although it sounds like you already have. You're doing all the hotels in Europe?"

"I—um, what?" That *creative* remark had thrown her, which had been his intention, she was sure. "No, I only have English and French and, um, can't be away longer than three weeks."

She and Zoey wouldn't starve if he fired her, she reminded herself. The knowledge calmed her nerves. She wouldn't even lose her house, and she always had the fall-back plan of moving in with her ex-mother-in-law, which would suit Zoey just fine because she loved the farm. She'd been beside herself that she would stay with her grandma for three weeks. No, this was a minor, very awkward speed bump that Natalie would get over as quickly as possible.

"I've always wanted to travel, so..." She cleared her throat as she realized that was too much information and headed back to bare facts. "They're trying to implement before the end of the year. There's a whole team. One person couldn't do it all."

"So you're here to work and see the sights. Not have an affair. That's what you're telling me?"

"Yes." From somewhere deep in her subconscious, a fresh blush rose. "Of course I'm here to work." Maybe she had thought this trip was her chance to have a grown-up affair away from her daughter's impressionable eyes, but that was very much a midnight fantasy and not something she intended to pursue. This trip might be the opportunity to cast off responsibility and act like a single woman instead of a struggling mom with bills and a flake for an ex, but she'd settle for a date with someone she wouldn't have met otherwise.

He didn't need to know any of that though.

Her cheeks stayed hot and hurting, nevertheless. It wasn't easy to meet his gaze and pretend a full-fledged affair was completely off the table, especially when there was a knowing glint teasing crinkles into the corners of his eyes.

"Even if I was looking for romance," she blurted. "Which I'm *not*, I'd hardly start with the owner of the company, would I?"

"I don't know. Would you? Let's have dinner tonight and talk about it."

Her stomach swooped and her heart stopped, as though she'd hit an unexpected wall.

That's how it's done. She'd been observing, trying to crack the code of dating and casual invitations. It had seemed complicated, but he made it look easy.

Practice, she surmised cynically.

But go out with him? *Impossible.* Her heart restarted, pounding with sudden panic, partly because, well, look at him. He was gorgeous and obviously knew his way around the entire city, not just the block.

Danger. If she could have escaped this airless room crowded with empty desks, she would have.

Somehow she managed to hang on to her composure and scoff, "Is that a test? I realize Theo— And yes, at this level we all refer to your family by your first names when you're not around to hear it." She encompassed the ground floor with a sweep of her splayed hand in a flat circle. "*Theo* might have married a woman who once worked as a chambermaid, but we're all well aware that was an exception. *I* have no such ambitions. You're quite safe from me, and so are the rest of the men in your family."

There. She folded her arms to close the topic.

He folded his, bunching those gorgeous shoulders in a way that made her throat go dry. "You're funny," he said.

"I'm completely serious!"

"I know. That's why it's funny. Calling marriage to any of us an ambition is hysterical." He didn't laugh. He only gave his mouth an ironic twist, which drew her notice to the shape of his lips. The lower was fuller than the top one, but the upper had a shallow space between the two peaks, perfect for a fingertip. The corners of his mouth extended into short, deep lines that gave him that look of being perpetually amused by the lives of the mortals around him.

His smile grew and he jerked his chin in a nudge of insistence, voice pitched intimately low, filled with knowledge that she was responding to him. "Have dinner with me, Natalie."

She was *mooning*. And he'd noticed. Of course he had. He was a serial pickup artist. Where were the natural disasters when you needed them? It was definitely time for the earth to open up and suck her underground.

"Dating among coworkers is frowned upon," she managed, delighted to have found both the excuse and a steady voice. "I'm sorry you thought I was making a play for your brother-in-law, but I'm highly cognizant of company policy and have no intention of violating it, even if he were available. Now, if we're finished, I really should get back to work."

"You're sorry for my mistake? This really is the beginning of a beautiful friendship. Come on. Dinner. It will be my apology." He splayed his straight fingers against his wide chest. A gorgeous chest, she was sure. He looked like he worked out. Often. His physique distracted her from how suddenly he'd turned on the charm. "Where's the harm in the boss taking an out-of-town employee to dinner? It's networking," he cajoled.

"Is that what it would be?" She couldn't help her snort of laughter. She'd thought he was merely a playboy, but he made the sharing of his favors sound like some kind of a job perk.

His expression changed slightly as she laughed, becoming less arrogant as his regard sharpened with male interest and something more acute, as though he was reassessing her. It made her think she might be holding her own in this match of wits, surprising him.

Which gave her a thrill that she did her best to ignore.

"Look, I'm flattered," she rushed to say, glancing away so he wouldn't see *how* flattered. As sophisticated as she dreamed of being, she wasn't prepared for someone like him. "But I've seen the women you date and I'm not in their league. Which, by the way, is another reason I would never set my sights on your brother-in-law. So thank you for this extremely interesting conversation, but I need to get back to work. I don't want to get fired," she added pointedly.

"Not in their league?" he repeated, frowning in disagreement as he gave her yet another thorough assessment in a way that set her alight. Her entire body actually hurt from the blood rush that prickled through her.

She'd starved herself and worked out like mad before leaving Montreal, determined that if any sort of corporate limelight fell upon her—or any sexy Frenchmen—she'd have nothing to be insecure about. Nevertheless, she experienced a pang of insecurity under his review, worried she wasn't up to standard.

He dragged his gaze back up to hers and let her see undisguised male desire.

Tingling excitement encompassed her. It wasn't exactly confidence, but it wasn't uncertainty, either. It was a delicious and involuntary "yes, please" that scared the hell out of her.

"You're very much in an elite league of your own, Natalie. Or are you making excuses to spare my feelings? It would surprise me if you are. You don't strike me as someone who would bother. Not considering the frankness we've already arrived at."

That made her chuckle drily, but she suppressed it with a sheepish dip of her chin. "You're right. But read my personnel file, Mr. Makricosta—"

"Demitri," he corrected.

"I don't live nearly as fast as you do. Demitri." She tried to make her voice diffident and amused, but Demitri was a surprisingly erotic name for a man with an American accent. "If I thought you were issuing a genuine invitation—and one that was only for dinner," she added with a you-can't-fool-me look. "I would be tempted. My coworkers here have families to go home to. It would be refreshing not to eat alone. But I suspect you're mocking me. Or maybe punishing me for said frankness?"

He was taken aback by that. "Why wouldn't I want to take you out? You're beautiful, amusing and you have a pretty laugh."

The sincerity in his tone made her heart swing inside her chest, dipping and lifting in a way that made her set a hand on the edge of her desk for balance. She grappled for humor to deflect how thoroughly his simple compliment disarmed her.

"And you want to hear that laugh in bed?" she challenged.

"Ha!" His chuckle was surprised and real, his grin appreciative before it turned hot and hungry. His gaze closed around her like a fist.

"I'll have the car brought to the curb for seven."

CHAPTER TWO

DON'T BOTHER.

That was all she'd had to say before he had winked and left her alone in her office. She could have chased him down, although she'd kept her eye out for him the rest of the day, filled with misgivings, but hadn't seen him. The intercompany email was the simplest option. It didn't even require the awkwardness of explaining herself. All she would have had to type was I can't make it.

She hadn't.

Why not?

Oh, she'd come up with dozens of rationalizations including, "it's only dinner." She was lonely and homesick. Travel for work wasn't as glamorous as she'd expected, especially without someone to share stories with, and calling Zoey twice a day wasn't nearly enough. She was used to her daughter disappearing for a weekend with her father up to the farm, but going on ten days without being able to hug her girl was a form of slow torture.

Therefore, she reasoned, she was entitled to a night out on the company that had separated them. She'd already put in tons of extra hours on this project. She and Demitri would probably talk about work anyway. She certainly wasn't looking at this as a real date. Definitely not one where she might get lucky.

She shaved her legs anyway. Then put on the sexy black underwear she'd bought here in Paris and topped it with a black lace sheath over a black slip. She stepped into the heels she'd picked up at the consignment store before leaving Montreal, the ones she'd debated whether to bring at all because they were too high to be practical for anything less than a night on the town. With her fake diamond earrings winking from behind the fall of her freshly washed hair and her makeup more dramatic than usual, she was as date-worthy as she'd ever been.

Then she stood at the curb like an idiot for ten minutes.

Wow. What a prince. And she had developed quite a jerk radar after her brief marriage and lengthy attempt to finalize her divorce. Well, she'd wanted a taste of the dating scene. Who knew it was this bitter? But it was exactly this well-honed resentment of thoughtless men that steeled her spine and made her demand better for herself whenever she had offers back home.

Pivoting to go back inside the hotel, she entered the rotating doors as Demitri entered them from the inside. She ignored him as she passed him and kept walking into the lobby.

"Hey!" he circled back to call after her. "Natalie. Wait."

"I was stood up," she said over her shoulder, then paused to swing around and level a glare at him. "Lesson learned. If that was your intention. Good night." She swung back toward the elevators.

"I stood at your door thinking the same thing."

She checked her step. Turned to search his expression. He looked annoyed, not smug or smarmy. She didn't want to believe him, too aware that giving men the benefit of the doubt was an invitation to be walked over.

"You said to meet you at the curb," she reminded him coolly. Her entire body prickled with awareness that the front desk and bell staff could see them, if not hear them.

"No, I said the car would be there." He came even with

her and scowled. "What kind of men have you dated that they pick you up on the sidewalk?"

That gave her pause. For all her ideals, she still expected the very worst from men. Maybe she ought to give Demitri more credit.

He offered his arm, gaze still vaguely hostile.

After a brief hesitation, she transferred her pocketbook to her other hand and tucked her fingers into the crook of his elbow, nervous now because she wasn't sure how to take him. Was he one of the few good ones after all?

With *his* reputation?

He skimmed a glance down her front to where her dress was revealed by her open raincoat. "I'll forgive you for underestimating me since you look so lovely," he commented.

It wasn't the most extravagant compliment, kind of backhanded in the way he suggested she was seeking his forgiveness, but she warmed under his words. And couldn't help taking a visual snapshot of him in his black pants and black buttoned shirt under a smoky gray suede jacket that was so buttery soft it made her want to caress his arm. He smelled fantastic, too, all spicy and masculine, jaw shiny where he'd freshly shaved.

They turned more than a few heads walking out to the car, but she doubted it was because they made such a striking couple. She'd have to make a point of mentioning how innocuous this evening had been when training her coworkers over the next few days. He'd been just being nice, she'd stress. Even though she doubted a man like Demitri went out of his way to be nice. She suspected he was ruled by self-interest, and most of his interest was banked below his belt.

For the moment, however, she set all that aside and concentrated on not smiling like an idiot because she was on a date. With a handsome man. This was exactly what she'd hoped for from this off-site assignment, and it astonished her that it was happening. Her neglected femininity had been desperate for male attention and glowed with pleasure at getting some.

They didn't talk much in the limo. Her fault as she took in the color and lights of Paris. The restaurant was only a short drive anyway, a distance she would have walked in Montreal, even in this blustery fall weather and wearing these neck-breaking shoes. They were shown to a table with a stunning view of Notre Dame and the Seine. She tried not to gawk as they moved through the dining room, but along with gorgeous detailing that spoke of France's rich history, the place was loaded with movie stars. There were probably athletes and politicians, too, not that she would recognize them. Demitri seemed to have a nodding acquaintance with almost everyone in the room, but didn't stop to speak to anyone.

"Shall I order for you?" he asked as the maître d' left them.

"What kind of men have I dated that dared to let me read the menu myself? As if a woman could," she scoffed lightly.

"This is why I asked. Some of you feminists find it condescending."

"And you see it as chivalry?"

"I had an old-world upbringing," he stated with a ring of pride in his tone. "But I also like to know my date is ordering something I'd like to eat, since she won't finish it," he added with a supercilious lift at the corner of his mouth.

"Ha! You don't know me very well, do you?"

"I'm working on it," he assured her with a look that reached across and held.

"You read my personnel file?" she challenged, heart skipping. He knew about Zoey? Her breath stopped.

"Too easy," he dismissed, leaning forward in a way that seemed to catch her in a magnetic field that pulled her into him. "I like a more personal approach."

So he didn't know she had a daughter. Natalie toyed with the idea of blurting it out, but didn't want to cool the sizzle between them. It was too exciting, playing with this particular fire.

"I'll bet you do." Her voice came out papery and soft. He probably knocked women over with gently blown kisses. Her pulse was racing and her skin glowing hot from the inside. The way the banter lobbed back and forth between them entranced her, but he was an expert, she reminded herself. This wasn't anything so grand as chemistry.

"If you think I'm such a womanizer, why are you here?" he asked, eyes narrowed to hide what he was thinking.

"Honestly?" She schooled herself not to look or sound desperate, even though she was bordering on despair where men and relationships were concerned. "I live like a shut-in, working from home a lot of the time. I'll never get another chance to dine like the one percent and, quite frankly, you hit the nail on the head about the men I date. I thought I'd see what it's like to be the girl for a change."

He raised his brows.

"Let you hold the door for me," she explained. "Pay. Even though I know it'll really be the company paying. But you do know this is only dinner, right? I work for you."

"You work for my brother," he stated firmly, not thrown off his stride at all by her bluntness. "IT falls under finance. I head up marketing." Despite his affable tone his gaze was dead level as he added, "My threats earlier were empty. I have no authority to fire you. By the same token, I have no way of helping you advance. If this turns into more than dinner, there's no professional advantage for you."

The warning pushed her back into her seat, putting her in her place. Yet she was strangely relieved. Embarrassed, yet amused.

"Look at all we've got on the table and we haven't even ordered," she said with a pert lift of her brows.

* * *

Demitri released a "Ha," and looked away, astounded by how thoroughly this woman was keeping him on his toes. Fortunately the waiter arrived to advise them of the evening's specials.

"Please," Natalie said when Demitri glanced at her. "Order for me. I'm curious."

He nodded in satisfaction even though his brain was barely able to pull it together to order at all, only managing to choose the starters with a suitable wine before he turned back to her, trying not to fall into her spell like a fisherman off a boat.

When had she hooked him? That first laugh? The doe-eyed virgin look when he'd asked to speak to her? Definitely by the time she'd cut him down to size with a few swings of her rapier tongue, he'd been curious. Everyone loved him. Instantly and thoroughly. Even his family only acted irritated as they made every effort to draw him further inside the fold. Hell, women he slept with and left within hours remained affectionate and syrupy when he crossed paths with them later.

But not Natalie. He didn't think it was an act, either. She'd been furious and insulted by his accusations today, then mistrustful and apprehensive of his invitation to dinner. When she hadn't answered her door, he'd been stunned. No one rejected him, no matter what he did. And he searched for the line at every opportunity.

Finding her at the front of the hotel had been entirely too much of a relief for his comfort. Then she'd demonstrated that she was perfectly ready to leave him in the dust for being thoughtless. The warning lights were still flashing. Off her and inside him.

Only dinner, she'd claimed.

Take heed, he told himself. He avoided women with

standards, being genetically incapable of living up to anything but the basest expectations of him.

Her honesty and playfulness were incredibly refreshing, however. And she was beautiful, with that skin like creamed honey and her eyes reflecting the sparkling lights from beyond the window.

"Tell me about yourself, Natalie," he commanded softly.

Something like indecision passed over her face before she brought her gaze around to his. Her expression smoothed to an aloof facade, as though she'd mentally tucked away everything personal and only left the basics.

"There's not much to say. I grew up outside of Montreal with my mother and brother. I divorced pretty much as soon as I married and worked on contract with Makricosta for two years before I was hired for a permanent position with the Canadian branch. Sometimes I go on-site across the country, but most of what I do is handled over the phone and through screen-share from my home office."

"Turn it off and turn it on again?" he guessed.

"Exactly. Along with some talking off the ledge when files are corrupted or a job change demands a revision of an email signature and they can't find where to update it. The excitement in tech support never stops, let me tell you. I couldn't figure out why my ear felt weird the first few days I was in France and finally realized it's because I wasn't wearing my Bluetooth."

There was more, he suspected, but before he could dig, she turned his inquiry around. "You?"

"Why don't you tell me what you know? Through your carefully vetted research," he drawled, and liked the way her full lips pursed in compunction. He wasn't bothered. Of course the employees gossiped about him. He made about as much effort to be discreet as he did toward curbing misbehavior overall. The whole point was to let his escapades be known in order to reach maximum exasperation factor.

Which was juvenile, he realized, reflecting on it under Natalie's regard and feeling the first traces of shame, but he had his reasons for making himself the target of attention.

"I don't actually know that much," Natalie said. "Your family keeps a low profile. Your brother turning up with a baby with the chambermaid was a hot topic for a while, but since I don't work directly in the hotels, I don't have close friendships with anyone at work and only get the odd bits of gossip fed back to me. There are some people I talk to all the time, and when I'm solving a crisis I'm very popular, but mostly I'm regarded as a necessary evil. Right now, making all these changes to the main system? It's a good thing I have a thick skin because I'm not anyone's friend. Which sounds like I'm talking about myself again. What a bore I am!"

"I'm interested," he assured her, surprised by how true the comment was. "How old were you when you married?"

"Not old enough," she said with a circumspect lift of her lashes. "Nineteen. Have you ever been married?"

"Hell, no."

"Wish I'd had your sense." The wry curl at the corner of her mouth and couched bitterness behind her eyes suggested she was being completely forthright.

A woman after my own heart, he thought ironically.

"What happened to cut your marriage short? Infidelity?" Hell, at that age he had broken up his brother's impending marriage, coldly and deliberately.

Natalie didn't answer right away. Her lips pursed in old disappointment as she stared out the window. "The short answer is he didn't come to my mother's funeral," she finally allowed.

When she swung her face back to him, it was as if she was saying, *There. I did it.* As if her telling him without showing too much emotion had been very hard.

A weird, answering pain lurched in his chest.

He was a student of human behavior. People thought he was superficial and lacking in empathy. He was fine with the misconception. Deep thoughts really didn't interest him, but he was very good at reading people. Years of living in a house where emotions were so deeply hidden you needed a pickax to find them had honed his skills. The side benefit was that it made him good at his job. Good with women.

Natalie didn't want his sympathy, however. The keep-away vibes rolling off her were obvious and troubling. Especially because, for once, he knew exactly how she felt.

"I couldn't face my mother's funeral alone. I brought a date. How twisted is that?" he confided.

"Adara and Theo weren't there?"

"No, they were." And Nic, the older brother Demitri hadn't known about. He averted his mind from how disturbing it had been to have a stranger enter their inner circle, as though a member of the audience had walked on stage and begun acting with the players, throwing off his lines. "We're not close in a way that would have made something like that easier." He'd barely spoken to them at all, too stunned and filled with questions he refused to ask.

"But you said you grew up with your mother and brother, so he must have been at the funeral with you?"

She flinched and sat back, distancing herself even more. She straightened her silverware and looked quite pale despite the golden glow of candlelight on her skin.

"He died the year before. Can we not talk about this please?"

"I'm sorry." When had he ever been so aghast at stepping on someone's feelings? Or apologized so sincerely to a woman? But his hand was over hers before he knew he was going to reach out to make a connection. "Really. Theo drives me bat-guano-crazy, but I don't know what I'd do without him."

She laughed. It was more of a sniff, and she brushed at her cheek, eyes wet and glowing when she lifted them. "Thank you. It was six years ago, but I still miss him and think about him every day."

The waiter arrived to distract them. By the time they were alone again, Natalie had her bravest smile back in place. "Tell me why your brother drives you crazy."

He shook his head. "You'll have *me* in tears," he dismissed.

"Your job, then. Will you talk about that?"

"You can't be interested," he deflected. Where were questions like "Were you in Cannes for the festival?" "Where do you summer?"

Natalie shrugged. "I'm certainly not interested in myself. This is the most excitement I've had in my life. True story," she assured him with a confirming nod. "You travel, at least. Meet famous people."

"People who think they're famous are boring as hell. *That* is a true story. But come on. You must have at least one deep, dark secret that makes you interesting."

"One," she allowed promptly, suppressing a smile. "But it's not very dark. Dirty blond at best. And I'm not going to tell you." She had decided that, since this was her one chance to act like a carefree young woman instead of a mom. It was harmless, she told herself. This was only dinner.

"I want to hear it," he insisted.

She shook her head, firm. "You'll think differently of me. But what about you? Any dark secrets falling out of your pockets?"

His guard was so low he almost told her about Nic. The fact his siblings had kept the man's existence from him had completely unraveled his view of his life and his place in the family. The exclusion had rocked his foundation, and he'd begun mentally separating from them, thinking more seriously about starting his own marketing firm.

Gideon had called a few weeks later to announce Adara's pregnancy and to inform Demitri that he would be expected to step up and take on extra hours in the family business. Demitri had been needed again. Integral to the business and to his sister. Things had gone back to normal for a while, but then Adara had started trying to get everyone together. She and Theo were as thick as thieves with their parenthood jokes, and he was once again on the outside looking in.

They weren't even leaning on him at work anymore. Quite the opposite, which was eating at his sense of self. With practiced ease he turned his mind from all of that, distracting Natalie with some of his stock stories that always drew a laugh. He knew loads of celebrities and had made a career of partying with them. His siblings had certainly never loosened up enough to ensure their highest-paying guests had fun.

That was Demitri's job: creating distraction. Drawing and holding attention.

Natalie was rapt, thoroughly engaged with everything he told her. It wasn't a strange occurrence for him. Everyone, women especially, responded to him. He'd recognized it early and used it to this day. The difference tonight was how much he enjoyed her attention while at the same time resenting that she wanted him to talk when he wanted to hear more about her.

They lingered over their meal, finishing the bottle of wine and nursing coffee, steering away from personal topics in favor of movies and news scandals and places he'd been that she'd like to visit.

"You're a single woman. Get on a plane," he ordered. "What's holding you back?"

"I did get on a plane," she argued good-naturedly, shielding her eyes with a downward sweep of her lashes. "I'm here. Dining on the Seine. Thank you for a lovely evening," she added, flashing her gaze back up to his. "This is what I'd hoped for when I applied for this trip."

She'd been looking for a man to seduce her. He could see it and a pulse of sexual excitement pumped through him. But seduction required patience, he reminded himself.

"Do you like dancing? We could go to a club."

"I… It's a work night," she argued, but the slant of her gaze told him she was tempted.

He smirked. "I begin to see why you don't have a life." He signaled for the check.

"Note to self—boss thinks a work ethic is overrated," she chirped.

"I'm not your boss," he reminded. "C'mon. I know you want to tick the box on dance in a Paris nightclub."

"Yes, but…" She canted her head at him, nose wrinkled. "I'm not dressed for it."

"Believe me, truly cool people do not dress for clubs. They drop in on impulse."

"And get turned away at the door for not being on the list."

"You're adorable. I'm *always* on the list."

She had definitely had one glass too many if she was tee-tering into not giving a damn about work or propriety, but Demitri was a difficult man to say no to. He took her hand and wound her through the restaurant, tucking her into the back of the limo and angling his body so he looked at her the whole way to the club.

"This is a bad idea," she insisted, trying desperately to hang on to a few grains of common sense while turning a challenging look on him that only clicked into a locked gaze with his.

His grin widened. "Because it's turning into more than dinner?"

"You're the kind of man who always gets what he wants, aren't you?"

"Yes," he answered without reserve.

Be careful, Natalie. Be very, very careful.

"Well, I'm only going along out of curiosity," she excused with a toss of her hair. "Don't say I led you on. Oh, we won't even get in," she added as they pulled up at the entrance where a hundred people stood in the rain, all dressed to the nines.

He made a pithy noise and waited until the chauffeur had opened the door and held an umbrella for them, walking them to the door.

"Jean," Demitri greeted the doorman, slipping him a bill without even pausing.

Pounding music accosted them as they entered the dark interior. Flashes of neon pierced the violet glow while strips of white stood out in stark contrast. As they wound through the crowded tables and bouncing bodies, a stunning woman with a lot of dark skin exposed by her French maid inspired two-piece bikini lowered her serving tray and kissed both of Demitri's cheeks. They had a brief conversation, she pointed, he nodded and then he tugged Natalie along with him as they continued toward the back of the club.

He said something into her ear, but she must have heard him wrong. She looked to the stage, but that DJ couldn't be the pop star he'd just mentioned.

Maybe it was, though. A chart-topping band occupied the VIP section and rose to greet Demitri with exuberance when he arrived, insisting they join their entourage, which included a dozen people, three of whom she recognized, two from television and one from a blockbuster movie.

More champagne was ordered and she was pressed into a chair next to a movie star.

Oh, sweet Lord. What kind of life had she stepped into that she was partying in Paris with celebrities? No wonder women dropped like flies for Demitri. He plucked them out of their boring little lives and set them into fantasy worlds where money wasn't mentioned and rich, gorgeous men flattered you shamelessly.

Not that she felt the same frisson of awareness and excitement when this very handsome actor leaned in to fawn over her, but the way he kept asking her about herself, as though he was genuinely interested, was enormously gratifying to her small-time ego. When he asked her to dance, of course she said yes. What a story to tell her grandchildren! *I once danced in Paris with a movie star.*

He was a bit handsy in real life. Drunk, she assumed. Not outright offensive but awfully familiar awfully fast. He wanted to dance right up against her and she told herself to go with it. This was how the high rollers lived, right on the edge, she supposed. And honestly, if she wanted to flirt with a wealthy stranger, this guy was probably a far simpler entanglement than Demitri.

He roamed his hands over her hips, skewing her dress up her thighs and she let him, hoping for a flicker of the physical spark she felt with Demitri.

An arm shot between them, separating her from the actor and none too gently forcing the man back.

Demitri stepped into the space he'd created, his posture one of startling aggression even though he said nothing, only stood there like a wall between her and the movie star.

"I thought you were done with her," the actor excused, holding up his hands.

Oh, *yuck.* Instantly feeling worthless and dirty, Natalie turned away.

Her arm was caught in a hard grip and Demitri said next to her ear, "We're leaving."

You think? she wanted to snap, but didn't bother. She was so offended and disgusted she wanted to evaporate. Maybe she owned some responsibility for that ugly remark since she hadn't exactly been discouraging the actor. Even so, it didn't excuse his talking about her as though she was something to be picked up and passed around. She wasn't an object.

And what did that say about Demitri that his women moved through the ranks?

And, if that was normal behavior for him, why was he acting all possessive? Because he hadn't actually had her yet? What if she'd been into that other guy? He didn't have to come on like he owned her, escorting her to the car as though he'd just bailed her out of jail. Giving her a shoulder of glacial ice because she'd danced with his friend.

"You know…" she began over the sound of the tires hissing through the wet streets.

"Not right now," he said in a deadly tone.

Seriously? She glared at his incredibly still posture, eyes facing front, jaw set, hands in loose fists on his thighs. As the silence thickened, she realized that hissing sound was his breath moving in measured soughs through his flared nostrils.

That signal of barely controlled fury gave her pause when she really wanted to rail at him. He'd set her up to be hit on and now he was mad it had happened, as though it was her fault. They drove in silence until they reached the hotel. As they entered the lobby, she said frostily, "Don't bother walking me to my room. Thanks for dinner."

"Suit yourself," he said through his teeth, and walked toward the elevators.

She stared at his back, brain throbbing with the knowledge it was better to leave it like this, him going to his room where everyone could see she was *not* following.

But she still needed to take the elevator to her own room.

Her feet carried her in swift clips of her heels across the marble until she was right beside him.

"I'm a free agent," she whispered. "In case you missed the part about this evening not coming with any guarantees. So how about you knock off acting as if I'm a tease who bruised your ego by dancing with your best friend."

Demitri slowly turned his head and watched her eyes widen like a gopher realizing she'd called down a raptor and was being swallowed by its shadow. Her throat worked and she pulled her elbows in against her body, telling him exactly how menacing he must look. But even though he was holding himself firmly in check, he couldn't shake the fury that had lit in him with a gasoline-fueled *whoosh* when he'd glanced over and seen that Natalie was gone.

Finding her on the dance floor being pawed by that overpaid puppet had further infuriated him, making an unfamiliar phrase explode in his head: *She's mine.*

He'd watched himself from a distance behaving like a jealous lover, unable to countenance where this streak of possessiveness had come from, but his desire to do violence had been disturbingly strong.

Especially when he'd heard the actor's tasteless comment.

Natalie's recoil had been a visceral stab to his gut, making him see how he was tarnishing someone nowhere near as cynical and jaded as he was. He'd been instantly disgusted with himself.

"Is that what you think? That I'm angry with *you*?" The skin across his cheekbones felt tight and he heard how low and chilling his voice was, coming from a churning, ugly place deep in his chest. "We had to leave, Natalie, because I was going to kill him."

The elevator doors opened, but neither of them moved. She stared into his eyes and he let her see the banked rage burning in his.

The doors started to close, and he shot out a hand to catch them back. Waving her into the car, he leaned in and pressed the button. "Good night."

"Wait," she insisted, holding the doors herself from the inside. "I probably kind of let him think—"

"No, you didn't," he said flatly. "I did." And he was so filled with self-contempt, with *shame*, he didn't know how to deal with it.

"What?"

He looked away, regretting he'd said anything. But he couldn't let her think he was calling her out for drawing that man's attention when he was the one who'd put her in the actor's line of sight in the first place.

Inhaling to gather his composure, he stepped into the elevator and punched the button for the penthouse, folding his arms and bracing his feet as he faced her. The elevator began to climb.

"I don't typically care if the women I take to these things choose to leave with someone else. That guy knows it. Hell, most of the women I date come on to me for an introduction to a crowd like that. *I don't care*," he insisted, because until this evening, he genuinely hadn't.

"But tonight you did?" She was very somber, looking up at him with something that approached concern. As though she sensed he was facing a demon, which was as painful as actually looking into the hard light of self-reflection.

"Tonight I saw how tawdry it is," he acknowledged.

The elevator stopped at her floor, making her take a half step for balance. The doors opened, but they stayed in the suspended elevator, the air so thick with tension it held no oxygen.

"He embarrassed me," Demitri admitted, teeth locked and trying to hold in the uncomfortable revelation. "He made me embarrassed of myself. You said you weren't in the same league as the women I usually date, and that's true."

She flinched, taken aback.

"You're well beyond anything they could aspire to," he expounded. "Not as worldly, I'll give you that, but you have the kind of standards the people I call friends wouldn't even begin to understand."

"That's not true," she argued. Glancing out to the hall, she motioned that he should release the door. She seemed embarrassed, as though she wanted privacy.

As he allowed the doors to close again, she clasped her hands before her, shoulders hunched and defensive, brow crinkled and looking mortified.

The elevator began the rest of its climb.

"I'm not worldly, that's dead-on. But I don't have any kind of great standards. I came to France kind of fantasizing about having an affair, just like you accused me this afternoon. I mean, obviously not really expecting anything to happen," she stammered, wringing her hands. "But as I was dancing, I was letting myself think it could. I'm sure I gave him the wrong impression."

His brain went supernova, exploding in his head, sweeping out any other thought but that he could have her.

"If you want an affair, Natalie, I'm your man." His voice plummeted into throaty depravity, the want in him so quick and intense it tightened his airway.

Her lashes quivered and her pupils expanded. "I... It was just a fantasy," she insisted—voice, tone, protest thin and insubstantial.

The elevator stopped again.

He pinned the door automatically with the well-practiced step of his foot into the sensor and the rest of him in her space.

She was off balance, breasts rising in a startled gasp as her hand went behind her, searching blindly for the rail.

He braced his hands against the wall on either side of her head and took his time gazing on her wary expression, letting her get used to the idea. Some primal part of him deliberately forgot why he'd meant to let her go home alone.

"The first time I saw you I thought you would have such soft skin." He leaned close enough to draw in the scent of her flushed cheek, letting their body heat build in the tiny space he allowed between them. Seduction was about giving a woman time to feel the want, then providing the relief.

"I'm not sure," she whispered, but her gaze was on his mouth. Yearning parted her lips. "I didn't mean for you to think…"

Patience, he warned himself, practically trembling with the avalanche of desire building behind his wall of self-control.

"I want this…" she whispered.

He moved in with the skill of a man who always got what he wanted, not by force, but persuasion.

Her mouth was a tender morsel that made his breath hiss out in gratification as he nuzzled it with his own. She responded hesitantly, then with openness, inviting his full possession, letting him guide her toward the sensual world he longed to explore with her. She was delightful, shy yet generous, eyes closed tight in pained pleasure. When a little sob of capitulation left her, when she brought her hands from behind her back to his chest and splayed them in a promising caress, he drew back just enough to speak.

"Come with me."

CHAPTER THREE

Don't, she thought.

But in the back of her mind, she asked herself, *What's holding you back?* She had mentally allowed for something like this to happen. Heck, she'd actually bought condoms, thinking at the time that it was a ridiculous prospect, but secretly dreaming of being swept off her feet by a suave foreigner. Demitri was a prime example of the sophisticated man she'd hoped to meet. Plus, he actually knew how these situations worked.

But she hadn't expected an affair to actually happen. She was normal, boring, run-of-the-mill Natalie. Not some irresistible, exciting woman who captivated a man.

Demitri looked at her as if she was that and more. He made her feel beautiful and alluring, as though she was the kind of woman who deserved a man to love and cherish her. That fantasy was as seductive as the genuine tingles of arousal he provoked in her.

When he closed his hand around hers and backed out of the elevator, drawing her with him, she let it happen.

Knees weak, heart pounding, lips still burning, she allowed him to lead her down the hallway, half convinced this was a dream because things like this didn't really happen. Not to her.

They passed recessed doors that led to private suites. She'd only been in one Makricosta penthouse ever, to resolve a Wi-Fi issue for a client she hadn't even seen. She knew *of* the family suites in each of the hotels, but hadn't ever expected to see the interior of one.

Demitri let her in a door marked Private Residence.

She took in the overstuffed semicircle couch and round coffee table, the dining area and table for twelve, the marble mantel and matching accent tables. Table lamps provided soft light against the draped windows. The art on the walls looked expensive. The suite was tasteful and welcoming, if cold. Not as generic as a hotel room, but not really lived in.

"Take your coat?" he offered.

She set her pocketbook on the chest beside the door and offered her back, nerves strummed by the brush of his fingertips as he lowered her coat off her shoulders. The brush of silk lining down her arms caused her to shiver, making her nipples pull tight. Everything in her tensed with anticipation while nerves had her heart hammering in her throat.

Was she really doing this? She ought to tell him that she didn't do this. It wasn't her. He'd be disappointed.

Working up her courage, she turned, hands clasped before her.

He was looking at her legs, coat suspended from his hand. As she turned, he lifted his gaze to hers, locking her in a heated stare, not looking away as he tossed her wet coat toward the leather sofa.

"You shouldn't do that," she protested, taking an automatic step to fetch it.

He stepped into her space. The air between them thinned like smoke, leaving a vacuum that pulled them into the space, energy sizzling and popping with sexual awareness.

He was so gorgeous. Not just that sculpted jaw and his intense dark eyes, but the kissable shape of his lips and the scope of his shoulders. His wide chest and flat abdomen and long legs.

I don't know what I'm doing. She tried to find the words, tried to make her throat work, but he touched a fingertip under her chin.

The brush was feathery and gentle. She hadn't expected finesse, but honestly, a man didn't rack up a conquest list like his by being a brute. He was showing her all his best moves, she reminded herself, but she still felt deliciously branded by his fingerprint. Lifting her gaze, she wound up fascinated by his mouth again, and it was coming closer...

Oh.

When had she even been *kissed* since having Zoey? Really kissed?

And so well?

He really knew what he was doing, persuading her with varying pressures and parted lips to follow him. Open. Let it deepen. Rock and soothe and moan involuntarily because it felt so good.

Seductive.

His arm hooked behind her and drew her into the hard wall of his chest. *So* good. And why? Why did the sheer hardness of him, the tension of strong muscles and flat breastbone and firm flesh, make her soften and weaken and melt into surrender?

So much strength harnessed and held in check for her.

He stroked his hands up and down her spine and she kept leaning closer and more fully, giving up more of herself until she was plastered to him, completely undone. Then he slid one hand down to clasp over her buttock and a heated zing of pleasure pierced deep in her belly, sending a flood of sexual awakening into her erogenous zones.

This was what she'd wanted. Sexual feelings. Womanly feelings. To be seduced so she wouldn't have to think about right and wrong. Grateful to him for making this easy, she wound her arms around his neck and licked into his mouth, letting him know she was utterly receptive.

He grunted, hips jerking into her in a way that spoke of his excitement, which excited her in turn. With a bolder touch, he cupped her backside and found her breast, possessed it, stimulated her through the fabric of her dress so she wriggled against him with impatient desire.

They were breathing heavily, barely breaking to gasp before diving into another long kiss. She ran her hands over him, greedily taking her fill of his physique, not letting herself think about how to make this count. Rather, she steeped herself in the moment and savored every sensation, drinking in his heady scent, peppery and spicy, but musky and exciting at the same time. She bumped her thighs into his iron-hard ones, liking the sense he was undentable. Impervious.

Their tongues tangled and she groaned in sheer luxury, letting herself burn alive in the bonfire of desire building between them. His implacable strength seemed to overwhelm her for a moment, making her stumble, then she felt something against her bottom.

He lifted her, dress riding up at the same time, and sat her on the cold marble of the table by the door.

Before she could decide what she thought of that, he pushed her legs apart and stepped between them so they were eye to eye, mouth to mouth...

Kissing again. Deeply. Unreservedly.

The fine lace of her new Parisian panties snapped.

She gasped and closed her teeth on his bottom lip, waiting... *There*. He touched her, stroking lightly, just a tantalizing caress that made her flesh pulse for more. After a long, breathless moment he easily deepened his caress into her slippery folds.

Encouraging him with moans of pleasure, she inched forward and layered on openmouthed kisses, letting him know how good he was making her feel as he caressed her.

Velvety waves of pleasure rolled outward from his touch, making her limbs weak and tingly, her core tight and eager.

With clumsy fingers, she undid his shirt buttons, wanting to taste his skin.

He took his hands off her long enough to yank his shirt open, revealing his muscled chest. Natalie couldn't help but gasp and hook her heels against the backs of his thighs, urging him back into her space so she could splay her hands on him and take in all that burnished skin.

He resisted long enough to take something from his pocket, then he opened his pants. Despite how aroused and excited she was, a tiny niggle of nerves hit her as he revealed himself. They were doing this. Now. Here.

Jerking her gaze up from the condom he was applying to his very admirable erection, she looked into his face and saw a kind of blind passion that made her heart skip, as if a bucket of water had hit her, but it was hot enough to scald. He was as hungry as she was. Barely holding on to control. It was heady and exciting.

"Demitri," she managed weakly.

"You're incredible," he muttered, hooking one arm behind her to draw her to the edge of the table. Then his gaze caught hers and something like panic edged into his. "You're not with me?"

"No, I am. I want you. This. Now. Please."

His breath flowed over her lips as he released it in an expulsion of jagged humor and relief. Firm pressure nudged at her opening and she closed her eyes, not wanting him to see how desperate she was right now. Aching with need.

He pushed with inexorable power into her. A smarting sting took her by surprise, making her catch her breath and set a hand on his shoulder.

Rearing back slightly, he said, "You're not a virgin."

"No!" Her gasping laugh came out as a papery husk.

"It's just been a long time. Please don't stop. I really want this."

He made a noise between frustration and despair as he covered her mouth, kissing her with hungry desire, trying to persuade her body into softness.

She enfolded him with her limbs, drawing him in, making the penetration happen despite the discomfort so they were locked tight, both pulsing in expectation. *Yes.* She'd needed so badly to be held tight against a warm body, a man's hands caressing her as though she was treasure, his hardness filling her where she'd felt empty forever.

His head tipped back and he groaned at the ceiling. "You're killing me."

She smiled, easing her tight grip on him, but squeezing internally, signaling that she was ready. Needy. Scraping her nails against his sides, she bit his pecs, inciting him.

He drew in his breath as a fierce hiss, slitted eyes staring deeply into hers as he practically pulled her off the table and onto his firmly planted, hard body. Then he caged her with hard arms, one hand low enough on her tailbone to brace her on the edge of the table, the other hooked behind her knee, holding her open. From there it was primal, but so good. Basic he might be, but selfish he was not. Each thrust was possessive, controlled and deliberate. And he watched her the entire time, as though he was willing her to lose herself in their lovemaking.

She couldn't hang on to control, not when the crashes of their hips sent detonations of joy splashing through her. Feverish and acutely sensitive, she felt everything from the friction of her silk slip to the damp sheen on his hot skin. He ducked his head to set his teeth against her neck. She knew a love bite would be bad, but she arched to make it easier for him to mark her. She'd never felt so glorious, so sexy or desired or alive.

They made love with lusty groans and fevered gasps as

she greedily fought orgasm, loving the way he made her feel, filling her up and stroking his hand restlessly up her inner thigh, under her dress. Swearing gruffly against her cheek, he found her mouth with his own and her breast with his hand, pushing her bra cup up so he could pinch her nipple, seeming to shake with need as he quickened his pace and claimed her mouth as though she was his last meal.

"Now, Natalie," he broke away to demand. *"Now."*

His voice sent prickling sensations down her spine. The coiled sensation where he moved inside her deepened to a kind of tension she couldn't resist. This was good, but the other side would be better. When he thrust deep and held himself there, held her tight to him, nudging her through the door of ecstasy right along with him, she gave herself up to it, clinging as though they were falling from an airplane into the sky.

For a blind second it was that fathomless. Then the tumble of orgasm struck, near wrenching in its power. The release and contraction inside her redoubled as Demitri pulsed and rocked, his body arched against hers in ecstasy, his cries triumphant, extending her sensation so she could only gasp and tremble, utterly helpless to their combined climax. He held her so tightly she was sure she'd bruise, but she didn't care. Nothing hurt. All the dark spaces inside her glowed hotly. Her entire being flooded with bliss and perfection. She never wanted it to end.

But the quivering pulses eventually died away. Her awareness returned to their ragged breaths and the hard marble under her bottom and the coat of sweat on his skin against her own layer of perspiration.

Embarrassment struck like a hammer. She'd been so easy. She'd just had a one-night stand—literally with him on his feet.

Lifting his head, Demitri stole a few tissues from the

box near her hip and eased from her. When he stepped away and turned his back, she forced her weak legs together and prayed they'd hold her as she unsteadily found her feet.

He walked into the first door down the hall. A powder room, she imagined, but didn't stick around to find out.

Mortified, she grabbed her purse and left without a word.

Demitri was barely forming thoughts. Deep in the back of his mind he knew what had happened with Natalie was wrong, but that wasn't why he'd sought a moment to pull himself together. He was fairly shameless when it came to right and wrong, but not usually so audacious as to take a woman inside the door like a sailor with a doxy. He might get his date into the mood in the lounge, but he never lost control there, not so completely.

That loss of sense made him uneasy. He loved sex, loved the escape and pleasure a woman's body offered him, but what he'd just done with Natalie had been the wrong kind of mindlessness. As impulsive as he was accused of being, he typically knew exactly what he was doing at all times. How much damage and why.

In this case he'd cast any sense of consequence to the wind. She'd waved him in and he'd slid home.

And he wanted to do it again. In a bed this time. Again and again.

That was unsettling. He had a very healthy appetite for sex, but sex was sex and women were women. He never, ever thought things like, *I want her.*

Probably best to walk her back to her room and cut this short.

Avoiding his own gaze in the mirror, he closed his pants, but left his shirt open. One damp hand lifted to rub away

the itch of drying sweat on his chest as he walked back
to the lounge. His muscles still felt quivery and weak…

Where was she? Her coat was still there on the sofa,
so…

"Natalie?"

In the bedroom? A strange relief flicked through him.
The night wasn't over after all. He ought to be uncomfortable with her making assumptions, but all he could think
was that he could sate this disturbing desire to have her
again. How could he be this restless and hungry when he
was still buzzing with orgasm?

She wasn't in his room.

Of course, she wouldn't know which one was his.

"Natalie," he called, pushing open all the doors as he
went, even the ones to the room the children used, but she
wasn't in any of them. Kitchen?

As he went through the lounge, he glanced at the table
by the door and noted her purse was gone. A sick lurch
hit the pit of his stomach and panged a little higher when
he saw the scrap of black lace he'd snapped and discarded
on the floor.

Oddly uncomfortable with the evidence of their passion
lying where housekeeping could find it—*really* not like
him to have such a sudden and acute need for privacy—
he stuffed the lingerie in his pocket and glanced into the
hall outside the suite.

Empty.

Grabbing his room card, he went all the way to the elevator and hit the button. The doors opened immediately,
so the car hadn't moved since they'd left it less than thirty
minutes ago.

Baffled, he went back into his suite and did another
search.

Had she taken the stairs?

He dialed her room.

She answered with a brisk "Hello... *Bonjour.*"

"Natalie?"

A tiny pause, then, "Yes?"

"It's Demitri."

"I know. I recognize your voice."

Another pause, this one longer. He was waiting for her to explain why she'd left, but there was an expectant curiosity on her side, as though she was waiting for him to tell her why he'd called.

It dawned on him that she hadn't expected him to call.

When had he last called a woman in a timely fashion after a tryst, let alone within minutes of their parting?

"Oh, I forgot my coat!" she groaned in realization. "Rookie mistake. I'm sorry. That could be awkward, couldn't it? Can you sneak it into the small meeting room on the second floor first thing tomorrow morning? That's where we're doing the group training sessions. I'll pretend I brought it so I wouldn't have to go to my room before leaving for lunch."

"Sounds elaborate," he commented with false calm, feeling like the rookie here as a hot, spurned sensation followed the word *sneak*. He told himself to go along with her plan and count himself lucky she hadn't read more into their evening than was warranted, but he still found himself speaking in a low, uncomfortably dry voice. "I could bring it to you now. Or you could come back."

"People are going to talk enough after seeing me go to dinner with you. I'd rather pretend nothing else happened."

Ouch. He scowled across the empty lounge of his quiet suite.

"Is that why you left without saying good-night?" he asked. "You were afraid of being talked about?" Repercussions were not something he worried about. What she needed, he decided, was a demonstration of how quickly his credit card could swipe away any worries she might have. There really wasn't much that couldn't be resolved that way, and he was realizing that he'd happily pay whatever it took to get her back to his room and into his bed.

"I sure as heck didn't relish doing the walk of shame in the morning," she replied, delivering a second, startlingly efficient kick to his gut. Most women regarded sex with him as a badge of honor. Having her treat it as if it was something dirty was surprisingly demoralizing.

"I'm sorry if it was rude to leave like that, but it is a work night so I should, um, get some rest... I had a really nice time, though. Thanks." *Click.*

Seriously?

He set down the phone and stared at it, tension increasing by the second.

"Let it go," he said aloud, but his brain yelled, *Seriously?*

He looked at her coat draped over the back of the sofa. Defiance took him across to pick it up. Her scent wafted into his nostrils, confusing him with a swirl of misgivings and conscience and sexual hunger.

He put it down as though it was soaked in combustibles. His hands continued to tingle even when he closed them into fists.

She was doing him a favor, he told himself. They'd had no business taking a professional relationship to such a personal level. Leaving it as a one-night stand was absolutely the best thing to do.

Hell, the best thing *he* could do would be to put on a fresh shirt, go back to the club and pick up another woman. He would, he decided.

But didn't move.

In his head, he heard that movie star say, *I thought you were finished with her.*

The graveled anger returned to the pit of his gut and he didn't understand it. Yes, he picked up social climbers and took them to suites and nightclubs and lost them to celebrities. It was all part of catering to Makricosta's elite clientele. But Natalie wasn't part of that world.

The inconvenient integrity he'd shoved aside when she'd told him she wanted an affair returned with a twist of vengeance. Exploiting the innocent was one of the few things he tried not to do. The vulnerable were meant to be protected. His upbringing had taught him that much.

That was why he worked so hard to prove he wasn't innocent or vulnerable. He was jaded and impervious.

Why was he dwelling on any of it?

He crossed to the bar and poured himself a drink, scowling at Natalie's coat, thinking, *I'm finished with her.*

While her voice repeated in his head. *Walk of shame, walk of shame, walk of shame.*

Natalie was proud of herself for thinking to take the stairs last night. She'd run down them as though she'd been pursued, and had told herself she was shaking and breathless from the exercise, not as a reaction to intense lovemaking and a kind of shock.

That wasn't supposed to have happened!

Dinner, okay. That was fine. Going to the club had been ill-advised, but not terrible. A kiss good-night? Generally acceptable after a date, even if kissing that particular man was a bad idea.

Sex? She honestly hadn't planned that and couldn't believe she'd been so swept up that she'd gone through with it. In the front room!

At least anyone watching the elevator lights would have seen it stop at her floor then stop at the penthouse without any sign of it returning down to hers. And people *would* watch for little signals like that. As much as she loved her job and the people she worked with, she knew they were the usual assortment of society. Most were wonderful and generous, but some lived for gossip and drama.

Thank goodness a scarf was part of her uniform. It neatly covered the mark on her neck—something she really ought to feel more disgraced to be sporting, but she felt too physically good. Floaty and delicious, body aching in the best possible way.

Her heart ached in a different way. A rebound loneliness had struck overnight as she'd left euphoria and stepped back into reality. Her hookup with Demitri wasn't a forever thing. It wasn't even the beginning of a romance. She was just one more in his line of conquests. Tuesday night.

You used him, too. It's fine, she assured herself as she went about her morning. Her life had been one of constant responsibility and family obligation. Growing up, her brother's needs had always taken precedence over hers, and now Zoey's were the priority. Last night had been a rare chance for Natalie to completely indulge herself. It had been deeply satisfying in a poignant way. Not tawdry, as Demitri had intimated, but temporarily, out of necessity. She had a daughter and a life to go home to.

And men, she knew from experience, were just one more person with needs that wound up being put ahead of her own. If she had a selfish streak, it was in refusing to court deep involvements because she knew how easily she became a pushover once her heart was involved.

Even Demitri, who wanted nothing more from her than she'd got from him, had become someone she was going out of her way to protect. Not that she wanted to broadcast what she'd done with him. It was far too private. For a little while she'd let herself believe in the fairy tale, the one she kept closest to her heart and didn't reveal to anyone because it was so far-fetched. Other people got the dream ending, but not her. She knew that, but she'd been able to pretend for a little while that it was possible, and because that little glimpse of happily-ever-after would have to do her for a lifetime, she had no regrets that she'd taken the opportunity.

It left her emotions raw, though, and her heart in need of extra guarding. When her coworkers pried about the dinner, she insisted he was just being nice, and then pretended an annoying email had come through from her ex. After that, she was able to keep her focus on training.

Still, her colleagues watched her with avid curiosity as she went through her slides and explained the advantages of the new system. All the while, she was acutely aware of the empty chair near the door with her coat shouldered over its back. When they broke for lunch, one of the women who shared her office downstairs hung back.

"Is it true you had a date with Demitri Makricosta last night?" Monique asked in an excited hush of French.

Natalie blushed and shook her head insistently. "It wasn't a date. He bought me dinner, but it was a work thing. I'm doing a report for head office," she prevaricated.

"Oh? What kind of report?" Monique was friendly, but on the nosy side. The kind of person who needed to know things before everyone else. She'd pressed for all the details on the training before Natalie had got herself properly organized at her desk the first day.

"It's confidential," Natalie dismissed, letting her hair swing forward as she pretended to search her coat pockets. She had a hard time with simple fabrications like Santa Claus. Outright lies weren't easy for her.

"So Demitri didn't make a pass? Nothing suggestive at all? I find that hard to believe, given his reputation."

Well, *that* was certainly to the point.

"It's his voice," Natalie dismissed, smiling tightly as she applied lip balm she didn't need. "He doesn't mean everything he says to sound like a come-on, but it does."

"Does it?" a masculine tone asked behind her, making her whip around and ignite with heat. Not just because he'd caught her talking about him, but because he was a blast of supermale hotness. He hadn't shaved, his hair was finger combed, and his jeans clung like a second skin made of faded denim. Dark circles underlined his eyes, and his striped shirt was creased as though it had just come out of the package. He leaned against the door with smug corporate ownership despite his casually disheveled appearance.

That sexy tilt of his wide mouth was very self-satisfied, kicking her pulse into a gallop.

In a very deliberate way, he turned his attention to Monique. She blushed, too, standing a little taller, tummy sucked in and lips bitten flat with remorse.

"What do you think?" he asked Monique. "I only came here to ask Natalie to join me for lunch so we could talk more about that report she's writing, but do I sound inappropriate?"

He did. He totally did. Especially when he looked back at Natalie and she read sizzling memory in his eyes. His gaze stayed fixed to hers, but it felt as though she was naked and he was looking her over from nipples to knees.

Monique swallowed audibly.

"Lunch has been provided," Natalie managed, stowing her lip balm in her purse with hands that trembled. "Everyone's gone in down the hall, but I should join them. I promised to answer any questions they might have about my presentation."

She silently willed him to move so she could escape his aura of assertive sexuality.

"Theo sprang for lunch? He's usually such a cheapskate." Demitri stepped back from the doorway into the hall.

Monique giggled as she exited the room. Natalie was able to take one small breath before Demitri fell into step beside her.

Why was he here? It took everything to act casually as

the din of chatting people died off when they entered the banquet room.

"Good afternoon," Demitri greeted the crowd in French. "I'm stealing lunch. And Natalie. Fifteen minutes," he added when she turned a startled look on him. "In my office. We'll talk while we eat."

Unable to protest in front of their audience, she waited until they'd gone up a floor with their filled plates to the accounting offices above the conference level, passing a few curious pairs of eyes along the way.

The administration offices devoted to the siblings' workspace had a small executive lounge as its hub. Demitri walked her through it, then tagged his card on a reader before holding open the door with his name on it.

"What are you *doing*?" she asked as his office door clicked shut behind them. He was completely undermining the composure she'd worked so hard to put in place all morning.

He set his plate on the edge of his desk. She rattled hers onto the small circular table in the corner, but didn't pull out a chair. A surge of defensiveness accosted her, making her keep her distance and stay ready on her feet.

"I don't know," he grumbled, pushing his hands into his pockets as he confronted her with a hard stare. "I never sneak around. This is new territory for me."

What was that supposed to mean? She had reconciled herself to their thing being one night and him never talking to her again. His call last night had shocked her to her toes. This was even more baffling.

She had the sensation that her shoulders were up around her ears, locked with tension, but she couldn't make herself relax. Her heart was pounding, her body flushed hot and cold, her ears filled with a rushing sound... All of her was reacting to him in conflicting signals of excitement and danger while her brain hammered with the knowledge that last night shouldn't have happened. It had been self-delusional on an emotional level and just plain unprofessional.

"I don't…" She had to clear her throat, completely out of her depth here. "I don't know what you're saying."

He frowned. "Do you want it in French? I'm saying that I've never tried to hide the fact that I'm seeing a woman, and I don't like it. Don't expect me to be good at it."

"We're seeing each other?" Her ears rang with a repetition of the phrase, trying to make sense of it.

"Having an affair, then. Whatever you want to call it." He shrugged his big shoulders, the movement jerky and dismissive.

"Is that what *you* call it? I mean, do you even do that? See women more than once?"

"Not often," he allowed, not flinching from her bewildered stare, utterly unfazed at being called a philanderer. "But you said you wanted an affair while you were here, and last night was good." His eyes narrowed a fraction. "Very good. Wasn't it?"

Her heart seemed to break through the thin skin of her throat, pounding in a state of painful vulnerability under his challenge. His statement was nothing so insecure as a request for confirmation. He knew damned well he'd rocked her world, and given the intensity of his gaze, he was one feminine sigh of surrender from doing it again.

"Is there *any* chance you'll quit your job so we can do this in the open?" he asked gruffly.

"I… What? Ha!" The sound escaped her in a burst of disbelief as her consciousness landed firmly back on the hard floor.

She looked around, taking in weird details of his office that she couldn't have known if she was dreaming, like a slanted drafting table with a big scratch pad splashed with various streaks of color, a whiteboard scrawled with uneven boxes and illegible labels, a wall strung with threads, magazine clippings pinned along them. The shelves held dozens of odd items from water bottles to smartphone cases to beach balls, all wearing the Makricosta logo.

"Have I got this right? Are you seriously asking me to make a permanent change to my life for something temporary? That's not a demand for commitment," she rushed to add, holding up a forestalling hand. "I'm just saying, do you hear yourself?"

She almost added, *I'm a mom*, but it really didn't fit with the way she'd behaved last night and only made her more self-conscious with what was happening now. Especially because there was a small part of her that thought, *in another life...* She would never, ever wish away her daughter, but a wistful desire to see what might have been had underpinned all her very sound reasons for taking this assignment in France.

And here was the answer. This was what she could be: an independent woman who was carefree enough to take up a man's exceedingly frivolous offer of... What was he even suggesting?

"How would that even work?" she quizzed with bemusement. "I'd quit my job and you'd set me up somewhere, pay my bills?"

He barely moved, just offered a cool nod of assent. "You'd travel with me if I required it."

"Oh, my God." She'd been joking. Ridiculing the suggestion.

A gush of icy cheapness went through her as she absorbed the full impact of the scenario. This was what happened when you thought the grass was greener on the neighbor's lawn. Turned out it was actually an overflow of the septic tank.

She headed for the door.

Before she could turn the knob, his hand was over the

crack, his body looming next to hers in a radiation of heat and crackling male energy.

"Why does that offend you? I want to see you again and not on the sly. Whatever the obstacles are, I want to remove them."

She glared over her shoulder, trying to hang on to her insulted indignation, but he was so obviously uncomfortable it gave her pause. Her senses took a hit of his male energy at the same time, flooding her with memories of how yummy it had felt to be stroked and possessed and drawn into shared climax. Her breathing changed and so did his.

"Why?" she demanded. There were thousands of other women out there. He should know. He'd bedded most of them. Was he running out? Was that what motivated him to chase her?

"You know why. We didn't even make it to the bed, for God's sake."

Do not think he's calling you exceptional, Natalie. She had never been at the top of any kind of list, not even Most Reliable. She was straight-up, middle-of-the-road, work-hard-for-second-place stock.

But he was staring at her mouth like a kid at the penny-candy window, making her lips tingle and her insides twist in anticipation. She shook her head in disbelief, but he took it as refusal.

"Damn it, Natalie!" He shoved back from the door, crossing the room in a few steps, then swinging around to confront her. "Why the hell not?"

The feminist in her said, *I don't have to have a reason*, but she was so astonished by his reaction she could only speak the truth.

"Demitri, I don't *do* this. Forgive *me* for being lousy at *this*, but I don't go home with men. I thought…" She winced inwardly, not wanting to sound as though she was okay with a one-night stand. It made her sound as cheap as he was treating her. "I had this vision of getting away and being someone different, maybe having a fling since I haven't…" No. She would *not* admit it had been years. "Being away from home allowed me to behave in a way I wouldn't normally, but I can't continue doing it," she asserted. "Last night was just…"

What? An opportunity? An experiment? A much-needed climb back into the saddle of a horse she'd learned the hard way was expensive and ornery?

"It was a fantasy," she said, repeating what she'd told him last night. "One that shouldn't have played out, but I did it, and now I'm awake and it's time to be sensible."

Funny, Demitri thought. He'd spent the night coming to the realization that, for once, something real was happening to him. Being with her hadn't been an escape. It had been somewhere he wanted to go. That worried the hell out of him, but it had also pushed him to find her this morning and negotiate how they could continue seeing one another. And now he was remembering why women with standards were a pain in the butt.

"What's wrong with continuing the fantasy?" he demanded.

"You own the company I work for," she reminded.

A wash of relief went through him as he quickly dismissed that as an obstacle. "We've covered that. You work for my brother. And if you want to keep your job, fine. We'll work around it," he said, reluctant but resigned to that inconvenience. At least with that concern out of the way, he could give in to the pull between them and saunter into her space, brushing past her anxious "Demitri—" with a firm promise of "I'll show you a fantasy fling you won't forget."

"Don't." She pressed herself into the door, avoiding his

touch. "Please don't touch me. I have to face people when I leave here and—"

"You don't want to go back there obviously aroused?" he challenged, needing to hear it. To see it in the helpless flush and disconcerted cast of her gaze around the room before she brought it back to his, eyes deeply shadowed with painful desire.

He pressed his hand flat to the door beside her head, leaning close enough to smell the warm peach scent of her skin, aching for the graze of her rising breasts against his chest. Below his belt, a heavy rush of blood pulled him tight.

Flustered and anxious, she still managed to send a coy glance south. Her body arched ever so slightly so she brushed against him. She released a powerless whimper on a sobbing "Yes."

"I want you very badly, Natalie. Not after five o'clock. Now," he told her, willing her to fall in with his demands. To let him bend her over the desk and take both of them where they were screaming with agony to go.

Natalie heard the words and flinched inside, telling herself to remember who she was dealing with. She set her jaw and leveled her chin, forcing herself to stare into his black-coffee eyes. "Is saying that part of giving me the fantasy? Because I prefer honesty, Demitri. I'm pretty sure what you want is sex, not me."

He narrowed his eyes, displeased, but he only levered himself straight and said, "Do you know what vacuous means?"

Apparently it was a real question. He waited until she said, *"Yes,"* with an exasperated frown before he continued.

"Most of the women I've been with don't. And it shows. You're sexy as hell, but you're also interesting. Give me your number. I'll text you where to meet me tonight."

Just like that? Breeze right past *shouldn't* to *will*? Misgivings danced in her periphery, but there was no sick knot of guilty conscience that would have stopped her doing something truly immoral. Two unattached adults spending time together for a few nights was allowed, she rationalized. She'd be leaving on Saturday. Three nights out of her life to keep her warm for the next thirty years. It might make her cheap, but it would make her happy. She'd regret saying no.

When would she ever again have a chance to be with a man on her terms, without it impacting her daughter? This was the only time she could do something reckless and imprudent, selfish and deeply sexually satisfying.

With giddy excitement expanding in her chest, she heard herself giving him her number, saying, "You could have got that from my company profile. You realize that, don't you?"

"I told you, I'm not going to read about you when I can see you face-to-face and ask." His eyes came up from his smartphone, gaze warm with satisfaction and lit with anticipation. His carnal expression was exhilarating, but unnerving.

"You're really not going to read it?" she asked.

"Is there a reason I should?"

"No," she said with false calm. Three nights of sidestepping honesty and pretending she didn't have a daughter. That made her squirm internally, but she instinctively knew it would change everything, and she wanted the fantasy. She wanted to be a single woman alone in Paris having an affair with a hotel magnate.

And what an affair! They didn't come up for air until two in the morning, when she rose to dress, muscles aching, nipples abraded and loins tender. Oh, it was an amazing feeling. Her skin felt like velvet on the inside, luxurious and petted smooth.

"I don't like you going back alone at this time of night. Stay."

"I'm not going to walk. I'll take a cab," she said, even though it was only a few blocks. He'd booked this suite in a competitor's hotel for the rest of the week, he'd informed her when she had arrived to a candlelit dinner looking out on the Eiffel Tower.

They hadn't eaten any of it, consuming each other with a crazy appetite she put down to her years of abstinence and his years of building a healthy one. In her heart she knew this was bad, being such an easy conquest for him, but, dear Lord, he knew how to make it good for her.

"Bring a bag tomorrow," he ordered, following her into the lounge, casual in his nudity. "So you can go to work from here in the morning."

The man was incredible. Completely un-self-conscious, possessing more command unclothed than a decorated general. He was playful when he was relaxed, like right after sex, but he got straight to the point if things weren't going his way.

He was spoiled. Privileged and spoiled, yet so generous in bed *she* felt like the spoiled one.

He was dangerous, that was what he was. If she wasn't careful she'd start fantasizing about more than two more nights with him.

She crossed to the untouched table where the tea lights in their globe of water had gutted out. Stabbing an olive with a fork, she waved the little green orb at him.

"That's two meals you've made me miss—lunch this afternoon, now dinner. You'll be lucky if I don't go on strike for better conditions." She popped the olive into her mouth.

"Here I thought the package of benefits was enough to keep you satisfied."

Said package was twitching to life, making her grin right along with him. They locked gazes, and the prospect of returning to the bedroom crackled like a welcoming fire. But one of them had to show some control.

"Yeah, well, I guess I'm one of those high-maintenance women who can't be pleased."

"Ha! That is far from true, Natalie," he said in that husky tone he used when all his blood was rushing into one particularly prominent place.

"You're saying I'm easy?" Even though they were her own words, they went through her like a white-hot spear. She looked away from him, startled to feel the backs of her eyes sting. Why? Because she'd just remembered she was one in a legion of women for him? Because this was as good as it would ever get for her?

She dropped her fork with a clatter and headed for the door.

"Hey." He caught her up before she reached it, scowling when she stiffened with resistance against his hold. "What's wrong?"

"I just need some proper sleep," she dismissed. "I get emotional when I'm tired." And she was suddenly so homesick she could cry. She wanted desperately to hold Zoey. Right now. Her arms ached with need to feel the wiry strength of her girl. That was who she was: Zoey's mom. That was where she belonged, and she didn't need a man in her life, in any capacity, to make her life bigger or better.

She told herself.

He cupped her jaw and smoothed his thumb along her cheek. "Give me a minute to dress. I'll come with you."

"No, I'm fine." She couldn't let him become something she thought would fulfill her. She already had all she would ever need. Smiling flatly, she pressed the middle of his chest, tempted to let her touch linger on his taut skin, still able to taste his flavor on her lips, but she was her own person, apart from him. Had to be. "Good night."

CHAPTER FOUR

DEMITRI WAS TYPICALLY the one who needed space. That was how it had always been. Yet Natalie pushed him back a step and walked out.

Usually he created distance when the microcues of emotional discord began to manifest. He was deeply attuned to them, whether he wanted to be or not. His childhood had predisposed him to picking up the slightest shift in the air, when bad could go worse within the space of a heartbeat.

He'd learned to defuse those explosive situations with an outrageous comment or an injection of chaos. He stirred the soup very deliberately, taking control of the moment by drawing attention and forcing the detonation. The shrapnel never landed on him, so it had always worked for him to push the plunger or pull the pin.

This was different. Everything about Natalie was different. She wasn't clingy. She was defensive. Oddly quick to isolate herself even though she projected genuine warmth and affection. One second she'd been teasing, the next revealing a kind of desperation, but not looking to him to resolve it for her.

That was often the impetus for him to dust his hands of a relationship. The moment things grew complex and a woman grew needy, he slipped away. But Natalie hadn't looked to him for solace. She'd looked off into the distance, as though he was the last place she'd expect to find whatever it was she needed.

A bizarre, painful hollowness sank into him, urging him to follow her to the hotel and catch at the connection they'd had and lost without him understanding how or why.

Damn it, he didn't *do* introspection and angst. Especially over women.

Nevertheless, he found himself returning to the hotel first thing, snapping out arrangements that brought her into the hotel dining room with a harried look on her face. It was just before 8:00 a.m. Her hair swung in the sweep of gold he'd run his fingers through just hours before, and her warm brown eyes refused to meet his, instead taking a run around the table of three managers he'd assembled on the fly.

"I'm sorry. I just picked up the message about this breakfast meeting. I'm not prepared at all," she said.

"No problem, Natalie. It's informal. Adara asked me to check in on the software transition while I'm here, so I thought we'd have a quick round table over eggs and coffee." It was an outright lie, but he'd wanted to see her and figured she'd balk at something more private or intimate. This was an excuse to sit beside her, brush his sleeve against hers, memorize her lipstick print on her coffee cup. He resented every second of not having her to himself, but it was better than nothing.

She was the first to leave, anxious to get to her training session on time, she said, tilting her head over her phone as she left without looking back.

His mobile vibrated. He took his eyes off her and pulled out his phone to glance at the screen.

What was that? her text asked.

He grinned.

The first of three square meals, he thumbed into his keypad, inordinately pleased to flirt with her this way. I don't want you going on strike.

Who can I expect at lunch?

Who do you want?

Her reply took a few minutes, then, Just you.
He began to breathe again.

Meet me in our suite.

"I feel so Parisian," Natalie said as she put herself to-gether, one eye on the clock ticking toward the end of her lunch hour. She was pretending her attack of insecurity this morning hadn't happened, and he seemed to be going along. "Meeting a man in a hotel in the middle of the day is very French, don't you think?"

"I don't know. I've never done it."

"Met a man?" She laughed, pausing before applying her lip gloss to sit on the edge of the bed instead. "A woman, then."

He came up on an elbow, the sheet tangled around his hips, his physique seeming sculpted by an old master. His kiss was lazy and lingering, but he searched her eyes, mak-ing her drop her gaze.

"Are you embarrassed to be doing this, Natalie? Ash-amed?"

"No," she said, but even she heard the *not quite* tagged on to the end. The clock was ticking. No time to search out the words to explain how she was betraying a part of herself. "Are we meeting here tonight?"

"Would you rather go out?"

She shook her head, feeling foolish for her stricken neediness this morning when she'd wished for a moment that she was the only woman he'd ever known. When she'd wished she was the type to expect the best and had every right to receive it. When she'd wanted to be someone he found hard to please but longed to anyway.

It had been a silly moment of conditioned anxiety for a man to complete her when really she knew that was the real fantasy. Her father hadn't stuck around to help her mom. Her own husband had never really been there for her. If she sometimes yearned for someone to walk through life with her, to be there when Zoey was grown and spreading her own wings, well, maybe she'd look for that companion in twenty years.

Right now, this was enough. She had a gorgeous man showering attention on her, even if it was just physical. The here and now was pretty damned good. You had to embrace these things, even if they weren't perfect. That was what she'd learned from her brother. Merely having a good day was a gift. Take it and run.

And Demitri made her day *so* good. When he rolled her beneath him late that night, she was still trembling and damp with having taken her fill of him, but she was glad it wasn't over. He was still hard inside her, his body primed with tension.

"My turn," he said, closing his arms into a tight cage around her. "But that was insanely hot, watching you lose it like that on top of me. I don't have much control left. This might get rough."

"Okay," she said dreamily, hugging her quivering thighs to his hips, surrendering herself utterly to his control.

He groaned out a curse and clenched his hands on her shoulders. "Except I want to stay like this, so aroused I'm going to snap. What are you doing to me, Natalie?"

"Can't last to take me with you?" she teased.

A feral light came into his eyes, and when he moved, he wasn't rough, but he was deliberate and thorough, thrusting deep and driving her inexorably along the path he was taking. It was almost too intense to bear, but soon she was gasping, "Don't stop. Please, I'm so close."

"Now, damn it. Now."

He did get rough at that point, and she encouraged him, eyes open but vision white as they shattered together, crying out with jagged ecstasy while they turned over and over in the abyss of pulsing pleasure. The waves of joy went on forever, holding them in a paralysis of tense and clinging rapture, only fading enough for their hold on each other to relax, but they were still locked tight, his weight upon her, both of them weak, breaths uneven, hearts still pounding hard against the other's.

Dimly she grew aware that she wasn't going to get her breath back as long as he stayed on top of her, but she didn't care. He was sweaty and heavy, and her hip was cramping, but she didn't want to move.

"I'm a little bit afraid you're going to kill me, Demitri," she finally whispered, only half joking. This intensity between them put her utterly at his mercy.

He snorted and shifted half off her, sliding a lazy hand up to cradle her breast. "I've been thinking the same thing about you since that first night."

That made a funny bubble of optimism lift her heart, but she quickly ignored it. Turning her head, she kissed him once. More of a quick nip.

"Seriously. I *have* to eat. That croissant at lunch was not a meal," she complained.

He groaned as he rolled away from her. "You are *so* demanding. If you recall, I offered to take you out to dinner this evening, but you chose to jump my bones."

She had, and she didn't feel like dressing to go out now. They wore hotel robes on the sofa and ate picnic-style food he'd ordered this afternoon: cheese and bread, pickles and caviar, wine and strawberries.

Tell him, she thought, feeling close enough to risk it, but tested the waters first by asking, "You have two nephews, don't you? Do you spend much time with them?"

"And a niece." He paused, gaze drifting into the distance while a darkly introspective look came over his face. "But that's a long story. One I don't even know how to tell. And no. I have as little as possible to do with them."

Her heart dropped. "Really? You don't like kids?"

"I don't think they're a scourge on the planet that needs to be wiped out. But I don't..." He scowled again. "I honestly didn't think any of us wanted kids. I knew Adara was trying, but I thought she was just buckling to pressure from our father. He wanted an heir. I didn't think she genuinely wanted a baby. Realizing she did... And then Theo turning up with one. I was downright stunned. Worried even, because—"

He rubbed a hand down his face, stopping himself from continuing.

"Because?" she prompted, curious, especially when he revealed a flicker of conflict, something like remorse.

He shook it off. "Family skeletons. He's turned out to be a better father than I could have imagined, but it's been an adjustment for me. Suddenly I'm supposed to be this involved uncle and I have zero interest in the role. I will never be like them. Why? Are you dreaming of picket fences?"

There was a cool warning underlying his question that made her smile flatly. "I did at one time," she admitted. "But my father left my mom and my ex..." She sighed with all the dispirit he'd left her with.

"Did he hurt you?" His tone shifted to something that was both warmly protective and chillingly dangerous.

"No," she assured him. "Well, with his thoughtlessness. He's pretty self-involved, but he's actually..." A good dad. Not a great one. *Discipline* and *structure* weren't in his vocabulary, but Zoey knew without a shred of doubt that she was loved to bits, and that counted for a lot when love for his daughter had failed to keep Natalie's own father in the picture.

"My mother-in-law says we have to respect Heath's energy. That we're all on our own journey." She rolled her eyes, but then grinned with affection as she thought of Heath's mom. If she couldn't have her own mother, at least she had the best possible surrogate. If she'd had to leave Zoey solely in Heath's care for three weeks, she wouldn't have come, but Zoey's connection to her grandmother was special and deserved to be nurtured and reinforced. "He actually has a very nice family. I think that was what I was really marrying. His mother is a foster mom and takes in every stray orphan that happens by. I was in a pretty bad place, having just lost my brother when I started dating Heath. She was there for me after Mom died, too, so I can't hate him when he's the reason she's in my life."

"Very magnanimous."

"I try. But in answer to your question, no. Remarriage is not something I'm aspiring to." Especially with a man who had such low interest in children. "If you give someone the power to make you happy, you give them the power to make you unhappy. I don't want to be unhappy. So you're safe," she said, swallowing disappointment that she couldn't even talk about her daughter. She missed Zoey more and more each day.

Not that she'd be sidestepping that topic much longer. Tomorrow would be their last day—and night—together.

Except, unbelievably, it wasn't.

"What are you doing?" Demitri asked, emerging from his shower to find Natalie dressed in sweatpants and a slouched hoodie with a maple leaf on the front.

He'd left her sleeping since it was still two hours before she needed to start work, but he'd woken and checked email only to become annoyed at his brother questioning why he wasn't in Athens for a meeting. His first instinct had been to roll onto Natalie and forget about everything, but he was already making more demands of her than he had with any other woman, and that disturbed him. He'd hit the shower as much to prove his ability to resist her as anything else.

She didn't have the power to make him happy or unhappy, he kept telling himself, oddly unable to quit turning that remark over in his mind.

Now she was dressed and putting on her shoes, and his need to possess her climbed several notches.

"Being a master of disguise, I'll pretend I've gone for an early-morning walk to pick up some pastries," she explained. "Then it won't seem weird that I'm coming to work from up the block."

Impatience pushed out of him in an annoyed sigh. "This is ridiculous."

Surprised hurt flashed across her face before she schooled her expression. "It's only one more night."

A spike of ice nailed him in the chest. "What do you mean?"

"I leave for Lyon tomorrow. I thought I'd pack over lunch so I can come here right after work. I could check out properly and stay here my last night if you like, but that seems kind of—"

"What do you mean you're leaving tomorrow?"

"I'm catching the train. I did the same thing coming here, arrived on Saturday so I could get settled and see a few sights before starting work Monday."

"There's nothing to see in Lyon."

"Only two thousand years of history." She held his gaze, an unvoiced question in her quirked brows. *Are you asking me to stay?*

She didn't ask it and bent to tie her shoe instead, then

stood to shoulder her bag. "I won't bother checking out. I'll just come over for—"

"What time are you off?"

"Might be as late as six."

"Do you ski?"

"That's random," she remarked. "I can, but not very well. Why?"

"We can go to Switzerland for the weekend," he decided.

"Switzerland? That's crazy!"

"You're thinking like a colonial. It's not that far. I'll take you to Lyon myself. On Sunday."

"But—"

She looked so fresh and innocent, face clean of makeup. For a minute he wondered what the hell he was doing with her. As cynical as she'd sounded about marriage last night, the way she was hiding their relationship told him how uncomfortable she was with what they were doing.

"You don't want to?" he demanded gruffly, bracing himself.

"No, I just didn't realize you wanted to…" She shrugged. "I thought you'd have somewhere to be by now."

According to his brother, yes, but she wasn't talking about work or any sort of external commitment. She was inferring she thought he'd be tired of her. He should be, and it made him uneasy that he wasn't.

On the other hand, a tension he hadn't quite acknowledged eased in him as he made plans to continue seeing her. He was already looking forward to being open about their relationship in Switzerland. This cloak-and-dagger lurking in shadows was not his style at all.

Wait. Relationship? *Arrangement*, he mentally corrected.

She canted her head. "You're scowling. *Do* you have somewhere to be?"

"No. I do what I want," he assured her. "And I want to take you to Switzerland."

"Do you?" she murmured, eyes dancing with laughter at him.

He scowled. "If you don't want to go, say so." And he'd commence with convincing her.

"I'll go. I just didn't expect this. Text me where to meet you when you've made the arrangements." She came across to lean into him, mouth lifted to press against his.

He took over the kiss. It had to last him all day, so he made it thorough.

"You can't buy me skis," Natalie protested.

"Why not?" he looked genuinely perplexed, even glanced down at his credit card as though he was checking to make sure it hadn't been declined.

"Because…" It was obvious, wasn't it? If he wanted to pay for a hotel room so they could sleep together, fine. And since he said his brother owned the helicopter that had flown them here, she supposed it was between the two of them to figure out how to pay for the fuel, but buying her ski equipment was weird. "What will I do with them after? I can't take them home."

"Of course you can. You ship to Canada, don't you?" he asked the clerk.

"Of course," the clerk assured her.

And the cost for *that*? Natalie drew in a slow breath. "I don't need skis at home, Demitri. I'll just rent a pair for the weekend."

"The line is too long."

"I don't mind standing in it. You do your thing and I'll do mine. We'll find each other on the slopes once I'm outfitted."

"*This* is my thing," he said with impatience.

"Getting your way is your thing?" she surmised.

"Exactly. Ignore her and outfit us both," he ordered the clerk.

"Demitri—"

"Come here. I want to show you something." He drew her over to the window, where snowflakes fell in glimmering sprinkles along the runs lit by high-powered lights. Against the indigo sky, the moonlight glinted off veins of ice in the jagged mountaintop. "Do you see that?" He pointed upward, to the ceiling.

"What?"

As she lifted her face, he kissed the daylights out of her. When he finally drew back, she blinked in shock, kind of embarrassed by their display, but also moved by the tender look in his eyes and the sweetness of his caress as he tucked her hair behind her ear.

"I just kissed you in public," he said. "We're here to be together."

"You could stand in line for rentals with me," she suggested with a cheeky grin.

"I do enjoy your sense of humor, Natalie." He reached past her and snagged a pair of lavender ski pants, the kind that clung unforgivably. "Try these on."

She glanced at the price, winced and said, "Okay, but I'm buying them."

"Again, completely hysterical. I invited you here. This is my treat."

Just going along with his demands didn't feel right, but what woman ever said no to Demitri? Before she knew it, she was decked out from head to toe, including goggles *and* sunglasses.

"It's night," she protested when he placed the shades on her nose.

"But the slopes will be bright tomorrow, even if it's overcast."

She gave up arguing with him, and they spent a couple

hours rediscovering their ski legs, left their equipment in a locker he rented and picked their way back through the pubs in the village to their hotel, eating fondue and drinking toddies while sampling live music. When they fell into bed, they were almost too tired to make love.

Almost, but not quite.

She fell asleep with her nose tucked into the damp warmth in the middle of his chest.

"You don't have to stick to the baby slopes for me," Natalie said as they leaped off the chair and snowplowed to a viewpoint. Far below, nestled in the valley, the village sat with comfortable old-world ease. Smoke puffed from small brick chimneys and snow-blanketed roofs poked up against sharp white peaks and brilliant blue sky. It looked like something off a Christmas card. "Go off and do some jumps or something. I'll be okay."

"The past two runs have been midlevel. I think you're ready to try something more challenging."

"No, they haven't," she denied, swinging her attention to him, then catching her breath at how urbane and good-looking he was.

His black bib-style ski pants over a white form-fitting insulated shirt, coupled with his sunglasses and natural air of command made him look like one of those intensely attractive villains from a British secret-agent film.

"I, um, don't ski well enough for midlevel." How had she even wound up here? The family hill she had skied during school trips at home had been a financial stretch. This place was practically coated in genuine silver, every piece of equipment sporting a designer label and mostly being used by licensed representatives, as far as she could tell.

"What are you talking about? You're cautious, but your skills are strong. I'm impressed."

He gave a passing nod of greeting to—good grief, was that a *royal*? Demitri had invited a gold-medalist and his wife to join them for lunch when they had bumped into them at the chalet, and a Swedish model had fawned over him in a gondola car. This mountain was a mecca for Europe's elite.

"Sorry about that," he murmured as an entourage in black followed the athletic frame of the prince down the slope. "I would have introduced you, but protocol says he takes the lead on that, and he's obviously preferring to be left alone right now. Ready?"

"Wait, no! Steep sounds scary," she said, catching at his sleeve and releasing a gurgle of nervous laughter, still taking in how he hobnobbed with the crustiest of the upper crust. "I'm cautious because it slants downhill. I'm used to ice. Flat." She lifted the hand not holding her poles and cut it straight across the air to demonstrate.

A snowboarder kicked off the ledge beside them and began to fishtail down the sharp incline, spraying powder back and forth with a *swish-swoosh*. Demitri had said he usually boarded, but he'd chosen to ski this weekend since that was her preference. She feared she was holding him back. He detoured for the occasional jump or slalom through a copse of trees, but kept returning to her side almost before she realized he'd disappeared, and always stopped with her if she needed a break.

"Ice? You mean skating?" he asked. "Do not tell me you played hockey."

"I'm Canadian. Of course I've played hockey. On a pond, not in a league, but I really meant ice dancing in a rink." She'd always thought the carving of skis into snow felt a lot like working skate blades against the ice, but speed gathered rather swiftly on a slope. She was so busy controlling that she wasn't paying attention to the signs, trusting Demitri to keep her from getting lost and keep her on the easy runs.

"Ice dancing," he repeated, taking in this new information with a bemused look. "How long did you do that?"

"Almost six years, I guess?" She wrinkled her nose. "Until Dad left and there wasn't really the time or money. I had a friend who drove me for a while, then I took the bus by myself, but Mom didn't like me sitting at the bus stop at five in the morning and…" She'd needed her. Gareth had. "It just didn't work."

"That's too bad."

"That's life," she said, shrugging it off. "It doesn't really bother me except, well, like today when we met your friend who medaled. I don't know if all the training in the world would have got me half that far, but he's just a guy who worked really hard. He made sacrifices, I know that, but it makes me think that if I'd been able to stick with my own training, I might have got a blue ribbon somewhere along the way. I really liked it and would have done the work. I wished I could have kept it up, but my life has never really allowed for the chasing of dreams."

He was looking at her as though he wanted to ask more, and she didn't want to talk about it or she'd get emotional.

"Okay, I'll try the top-level run," she told him decisively. "But if you get bored waiting for me to pick my way down, promise to go ahead. I'll meet you at the bottom."

"I'm never bored with you, Natalie," he admonished. "That's why you're here with me."

"Such a flatterer," she said, hoping he'd blame the tremor in her smile on the cold.

"It's the truth. But with the ice dancing, is it something you could take up again?"

"Gonna offer to be my sponsor? No," she said firmly. "It's not." She shifted her weight and moved in a comfortable glide so her skis were alongside his. Facing him, she leaned over, offering her mouth for a kiss. "But it's nice of you to encourage me."

"I'm not being nice. I'm telling you you're not too old. Seriously, what are the obstacles? The cost?"

If only he knew.

"You better take advantage of this now," she said with a touch of her gloved fingertip to her lips, not wanting to discuss any of her discarded aspirations. "In case I break a leg and have to spend the night in the hospital."

"I'm not going to let you break a leg. You know exactly where I want you tonight." He covered her lips with his own.

Demitri was in the kind of sleep he rarely found. Conditioned by his childhood to be a light sleeper—always on guard—he didn't often hit the really deep levels of REM, but he'd had an early morning, a lot of exercise, plenty of good food, a few glasses of wine in the hot tub and a delicious release with Natalie's humid gasps of pleasure against his ear. The room was cold, the bed warm, the smooth lobes of her bottom were spooned into his groin, and her breast was in his palm. He had found perfection.

Then a song like something off a kid's cartoon penetrated his consciousness. He fought acknowledging it, but Natalie shifted, coming up on an elbow to fumble for her phone on the night table.

"I'm sorry. Don't be mad," she said.

"Just make it stop," he growled, dragging her back into the hollow of his body, resealing the heat of her nude skin against his own.

"No, I mean I should have told you. Don't freak out."

What the hell was that supposed to mean? With his nose buried in her hair, he felt the tug of incomprehension pulling against the weight of falling back asleep.

"Hey, baby," he heard her say.

Baby? His mind sharpened.

"Hi, Mom," a little girl's voice said.

He snapped his eyes open.

CHAPTER FIVE

As Demitri left the bed behind her, Natalie tilted the screen on her phone so Zoey wouldn't see she had company. The fog of sleep was still befuddling her, but she was a mom, capable of pulling it together when her kid needed her in the middle of the night.

"Why are you up so late, sweetie? It's past your bedtime. Are you okay?" She'd talked to Zoey before leaving Paris, explaining she was going away for the weekend so might not be able to answer any calls. The fact her daughter wanted to connect anyway alarmed her.

"Daddy said I could stay up 'cause it's the weekend."

The door to the bathroom clicked firmly shut.

Natalie suppressed a wince and focused on her daughter. Zoey wasn't bathed, let alone in her jammies. "Where's Grandma?" She, at least, appreciated the value of a well-rested child.

"Auntie Suzie's baby is coming so she walked over to look after Bobby. She'll be back in the morning. Daddy said I could call you and tell you."

"Oh! Well, that is exciting news." They'd all known this might happen, so Natalie wasn't completely surprised. Heath was with Zoey and the worst that was going to happen was a late bedtime without a bath, but it still annoyed her that he saw no value in sticking to routine. "Babies usually take a long time to arrive, though, so you can't stay up and wait.

I want you to go to bed now, and I'll call you in the morning, okay?"

"But, Mom…" Always Mom lately. Never Mommy anymore. Five years old was way too young to make that transition.

"Listen, we'll compromise. You can skip your bath and have one tomorrow when Grandma is there to help you. Get yourself into your jammies and ask your dad to read stories, then you can play two or three games on the tablet if you want. You don't have to sleep, but I want you in bed." It was a trick. Zoey always dropped off like a rock once she was under the covers, especially after an active day on Heath's mother's farm.

Zoey agreed reluctantly. They said their "I love yous" and Natalie ended the call. Sitting up, she stared at the bathroom door, stomach as heavy as the pit of doom. Now what?

As the silence prolonged, the door opened. Demitri hesitated in the frame, naked and powerful, glancing at her with a chilling flatness that turned her to stone.

Her heart plummeted while varying levels of culpability, indignation and vulnerability washed over her. She should have told him, but he didn't have to act as though she'd committed a federal crime. As though he was not only furious, but wanted nothing to do with her now.

His view of her had changed, exactly as she'd feared. No matter how common single motherhood was these days, a stigma still existed. A judgment. Maybe she wasn't easy, but she was a woman who made bad choices where men were concerned. Someone who didn't have it together. A failure, and therefore her daughter didn't stand a chance. Natalie had been exposed to all those angles of prejudice at one time or another.

And she couldn't deny that she made bad choices where men were concerned, could she? Look at this one, giving her the silent treatment rather than asking her why she hadn't told him.

He moved to the chest of drawers and fished out a pair of shorts, stepping into them, and then continued to dress with efficient flicks of a collar and a snap of his jeans, all without looking at her. When he sat to put on his boots, she got the message.

"You don't have to go. I'll leave," she said, flipping back the covers and rising to search out her own clothes.

"It's fine. Stay." He stood and reached for his jacket off the hook on the wall.

She snorted, the furthest thing from amused. Angry, actually, that he didn't even want to talk about it.

Really bad choices, Natalie.

Wearing only her bra and underwear, she pulled her suitcase from under the bed, anxious to get away now. Feeling stupid and discriminated against. Feeling really, really hurt and disappointed, because yes, a very misguided part of her had thought he might like her enough that it wouldn't matter that she was a mother. It wasn't as if she was asking for marriage and a father for her child. Just a bit of companionship without being labeled or dismissed.

"What are you doing?" he asked, hand on the door latch.

She was obviously packing, but didn't see the point in being sarcastic about it. There was no reason to have a fight over this. She'd kept a secret and he was reacting exactly as she'd expected. Now they were done. It hurt, stung like hell actually, but there was nothing she could do to fix it, so she accepted it.

"Natalie," he said, demanding she respond.

"I'll get a room for the night, then make my own way to Lyon tomorrow," she said in as level a tone as she could manage. The nice people at her credit card company would be thrilled to extend her the cash. "You don't have to give up your room or your weekend."

"This was the last room. You're not walking down the street in the middle of the night with your luggage. *I'm* leaving. Stay here."

She turned, finding him with one hand still on the door latch, the other clenched so tightly around his dangling jacket his knuckles showed white. His face was all taut angles, his shoulders as stiff as iron, his will for her to do as he said practically resounding off him like rings of a bell.

"I want to leave," she said, not happy with the way her voice came out all papery and husky, but rejection did that to a person. She realized she was shivering and grabbed her long-sleeved undershirt off the floor to struggle into it. She found a pair of jeans in a drawer and shot her legs into them, then had to bounce on her feet to shake her butt into the seat of them. The rest of her clothes went from the drawer as an armload that got dumped into the suitcase.

"Natalie, stop." He was suddenly right beside her, tall and broad and reaching toward her.

She jerked away, pivoting to confront him. "I'm making this easy for you," she said with razor sharpness. "Stop making it hard for me."

"I have a right to be shocked," he said with a fling of his hand toward her phone. "Why the hell didn't you tell me?"

"Because I knew you'd act like this. Think differently of me," she blurted with a pointed, significant look. She couldn't hold his stare, though. Shame washed over her. All the guilt of denying her daughter weighed into her, slumping her shoulders so she skulked around him and into the bathroom to gather her things there.

Demitri listened to her clatter together all the millions of bottles and compacts and tubes she'd scattered across the tiny vanity since they'd arrived. His heart was pounding and a sick knot churned in his gut. Nausea had arrived with his realization that she had a child. Confusion and panic—yes, he was in a state of panic—had him desperate to walk out and pull himself together. Get away from whatever this was.

But she wouldn't be here when he was ready to come back.

That should be a relief. It should be exactly what he wanted because, damn it, that was how he coped best. Walk away. Pretend it hadn't happened. Leave the devastation for someone else to clean up. But *she* wanted to leave, and he was stuck to the floor, aware he didn't want her to go.

She wasn't the flirty, gamine, sometimes-nerdy single woman he'd thought he was maneuvering into a long-term position as his mistress. While he'd been delighting in finding a woman who had attained the perfect combination of being interesting while remaining disinterested in deep commitment, she'd been hiding that she actually carried the most indelible responsibility possible.

He was completely flummoxed as to how to proceed.

She came out of the bathroom and brushed by him without looking at him, almost as though she was too ashamed. *I knew you'd think differently of me.*

He was seeing her differently, but not in a bad light. It was more... Hell, he didn't want to examine any of what he was thinking or feeling. Face forward and keep moving was his motto. He never looked back and self-examined.

Scratching a hand through his hair, he watched her struggle to zip the poorly packed case and the word burst out of him. "Stop."

She only set her chin and worked to press and joggle the zipper tab with more determination.

"Natalie, would you give it a rest for a minute and just tell me—"

"What?" she demanded, quarter turning from the case and folding her arms, pure belligerence in her tone. "Tell you why I'm in Europe pretending to be a single woman who can have affairs?"

"You're not single?" That lit his fuse with a burn so deep and hot, he stopped breathing.

"No, I am. I'm single," she assured him with a widening of her eyes that told him she'd seen the switch inside him and was alarmed by it. "I meant about not mentioning Zoey. That I've been acting as if I don't have any obligations when I actually have a five-year-old." She pressed a hand to her forehead. "But I did tell you that first night that this is just a fantasy. A chance to live in a way I could never touch in my real life."

He told his muscles to relax as he watched self-consciousness flicker across her face. She met his eyes with a small plea for understanding in hers.

"I'm not proud of that. Or of hiding her from you. Heck, leaving her for three weeks with my mother-in-law has been eating me up, but that, at least, was for the sake of my career. It's actually what Gideon talked to me about that day you saw us."

She flicked another glance at him before she continued in a rush, as if she'd been dying to get this off her chest.

"Twice before this I couldn't take a special assignment because Zoey was too young for me to leave her. I was almost passed over for this one and wrote Adara an email about how it feels like discrimination when a married man with a child my daughter's age would be chosen without any hesitation, but I wasn't. She arranged for me to have this spot and asked for my input on rewriting the policies so they're more supportive to single-parent employees. They want to encourage everyone trying to advance in the company, especially if they're caregiving at home, because poverty doesn't help anyone in that situation."

Demitri nod-shrugged, vaguely aware of a discussion about that at board level, but it was so beyond his sphere of interest he'd let his siblings run with it. It wasn't the most impactful detail now.

"Your daughter is *five*? How old are you?" He'd guessed her to be twenty-five or six, but to have a daughter that old, she must have been a baby herself when she got pregnant.

She tucked her chin. "Twenty-four."

He couldn't help the way his brows lifted in shocked dismay.

"There was a party the night we all graduated high school." She shrugged. "My brother had just died and I was..." Her shoulder hitched defensively. "I'm not proud of that, either, but it happened and we got married because that's what you do, right? I wanted someone to take care of me, but Heath wasn't interested in taking care of either of us. He barely takes care of himself." She combed impatient fingers through her hair. "I shouldn't say it like that. I mean, he's not going to let Zoey play with matches or anything," she grumbled. "But he doesn't hold down a real job. 'Flash cards and dental appointments can be done another day, let's go fishing instead' is his attitude. He loves her and will always keep her safe, but I can't count on him when it comes to the day-to-day stuff."

The baleful darkness in her tone hit Demitri below the belt, bludgeoning him with the knowledge that he'd never been someone to count on, either.

"And this wasn't... I wasn't looking for someone to take care of me here," she rushed to add, indicating the room with a circle of her finger. "Skiing the Alps is nice, but I learned to live without any sort of frills a long time ago. I'm actually good with taking care of myself and Zoey. One of the reasons I don't date is because I don't want the hassle of trying to fit someone else's needs into our lives. We're solid, and even when I focus on my career it's really about her. Better income translates to more opportunities for her, a better education down the road. I'm trying really hard to make decisions that are best for her. But then

I had this little spell of time here to think about myself for a change."

She smiled with pained truth.

"You live single and carefree every day," she pointed out. "You probably don't realize how alluring the lifestyle is. Parenting and mortgage payments are not glamorous. And look at how you've reacted. You thought I was super-hot when you thought I was single and now you're turned off because I'm a mom. I wanted to *feel* hot and fun for a change."

"I'm not turned off," he growled, moving into the chair where he'd sat to put on his boots. His feet were heavy, his jacket on the floor where he'd dropped it.

He braced his elbows on his knees, deeply bothered and uncomfortable, still not keen to delve into why he was struggling with this, but he couldn't avoid dissecting it.

While she was already turning back to her suitcase to fiddle with the zipper, apparently resolved to leave.

"I don't mess around with moms, Natalie. I hear what you're saying," he hurried to state, forestalling another "you're a fantasy" remark. For some reason that was starting to annoy him. "The women I usually get involved with are as superficial as I am. You're not shallow in the least, and I knew that the first day we spoke, but I ignored it because…"

"Sex," she provided. "I know. That's why I'm here, too."

It was more than the sex. He liked her, but the sex was pretty incredible. Did she even realize how good? His conscience twinged as he processed that it sounded as though she'd had one lover before him, a boy-man who had never got past seeking his own pleasure.

A dark ache rose behind his breastbone. No wonder she was so enthralled with him. It had nothing to do with substance on his side or even his money. It was purely because he happened to take a great deal of pleasure in giving women pleasure, and she was starved of it.

He swore at the floor between his feet, oddly embittered by the thought.

She sighed. "I should have told you. I'm sorry. You're feeling guilty and you shouldn't. This was my decision, Demitri."

He lifted his head, grumbling, "Maybe your ex never gets a chance to take responsibility. Did you ever think of that, Natalie?"

She dropped her splayed hand from the middle of her chest, expression blanking with surprise. "Fine. Wallow in guilt, then. This is all your fault."

It wasn't, obviously, so he shouldn't be feeling anything beyond mild inconvenience that he was losing a delightfully compatible lover.

He rubbed his thighs, growing more keyed up as he watched her open her case and rearrange things, shoulders bowed with rejection.

Because she had a kid. And rather than try to pull him into that vortex, she was telling him why she never would. There was a quiet ferocity in her defensiveness. She was sorry she'd hidden her daughter, but everything she'd said told him she was deeply proud and committed to the girl. It was sweet and endearing, and he couldn't leave her thinking that he found something wrong with that.

"Nat, listen," he said to her back. "I'm allergic to family. Mine's a horror show. Like, we should be in therapy, but that would mean talking about it. If I could cut all my ties to them, I would."

"Don't say that!" She swung around. "If I didn't have Zoey, I'd be completely alone, and that's awful. Don't wish your family away. Don't."

"Obviously we have different perspectives," he dismissed, not comfortable with her vehemence. "What I'm saying is this does change things, but because of *my* history, not yours."

She hooted, swinging around to say, "It's not you, it's me? Is that what you're saying?" Heaving her suitcase off the bed, she let it hit the floor next to her with a thump that jostled her narrow body.

"Stop." He stood, hissing with impatience at her determination to leave.

"Look, I'm not going to tell the guy who paid for the room to get out of it," she stated. "I'm a big girl and can solve my own problems. I wasn't sleeping with you for this ski trip or even a new scarf." She pulled the silk one he'd bought her from its bunched home inside her coat sleeve and left it on the dresser. "I just wanted a nice memory. Let's keep it as one by ending things here, with civility. A clean break."

He had never realized how much that silly saying could feel like an actual bone snapping inside him, leaving a screaming agony that reverberated through his entire body.

"I brought you here," he said through his teeth. "Stay in this room, get some sleep and I'll take you to Lyon in the morning. Meet me in the lobby at eight. That's the end of it." In more ways than one.

He walked out.

CHAPTER SIX

DEMITRI HAD TWO limos waiting at the helipad when they arrived in Lyon. Aside from a few neutral remarks—*good morning, ready?*—they'd barely spoken. A maid had come to the room to pack his things. He'd piloted the helicopter and Natalie had tried to convince herself she was airsick, not lovesick.

They arrived at the Makricosta Heritage in Lyon one behind the other. He had no reason to check in and only a small duffel that he took straight to the elevators. She had new colleagues to meet and a room to be shown to. If she was distracted while she waited and her gaze followed the youngest Makricosta brother as he strode across the lobby, it was hardly suspicious. Every female employee's head was programmed to turn in his direction when he graced a hotel with his indifferent presence.

Her room, a standard queen in the upper middle of the main tower, had a pretty view of spires and red-tile roofs winding along the Rhone. Liable to break down if she moped in her room, really needing distraction from her melancholy thoughts, she asked to be shown to the desk she'd be using.

The administration floor was mostly deserted. The weekend manager pointed out her cubicle and leaned in with a conspirator's whisper. "I'd keep my head down and finish as quickly as possible, if I were you. The boss is in and does *not* look happy." He nodded toward the end of the hall.

"Demitri?" She willed herself not to blush. "I saw him arrive." And the idea of him looking as despondent as she felt should *not* be such a boon to her ego.

"Adara," he corrected under his breath. "But she's got him in there, and the staff in Paris said heads will be rolling, but they're being very tight-lipped about what happened. You were just there, weren't you? Do you know?"

She tightened her grip on her purse. What was left of her conscience swirled down an imaginary toilet. The dryness in the pit of her stomach affected her voice.

"No," she managed, but it was more a mouthed word than spoken. Her eyes had to be huge and swimming in guilt.

Fortunately, he was craning his neck as he ensured the doors were still firmly closed down there. "Well, I don't want to be around when they come out looking for blood. I'd suggest ignoring the rain and heading out to see the sights." He gave her a nod as he walked away.

Adara *knew*.

Natalie wished she could run and hide from this, but it was not her way. When she made a mistake, she owned it, 100 percent.

On heavy feet, she started down the hall.

Demitri so didn't need this. He reached for the knob on Adara's office door, only getting it open a crack before his sister said sharply, "We're not done talking about this!"

She stood behind her desk, more imperious than he'd ever seen her, but hard to take seriously when she had yogurt on her lapel. Apparently she'd been in a hurry to leave her family in Athens this morning so she could lie in wait for him and ruin the rest of what had already become a lousy weekend.

"It's over anyway, so there's nothing more to say," he told her.

"There's plenty to say! You've opened us to a sexual-harassment suit!"

"She's not going to sue," he said impatiently. Natalie was good and decent and maybe a little too grateful for his attention. They'd parted amicably—or as amicably as he could feel when he was furious with her for being completely different from what he wanted her to be. He would still be brooding over that if his sister hadn't arrived and *commanded* him to meet her in her office. *Now.*

She'd been taking lessons from her husband, he imagined. At one time Adara had been quite the pushover, determined to run the hotels but hiding behind Gideon and his position as chairman to do it.

The PA who'd nearly destroyed their marriage had turned out to be the best thing for them, however. Adara had grown a lot more confident once she knew her husband was completely devoted to her and always had her back. These days she really was the face and voice of Makricosta's, strong and determined.

Admirable, Demitri would have judged her, if she wasn't being such a pain in his hide.

"Everyone in Paris knows you've taken up with one of the IT specialists. It will be across the entire organization within the week. Are there others?" she demanded.

"No. And may I remind you that Theo did it? Why the hell are you coming down on *me*?" He could hear his voice tightening with anger at the injustice, and searched for patience. For the laconic disinterest he'd patented for any occasion when his morals were called into question. This was what he did. He behaved badly and it rarely had serious consequences. He rode out the waves he'd created and got on with his day.

Today his sister's castigation got under his skin. Maybe

because he was already so angry—he would still be with Natalie if not for her revelation, and company regulations could go to hell.

"I suggest you draft a new policy," he stated with a patronizing smile. "One that spells out exactly when it's appropriate to dally with employees. Because right now it appears to be a gray area."

"First of all, Theo offered me his resignation," she said testily, counting on a finger. "Even though, technically, Jaya was no longer working for us when they got together."

"About twenty minutes technical, from what I gather, but *okay.* I'll resign. Are you done?" Demitri said, dead serious, but she ignored his offer and touched a second finger.

"And he *married* her. Are you in love, Demitri?" she scoffed with cold disparagement. "Are you settling down to have a family?"

A hard fist clenched around his chest, suffocating his lungs and squeezing his heart so it pounded hard enough to hurt. No, he wasn't in love. What kind of emotion was that anyway? It was something that had kept their mother with a man who used her attachment to torture the bunch of them. Natalie was far too sweet and special to abuse with such a vile thing as *love.*

As for family, it was nothing but obligation and politics and bad memories swept under a rug. Did Adara not remember where they'd come from? Family was the reason he was the black-sheep clown that drew attention so it didn't land on her and Theo.

Resentment came up in a rush, gathering strength from her scorn. Did she think he had never wished he could be good like them? All those stupid, asinine, outrageous things he'd done over the years had been for *her*—trying to protect the two of them. If he had to spell it out for her, fine.

"You know what it was?" he challenged, lying, but

wanting her to see for once that he was loyal to the family in his own way. In the only way he could be. "I was keeping another opportunist from trying to poach your husband. I took one for the team, okay? If you want to fire me for that, go for it."

Adara went chalk white. He realized immediately that he'd screwed up, hitting her where she felt most vulnerable.

Remorse arrived like a westbound train, but before he had a chance to backtrack, the door he'd started to open pushed into him, knocking him into taking a step forward, clipping his shoulder hard enough to make him swear.

"What the hell—"

Natalie.

She confronted him with such horrified hurt that his guts turned to water. Her expression was shattered, her lips white and parted in disbelief, plunging him into a bath of emotion far worse than remorse. He wanted to slink away in utter disgrace.

"Really?" she demanded.

He opened his mouth, distantly aware of his sister taking in a shocked breath.

His brain rapid fired with reactions, all of them too revealing. Adara would realize how much Natalie had come to mean to him, and it was too much to let anyone see. Even Natalie, because she was shaking in a tremble of shock and rage, skimming him with a contemptuous gaze, as though filth coated him, filling her with repugnance.

He couldn't let her see how much that hurt.

"That's all it was?" she spat with loathing. "Even though I *told* you—"

"No," he protested, reaching for her arm.

Natalie knocked his hand away, adrenaline making her instincts fast and violent. She wanted to hit him. Punch and kick. She really did. Her heart was racing, her entire body hot, her ears ringing, her muscles twitching in aggression. She was sure that he'd believed her when she'd denied having planned to seduce Gideon.

"I told you I didn't expect anything except..." *A good memory.* So much for *that.*

She couldn't continue. Her face crumpled. Her control unraveled.

She shouldn't have walked down here thinking she could explain. She shouldn't have stood outside the door eavesdropping, hoping to hear he *did* love her.

Quite the opposite. He had complete disdain for her. He thought she was some kind of husband stealer and had only slept with her out of familial obligation. That put her somewhere lower than a pity—

She ducked her head, nausea climbing as reaction settled in.

She turned and left. Bolted from his call of her name and the equally sharp cut of Adara's voice. She dived into the first ladies' room she saw, eyes burning with tears she couldn't hold back.

She was such an *idiot.*

And now she'd lost her job. She was sure of it. They weren't going to fire *him.* The affair had been consensual. In its best light it looked as if she'd been trying to climb the corporate ladder. At its worst, Adara would believe her marriage had been threatened.

Fighting back tears, Natalie reached for a hand towel, but couldn't look herself in the eye to dab at her makeup. Her face ached with the effort of holding back a flood of emotion.

Men. Why hadn't she learned her lesson from her father, who'd left, and Heath, who hadn't really been there? Had she really expected Demitri to show up for anything but what she'd been putting out?

Heels clipped toward the door, and she swiftly stepped into a stall. The main door opened and Natalie heard a woman enter. The door whispered closed and a lock was turned. There was a sniff and a rustle while Natalie held her breath.

Through the crack in the door, she saw Adara dialing her mobile. She spied her own handbag sitting next to the sink. Damn it, why hadn't she grabbed it? This was a nightmare.

"It's me," Adara's tear-strained voice said.

Natalie opened her mouth, not sure what to say, but Adara continued.

"I should have told you why I had to come to Lyon. I think I just fired Demitri. Or he quit. I'm not sure." Another sniff, then an impassioned "No, it's not okay, Gideon! I feel awful."

Natalie let her head drop into her hand, wondering if this could possibly get worse. She didn't want to listen to this!

"Do you remember Natalie from the Canadian...? Yes? Demitri has been seeing her and— Oh, hell. I have to go. No, I'm fine," she added quickly, voice steadying. "But Natalie is in here. I can see your purse, Natalie," Adara said, making Natalie wince behind her hand and stay exactly where she was. Beyond the stall, Adara continued to her husband, "I'm fine, Gideon, honestly. Just upset. But I have to talk to Natalie. I'll call you back in a few minutes."

An expectant silence manifested.

Feeling cheap and pathetic, Natalie pulled the creaking door inward and exposed herself. "I swear to you I did not have designs on your husband. I would never, ever go after a married man."

Adara's mouth pinched. Her eyes were red and her makeup threatening to run, but she was still incredibly beautiful in her quiet and conservative way. Long dark hair, clear olive skin. She was class personified, and Natalie felt incredibly cheap being in the same room with her.

Adara pulled open a drawer and took out a makeup bag

along with a white facecloth. Her reflection smoothed to neutral, yet remained distantly defensive.

"Demitri said it to hurt me. He *wanted* to hurt me, which is why it did. He does a lot of infuriating things, but he doesn't usually set out to wound. Lately, though, everything he does seems to be an effort to push Theo and me away." She wet the facecloth and wrung it out. Her glance came up to meet Natalie's. "I didn't mean that the way it sounded. I'm upset." She held out the cloth to Natalie.

It seemed too nice a gesture, especially on the heels of such an insult. Adara was suggesting that if it hadn't been Natalie, Demitri would have taken up with a different employee just to alienate his siblings.

She really didn't want to think he was that childish or that mean.

She'd like to think Adara was only saying it to spite her, because she was angry, but Adara wasn't angry. She was watching Natalie with a pleading gaze, her expression so sympathetic it could only mean she pitied Natalie for becoming a weapon in a family feud.

Natalie came forward to accept the cloth, more to hide her face than dab at her ruined makeup. Adara pulled a second from the drawer and worked on her own, making Natalie feel even more foolish as they repaired themselves in thick silence.

"I don't..." Adara began, then tsked as her phone chimed with a request to connect. "Not yet, Gideon," she muttered, adding with a sober look toward Natalie, "He worries. Especially when it's family stuff."

After a brief bit of typing, which Natalie assumed was a text to her husband, Adara set down her phone and gave Natalie an apologetic look. "My business head is telling me to record this and say as little as possible, but I can't do that. Natalie, I'm sorry."

"For what?" Natalie asked, askance. "I knew what I was getting into."

"I highly doubt that." Adara offered a tight smile.

Natalie had to look away. Adara was right. She had thought that at the very least their fling was based on mutual attraction and desire. Instead… Humiliation ached through her and would for a long while.

"I can't protect all of womankind from my brother," Adara said gently, as if she knew what Natalie was suffering. "If he wants to pick up good-time girls looking for a night of partying, I can't stop him, but employees are off-limits. He knows that."

"*I* know it," Natalie insisted.

She was being punished for self-indulgence. It wasn't that she wasn't allowed to be happy. She just had to be happy with less than what most people got. She'd figured that out a long time ago. Wishing for things that other people took for granted, such as having a dad or a healthy brother or a functioning life partner was futile. But if she kept her expectations low, she could usually have that much.

If she hadn't stood outside that stupid door, yearning for love and marriage, she could have *had* the poignant memory she'd wanted from Demitri in the first place.

Adara dug an eyeliner from her bag, then leaned into the mirror to draw fresh lines around her lids.

Natalie opened her own purse and searched out a lipstick, but she really didn't see the point in fixing makeup she'd cry off as soon as she reached her room.

"It's not as if I expected anything to come of this. I just wanted…" Her mouth struggled to form words. Her hand was trembling, her whole body still reacting while her mind tried to latch on to logistics so she wouldn't melt into a complete mess. Dread and guilt mixed with regret and embarrassment. "Getting involved with him was my decision. My mistake. I just…" Time to grovel. And keep her expectations realistic—she hoped. "Will you let me put in a resignation rather than leaving me with a termination on my record?"

"I'm not firing you!" Adara lowered her hand and straightened to face her. "Don't be ridiculous. And you're not quitting, either. If you need some time, I'll arrange for you to go home early—and believe me, I'll understand. Take paid leave while the gossip dies down if you need to, but I can't imagine who we could possibly find to replace you. We'll have to make a statement of some kind, too. I'm sorry about that. Your privacy will be protected as much as I can manage, but as a company we can't be seen as trying to cover up, especially because he's family. Legal will have to walk us through exactly how that part should be handled."

"I didn't mean any of this to happen," Natalie blurted, feeling the press of tears rise to brim her eyes. "I'm so sorry."

"This is Demitri's disaster, not yours," Adara scolded. "I'm upset it happened, but not entirely surprised. I wish he would—" She pressed her lips flat and seemed to deliberately force her despondent expression into something more stoic. "I won't bore you with our family issues. But tell me, would you prefer to go home for the week or soldier on?"

Natalie desperately wanted to go home and lick her wounds, cuddle her daughter and let maternal love heal the cracks that romantic longings had fissured through her heart. But the fact that she still had a job was a miracle in itself. No way could she walk away from it and jeopardize it further.

"If you really want me to, I'll stay."

Demitri was drunk. Not stinking drunk, but drunk enough not to care how unhappy he was. It was the perfect state to be in as he sat beside the pool of a competitor's five-star hotel in the south of France. No chance of sitting beside one of his own—his brother had canceled all his key passes along with his company credit cards.

That was after his brother-in-law, Gideon, the *real* head of the Makricosta organization, had had him escorted off the Lyon property. There'd been a phone call first. He had to give Gideon credit for wanting his side of things, but Demitri had been in no state of mind to be civil. "Adara's not sure if she's fired you or you've quit," Gideon had said.

Demitri had told him what he could do with his job, so furious by the way things had gone, he'd cut all ties to Gideon, his siblings and the damned hotel chain.

Do you love her? he could still hear Adara saying. *Are you going to marry her?*

It was supposed to have been a simple affair, not something that would haunt him. Not something worth quitting his job over.

He didn't care about his job. Not really. Certainly not about the money. He had a trust fund he rarely touched. He'd only gone into the family business for them. Adara was the one who cared about the hotels. Theo, well, Demitri would never understand why Theo was still there. At least he, Demitri, *liked* the kind of work he did. He was competitive enough to make sure all his campaigns and strategies were exceptional, even if he was bored out of his skull with the subject matter. Aside from Theo getting on his case about budgets now and again, neither of them had reason to question the quality of his work. They were going to miss him long before he'd miss them.

Which was proved when he saw Theo scanning the crowd from across the pool.

Demitri let a smirk of satisfaction tilt his mouth. He had known they'd break first. Come begging.

Theo spotted him and a twitch of disgust tightened his mouth.

Oh, goodie. A meaty, overcooked lecture, coming right up.

He watched Theo wind his way through the occupied deck chairs and families around tables. Theo paused at one, speaking to a mother with a baby on her lap.

Missing his own baby so much he had to stop and tickle the chin of a stranger's? God, he was sick of how besotted they all were with their spouses and babies.

Theo handed over a business card to the man at the table, hands were shaken and the baby gathered up by Theo. He walked purposely toward Demitri, the baby beginning to reach back and cry as he realized he was being taken from his mother.

"Is Makricosta's starting a black market—?" Demitri began.

Theo plopped the bawling kid into his lap, making Demitri scramble to set aside his vodka tonic and hang on to the squirming boy so the tyke wouldn't pitch himself onto the marble pool deck.

"What the hell?" he said to Theo, raising his voice to be heard over the growing volume of the worked-up kid's bellow.

"Make him stop," Theo challenged.

Demitri would have risen and carried the brat back to his mother, but was a little too drunk to trust himself, especially when just keeping the boy in his lap was like wrangling a marlin.

"Make your point, Theo," he demanded.

"It's pretty distressing, isn't it? Is he hungry? Does he need a diaper change?"

"He wants his mother," Demitri said pointedly. "Take him to her."

"What if his mother is passed out from drinking and

pills?" Theo said, leaning a hand on the arm of Demitri's chair as he mentioned the unmentionable. "What if you're a little girl and if you don't keep him quiet, your father is going to backhand you so hard you hit the wall on the other side of the room?"

"We're doing this here? Now?" Demitri asked, reminding himself not to crush an innocent baby just because his brother made him see red. Did Theo think he didn't remember? That he wouldn't have stopped their father if he could have? That he hadn't tried in the only way open to him?

"I'm sorry," a woman said, pushing in to break the men's intense eye contact. It was the boy's mother. "I can't bear hearing him—"

"It's fine. Perfect," Theo said, straightening into his hotel-controller role. "I appreciate your loaning him to me. As I said, just call my personal number when you've decided where you'd like to stay. Two weeks, any Makricosta resort. Room and meals on me. Thanks."

"That's awfully generous for such a penny-pinching bastard," Demitri said as the woman walked away and the baby quieted.

Theo ignored that and only said, "Adara is worried about you."

"Really? Weird, because she sounded more worried about the reputation of the hotels when we last talked."

"She doesn't deserve the silent treatment. Text her and let her know you're alive."

"Take a look, Theo," Demitri said with a wave at his mostly naked, semireclined form on the lounger. "I'm a grown man. Why don't you two stick to playing mommy and daddy with your actual children?"

"Why do you always have to make things harder, not easier?" Theo muttered, crossing his arms and shaking his head with disgust.

It might as well have been one of those backhands Theo had been talking about, only for once, it had landed on him. *You have to be good, Demitri.* Yet being bad had been the only way he'd known to defuse their father's lashing out.

The guilt that had always sat in Demitri for getting away with so much, setting him apart from his siblings, slithered in him like a venomous snake, sinking fangs behind his heart. He'd always known in the darkest corners of his soul that Theo must blame him. Must secretly hate him. That was why he hadn't asked all the questions he had about Nic, fearing the answer would be, *because you're not one of us.*

"What do you want from me, Theo?" He wasn't going to beg for their acceptance. Adara had made it pretty clear what she thought of his ability to contribute to family. Did their tolerance of him hinge on his doing as he was told? "Do you want me to toddle on back to my room? You know he's dead, right? You're not going to get belted this time if I stay here and do whatever the hell I want."

It was too far. He saw the same look come over Theo that Adara had worn when he'd made his brash claim that Natalie had been trying to move in on Gideon. He hadn't been aiming for Theo's internal organs, but that was where his sarcasm had landed.

"Damn it, Theo," he said tiredly. "You started it—"

"No. You're right." Theo blinked once and revealed a gaze that was so devoid of emotion, Demitri knew he'd been wiped from his brother's short list of people he'd die for. "You do whatever the hell you want. Sit here and drink like him and act like him and don't give a damn about anyone else. We're better off without you if that's your attitude. I'll let Adara know she's wasting her time being concerned. I look forward to not receiving your calls."

"You look like a waiter," Demitri wanted to call at Theo's white shirt and black pants as his brother retreated.

He didn't trust his voice, though. When he reached for his glass, his hand shook and the taste of it made his gut churn hard enough he thought he might throw up.

If they had just left him alone about Natalie...

But he knew who had really caused this chaos. They all thought they knew about protection, but for years he'd done everything he could to keep his sister from getting knocked around and his brother from being beaten.

They didn't need his high jinks anymore, though. They were settled and happy with their little families. He only had a place among them on their terms.

He hadn't felt alone with Natalie. Not that he'd ever considered himself reliant on anyone. Until her, he'd *always* felt one step removed. Different from his siblings, not like other people.

But he'd *had* Adara and Theo. He'd always had their back, and he'd always wondered what it would take for them to turn theirs on him. It had been his secret fear: losing them.

Which was why their picket-fence marriages grated. He could trace all the twists and turns starting pretty much from when their father had died and Adara had looked up Nic, bringing him into their lives as if he had a place there. But those were just steps that had led to this moment, when his siblings not only didn't need him anymore, they didn't want him.

Natalie had wanted him. Not the way that other women did. Not because of his money. Maybe because of his proficiency in bed, but also because he'd made her laugh.

She'd made him laugh. She'd been a bit of a feminist, quite a history buff, quick to weigh in on current affairs. She'd been thoughtful and sensitive, and he'd wanted more time with her.

God, he hated himself for hurting her.

Pushing his thumb and forefinger into the corners of his

eyes, he tried to quell the pressure there, wishing futilely for someone to sort out this mess he'd made.

No one was going to show up this time, though. He was exactly where he'd always feared he'd wind up.

Completely alone.

CHAPTER SEVEN

AFTER LEAVING LYON, Natalie had managed to avoid going into any of the hotels for more than a month, thanks to a snowstorm that had turned the company Christmas party into a bust.

The whispers and stares had been pretty bad by the time she'd left France, but she'd taken it on the chin and powered through her assignment. Adara had defused some of the gossip by making a statement that Natalie's special contribution working with high-level management would ensure all employees, regardless of obligations at home, would be given the same opportunities in future.

This, along with a statement that Demitri had left the company to pursue his own interests, had all become old news by the time Natalie was required to show up for the quarterly departmental meeting at the Montreal location.

The meetings were as predictable as clockwork, always taking place on the second Wednesday of the first month. They always had morning one-on-ones with various departmental managers, then a catered lunch followed by a presentation of slides and reports. Theo called in his contribution by webcam, taking questions before turning the afternoon over to the Canadian IT manager, who always closed with breakout brainstorming sessions based on the morning's findings.

Each of these teams was making their presentations

when Natalie was handed a message by a bellman who'd slipped in to find her.

Your car will be waiting at the main entrance at four-fifteen.

What car? She didn't get a chance to ask and had to make her way to the front of the hotel when the last presentation finally finished. The limousine windows were blacked out and the chauffeur forestalled the bellman to open the back door himself.

Natalie caught sight of male legs on the far side wearing black jeans and motorcycle boots. She bent to see Demitri glance up from his tablet. The collar of his sharp peacoat was turned up against his scruff of stubble, making him look as rakish and devil-may-care as he truly was. His hair, needing a cut, looked ruffled by fingers, making her think of all the times she'd done it with her own.

Her heart rose to throb painfully in her throat, leaving a hollow feeling in her chest that threatened to cave in upon itself. She strangled out, "No." Then she straightened to force a smile for the chauffeur, repeating a tight, "No."

It was the only word she could manage. Her limbs began to tremble.

"Get in the car, Natalie. Or I will get out," Demitri threatened, voice so low she barely heard it, but so implacable she had to take heed.

Alarm, the kind that accosted with sharp tingles down her arms and legs, had her looking around at the curious doormen and her IT colleagues who were leaving the hotel for the transit stations, glancing at her as she stood next to the open door of the limo. She could hear their thoughts, wondering how she afforded a private car.

She did *not* need to stir up gossip again.

Ducking to speak to Demitri, she claimed, "I have my own car."

"You take the bus into the city in the winter so you can read, rather than having to pay attention to road conditions." He tossed his tablet onto the seat opposite. "You told me. Want me to get out and reminisce about the other things you shared with me?"

She narrowed her eyes into lethal death rays at him.

He reached for the door latch and gathered himself.

"I have places to be," she told him, making him pause and look at her. "A *daughter* to collect and make dinner for."

If that had any impact on him, it didn't show on his impervious expression. He only stated, "I'll take you wherever you want to go. But I want to talk."

About what?

She didn't suppose she'd find out unless she climbed into the car.

A sharp wind was cutting through the breezeway, pulling at her hair and the open lapels of her coat.

With an annoyed huff, she swung her laptop bag on to the seat next to him, then plopped herself into the seat opposite so she was diagonal to him, about as far away as the confines of the car would allow. Warm, at least, if not happy.

She gave the chauffeur her address and he closed the door. The privacy window was already up, and seconds later, the car pulled onto the road.

Natalie folded her arms and stared sulkily out the side window. "Someone told me once that only lowlifes pick up women at the sidewalk. He would know, I suppose."

A pause in which she refused to look at him. He was probably laughing at her. At the sort of treatment she accepted from men.

"You look good, Natalie," he finally said.

She snorted, because she'd been feeling wan before

she'd even made the trek into the city this morning. Zoey had been sick earlier this week, was finally well enough to be back at school, but Natalie was still shortchanged on sleep, always too worried when her daughter ran a fever to rest properly, and sitting backward in the car was making her ill.

Without explaining, she shifted to the other seat and snugged her coat collar up around her throat, returning her disgruntled scowl to the window. It had snowed while she'd been inside all day, just enough to drape the city in a fresh layer of white. Just enough to snarl traffic and persuade more people than usual to use transit rather than drive. The commute would have been a killer. She was secretly thrilled to have door-to-door service.

"I was angry with my sister and looking for the quickest way to shut her up," Demitri said quietly beside her. "That's the only reason I suggested you were going after Gideon. I didn't mean it."

If that was supposed to be an apology, he'd missed the most important word.

"She could have fired me." Her voice cracked, more from hurt than anger, but she hoped he didn't realize that. "I need my job, Demitri. I have a mortgage and a child to feed." Did he think she hadn't spent countless nights having this conversation in her head, where she railed at him and told him what a jerk he was?

Yet, when he sat beside her smelling all masculine and foreign with his special European blend of aftershave and a take-away espresso in the holder beside him, she couldn't help remembering how those scents had surrounded her in bed, clinging to the sheets and her skin. Making her close her eyes in dreamy memory of physical satiation.

"I'm lucky she didn't take you seriously," she muttered, scoring herself with the memory of that day even though it was something she had spent a lot of time actively forgetting. "But your real motivation is just as awful, so *whatever*, Demitri."

"What do you mean?" he asked in a dangerous tone that almost made her look, but she kept her head stubbornly turned away.

"Adara told me how you were looking for ways to dig at her and Theo." She worked hard to keep her tone flippant, trying to act as if this was merely something annoying rather than devastating. "That you probably would have slept with any employee just to tick them off." It made her raw inside to say it. She was insulted and sad. Very, very hurt.

"She said that?" His voice hardened with ire, stilling the swirling ache in her heart. "Look at me," he commanded, making her turn her head with a reflexive jerk. Outrage pulled at his expression. "She said that to you," he confirmed, looking straight into her eyes with aggressive demand. He was incensed.

Which was disconcerting. A little alarming and even heartening, since he seemed so insulted, but she reminded herself he was no choirboy. He passed along his dates to rock stars, among others.

Mentally willing her pulse to settle, she lifted her chin, trying to appear as unaffected as she wanted to be.

"Are you saying she was wrong?" She tried to sound bored, and hated that silken threads of optimism wound through her. And she braced herself for hard truth if he allowed that, no, Adara hadn't been wrong. Natalie had been trying to reconcile herself to that reality for weeks, and it still shredded her insides. "You weren't using me?"

"No. I wasn't." His gaze flinched away from hers as he looked forward. "Maybe I can see why she'd think so, but to say something like that… That's offside, Nat. I'm really angry with her for that."

She sputtered a laugh of disbelief. "Why? You said something awful and so did she."

"I didn't say it to your face. I didn't *mean* it," he shot back, dark fire brimming in his eyes as he looked at her again.

His fury was a stab into an abscess. Revisiting that day hurt so much she could barely stand it, yet his anger on her behalf released a painful pressure she'd been trying to get used to since it didn't seem as if it would ever go away.

That bleeding of acute pain edged her dangerously close to forgiving him, though. To thinking everything that had transpired had been okay. It hadn't been.

"Adara wasn't trying to hurt me," she muttered. "She was a lot nicer to me than I deserved, considering what I'd done. What *we* did." She drew in a long breath that burned. "We never should have…" She flicked her free hand at the interior of the limo, "This shouldn't be happening, either. There's no point. Why are you even here?"

Demitri studied Natalie's face, not liking to see her so unhappy, mouth pulling down at the corners as she looked away again. He'd been starting to think she wouldn't show, trying to find her home address on his tablet, when the door had opened and he'd heard her voice calling goodbye to a colleague.

The brooding disinterest that had weighed on him for weeks had lifted like clouds revealing the sun. His blood had burst with a zing of enervation in his veins and his nostrils had sharpened in search of her scent. For a moment he'd seen only her torso and legs, uniform eschewed for a chic pair of knee-high boots, tights, a tweed skirt and a cashmere top, all glimpsed from the open flaps of her long red woolen coat. Lissome thighs. Round, deliciously weighty breasts that he loved to cup and fondle.

Then she'd bent down to look into the car, and her curious frown had flattened to shock followed by complete rejection. *No.*

Not something he'd heard often in his life.

And now, *there's no point.*

He sighed, not having entirely thought this through. He'd simply realized a few days ago that given Theo's precision schedule for his communication meetings, there was an excellent chance Natalie would be in the Montreal conference rooms today. He was doing a lousy job forgetting about her, and he'd never been one to sit back and ponder when he could be taking action, so...

"Knowing what you thought—well, what I thought you thought—about my reasons for sleeping with you, made me feel..." The unbearable churn of guilt and shame returned full force to grind within his chest. "It made me feel. Period. I don't normally have a conscience or listen to it, but hurting you has been sitting on mine."

He let her see his regret.

Her mouth quivered briefly before she pressed her lips flat and looked away.

"Apology accepted, as thin as it is," she said stiffly.

"I rarely apologize. I can't be expected to be good at it," he retorted, stung. This conversation was not alleviating his inner turmoil at all.

"Sorry," she grumbled, smoothing an eyebrow, then glancing at him, somber and sincere. "I don't like conflict or bad feelings. I mean it. Apology accepted. You didn't mean for me to overhear you, didn't mean what you said. Adara had it wrong. Whatever we had was just...whatever it was."

"It was good, Natalie," he told her, reaching across to cover the hand she dropped to the seat between them. "You know that."

So good he hadn't been with another woman since. Which was driving him insane. He was *not* used to going without sex, and every woman he took out, trying to forget Natalie, was such a poor imitation he couldn't bring himself to do so much as kiss them. He'd come here thinking there must be a way…

Her eyes widened as if she was reading his thoughts. She snatched back her hand.

"Oh, no," she said firmly. "The position of man-child is already taken in my life, Demitri."

Perhaps the blow wasn't undeserved, but it was brutally placed on an open wound Theo had kicked through his psyche. Given the breadth of responsibility he *felt* like he'd carried all his life, he was stung by how little she thought of him.

"That was cruel," he told her, not entirely successful at affecting a casual tone.

"Did you honestly think we could just pick up where we left off? Are you forgetting I have a daughter? She's the reason you broke things off in the first place."

He clenched his teeth. There was a very convenient emotion called denial that had allowed him to set her daughter on a shelf while he had traveled here from New York. It wasn't that he wanted to pretend the girl didn't exist. But every time he tried to imagine how the edges of his life might accept the invasion of her daughter's, he recalled Adara's disparagement of his ability to be a family man. If his own sister couldn't see it in him…

Then Theo's "act like him" comment would echo in his head.

That one still burned. He would never, ever hurt a child, and that wasn't really what Theo had been suggesting. No, he'd been tarring Demitri with the man's selfishness and bent values of pride and superiority over empathy and caring.

The vilification kept rubbing at Demitri's rawest edges because he couldn't refute it. He didn't know if he had anything meaningful to offer a child.

But he wanted Natalie. So he was willing to try, or better yet, stay the hell out of the way so he didn't cause any emotional scars to the girl.

"I realize she's your priority," he said, trying to convey his willingness to accommodate. "But surely there are times when you have an evening free? When she's with her father?"

Natalie's eyes grew glossy as she stared at him. Her brow crinkled in a flinch and she looked down, bottom lip pouting out while she twisted her fingers in her lap.

"So that really is what you're suggesting? Except, rather than sneak around on your family, we should hide from mine."

"You're making it sound… No. Look, I can see why single parents don't want a revolving door of partners paraded in front of their child. If you want me to meet her, fine. I will." Even though it made him feel like he was offering to lock himself into the Mixed Marital Arts ring with the reigning champion. "I want to see you, Natalie. I've quit Makricosta's. There's no reason we can't date."

"The sex wasn't that good, Demitri. Find someone else," she dismissed with a fracture in her tone.

He had to check himself so he didn't leap out of his own skin.

"Do you need a *reminder*?" he challenged in a voice that rose with astonishment and dismay.

She shrank into her seat, giving him a helpless look not unlike the one she'd worn that first night when he'd dragged her into his room.

He remembered every single thing about every single encounter with her. Did she think that was normal?

Her brow crinkled with disgruntlement and she set her chin mutinously, but there was something incredibly vulnerable in her expression. She was trying to resist him and finding it hard. If he had any morals, he'd protect her against the lothario in him.

Damn it, he was so desperate to kiss her and *show* her…

Jamming a desultory foot against the opposite seat, he tilted back his head and groaned at the roof. Since when did he show mercy? Care? Use words to communicate rather than actions?

"I realize that walking out on you that night, when you took that call from her, was insulting," he said, searching for the right thing to say. "I've been regretting ever since that I didn't stay and try to find a compromise. I want to keep seeing you, Natalie. I like what we had. You told me you weren't looking for marriage and picket fences, either. Was that a lie?"

"No," she admitted after a weighty moment, voice low. "I have my own version of that already." She nosed toward the suburban street the limo had slowed to navigate.

It was a quaint old neighborhood of new mansions and restored heritage homes, mature trees and lopsided snowmen waving from the front yards. Not far from the city center, he noted. Quite the upscale location.

"Exactly how much does my brother pay you?" he asked.

She chuckled self-consciously. "My grandfather was an architect. He built the house and my mother inherited it, then it came to me. My mortgage paid for a new roof and some other updates along with the estate taxes, but the actual house was paid off years ago."

The limo turned into her drive and stopped. He leaned forward to look up at the charming two-story—three, since she appeared to have a basement. Steps rose to a covered and recessed front door. He liked how she'd married the 1940s architecture with efficient replica windows and modern siding.

"Invite me in to see it," he said as the chauffeur left to come around to her side.

She shook her head, gaze flicking to the back window of the limo. He glanced across the street to where a pair of little girls, bundled in snowsuits, climbed the berm of plowed snow to exclaim at the fancy car.

"Zoey walked home with her friend's mom, but will be hungry for dinner."

Inexplicably, he found himself about to insist she introduce him to her daughter, but he could already see the shadows of refusal building behind her eyes.

"When can *we* have dinner? Friday?" he asked, holding her pensive gaze. Willing her to capitulate.

She hesitated. "I don't know where this could go."

"Don't you?" he wanted to ask, but schooled himself from stealing a kiss to demonstrate.

She gave him a look that was a mixture of scold and hurt and yearning. Then she shot another look out the back window. "I have to go," she insisted, reaching for the door latch.

The moment she did, the chauffeur, who'd taken himself around to wait for her, opened her door.

"Friday," Demitri said, helping her gather her bags. "I'll be here at six."

"I…" Her attention was torn between him and the girl across the street. "I'll meet you in the city," she finally ceded.

He howled with triumph inside, but shook his head sternly. "You know my feelings on that. I'll be here."

She might have protested, but a happy cry of "Mom!" cut her off.

She straightened and urged the chauffeur to close the door, calling, "Stop and look for cars! Is it safe? Then yes, you can come across."

A moment later, she took a full-body hit in the middle from a girl with a purple hat and a yellow jacket who wrapped her arms around Natalie and beamed up at her. Her reddened nose topped a profile that was a rounder, younger version of Natalie's. He hadn't anticipated that she'd look like her mother, or have that same bright glow of optimism that he found so likable in Natalie.

"Why did you come home in this big car?" her high voice asked, audible through the glass. "Can I see inside?"

"A friend gave me a lift. How was school?" Natalie steered the girl to start up the front steps with her.

Natalie's daughter stopped and turned as the limo began to back out. She waved, but Natalie only watched, a troubled look on her face, bottom lip worried by her teeth.

Arriving home to find Zoey outside at the neighbor's had forestalled Natalie really working through everything that Demitri had said. She kept trying to tell herself that it didn't matter that he hadn't *meant* to hurt her. Or that, according to him, he hadn't used her, either. He thought what they'd had was *good*.

He still didn't want a future. He didn't want anything more than the casual arrangement they'd had in Paris. Actually, he wanted less, since he lived in New York. How would a relationship—an affair—even work? She definitely shouldn't cheapen herself by agreeing to one.

Except when he'd reminded her that she'd claimed not to want marriage and more children, an unexpected greed for *something* had risen in her. No, she wouldn't dare ask for the full package. Look how dreaming too big had stung her in Lyon. But it felt awfully good to have someone tell her she looked good, stroking her ego and her skin, before kissing her in a way that made her blood race.

Oh, she knew exactly what had happened. The charm train had rolled into the station and she was tempted to climb aboard, forgetting that she'd been dumped from it once before.

She agonized all day Thursday, then spent every spare moment on Friday drafting lies and excuses, going so far as to type them into her phone, but never hitting Send.

I have to work late.

I'll be in the city anyway.

I'm sick.

Zoey is sick.

Zoey was away for the weekend at her grandmother's. Yes, a wicked part of Natalie had wanted to be available to whatever Demitri might plan, but now that her workday was done and she was ruminating in front of her closet, she had to ask herself what the heck she thought she was doing.

She'd made her peace with being single after breaking up with Heath. Demitri had stirred up a pile of longings in her while they'd been in France, a vision she'd blacked out because it was so far-fetched, especially because it starred him. It would definitely be better if he disappeared as abruptly as he'd shown up.

Which was exactly what she'd tell him over dinner, she assured herself.

Then he showed up looking all alpha and sexy in a cream-colored mock turtleneck under a fitted blazer in chocolate brown. It had a casual formality that lent him authority and command. And he brought flowers and a bottle of wine, which nearly finished off whatever defenses she had.

"No chocolates?" she mused facetiously, trying not to melt into a puddle of submission.

He looked at the items in his hands, expression blanking with surprise. "They're in the limo."

"No way!" she burst out with a laugh. "I was joking."

He stared at her, making her self-conscious. A pleased, answering smile twitched his mouth. "That laugh gets me every time," he said, voice husky and intimate. Affected?

"I'll be right back." He pushed the wine and bouquet into her hands and left.

She did the only sensible thing she could do. She moved through to the kitchen to put the flowers in water, using them as a shield of busywork so he didn't completely disarm her when he returned.

Snowflakes glittered in his hair when he came back. He set a large, flat wooden box on the kitchen table.

Her eyes popped when she saw the gold-embossed name. He'd bought them a pair of those truffles from a specialty shop in Switzerland as if it was penny candy, even though he'd turned over a very large note for them. Eating hers had been a peak life experience. Now he'd brought her a whole *box* of them?

Shrugging out of his jacket, he draped it over the back of a chair and reached for the wine, beginning to peel the foil off the neck. "You look fantastic."

"Tickets, please," the conductor said, and she found herself with one foot on the Demitri Heartbreak Express, all of her tingling with excitement.

Check yourself, Natalie. Where on earth did she think this train was going? This wasn't France and fancy-free time. This was nine-to-five, get-the-groceries, be-a-mother-and-set-a-decent-example time. Sure, he had money and turned up with fringe benefits, but she couldn't count on him any more than she could on Heath.

"I bought it in Lyon," she said of the dress. She'd found it on one of her many excursions out of the hotel to avoid all those speculative looks. *Remember that?* she scolded herself.

The dress was a thick knit that fell to just above her knees, the wool speckled with green-and-gold tones. She'd paired it with a filmy gold scarf and a narrow belt. Her tall boots, pretty much her regulation attire from November to February, would jazz it up, but it wasn't deliberately sexy or seductive. She might as well be in a bikini, though, given the way he scoped her from top to bottom and back.

"The chauffeur is waiting, isn't he?" she hazarded as he opened a drawer in search of her corkscrew.

"I pay him very well to do exactly that."

Of course he did. Nipping the ends off the stems in the arrangement, she set the whole thing into her largest vase and filled it with water.

"How, if you don't mind my asking? There was an announcement that you'd left Makricosta. Did I get you fired?"

"No, I did that all by myself," he assured her, opening a cupboard at random, forcing her to point out the correct one. "Actually, it was a mutual parting of ways. I've wanted to leave for a while, but didn't feel right about it." He carefully positioned two glasses on the table. "I'm starting my own firm, so I can pick the jobs that interest me." He lifted a dark look at her that was vaguely insulted, but amused, too. "So I'm temporarily unemployed, but I'm not here to couch surf at an old flame's if that's what you're thinking."

She bit her lips together, suspecting she was being chastised for her man-child remark. "So I shouldn't feel guilty about the way you left? You and Adara have made up?"

"No," he said shortly. "I mean, no, you shouldn't feel guilty. My leaving was a long time coming, and no, my family isn't speaking to me right now." He poured and offered her a glass. "But I'm angry with them, too, so the radio silence is also a mutual thing."

She dried her hands and accepted the glass of chilled, lightly sparkling rosé, glancing up at him with concern.

He offered a blithe smile, uncaring, always trying to pretend he was superficial and lazy, spoiled and arrogant, but he had so much more going on below the surface.

"Demitri…" This would be a massive invasion of privacy, going a lot deeper than any conversation they'd delved into in Europe, but she felt she had to know. It was the reason he'd ended things so abruptly in Switzerland. Searching his eyes, she asked, "What makes you so averse to family? What happened with yours? Why are you so angry?"

His lips thinned, rejecting her question, gearing up to refuse to answer, she thought.

"They kept something from me," he surprised her by replying. "Until a few years ago, I didn't know that I— we—have an older brother. Half brother." He tilted his glass, staring into it so hard it should have sizzled and boiled dry. "Nic Marcussen."

"Nic... *The* Nic Marcussen? The media guy? Who owns, like, half the world's magazines and news channels?"

"Yes." He sipped, blinking to contain what she sensed were volatile emotions.

"That's quite a secret big brother."

"Right?" he challenged, fury creeping like lava under his tone.

"Why didn't they tell you?"

"*I don't know.* But he's back in our lives—their lives— and I don't know what the hell I'm supposed to do with that, so I've been keeping my distance." He set aside his glass, pushing his hands into his pants' pockets broodingly. "Adara seems to think we should all get together in some sort of family reunion. I've been resisting, finding other things to do, which annoys her. That's why she thought I was using you to get at her and Theo, but I'm not *that* childish. I just don't want anything to do with him."

Not all families were as close as she'd been to her mother and brother. She knew that, but it still made her sad for him and his siblings. And keeping such a huge secret was a curious mystery that made her want to quiz him further, but he changed the subject.

"Show me around. Is this flooring maple?"

* * *

Thankfully Natalie could take a hint. She took him upstairs for a brief glance in the three bedrooms, a tidy master just airy and pastel enough to confirm it belonged to a woman.

"Queen," he commented, eyeing the mattress, thinking it would do.

"Because my daughter sneaks in," she said with a don't-even-think-it smile.

He was thinking it. Of course he was. That dress she was wearing was a statement in subtle eroticism, clinging to her curves in a mysterious way that hinted while hiding, driving him insane with desire to press and feel and stroke.

He let her take him along to the princess-themed girl's room full of stuffed animals and well-stocked bookshelves, and then another bedroom converted to her home office.

His interest in the house had been piqued from his first glimpse. He'd thought it was basic curiosity in things like architecture and workmanship, but he realized he'd really wanted this glimpse into Natalie's true self. He wanted to know why she held such a grip on him. Despite her sunny nature, she kept a lot of herself private. Her child, for instance.

Her office was as efficient and practical as he knew her to be on the job, but the framed child's artwork down the stairs and newspaper article above the fireplace congratulating her grandparents on their fiftieth wedding anniversary reflected her less obvious, but very endearing qualities: warmth and sentimentality and hints of a romantic.

"The dining room is a mess. I've taken up scrapbooking." She flicked on the light, but hung back as though she'd rather he didn't enter.

"You know you can do that sort of thing on computer now?" He purposefully brushed past her through the arched doorway, taking advantage of the movement to graze a light touch on her shoulder and upper arm, liking the way she jumped under his caress.

"I spend all day on computers. I like doing something real. Don't look. You're Mr. Marketing and Ad Campaign. I'll never measure up," she protested, catching up a handful of crumpled paper in a tight fist.

When they called it scrap, they meant it. The table was covered in bits of colored paper, buttons and ribbons, and novelty stickers, but the chaos was nothing he hadn't seen on his own desk when he needed a cut-and-paste mock-up.

"You have a good eye for composition," he said sincerely, taken with a collage of black-and-white snapshots of her grandparents that she'd arranged with silver borders on a sheet of pale green.

"It's, um—" she edged protectively toward a finished book "—just something to do with all my mom's boxes of photographs."

He spied the photo on the front of the finished book, a baby in an incubator. Something in the colors of the snapshot told him it was real, not a print from digital. Older. He set his hand on the book to draw it across the cloth on the table so it was before him. "Gareth," he read. "Your brother?"

"Yes, it's…" Her hand wavered as she decided whether to stop him opening the cover. "I wanted something that Zoey could keep, so he's not forgotten."

Her voice had gone husky. He could tell she wasn't comfortable with letting him see, but he couldn't resist turning the pages, admiring the care she'd taken with designing each page, but more ensnared by the story she told.

Natalie had said her father had left, and there was no evidence of him here. As for her brother, he had spent his life in hospital and sick beds, occasionally a sofa or a picnic blanket. Her wearily smiling mom was usually behind the camera rather than in front of it, capturing her underweight but grinning son and his vibrant, obviously devoted older sister. In the early ones Natalie cuddled and coddled him; as they grew up, she did terrible things to his hair with clips and bows. She made faces at him over a hand of cards, sat with him in front of a bin of building blocks and eventually aligned herself behind a computer screen next to him.

That was where her interest in IT had come from, Demitri would bet. She couldn't throw a ball with this boy. She would have had to race him in video games.

"You told me your brother had died, but I didn't realize he'd been sick all his life." He looked at her with new eyes, amazed by how effervescent she often was after everything her small family must have endured. "What was it?"

"A congenital heart defect, but there were other things that came along with it."

"Was it…" He could see her shutting down. "You don't want to talk about it. Too painful?" Of course it was.

She nod-shrugged. "I don't mind talking about him, but his illness was my whole life for so long… That sounds awful." She shrugged jerkily. "As if I resent him, and I don't. But my entire childhood revolved around his appointments and surgeries and recoveries and lack of a future. Everything that needed to be said about his condition was said while he was alive. The only important piece now is that I loved him."

She stroked his image, her smile brave and crooked, causing something to shift in his chest. It hurt and made him reach out, drawing her in so he could soothe.

"Oh, Nat," he murmured, setting a hand on her silky hair, tucking her crown under his chin in an unfamiliar need to comfort. "And then you lost your mom."

"She was tired," Natalie said on a breath of sorrow, dropping her hand onto his waist, not quite accepting his embrace, but he thought it might be more about fighting her own emotions. Her voice wasn't steady. "She fought for Gareth every day. Urged him to keep fighting, and took on the system that didn't expect him to make it past two or three years old. If there was a treatment or surgery we hadn't tried, she made it happen. Then he was gone and I was married, and I think she thought she could rest. She didn't have to worry about either of us. I went away with Heath just after Zoey was born, up to his mother's farm, and Mom got the flu."

Natalie drew away, brushing fingertips under her eyes where her makeup was threatening to run. "She'd had enough of hospitals." She closed Gareth's book and set it aside, as though she was trying to set aside her grief. "She wouldn't even go to the doctor. I came home and got her admitted, but she had pneumonia by then and it killed her."

And Natalie's husband hadn't come to the funeral.

"I'm so sorry, Natalie."

She gave a muted shrug. "She's with Gareth now. We should go, shouldn't we?"

Her defenseless expression bordered on persecuted. She needed time to regroup the way he had after talking about Nic.

He didn't want to leave. He wanted to hold her again. Touching her had felt good. Right.

They were both raw from delving into things that he was still shocked he'd revealed, though. And getting physical right now would be less about the kind of escape he longed for and could take the intimacy of their conversation to an unforgettably deep level. Something he couldn't come back from.

"Probably a good idea," he agreed, following her to the front door and watching her zip into shiny black spiked-heel boots that hugged her calves and cocked her curves into a sassy posture when she straightened. That backside of hers never quit. Shame to cover it, but he held her coat and drank in the scent of creamy vanilla in her hair, so familiar he forgot for a moment where he was. Things in him that had been wound tight relaxed. A smile touched his lips as he thought about brushing aside her blond tresses and setting his lips on her nape.

She went still, and he glanced up to see they faced a mirror. He stood behind her and to the right, not unlike the photo of her grandparents. Whether she'd seen his expression of desire, or saw the similarity to the longtime couple's pose, he didn't know, but he found himself taking a mental snapshot of the two of them looking at each other so nakedly, his hands on her shoulders, her expression still shadowed by emotion, his own filled with tender affection.

It struck him that you didn't get to fifty years by staying detached. You shared the things next to your soul. In his previous life, he wouldn't have encouraged her to give him the details of her most terrible heartaches. But it hurt him to see her suffer. He wanted to hear what pained her so he could carry some of the burden for her.

Disturbed, he looked away, feeling her pull away from his light touch at the same time.

Natalie was changing him. He didn't understand why or how, but he'd felt it after their breakup, sitting in New York unable to stop thinking about her.

In the car, he studied what he could see of her profile in the dark silence, trying to work it out, wondering if there was a Freudian element to it.

"Did you have to look after your brother a lot?" he asked her.

"Yes," she said simply, adding, "when Mom went to work, which was three nights a week and every weekend. Someone had to make sure he took his meds or monitor his temperature and pulse if he was recovering from surgery. Mom was spread so thin, I did a lot of the housekeeping and cooking, too. Then I had Heath and Zoey to look after. I still have to remind Heath to pay his rent," she said with a little tsk. "I've never *not* felt responsible for someone. That's why, well, it's what I was taking a vacation from," she admitted in a small voice. "In France."

He could help her carry some of that load.

"How old were you when it started? When you had to be a little mom to your brother?" he asked.

"I don't know. After Dad left, I guess. Seven? Gareth would have been three."

He rubbed his thigh, confiding family secrets before he lost his nerve. "Adara was younger than that when she started looking after me. Five or six."

Natalie turned her head, voice colored with surprise when she said, "Really? Where was your mom? Working?"

"Passed out." He could still see the unresponsive shape in her bed. When Theo had called him to tell him she was gone, he'd had to catch back a tasteless, "Are we sure this time?" because he'd thought her dead so many times as a child.

"She liked to wash down her pills with vodka. Dad liked to drink, too," he stated flatly. Then he closed his eyes and walked through the door he'd only peeked through that day by the pool with Theo. "He got violent when he'd had enough of it. If Adara didn't keep me quiet, she got smacked. If Theo failed, he caught Dad's belt."

"Oh, my God." Natalie caught her gasp with her cupped hand, understandably speechless. Her eyes glowed white at the edges, not that he was able to meet her gaze for long.

Why had he been so cavalier that day with Theo? It had been cruel, and he didn't blame his brother for not returning the one call he'd placed to try to make amends. The truth was he didn't understand why his brother hadn't rejected him the moment it had happened.

Demitri never looked back on his childhood. Ever. But

he made himself remember that incident now. Made himself feel the guilt. He'd left his room, even though Theo had tried to stop him, but Demitri had been determined to find Adara. Not their mother. His sister. Because Adara had been the one he relied on. She'd been the closest thing to a mother he'd had while theirs had been a slurring mess who'd rarely left her bedroom.

And Theo had taken the punishment for Demitri's transgression.

Who *did* that to a little kid? Why hadn't someone called child services?

Why hadn't *he* been the one to catch hell?

Fierce, angry tears came into his eyes so hard and fast he had to avert his face to the window and remind himself he'd been three years younger than Theo's eight. He hadn't really known what he'd been doing. He had barely understood what had been happening when Theo had screamed in their father's den. It was only later, when Adara had pleaded with him, "You have to be good, Demitri," that he'd begun to comprehend that Theo's injuries, the stripes on his back that were visible to this day, had been his fault.

And despite Adara's pleading, he'd never been good. He didn't think he ever would be.

CHAPTER EIGHT

"AND YOU?" NATALIE asked with trepidation, lowering her hand, needing to know, to understand him, but certain she wouldn't be able to withstand whatever she heard.

Demitri shook his head, expression impossible to read.

"He loved me." He made a quick noise of negation, clarifying in a bitter tone, "I mean, he loved to throw me at Adara and Theo in ugly little ways. 'Demitri got a trophy today, Theo. What did you get?' 'Have you fed your brother today, Adara? Why are you eating if he hasn't?'"

Natalie couldn't move. A cry of denial that anyone could put children through such mental and physical torture locked her throat.

"That's really horrible," she managed.

"It's sick," he hissed, revealing a pressure of anger she suspected had been bottled tight for years. "I *tried* to make him hit me. I dented his car and drank his booze, skipped school and broke the front window. He was the only one home that day, half a bottle in him. It wasn't even lunch. Winter. Snow was blowing in. You know what he said? 'Call Theo. Tell him to come home and fix it.' That's crazy, right? Like, legitimately not sane?"

Finally he looked at her, and while his brow was an anguished line, his eyes were glazed with wrath. The devil-may-care veneer was cracked wide-open, revealing that the man inside did care about things. He cared a lot.

"Demitri, I'm so sorry," she could only say, while the back of her throat stung.

The car stopped.

He seemed to shake himself out of his past. "I shouldn't have told you that."

She reached out to cover his hand, folding her fingers over his stiff ones. "It's okay." She got the feeling he'd never told anyone. "Did no one ever report him?"

He shook his head, turning his face forward, but his hand shifted in hers so he could pinch her fingers in a tight grip. It was as though he was holding on to a lifeline so he wouldn't be sucked under and drowned.

"We had money. The privilege of the rich extends to not having your actions questioned. I've learned that. Even when you're leaving marks on your kids, you can get away with it. I remember waiting for Adara at school one day. Her teacher told her she could stay in class as long as she wanted, but Adara told her it was better if she got me home on time. The teachers knew. They didn't do anything."

"You never thought about making a call yourself?"

The corner of his mouth twisted. "By the time I realized I could, I'd developed my own way of dealing with it. The old man would be reaching for Adara and I'd spill my milk. Instead of shaking her, he'd tell her to mop it up. Then we all grew into teenagers and Theo was big enough that Dad kept most of his bullying to verbal. Even at that, it never stopped. And they took it! It made me so crazy." His hand worked hers with hard agitation, but she ignored the discomfort, sensing this was a much-needed bleeding out of poison. "I'd say, 'Just tell him no,' and Theo wouldn't even hear me. He'd just keep doing whatever he'd been told to do. He took accounting! The man should be engineering fighter jets."

Natalie could hardly take in all she was hearing. She had grown up sad and frustrated with her brother's illness, but aside from resentment over her father leaving, their house had been loving. So loving.

She didn't know how anyone could live with something so twisted and painful. No wonder the Makricostas were standoffish and hard to read.

"And they never hated me, no matter how bad it got for them. No matter what I did. I slept with Theo's fiancée, for God's sake!" He glared at her, half his face lit by the slant of neon glow from the street, making him look satanic as he practically insisted she revile him for his actions.

"With *Jaya*?" Her mind started to explode, but he quickly dismissed that.

"No. Long before her. Someone Dad arranged." His grip on her hand eased. "I knew Theo didn't want to go through with it and asked him why he didn't just leave. He was in his twenties. I couldn't understand why he was still letting Dad run his life, and Theo said, 'If I don't get married, Adara will have to.' We'd seen the kind of Neanderthals Dad was trying to fix her up with. She was trying so hard, even that late in the day, to make us look like a nuclear family, never acknowledging that it was radioactive. I could see why Theo was willing to make the sacrifice, but I couldn't let him go through with it. So I slept with his fiancée and that broke them up. Then Adara married Gideon and I honestly don't know why Theo stuck around after that. To make sure Gideon was good to her, maybe."

"You could try asking him," she suggested gently.

He snorted. "I told you. They're not talking to me."

He rapped a knuckle on the window and the chauffeur opened his door. Demitri reached back to help her out, then hugged her into his side as he walked her into the restaurant.

They were both shivering, and she wasn't sure how much was cold and how much was reaction. Never in her wildest imaginings had she seen such a history on him.

It explained a lot, but raised more questions, most pressingly: Where were they going?

Not for their date, of course. She could see he'd brought her to Old Montreal. They entered a converted industrial building where they were ushered through a trendy lounge to an elevator. It opened into an elegant space of velvet chairs and crystal chandeliers, where a table had been reserved against the windows overlooking the St. Laurence.

But where were they going as a couple?

As they were seated she saw far too many similarities to their first meal. The waiter set her napkin in her lap and Demitri ordered wine and a mixed plate of seafood hors d'oeuvres for them to share.

Of course, she'd told him in Paris that she liked lobster and shellfish, and this place had a reputation for offering the finest of both. Perhaps he was being less high-handed and more thoughtful than she gave him credit for?

Linking her fingers together, she touched her knuckles to her lips, elbows braced on the table, and regarded him through the tangle of her lashes, intrigued by the dance of light and shadow from the candle flame against the carved angles of his handsome face.

"What are you thinking?" he prompted.

"Honestly? I doubt you've ever told anyone what you've told me tonight. I'm wondering, why me?"

His lip curled in self-contempt. "If you only knew how many times I've listened to some rejected pop diva or a humiliated politician going through a divorce. 'Thanks for listening,' they always say, while I shake my head at their bizarre desire to share their personal garbage. I have no idea, Natalie. I felt like I *could* tell you, I suppose."

She smiled wistfully, not entirely surprised. "I'm easy to talk to because I'm used to having the hard conversations. I never had the luxury of radio silence with my brother."

He looked up sharply.

"I didn't mean that to sound superior," she said with an apologetic quirk of her mouth. "I can see why your family would avoid talking about your childhood, but..." She leaned forward. "What if something happened, Demitri? Do you really want this animosity sitting unresolved between you forever?"

His face spasmed briefly and he looked to the window.

After a long minute, after she'd retreated into her chair and tucked her hands in her lap, he said, "No. Of course not."

He shifted, gave his jaw a brief skim with his hand.

"That first day we met? Gideon accosted me right after you'd spoken to him. He was pressing me to come to Adara's birthday party. I was annoyed and took it out on you. I don't want to go. Nic will be there." He grimaced. "But I keep thinking I should. It would mean a lot to her."

"You really don't remember him? I find that so strange. How is he even...? Did your father have an affair?"

"How sexist of you, Natalie," Demitri scolded. "My mother had the affair. My parents had broken their engagement and she had a fling with Nic's dad, from what I've been told. Then she got back together with our father and passed off the baby as his. Maybe she even believed it. She was pregnant with me when Dad realized Nic wasn't his. They sent him to boarding school. I guess we saw him a handful of times after that, but the closest thing I have to a memory of him is asking Dad, 'Who's Nic?' I don't know why it came up or who else was in the room. I just remember the look on his face and being scared. I was sure I was going to get it. Then he slapped me on the back and laughed."

"Your father punished them for remembering him," she said on a wisp of stunned disbelief. "But not you, because you didn't."

His face fell in shock. Obviously it hadn't occurred to him.

"That's really cruel, Demitri," she said, numb with incredulity. "You're entitled to feel confused and angry. All of you are. I can't believe anyone would act that way toward their own children."

"I always had a kind of survivor's guilt, because they suffered and I didn't." He frowned at the table. "I always thought I should have been punished the way they were. I looked for the line. I pushed and pushed to find it. And I always figured they should hate me because I wasn't catching hell the way they were. Now they do hate me, and even though I deserve it—"

The sommelier arrived with their wine, giving them both time to regain their composure.

"You should go to her party," she told him when they were alone again. "You don't have to get into all of this, but at least turn up."

He only gave her a disgruntled look, as though he knew she was right but was reluctant to admit it. Then his attention on her sharpened. He narrowed his eyes, holding her gaze with that willpower of his that was so implacable.

"Come with me."

"What? No," she said decisively, and then had to ask, "Why would you even suggest it?"

"Because we're seeing each other."

"No, we're not! We're having dinner," she insisted. "Once. Tonight. So I can tell you we're not doing this again."

Demitri sat back, face icing into hard angles. "Because you're afraid I'll turn out like my old man?"

"What? No!" The protest came out unreservedly. He was as capable as anyone of saying something awful, obviously, and far too used to getting his own way, but the times she'd seen him angry, he'd been tightly controlled, not one to resort to violence.

"I've cut way back on my drinking," he continued as if he hadn't heard her. "Not that I was ever a mean drunk. I hate losing my temper. I wouldn't so much as raise my voice to you. Are you afraid for Zoey?"

She could see genuine agony in him. Perhaps the only glimpse anyone would ever get of him with shaken confidence.

Natalie shook her head emphatically. "I don't think you would ever hurt me or Zoey. But, Demitri, that woman you met in Paris, that's not me. You won't find me as fun or accessible as I was. I can't play pretend again."

Demitri was feeling his way on very thin ice. Relief had deflated a lifelong tension in him as he realized that his father hadn't favored him because he saw something of himself in his son. That black mark on his soul was lifting, thanks to Natalie's insight, but it didn't mean he was reformed into the kind of man who would fit into her life. He respected that she'd engineered her personal world so she was self-sufficient. He admired her for it. And God knew he had never measured up to anyone's expectations unless they were basement level. He didn't blame her for her lack of willingness to take a chance on him.

But if there was a way he could keep seeing her, he wanted to find it.

"What do you want from a man, Natalie?"

"Why do you think I need anything from a man?" she challenged lightly.

"You don't need *anything*?" he asked with a skeptical cock of his brow. He swept her blushing cheeks with a masculine gaze of interest that hovered on lips she nervously dampened with her tongue.

"You seduced me in France because I allowed it," she asserted, adding blithely, "I can seduce myself if I want to."

"Flirt," he accused, delighted when she was cheeky and

suggestive. "You know I'd like to see that." She never, ever bored him. He adored that about her.

"I'm not flirting," she lied, mouth twitching with rueful amusement.

"It was a challenge, then?"

"No," she said firmly. "And don't think for a minute I don't know how to say that word when I need to."

"Cute of you to think so, but you're the biggest soft touch going, Natalie."

"I have a daughter to think of," she countered with a shift in her mood to grave sincerity. "As weak as I might be as a woman, as a mother I would lift cars and tear grown men apart to protect her. That's what I'm trying to say, Demitri. That's who I am here. Mom first. Woman second."

He pondered that, asking cautiously, "Do you want a father for her?"

"She has one," she said with a pragmatic shrug. "He's not perfect, but she gets more from him than I got from mine."

"Love, you mean." The word hurt to say because it was an emotion so foreign and incomprehensible to him, he doubted he could ever offer such a thing.

Natalie didn't laugh or mock. She didn't light up and say yes. She pursed her mouth as though trying to school her lips from trembling. He watched her throat work as she swallowed, and he sensed pain. It made his throat hurt.

"Love is nice," she said with a flicker of a smile. "But it doesn't mean anything. Heath tells me he loves me all the time. I still can't live with him."

"Does he?" Demitri began to fall, pushed so abruptly into a chasm of darkness he couldn't see or feel or breathe.

"He says it after he feeds Zoey junk food all day, or gets her from school but forgets her backpack. As if he's this great guy capable of loving me even though I'm angry with him. I thought my father loved me and he left because life got hard. Love isn't enough. I want someone I can count on."

She looked up at him, but he couldn't reply. What could he say? They both knew Demitri Makricosta could only be counted on to do what he shouldn't.

"Natalie..." He found himself laughing bitterly at what a mess this had become. He'd flown up here thinking he could fall into bed with her and stop feeling this angst and dismay with his life. Instead, he was baring his soul in a fight for a place in her life. "The way I've always behaved... I don't want to be that man anymore."

The persona he'd cultivated had worn thin even with him. No one ever gave him credit for the level of control he exerted, and he was tired of being underestimated.

"I can appreciate that, Demitri. I can," she said, so earnestly she moved him, giving him hope yet gently rejecting him. "But I can't afford to be your guinea pig. I can't invest my time and heart, my *daughter's* heart, while you figure out if you really want to stick around."

Was she asking for a deeper level of commitment? Marriage?

The thought should have put him firmly on the run, ending dinner before they'd eaten the appetizer that arrived with a waft of buttery garlic and salty tang.

He wasn't repelled by the idea of marriage to her, though. He liked sharing space with her, waking next to her, eating across from her. In France, he'd wanted to make her his mistress, but he could easily see something more permanent. Given how hard she'd had it, he would feel really good if she'd let him provide for her.

The stumbling block was her daughter. Maybe Natalie didn't expect a father for Zoey, but he would never convince her to let him infiltrate *her* small family if he remained estranged from his own.

* * *

Natalie picked at food so exquisitely prepared she ought to be moaning aloud, but her heart was weighted by Demitri's silence and everything tasted like cardboard in her mouth.

When their waiter came to remove the plates and ask after the next course, she was surprised that Demitri ordered entrées. He'd gone so quiet she had assumed the date was over.

"Really?" she asked when the waiter had left. "I thought you might want to call it a night."

"Natalie," he chided. "When I said I want to change, it doesn't mean I've lost my taste for getting what I want. I won't slink away and die because you expressed a few doubts about my reliability. Count on me to be persistent, at least."

She shouldn't laugh at that, but a mixture of relief and alarm twitched her lips.

He intended to *pursue* her. The scent of danger sharpened in her nose and her heart rate kicked up. She shook her head, fearful she wouldn't be strong enough to resist him if he had his mind set on possessing her.

She wanted to be possessed. Therein lay the problem.

"Don't make this hard for me, Demitri." It was a plea.

He picked up her hand, smiling ruefully as he drew it across the table and leaned forward to kiss her knuckles. "I could say the same to you."

He was asking her to allow him to break her heart. She *must* be the biggest soft touch going, because she sat there and let him continue to hold her hand, incapable of arguing.

"How's work?" he asked, taking her by surprise. "Catch me up on the gossip."

"Seriously?" she asked with a disconcerted laugh. "Why?"

"We've had enough of the hard conversations for now,

haven't we? Let's remind ourselves why we enjoyed each other so much in Paris. Tell me if that idiot Laurier is still rewriting all of my carefully worded campaigns when he translates them into French. That always annoyed the hell out of me."

Oh, he was a magnetic man. Far too capable of disarming and engaging. She found herself admitting, "Laurier's losing his mind at all the shake-ups in that department since you left, thinking he ought to have been promoted over Sanjit."

They wound their way through a million topics over dinner, taking their time, lingering over specialty coffee and crème brulée while the restaurant emptied. When he said, "Tell me about Zoey," she hesitated.

"What do you want to know?"

"Anything you would have told me in France if you hadn't been afraid to."

She shrugged, thinking of all the moments she'd almost said, "One time Zoey…" Wrinkling her nose, she admitted, "Last week she asked me where babies come from."

"Wow," he said, chuckling at the wry panic she recreated for him. "What did you say? Stork or cabbage patch?"

"I was close to my mom because she was always honest with me," she said with a helpless lift of her hand. "I had to tell her. It was a very basic version, of course. I skimmed over *a lot*."

He grinned at her, so much admiration in his look she had to glance away from the intensity of its glow.

"You're a good mom, Natalie. Contrary to what I made you think our last night in Switzerland, it's actually one of your most appealing qualities."

Tears sprang to her eyes and she swallowed, deeply moved. She tried really hard to be a good mom, wished daily that she had her own mother to ask for advice and second-guessed herself all the time. Demitri was hardly an expert, but it still meant a lot to her that he'd said that. No one ever did.

"Thank you," she murmured shyly.

"I would never try to get between you. I hope you believe that," he said solemnly. "What you have with her is precious. I'd do everything I could to preserve it."

Perhaps he wasn't an expert on good parenting, but he was very well versed in terrible. The flimsy defenses she had against him wavered and fluttered like the walls on a house of cards.

"I should pay before they turn the lights out on us," he said, reaching into his pocket.

A few minutes later, he held her chair and kept his hand at her back as he steered her toward the door. His touch sizzled through her dress and she knew there was only one way she wanted this evening to end.

Weak, weak Natalie. Was he playing her in his expert way, seducing her to his will? Or was this real?

When he'd helped her with her coat earlier, she'd caught a look so tender on his face, she'd been completely beguiled. Still, it surprised her when he turned her in the elevator and made no effort to disguise the warmth and desire in his gaze. He curled his fists into her lapels, then paused as though waiting for permission.

She looked at his mouth and licked her lips, sexual yearning swirling into her middle as she anticipated his kiss. "Yes, please," she heard herself whisper, and cringed inwardly at how blatant and needy that sounded.

He reacted with a look of aching hunger and lowered his head, covering her mouth with the hot mastery of his own. Where she expected to be crushed, he caressed, then gradually deepened the kiss into the sort of seductive coaxing he was so devastatingly good at delivering.

Her breath shuddered out in a warm hiss against his cheek and she leaned into him, increasing the pressure of their kiss, encouraging him to gently and thoroughly ravage her. Relearning all the hard muscles of his back and shoulders beneath his open jacket.

He made a growled, grateful noise in his throat that the staff must have heard, because the elevator had opened just then. She didn't care any more than he seemed to. He delicately plundered for every last dreg of her response and she gave it to him, recognizing that she'd been aching for this since four-fifteen outside the hotel two days ago. Since about five minutes after he'd walked out of the room they'd been sharing in Switzerland.

The doors started to close, and they reluctantly eased back, loosening the death grip they'd taken on each other. He stopped the door, but kept his gaze locked to hers. Her blood continued to sizzle in her arteries and she had to consciously lock her trembling knees. No way could she look at anyone as they exited, fingers linked, breaths hot enough to cloud the winter air as they climbed into the limo.

"Are you spending the night with me?" she asked in the safety of the darkened car. She refused to ask—beg— *will* you?

"I want to," he said, head turning toward her as he spoke.

She heard the unspoken *but*, and her heart went into free fall. This was why she had accepted their casual relationship in Paris. The minute she expected more from him, she risked being grossly disappointed.

"But?" she prompted, trying to pull her hand away from his warm grip.

He tightened his hold. "But if I spend the night, I spend the weekend. And next weekend, you come to New York and Adara's party with me."

She'd already told him Zoey was away until Sunday night, but "Next weekend I have Zoey. I can't go away."

This was precisely what she'd been trying to warn him about. She wasn't footloose and fancy—

"She can come. You have a passport for her, don't you?"

"I…" She did, and she was saving up to take her to the amusement parks in Florida, but "That's not the point."

"It's not any kind of point. We don't have to sleep together in New York if you think it would confuse her. Share the spare room in my apartment with her or I'll get you a hotel room if you prefer. And I'll pay for the flights. You won't be out of pocket."

"Demitri, I can't," she protested, forced to bring up the real issue. "There's no way I could throw myself, *us*, in your family's faces like that."

"What does that mean? You're embarrassed to be seen with me?"

"No! But our affair created a huge headache both at work and in their family life. The last person they want to see is the woman who caused it all."

"You didn't. I did. And I assure you, they'll be far more welcoming to you than they will be to me," he predicted in a rancorous mutter.

"They think I want to sue them for sexual harassment," she reminded, vehemently getting down to brass tacks.

"Exactly. And your turning up will reassure them that you're not holding a grudge."

She hadn't thought about it that way, but "It would still be awkward."

"Natalie," he said from between clenched teeth. "If I show up alone, Gideon will have me kicked out before I reach the elevator. If I have a date, someone he respects, he'll show some manners and give me a chance to apologize to my sister. You can rest assured that I will be bearing the brunt of the awkward."

"Still—"

"Damn it, Natalie. I don't like them thinking I was only

seeing you to hurt them. They were the last thing on my mind. I want them to see we're a serious couple."

Was that what they were?

Because she strongly suspected that was what she was really shying away from, she acknowledged darkly to herself. It was one thing to invite him in for the night, relive the fantasy and feel desired for a few hours. It was quite another to let a man occupy a more permanent space in her life. She might start to depend on him. Want stuff. Yearn for love and completion and other things that she secretly feared were never meant to be hers.

They didn't speak again until the car parked in her driveway. Demitri climbed out to walk her to her door, where he lightly cupped her face and said, "I can tell you want time—"

"No," she interrupted, grasping at his arm where he lightly touched her jaw. "If there's one thing Gareth taught me, it's that time is finite. Tomorrow might not come. You have to live today as best you can. I want you to stay. I do."

"Yeah?" His touch on her gentled and he drew her forward so he could press his lips to her forehead.

She closed her eyes, enjoying the simple gesture for a moment before drawing away with a smile and opening her front door. She stepped through and held it, inviting him in.

He hung back, making her frown in confusion.

"I'll just get my bag," he said.

"Of course you have a bag," Natalie snarked when he returned. She had the box of chocolates open and was unwrapping a truffle. She glared at him as she bit into it.

He stopped in his tracks, recognizing that perhaps there was something distasteful in the fact that he'd thrown it into the car without really thinking about it, packing it as routinely as he had a thousand times when leaving for an evening with a woman he desired. But her condemnation caught him off guard, making him shoot back, "It's called being prepared. Do you want me to get you pregnant?"

She paled and choked, covering her mouth before chewing and swallowing audibly. Closing the foil on the truffle, she placed it back in the box and said a firm "No."

For some reason that stung, even though it hadn't been a real question. He'd meant tonight, not *someday*, but her answer seemed to encompass both. It was a painful rejection.

He cursed and ran a hand over his hair, knowing what the real problem was here.

"I've slept with other women," he said flatly, continuing despite the injured glance she flashed at him. "But I've never slept with anyone who knows anything about me. If you think this is something I do all the time, it's not. Getting naked with someone is easy when you feel like the smartest, strongest, least-invested person in the room. I don't right now. Not with you." He glared at her, resenting how much guilt accosted him over those easy, meaningless hook-ups when he realized what he wanted from her. "I don't want sex from you, Natalie. I want to feel you and smell you and be inside you. I want to know you're mine."

He looked like a pirate. A sultan. A marauder bent on stealing her from her home. Or, at the very least, stealing her heart from her body.

"I'm scared," she admitted. "I don't want to start believing you'll be here and then find out the hard way that you won't." He hadn't even met Zoey. How could he be so sure they were a *serious* couple when he hadn't really seen her as a mom?

He opened his hands, coming forward to take her elbows as she draped her fingers on his biceps, surrounding her in his masculine scent and aura of command. "I don't know how to reassure you except to be here when you wake up."

Of their own accord, her fingertips moved restlessly on the stiff fabric of his jacket, wanting the man beneath.

He read her receptiveness in the betraying little motion.

He slid his hand down her forearm, linking their fingers as he canted his head toward the stairs. "Take me up with you."

This was how he did it, she thought as she led him to her room. He made her think she was in control when he was the one guiding the whole thing. Except, as they started to undress each other, he watched her closely, not rushing her, seeing if his caress against the side of her breast was welcome, stealing a kiss, but a soft, sweet one.

And when they were almost naked, he gathered her against his hard chest with arms that trembled and said, "I've missed you, Natalie."

"I can tell," she teased, trying to lighten the mood because she was so moved. She shifted a hand between them so she could caress the fierce muscle straining between them.

He closed his hand over hers, stilling her with a firm crush of his grip over hers. Then he caught her other hand and drew both her arms behind her so he could manacle her wrists. "My turn," he warned, fingertips playing against the lace triangle at the front of her panties, making her flinch with sensitivity. "Uh-uh," he scolded. "Stand still."

She bit her lips, whimpering as he slowly eased her panties down just enough to expose her to the tracing pad of his fingertip, delicately teasing her damp flesh into blossoming open, welcoming a deeper caress. "Demitri," she gasped, her vision going white as he aroused her with deliberate expertise.

"You were like this that first time. So wet. As if you couldn't wait for me to be inside you. I wanted to lick into this heat, but I couldn't wait, either." He pressed her backward onto the bed, releasing her hands so she splayed them, trying to keep her balance as he tipped her against the edge, skimming her undies from her legs and throwing them away. Then he knelt and pressed her knees open. "This time I will."

"Demitri—"

He draped her thighs over his shoulders, pulling her into the tender plunder of his kiss, demanding everything from her, making her abdomen knot into such tension she nearly screamed, then releasing her to such a burst of pleasure she did cry out, arching and throwing back her head with abandon, willpower demolished. Subjugated by passion into a vessel for his pleasure.

He rose to roll on a condom, taking a moment to study her utter abandonment before he covered her. Very much the marauder taking his slave. He caged her with his arms, all man, ferociously possessive. He drove into her with the thick flesh that her body had been aching for, pressing inexorably into her. It was the piece that she'd been missing, erasing the ache of solitude and filling her with joy.

Wrapping her legs around him, she pulled him in, accepting all of him, and he shut his eyes as if it was too much. He began to move and she closed her eyes, too, unable to bear the intimacy. It was too acute. He was taking something from her that she would never get back. Perhaps it was her heart. It might even be her soul.

For this kind of pleasure, this kind of closeness, she told herself it was worth it. She would give him anything, she dimly acknowledged, as long as he continued making her feel whole.

Demitri felt strange as he padded around Natalie's home barefoot and shirtless, sun streaming in through the front window to warm the hardwood floor. Last night had been intense, their appetites for each other as strong as ever and sharpened by emotion. Sex had been many things for him, usually escape or distraction, entertainment certainly. It had never been profound. It had never been a vehicle for closeness, for cementing a bond.

He kept having flashes of exposure, thinking of the things he'd told Natalie about himself. Then he would remember the way she'd opened herself to him, allowing his greed and dominance in her bed, letting him regain his masculinity while stroking and encouraging him, praising him for the pleasure he gave her. Snuggling tight against him with complete trust.

Something in him had been terrified she would reject him for all he'd told her. Her acceptance of him was disconcerting and oddly healing. It had pushed him from the bed before he'd had a full night's sleep, restless to do more to close the gap between them. He'd sent a few emails and texts, looked in her refrigerator and settled for three truffles, then called a cab to deliver coffee and breakfast.

When it arrived, he threw on his jacket and shoes and ran out to pay, coming back to a locked door.

"Hey!" He glimpsed Natalie's form through the window and knocked his elbow against the glass, showing her the fast-food bags.

She opened the door, a cross look on her face. "I thought you were ducking out."

"Excuse me?" He was astonished, considering what he'd been up to this morning.

"Well, the coffeemaker is right there. You ate three of my truffles," she accused.

"So you locked me out? Even though my bag is still upstairs?"

"I didn't notice that." She crossed her arms over the T-shirt she wore. It was her only attire. Her bare legs pressed together against the chill, toes curling into the floor. It took everything in him not to attack her on the kitchen table. "I heard the cab honk, then the front door.

I looked out to see you running out to it, wearing your jacket and—"

"You deduced the worst." She was never going to let him get away with a single thing. Privately that made him laugh, but he gave her his most aggrieved frown.

"Why didn't you wake me up if you wanted coffee?" she asked defensively.

"Sweetheart, I am many things, but stupid is not one of them. How many men get away with telling a woman to get up and make him coffee?"

"Fair point," she mumbled toward her toes.

"And I thought…" He ambled toward her, dropping the bag on the table before taking hold of her hips through the thin layer of cotton that barely covered them. "You would appreciate sleeping in, since I kept you up so late. And maybe you wouldn't wake up grouchy."

She diced him into little pieces with a glare.

He drew her closer, delicately crashing her against his growing arousal, liking the hitch of her breath. "And because I knew that once you were awake, I'd be hungry for more than an egg sandwich."

She ran her fingers over his collarbone and warmed the skin on his shoulders and upper arms with a soft exploration of her feminine hands. "You can always wake me for *that*," she assured him with a pouting moue that invited his kiss.

He brought her in tight now, enjoying the play of their bodies against one another as much as the play of the conversation. "I had something more important to do."

"Really?" Predictable frost entered her tone, making him chuckle. Her hands shifted to the middle of his chest, pressing.

"Yes," he confirmed, resurrecting his most bored and arrogant tone, purely for impact. "Among other things, I spent the morning redirecting my new staff to look for a property here in Montreal and see what is involved in drawing up incorporation documents for Canada instead of New York."

Her arms went limp. Her expression was dumbfounded. "Are you serious?"

"As a heart attack, baby." He surprised her with a dive to scoop her legs out from under her, giving her a little toss that made her scream before he caught her in the cradle of his arms and started for the stairs. "So don't ever doubt me again."

Natalie was suitably chastised for the rest of the day, cooking him a late breakfast, then suggesting some neighborhoods for his new offices. Maybe it was only something he was considering, but they wound up driving around the city in her car, scouting different blocks, then eating at a pub before going back to her place for a glass of wine, a movie and more incredible lovemaking.

She didn't allow herself any doubts until Sunday, after he'd woken her with a light tease of his tongue on her nipple, which led to lusty groans of ecstasy shortly thereafter. It was well into late morning and they were still dozing off their lovemaking, negotiating who would rise and make coffee, when he asked her what she wanted to do with the day.

"I have to pick up Zoey," she mumbled into her pillow. It had been hovering in her subconscious, waiting for the opportunity to be mentioned.

"From where?"

"Her grandmother's. It's a couple of hours out of the city." She lifted her head to see he wore his most neutral, arrested look, reserving his thoughts. "Heath is supposed to bring her back by supper, but he's always late. If I want her in bed at a reasonable hour on a school night, I have to get her myself." She looked toward the window, pleased to see streaks of sunlight behind the blinds, but sad to cut short their weekend. "It's not a bad drive on a nice day. I'll probably stay for coffee."

"With Heath? I'll drive," he stated before she could answer.

Jealous? She shunted off that thought, not wanting to build up his feelings into more than they really were.

"With his mother," she clarified. "Heath will be ice fishing up on the lake, which is why he gets Zoey home so late."

"I still want to drive." He swung his legs to the edge of the bed and rose. The cheeks of his butt were taut and firm. The muscles in his back flexed as he rolled his shoulders.

"Demitri…" She sat up.

"It's time for me to meet her, Nat." He glanced back at her, the implacability in his features not allowing for refusal. "Especially if we're all going to New York next weekend."

About that, she wanted to say, but he disappeared into the shower and didn't give her a chance to talk to him before they were in the car heading out of the city. By then she had gone around and through every avenue of thought on whether her behavior was wise. She kept coming back to his calling them a serious couple. He was considering working out of Montreal. If she didn't want to be with him, she should tell him to get out of her life right now, before he made big changes to his own.

She wanted to be with him.

She just wasn't convinced he would want to be with her *and* Zoey.

Despite Theo's comment still rubbing like sandpaper on his ego, Demitri knew he wasn't *really* like their father. The few times he'd had physical altercations had been with fully grown men who were drunk and trying to kill each other. He stopped violence, didn't perpetuate it.

As for relating to kids, okay, he didn't have the first idea, but Natalie was a two-for-one package, so he was going to have to figure it out. The one thing he couldn't be was too self-centered and inflexible to try. He really would be his father if he couldn't live with a child who didn't carry his own DNA.

Still, as casual and confident as he tried to appear about the whole thing, Natalie must have sensed his tension because she was very quiet on the drive, only speaking to point out a landmark or give him directions.

It was pretty countryside with rolling hills and churches nestled back in the trees and icicles hanging in claws from rocky escarpments. He could see why she was willing to let her daughter get away into this kind of fresh air and natural surroundings.

They arrived at a farmhouse where an older woman swept blown snow off the porch and Zoey threw a stick for a midsize mutt in the trampled snow.

Natalie introduced him to Claudette, who said she'd go in to put on fresh coffee, then she introduced him to Zoey, whose hair was covered with a crooked hat that Natalie called a toque when she straightened it.

"Grandma was going to take me to the barn to see the kittens. Do you like kittens?" Zoey asked, leaning way back to see his face.

"Who doesn't?" he asked, wondering if that was too glib. Frivolous banter was his fallback, but maybe you took a kid more seriously.

"Uncle Frank," she answered innocently. "They make him sneeze. C'mon. There's five. Like me."

"There's five of her?" Demitri mused to Natalie as they followed.

"You'll start to think so," she assured him, slanting a look up at him that told him she was reserving judgment, but watching closely.

He refused to be daunted. Surely Zoey couldn't be harder to schmooze than the average sociopathic celebrity demanding VIP treatment.

She wasn't. It turned out fine. Better than fine. They wandered the farm with her for almost an hour, admired the snowman she'd made with her cousins, located all the kittens in the barn and learned their names, waited while she gathered eggs and listened attentively when she explained each step of how her grandmother had turned the alpaca's fur into the matching hat and sweater she wore.

"You're being very patient," Natalie commented as they followed Zoey to the house.

He was startled by the remark, since he had yet to reach for any patience. He was here to meet the girl and he'd been getting to know what made her tick. She was five. He didn't expect her to discuss the day's stock-market numbers. She knew more about fish and hockey than a lot of the blowhards he'd met over the years and either laughed at his jokes or didn't get it and said something bemusing, which made him chuckle.

"I'm waiting for the hard part to start," he responded, indicating his watch. "It's been forty minutes and she hasn't asked for drugs, thrown a television off a balcony or gone viral on the internet with a nude selfie."

She snickered. "And that was just the one teen pop star?"

"Everyone always thought I was partying with them. I was trying to keep the lawsuits to a minimum."

They stayed for coffee and it was relaxed and easy. Claudette was one of those earth-mother sorts who made him feel at home immediately, not asking nosy questions or seeming overly curious about his relationship with Natalie. She projected warm acceptance, and he could see why Natalie treasured her.

Zoey colored at the table between him and Natalie as

the grown-ups talked, at one point asking, "Mom, do you want to help me?"

Demitri gave in to temptation and picked up a crayon. He hadn't messed around with them in years and the smell took him back to his own childhood, when Adara had tried to keep him quiet with drawing projects. He was missing work, he realized. There had been a part of him holding his breath as he and Natalie had looked at properties yesterday. Zoey had been the unknown quantity, but now he was beginning to see her as part of the broader picture, and felt more certainty he was making the right choice.

"Is that me?" Zoey asked, pausing her own coloring to watch.

He was showing off, sketching Zoey in primary colors. It was a shameless bid to win her affection, but where he thought the endgame was winning Natalie's, he found himself inordinately pleased by Zoey's "That's one for the fridge!"

Later that night, when Natalie showed him to the door, shadows edged her gaze as she asked a very weighty "Well?"

"Well, what?" he asked, deliberately obtuse. "Am I resentful that I'm being kicked out to a hotel? Just disappointed. I said I'd respect your boundaries where she's concerned and I will."

"That's not what I meant."

"I know what you meant." He stole a light kiss. "I'll be back tomorrow."

CHAPTER NINE

GOING TO NEW YORK was a step back into the fantasy world of Paris, which scared her. And she really should have seen the signs.

"Which one?" she'd asked, holding up two dresses from her closet. One was a very sophisticated blue cocktail dress she'd bought at a consignment store. The other was the black dress she'd worn on their first date.

"You're adorable," he'd replied with a shake of his head, going back to the travel arrangements he'd been making on his tablet. "I'll buy you something in New York," he had added in an aside.

"We could have shopped last weekend," she'd protested, but began to understand why even Montreal's excellent shopping wasn't good enough for him after he'd flown them in a chartered plane to New York and had shown them into his screamingly sophisticated penthouse.

How had she forgotten how rich he was?

They had spent the week having Parisian trysts in the afternoons before Zoey came home from school, then Natalie had cooked dinner for all of them. After a lifetime of catering to spoiled guests, one decently disciplined five-year-old was a piece of cake for Demitri. Zoey was quickly becoming one more female caught in the net of his effortless charisma. And so was Natalie, because he spent time on Zoey, not money, listening to her stories about school friends and playing games with her after her bath. The evenings had been domestic and nice.

And somehow Natalie had forgotten that even though Demitri might not have a real job at the moment, his family owned a worldwide chain of five-star hotels. He had a trust fund, an investment broker he talked to a few times a week and one of those credit cards without a limit. Also a top-floor apartment bigger than her house. With a pool.

"That's a lot of windows," Zoey had said when they'd entered his home, craning her neck up the twenty feet of panes that made Demitri's flat seem as if it occupied a place among the constellations. "You have a lot of books, too."

"I do," he'd agreed. "I've even read most of them, which I imagine surprises your mother. Have a look around. Don't go outside without me, though."

Zoey had run off to explore, but Natalie hadn't needed to catalogue the professional decor or the signatures on the paintings or eyeball the view from the terrace. She'd already been suffering a fresh set of panic as she had seen a brand-new reason his family might have no desire to see her at their little dinner. Peasant stock did not belong here.

Except it wasn't just a little dinner, she found out over breakfast.

Eggs benedict, strawberry waffles and pastries had magically appeared while she'd been trying to figure out Demitri's espresso machine. Zoey thought it was Christmas when the whipping cream came out of the delivery bin.

"How do you feel about dinosaurs, Zoey? I thought we'd visit the Natural History Museum today," Demitri said when they sat down to eat.

"Oh, that sounds fun," Natalie enthused. "I've always wanted to go there."

"I'm afraid I'll have to take you another time." He

stabbed a hash brown off her plate. "You have an appointment at the spa."

"Do I?" she said, lifting her chin in dismay.

"You're also meeting with a stylist."

"Is there something wrong with the way I look?"

"Not at all. Wear what you like. But I'll be in a tuxedo and all the other women will be in gowns. I thought you would prefer one."

"All— As in lots of women? I thought this was family dinner?"

"It's a white-tie ball," he said, as if she ought to have known. As if those happened in the normal world.

"For how many?" she exclaimed.

"Two hundred couples or so. You didn't ask," he protested at her glare. "It's not a secret. It's a charity thing for the homeless. Adara does it every year. Look it up."

"And Zoey is invited to this thing?"

"Zoey will meet my niece and nephews this evening along with their nannies, all bonded and vetted and valued for their attentiveness to the children. They'll only be a few floors away at the hotel, should anyone feel a need to check in." His tone said that he expected Natalie to suffer the separation anxiety, not Zoey. "Apparently Evie enjoys playing with her boy cousins, but would love to spend time with a little girl." To Zoey, he added, "Evie is three and likes princesses, too."

Demitri must have a secret fetish for them himself. An hour later, Natalie began receiving the royal treatment, from a mud wrap to a Swedish massage to drinking a mimosa during her pedicure. She couldn't remember a time she'd felt so pampered and renewed. All of her skin was waxed and lotioned, detoxified and revitalized. The stylist met with her twice before she dressed, taking measurements and consulting with the salon, agreeing with the plan to weave a sparkling ribbon into her updo so her hair became a subtle crown. Her makeup was a masterful understatement highlighting all of her best features, and finally, the dress…

Natalie hadn't worn a long gown since high school graduation, and that one had been a thrift store find in garish pink with puffy sleeves.

Demitri had much better taste. According to the stylist, he'd chosen her gown himself. Nothing so predictable as burgundy for winter, it was a shade between lavender and gray, the color muted by the crushed velvet fabric, but it made her eyes look like mysterious pools in the Scottish highlands. Strapless, with intricate detailing at her hip that gathered the skirt before allowing it to flare around her shoes, the confection clung to her curves to make the most of her silhouette. A matching jacket that really only covered her shoulders and upper arms ensured she wouldn't freeze to death.

Her shoes added height—a lot of height. They were deceptively simple black things, but the underside matched the color of her dress and the tops, open toe but closed back, drew a sparkling line from the ankle strap down one side of her foot and across her toes. More important, they looked as if they'd kill her yet made her feel as though she walked on clouds. She could dance all night.

She couldn't accept this, she kept thinking, reminding herself he would have done this for countless women before her. It still felt as though she was climbing too high, starting to feel special and treasured.

"The jewelry is on loan," the stylist said, trying a few different pieces before settling on an antique cameo on a thick silver rope chain and a pair of sapphire studs. "But I've done this for other clients and if I get it right…" She debated a bracelet, then rejected it. "The gentleman will buy them for you."

"Oh, I don't expect anything."

The stylist smiled with smooth acceptance of what she plainly thought was a lie. "Of course not."

Natalie found herself acknowledging it was a lie. Not the part about expecting jewelry, but the part about not expecting *anything*. She was starting to dream of things she had cautioned herself never to expect. Never to *want*.

Love. Family. Commitment. Marriage.

A life partner. Another baby.

Because she was falling in love with Demitri. Deeply and irrevocably.

Demitri might have spent the day brooding about the coming meeting with his family tonight if his mind hadn't been completely occupied trying to keep up with a five-year-old in a museum. And the Empire State Building. And a world-famous toy store. After feeding ducks in the park, he finally brought Zoey back to watch a movie on his flat screen, set a bowl of popcorn in her lap and went to shave and change.

When he heard the door and Zoey's gasp of "Mommy!" he smiled at the bittersweet sound. Bitter because time was running out—he would be facing his siblings soon—but sweet because Zoey's wonder was so delightfully expressive.

There was something pure about her view of the world that dusted the cynicism out of his own eyes. She had no reason to hide enthusiasm or curiosity or any emotion. She'd never been bruised by life, let alone deeply hurt by it. He found himself wanting to protect and preserve her innocent confidence in adults. Where anger and resentment had made him see his siblings as deluded in their joy of being with their children, he felt privileged that Natalie was sharing her daughter with him. He wanted to guard her, spend time with her and watch her flourish into the bright, funny, self-possessed woman she was meant to become.

The more time he spent with the two of them, the more certain he was that he wanted to come home to them every day. Which flummoxed him. He'd never seen himself married with a ready-made family.

Natalie would never see him in the role, either, if he quit on his family because things had turned hard. That made the stakes on tonight's reconciliation higher than anything he'd ever undertaken.

It was an unnerving state to be in, one he brushed away as determinedly as he smoothed his bow tie. Shrugging into his jacket, he walked out to the living, room where he took a punch to the heart. It was a ground-shaking reaction, considering he was a connoisseur of beautiful women.

But she was *so* beautiful. The color of the gown had caught his eye, making him think of chain mail and strength and Saint Jeanne d'Arc, while still reflecting the softness and light of Natalie's true nature. It enhanced her beauty, rather than outshining it, so the impact was the woman, not the dress. Curvy and desirable, but elegant and resilient and completely feminine.

She stole his breath.

And her laughter at her daughter's excitement, joyful and teasing and so loving, turned up the piece of himself that he'd buried long ago, exposing it to the sun so it burned and shook.

Natalie caught sight of him and straightened, mouth forming a pretty "Oh" that he wanted to kiss.

"I thought I was overdressed, but…" She swallowed, blushing a little while her gaze traveled over him like soft, feminine fingertips, touching all the places that responded most acutely to her every caress. "You look very handsome."

"You look perfect," he assured her, crossing to graze his lips against her cheekbone, lingering to take in the feminine scents designed to disorient a man. "Mesmerizing."

Natalie blushed again and ducked her head to ask Zoey to take their photo. The little girl was beside herself with admiration for the two of them, and then quivered with excitement at riding in the limo.

Demitri took them into the underground parking lot beneath the Makricosta Manhattan rather than having them dropped at the front doors. As they arrived, he made the call to his sister-in-law to have the VIP elevator opened. Demitri had figured there was only one person with enough clout to get them into the hotel without notice while remaining secure enough to know she'd be forgiven for interfering: Nic's wife, Rowan. She'd become Adara's best friend and she was also booking all the entertainment for this event, so one more group in the elevator wasn't suspicious.

This particular elevator was typically used to smuggle in celebrities trying to avoid detection by the paparazzi. They stepped directly into it from the car.

When they arrived on the penthouse floor, the door of the end one swung open before they reached it.

Nic. Damn. Demitri had asked Rowan to hang back and take them down to the party herself without mentioning to any of his siblings his intention to attend.

Looking rather like a vengeful god, Nic sent a level stare at Demitri that hit like a punch in the face. His features were oddly familiar, Theo-like yet older, with a Nordic cast to his cheekbones and blond hair.

"Your wife is expecting us," Demitri said, falling back on a well-used, affable expression of indifference.

"So she has just informed me." Judging by his tone, Nic didn't appreciate Demitri going behind his back in talking to her.

"I waited until Theo and Jaya had dropped off Zephyr and left," Rowan said in her welcoming Irish accent, smiling as she came forward from behind him. "But I don't keep things from Nic. Please come in."

Despite being famous from childhood, Rowan was always pleasantly self-effacing. Tonight she was as attractive as she always looked on-screen, wearing a gown that clung like emerald paint to her flawless figure, black hair loose and straight. Her smile seemed natural, but she *was* an actress. She had sounded eager to assist when he first contacted her, but now Demitri wasn't sure about her, given that she'd revealed his presence here to Nic.

"You must be Natalie. And Zoey," she greeted warmly.

Natalie seemed caught between intimidation and sensitivity to the undercurrents. Glancing at Demitri, she said, "I don't want to impose if we weren't expected."

Nic turned his sharp gaze on her, blinking as though he was taking a photograph. "It's fine."

Natalie might have relaxed if he'd smiled, but he didn't.

He only added, "I'll fetch Evie," and disappeared down a hall.

"We don't know much about the falling-out," Rowan said delicately. "But Nic and I are happy to help mend fences."

Were they? She really was a hell of an actress, managing to look and sound sincere when it was obvious Nic was the furthest thing from happy.

Natalie kept her eyes downcast, but Demitri was so attuned to her, he could hear her silent screams for him to get them the hell out of here.

Excellent job of showing her how well he integrated with his family.

"Look, Rowan, if—" he started, but was interrupted by Nic's return.

The ferocious bear had turned into a house pet while he was gone, judging from the doting tone of his voice as he carried his daughter into the lounge. "I want you to meet someone," he told the petite girl wearing a stained T-shirt and turned up jeans over bare toes.

Demitri really looked at the girl for once. Not the obvious details like her dark hair and Asian features—she had been adopted from one of the war-torn countries Nic used to report on when he'd been a feet-on-the-ground journalist. No, Demitri looked at the protective way Nic held her. The connection between them, demonstrated by the way Evie's arm curled around his neck and she gazed at him with utter trust.

If a hard case like this man could become a caring father to a child who'd had a rough start, surely there was hope for himself with Zoey?

"Who is it?" Evie asked, letting her gaze swing out to hit each of the adults, then tilt and fix on Zoey.

"Her name is Zoey. Uncle Demitri brought her to visit. Will you say hello?" He squatted so the girls were eye to eye.

"'Lo," Evie murmured, pushing a finger into her shy smile. She took it out to point down the hall, then mentioned her cousin, Theo's boy. "Zephyr's nanny brought face paints. I'm gonna be a cat. What do you like to be?"

Zoey looked up at Natalie, eager as a retriever. "Can I be a butterfly?"

Natalie hesitated, thick lashes sweeping up like a scimitar to shave Demitri's cheek, her flick of a smile telegraphing, *If only adult interactions were so simple.*

"Let's ask the nanny," Natalie said to Zoey, urging Evie to show them the way. "I'll give her my number so she can phone me if you need me."

Moments later, they reached the ballroom floor and exited the silent elevator behind Nic and Rowan. Demitri held back with Natalie, saying, "I'm sorry that was so…"

"Awkward?" Natalie prompted ruefully. "It's fine. He probably doesn't like secrets any more than you do."

Demitri hadn't thought of his request to Rowan as anything but trying to avoid pitting Nic against Theo and Adara on his behalf. Family relationships were bloody complicated.

Gripping Natalie's hand in his, palm to palm, Demitri drew her to the entrance to the ballroom, where a full concert band played over the din of conversation.

Security stopped him at the door.

"They're with us," Nic said.

"I still have to report that you're here," the tuxedoed man said to Demitri, making clear exactly how wide the chasm was between him and his siblings.

"I'll report myself," he said, impatience edging into his tone. He tugged Natalie along behind him, into the throng.

They turned heads. Not just because he was moving so determinedly through the crowd, either. People recognized him. The explanations for his abrupt departure from the company would have made the gossip rounds in many forms, he was sure.

The startled reactions worked in his favor, however. Once people noted he was here, they craned their necks to catch the reaction of the host and hostess. It pointed him like a compass to the small knot of people opposite the banquet table.

Gideon saw him first, narrowing a piercing, hostile glare on him even as a minion slid in close to whisper in his ear.

"I can see that," Gideon mouthed.

Demitri knew the moment Gideon identified his date. His demeanor changed from outright aggression to caution. He reached to his wife, getting her attention, excusing them from the group to step away and await them.

Adara looked up, started with recognition and then her posture softened in welcome.

Natalie tried to work her hand from his, and Demitri

realized he was crushing her fine bones. He softened his hold but kept her hand, linking their fingers, recognizing that he'd always flaunted brassy, interchangeable women at these occasions to shield himself from deeper emotions.

Real emotions.

Natalie was a white flag. Bringing her was a statement that he cared about her. He was unarmed. Vulnerable.

It wasn't a comfortable state. It was terrifying. If they rejected him, if they rejected *them*, he didn't know what he'd do.

The minute he was in earshot of his sister, he said, "You didn't deserve the way I treated you. I'm sorry." Old pain threatened to catch up with him as so much of what he'd faced with Natalie's help confronted him in the shadowed gaze of his sister.

Natalie's hand stopped squirming in his, and her other one covered the back of his, sandwiching him in subtle reassurance. Giving him the strength to finish.

"I just wanted to wish you a happy birthday, Adara." He reached forward with his free arm to catch his sister around the shoulders and draw her in, feeling her jerk in surprise that he would hug her, not having done so since they were both children. "If you'd rather I left, I will."

"Of course I want you here," she said after a stunned moment of surprise. Her arms went around him, hugging hard. She added shakily, "I'm so happy to see you, I'm going to cry."

"We can't have that," he scoffed, drawing back, moved that she'd forgiven him so easily. *Family*. It really was a luxury not to be taken for granted. He clawed for lazy humor so emotion wouldn't overwhelm him. "Your husband already wants to kill me for upsetting you. I'll write a suitably remorseful check to the shelter. Will that make you smile?"

Adara laughed and swept fingertips under her eyes.

Gideon's expression mellowed, then flicked to Natalie and came back with one brow raised in question at Demitri. *What are your intentions there*? he seemed to ask.

"It's nice to see you again, Natalie," Adara said, pulling herself together to demonstrate her perfect manners.

Natalie's covering fingers fell away from Demitri's and her other hand went limp in his. She lifted a brave but pained smile to her hosts. "I'm glad to be here. I wanted to take this chance to—"

"Do *not* apologize," Demitri warned her.

She flashed him a look of ire. "I can if I want."

"That's not why I brought you. And you know it," he told her in a growl. They'd shared so much, become so much, it would insult both of them if she made apologies for how they'd come together.

"Humph," she snorted, eyeing her fresh manicure of peach paint and glittering gold tips. "All those times you told me you weren't the boss of me, turns out you think you are."

"Really?" he challenged. "Take the blame, then. She cold-bloodedly seduced me for the sole purpose of destroying my career and hurting our family," he said offhandedly.

"No, I—" She frowned crossly at him, but before she could clarify, he continued.

"I have to fix this one, Natalie. *I* have to." It sucked. Royally. He hated it. But he was going to do it. She had to see that he was willing to go the distance.

"He's used to being the one at fault, Natalie," Gideon said, humor smooth and dry as always. "Let him have this."

"Thanks," Demitri muttered at his brother-in-law, finding the remark oddly heartening. Gideon wouldn't be making light if he still wanted to kill him.

"Theo has seen you. Were you going to speak to him?" Adara asked with a pull of concern between her brows.

"Yes," Demitri said firmly, setting a decisive hand on Natalie's back to turn her toward his brother. "But we'll come back. I want your opinion on my new venture," he told Gideon, genuinely respectful of the man's business acuity.

As they approached Theo and his wife, Jaya stepped forward to greet Natalie warmly. Jaya wore a lemon-yellow sari and her exotic looks were amplified by her husband's flawless, ironed straight tuxedo.

"I've been anxious for a debriefing about the work in France," Jaya said to Natalie. "We always promise we won't talk shop at these things, but five minutes, Theo? Please? Can I be horribly clichéd and ask you to come to the ladies' room with me while we talk, Natalie? I feel like I'm risking a wardrobe malfunction. I need to retuck."

"Your wife has never liked me," Demitri told Theo as Jaya made off with his moral support. It was probably for the best. Adara was soft and naturally forgiving. Theo's kinship would not be so easy to regain. He didn't relish Natalie watching him crash and burn.

But some said emulation was the sincerest form of flattery and Demitri wanted to emulate Theo. He would never be perfect the way Theo was, but somehow his withdrawn, reclusive brother had earned the devotion of a sweet, loving woman. Demitri needed to know how that was done.

"I've never liked you, either, if you want the truth," Theo remarked as the women disappeared.

"Is that the best you can do?" Demitri scoffed with a fake husk of a laugh, pretending the lazy blow hadn't landed hard enough to leave a mark.

"No," Theo said flatly.

Demitri rocked back on his heels, nodding as the silence stretched. "No, you can refuse to talk to me at all. It's a brutally effective punishment, Theo. I don't have a spare in Nic the way you do. Gideon can't stand me. You're all I've got for a brother."

Theo didn't look at him. He'd gone very still. Slowly he took a sip of the soda he held. "Gideon runs a tight ship. He doesn't put up with jackassery of any kind. I never make mistakes, so he doesn't have anything to call me up for. You've made yourself a pet project for him, though. That's the only reason he rides you."

Theo was letting a few emotions creep into the conversation—annoying ones like superiority and weary exasperation. It was his version of warming up. Demitri took heart.

"And Nic—" Theo began, but Demitri stopped him.

"I know. You would have talked about him if you could have. Frankly, I'm glad that you have at least one good memory from our childhood," he said sincerely, unable to suppress the deep anguish anymore, aware it flashed into his expression before he was able to control his emotions outwardly even if they threatened to overwhelm him internally.

Theo acknowledged the statement with a lowering of his brows and tightening of his lips.

"I shouldn't have said what I did," Demitri added, guts clawing with shame. "I don't expect you to forgive me, but I am sorry."

Nothing for a long moment, then, "Those things weren't your fault. I shouldn't have made out as if they were. We were kids. None of that was our fault. And you're not like him. *I* shouldn't have said *that*."

Their gazes met for a fraction of a heartbeat, just long enough to see the shattered emotion in the other and look away to hide their own.

A weird relief weakened Demitri's limbs. He'd needed to hear it. It allowed him to believe he might be good enough for Natalie after all.

"For what it's worth," Theo continued drily, "Nic has himself so together he makes me feel like the idiotic younger brother. So you'll always have a place in my life."

"Good to know," Demitri said with a catch of laughter, pleased to be back on trashing terms with Theo. "By the way, you don't pay Natalie enough. I'll be stealing her for the firm I'm starting."

"Is that what you're doing with her?" Theo asked, giving him a sharp look.

"No," Demitri said in a rare moment of complete sincerity. "I'm going to ask her to marry me." It made him proud to say it, and he liked the way Theo absorbed the news with a thoughtful, approving nod.

"Good luck." He even sounded like he meant it.

Natalie dropped her lipstick into her pocketbook and met Jaya's gaze in the mirror. "That's ten minutes. Have we given them enough time?"

Jaya's painted smile twitched. "Was I that obvious? I really have been wanting your impressions on how the new software was received."

Natalie shrugged, not feeling she'd told Jaya anything she wouldn't have heard through other channels, but the topic had been a nice path around the scandal that had arisen from Natalie's assignment in France.

"I think we were right to let them duke it out in private," Natalie said, referring to Demitri and Theo. "I just hope they have. Family isn't something you can have so much of that you can afford to throw any of it away."

"That's what I kept telling Theo after he ignored Demitri's call!" As they walked back, Jaya told her about a disagreement in her own family involving her cousin. It had gone on for years, breaking many hearts. She was so engaging, Natalie started when someone touched her arm.

It was Rowan. She waved them into conversation with

her and Gideon, leaning gleefully toward Jaya as she gave a little nod to something across the room. "Don't look now, but the planets have aligned."

Natalie followed their gazes to all four siblings standing in a group, talking animatedly.

"Oh," Jaya sighed, setting a hand over her heart. "I was starting to worry it would never happen."

"This will mean the world to Nic," Rowan murmured with a poignant creak in her tone.

"And Adara," Gideon said.

Demitri had needed this, too. Natalie felt a wistful pride in being part of making it happen. For a moment, she even felt equal to these other partners in this mystic circle, gazing with happiness for the group of laughing adults who hadn't known joy as children.

Not long after, they toasted Adara with champagne and sang along when Adara's favorite chart-topping crooner led the crowd in "Happy Birthday." Then the dancing started.

"Evie wants Zoey to spend the night," Rowan found Natalie to say. "Would you mind? She'll be heartbroken if Zoey leaves. One of us will have to go up to her."

Rowan had booked several rooms for the musicians she'd hired to entertain the crowd, but one of those suites had been set aside for Natalie and Demitri. If Zoey needed her mother in the night, they'd only be a few doors away. Natalie made the call to Zoey and had to pull the phone away from her ear when her daughter squealed, "She said yes!"

The enchantment of the evening deepened as Natalie absorbed that she would be making love with Demitri tonight. Resting her head on his shoulder, she surrendered to the sexual pull he always exerted over her. Her jacket was off and his lips touched her bare shoulder. Male fingertips caressed up her arm. She lightly traced the hollow at the back of his neck.

This was so perfect. So loving.

Holding eye contact with him was always a stumble into sexual heat. Tonight it was a blind gallop into a conflagration. He was so handsome, carefree in an authentic way that hurt to look at. Every point where she came in contact with him stung with need, tightening her airway and wetting her eyes at the magnitude of the moment.

She loved him so much.

"We have a room," she reminded in a voice husked with growing passion.

"Do you want to leave?" He searched her gaze, the delving deep enough to make her insides shake.

She nodded, ducking her head to hide her reaction, tracing a hand beneath his open coat across the tensed muscles of his waist.

The crowd had thinned. Nic and Rowan had already left, since they had to be up with the children in the morning. Adara hugged them and Gideon bussed Natalie's cheek with a kiss, sounding sincere when he said, "Thank you for coming."

She and Demitri walked out hand in hand, sexual tension climbing between them with each step. When they entered the suite, he threw the entry card on the table and said, "Come here, beautiful."

She spun into his arms, crashing herself against him so he grunted at the hit and wrapped her arms around his neck in abandoned joy. His mouth was everything she'd been waiting for, his hair spiky between her fingers, his body already aroused and thick against her—

"Easy, Natalie," he soothed in a masterful voice, arms hardening to still her from wriggling through his skin to adhere to his bones. His nose grazed her cheekbone; his brow touched hers. "We have time. Lots of time."

A lifetime? It wasn't like her to believe in permanence, but for once she let herself trust he would always be here for her.

And he wouldn't be rushed when it came to getting what he wanted from her. He *would* seduce her, holding her pinned to his steely body while he drew out his long, lazy kisses that thoroughly plundered her mouth.

She couldn't move in his hold, could only tell him with her lips and tongue and a ragged, lusty moan that he was torturing her. Her blood pounded her arteries in painful hammer blows of need. His heart slammed behind his chest wall, reverberating against her resting palm, the only evidence he matched her excitement.

That and their breaths mingling in shaken hisses.

"I want you so much," she whispered when he nipped at the straining cord along the side of her neck, then closed her eyes, abandoning herself to his caresses.

"This is all I've been thinking about since I first saw you tonight. Your skin. Your laugh. The way you catch your breath."

She did it now as he tilted her hips into his, sex to sex, need to need.

Stropping her face against his spicy-smelling neck, she said, "I want to be naked. I want to feel you."

"Yes." The word hissed out of him and he stepped back to turn her, lowering her zipper down her spine with sensual care, forehead tilted against her crown. His soft laughter pooled hotly against the back of her bare neck. "These dimples are my fatal weakness, Natalie," he said as her gown slid to the floor. He set two thumbs against the upper swells of her bottom, where the high cut of her French lingerie framed them. "After Lyon, I agonized that I would never see them again."

She smiled, made joyous by the confession.

His fingers moved into her hair, gently pulling pins and

dropping them. The quiet attentiveness, the tenderness of his touch, the graze of his clothing against her bare skin made it the most romantic moment of her life. She felt like a bride. Cherished. Loved.

Tonight she would let herself believe that she was. Somehow she was more than all the other women he'd been with combined.

Her own movements slowed as she grew determined to savor. Remember each touch. Each breath.

When he turned her, he grazed the backs of his fingers along the side of her breast. Leaned in to kiss her sweetly. "You're so beautiful, Natalie."

She believed him and undressed him between kisses, pushing his jacket off his shoulders, pulling away his bow tie, opening the buttons hidden in the ruffles of his shirt. When she got to his fly, he reached into his pocket to remove a strip of three condoms.

"Always prepared," she teased, pushing his pants down his hips.

"Wishful thinking that came true," he said, caressing her jaw and rueful smile. "I thought you'd be sleeping with Zoey tonight."

Kicking free of the last of his clothes, he set his feet apart and drew her into his nude body, making them both release shattered breaths at the contact of skin on skin. His fingers tangled in her panties and slid them down, urging her to leave them on the floor as he drew her to the bedroom.

The unhurried purity of the moment encased her in a glow, walking like the only two humans on earth to the bed. Her heart was wide-open to him, taking in his reverent study of her form as though it was a vow. She would never love anyone the way she loved him, she realized. Tears stung the backs of her eyes. Her feelings went beyond his primitive sexuality and masculine beauty. The fighter in her rested when he was near. Surrendered and trusted.

As he pressed her to her back on the soft mattress, parted her legs and entered her with his strength, she clenched her eyes against brimming wetness.

"Look at me, Natalie."

"I can't," she whispered. "It's too much."

"I've got you. I'm going to take care of you."

He would, she saw, when she dared to open her eyes. His dark eyes were deeply colored with sincerity. His muscles quivered as he held back. Always so generous, especially in bed.

She twisted, agonized by the acute intimacy and pleasure-pain of holding him within her, with the difficulty of stifling the words in her throat.

"You're holding back," he accused, thrusting with care to draw out each sensation. "Why? Give me all of you. Everything," he commanded.

She couldn't keep it in. She let go, moaning, "I love you. I love you." She shuddered as she released all her defenses, poured her love over him and prayed she'd get a piece of him in return.

CHAPTER TEN

DEMITRI HAD KNOWN tonight would be good. Sex with Natalie was easily the best he'd ever had. In those first days after their split in France, he'd told himself their lovemaking had merely benefited from the build of knowledge between them, as it typically could when affairs were drawn out. They'd learned how to tantalize the other to the limits of their sanity and enjoyed every second of it.

But here he was, missionary, barely having kissed her before he'd been inside her, and rather than emptying him, she had filled him. He was better than satisfied. He was moved—by words that she'd told him didn't mean anything.

He had little trust in the phrase himself. He'd heard it dozens of times from women in the throes of passion. He would have dismissed her saying it, but he couldn't. He wanted it to be true. He wanted to believe they really had been making love every time he'd touched her, building toward this moment, this emotion.

Because he was in it. In love.

It was the only explanation for his utter transformation. She wasn't changing him. He was changing himself for her, because she deserved better than he'd been.

He loved her.

Gently drawing away, he adjusted them, then gathered her against where his heart was only now easing to a resting pace. He'd never felt so fragile in his life. It was terrifying. Completely unfamiliar.

He wasn't an emotionally dependent man. He was connected to his siblings, their opinion mattered to him, and when he'd finally pushed them away to the point that they'd ostracized him, he'd quietly agonized.

But this, with Natalie, was so much more. From the moment he'd decided to find her—before that, even—he had been looking for ways not just to maintain their connection, but intertwine them. Knot her to him indelibly.

He wanted to tell her how much she meant to him, but he remembered so clearly her disparagement of her ex. It would gut him right now if she brushed off his saying something he'd never felt, let alone expressed aloud. If he wound up pushing her away with those words, he'd be devastated. But he still needed her to realize how far she'd brought him from what he'd been.

"Thank you for coming with me tonight, Natalie. I couldn't have made peace with my family without you."

She drew her arm off him and reached for the sheet. He pulled it around her and snugged her into his front more firmly, running a hand up and down her back, absently encouraging her to melt into him again, thoughts still drifting in a thousand directions as he tried to take in all the ways she'd enriched his life.

He tried to work up how to propose without risking his soul.

"All those times Adara nagged me about these little reunions, I couldn't see myself being a part of it. Now the pieces are falling into place." He should have stopped there, he would think later, but the next words came out of his mouth. "Should we get married? So it's not so confusing for Zoey? I'd like to be in your bed every night, you know."

Natalie shimmied away from the heavy weight of his arms, heart pared like an apple. For a moment all her brain could conjure was panicked expletives. He wasn't acknowledging her expression of love. He was saying thank-you, as though she'd brought him a fresh cup of coffee.

And starting to enlighten her as to why he'd brought her here: so he fit in with the siblings who had spouses and children. While she'd been falling in love, he'd been repackaging himself as a family man to find acceptance with his siblings. She didn't blame him. She was totally sincere in wanting him to strengthen his relationship with them on every level.

She just didn't understand why, *why* she had to be an instrument. A means to a prize rather than the prize itself. He'd told her last night that he was fixing his relationship with his family, but that had been a lie. Maybe just a fabrication. Maybe he didn't even see it, but she did. She always saw where her responsibility began and ended.

She wouldn't have been so hurt right now if he'd been honest with her about it up front. She probably wouldn't even have said no, because as he'd rightly pointed out, she was a soft touch, especially about things like family. If he'd told her this was why he'd needed her here, she would have found a way without letting her daughter attach to him and without giving up her heart to him.

But she couldn't do this for the rest of her life. She couldn't love him with all her heart and know he'd only married her for what she represented, not who she really was. She took on a lot for other people, but that was more responsibility than she was willing to carry. It wasn't fair to her and it would never be fair to Zoey.

"Demitri…" She swung legs that wouldn't hold her to the edge of the bed, then sat there, face covered. *Stupid, stupid Natalie.* Had she actually started to believe all the sparkle and glitter, laughter and lovemaking, added up to more than a nice chemical match with a very rich man?

"I know you don't want to get married," he said, coming up on an elbow behind her. "But for Zoey's sake—"

"For Zoey's sake I have to say no," she said, voice coarse. She stood, forcing her weak knees to lock, then searched out a hotel robe from the closet.

"Why?" The question was cold and hard.

"Because we'll end up divorced." She flung an exasperated hand into the air. "Listen, this is my fault. I started believing in the fantasy again. I know better than to imagine I'm ever going to get something real—"

"The fantasy," he interrupted, fairly spitting the word. "The one where you pretend you're one of those barfly tarts I used to pick up because acting like that is so much better than living your real life."

"Hey!" she cried, not liking how nasty this was getting.

"You don't like the way it sounds? Neither do I. You might have warned me that you were just enjoying the ride, Nat. Was saying you loved me part of the fantasy, too?"

So he *had* heard. And he was throwing it in her face. She jerked back as though it was a physical object striking her in the nose.

"Don't you dare act as if I'm the only one using someone!" She clenched her fists. "You only brought me here so you could look like the rest of them! I set my expectations very low. I've never had any other choice, but don't ask me to marry you just so you have a child to take to the family picnic."

"Because I'm that shallow," he said, throwing himself onto his feet, naked and furious, striding past her to walk out and find his pants in the lounge. Jamming his legs into them, he shouted, "You know what you want, Natalie? For me to be as self-involved and unreliable as your dad and your husband so you can tell yourself we're all alike and push us away. You can't count on others if you never *do*, you know. But you just love being responsible for everything, don't you? Well, good news, sweetheart. This one's all on you."

He slammed out of the suite.

Someone sat down beside him at the bar.

Nic.

Demitri silently swore. Things were just getting better and better.

Nic caught the bartender's eye and motioned to the drink in front of Demitri, indicating he wanted the same.

"Take mine. I don't want it," Demitri said, sliding it over a few inches. All his old coping strategies were shot and he hadn't found new ones beyond talking things out with Natalie, and he was so furious with her...

And so hurt...

End up divorced. Fantasy.

Nic didn't touch the drink. Didn't say anything. Only settled onto the stool, forearms on the bar, key card rotating on its edge between his fingers and thumb against the mahogany. His tuxedo jacket was gone along with his bow tie, his shirt untucked.

"Come to tell me you didn't like my talking to your wife behind your back?" Demitri guessed.

"No," Nic said with a measure of surprise, click-clicking the card against the glossed wood. "I didn't like it, but that's not why I'm here. Natalie called our suite. She wanted to come get Zoey— It's okay," he said at Demitri's curse, holding up a hand. "Ro talked her into letting the kids sleep till morning. She was inviting her over for a glass of wine when I left. I figured there weren't too many places a man goes when he's had it out with a woman. Found you on the first try."

"And why would you want to, Nic?" Demitri asked tiredly. It was late, Demitri was thinking. Far too late for this.

Nic pursed his mouth in thought, profile not unlike Theo's. Something in his features reminded Demitri of an old photo Adara had of their maternal grandfather. It was so odd. Made him feel less as though Nic was a complete stranger, even though he was.

"You didn't have to go behind my back, you know. You could have come to me," Nic said.

Demitri snorted, shook his head, baffled by the whole thing. He thought of Natalie telling him he had a right to his confusion and had to ask, "Why would I expect you to help me? Can I ask you something, Nic? And be honest. Do you remember me? Because I've got nothing."

Nic flinched, making Demitri feel as if he'd accidentally run over the guy's dog.

"Why would you remember me? You were a baby," Nic said, picking up the untouched drink and smelling it. Sipping once. "Yeah, I remember you. You liked to take your clothes off. Made us laugh."

Demitri choked on a chuckle. Couldn't help it. *True to form*, he thought, and immediately wanted to repeat the story to Natalie. It was the sort of thing that would make her laugh.

God, he loved her laugh. Loved her. *Hell*.

"Does Natalie know about any of that? What we came from?" Nic asked.

"She's the only one I've ever talked to about it." Something twisted in his chest, reaching out to her across the walls and floors, trying to get to her. He'd thought she understood him. Accepted him.

Nic's thumb worked the edge of the glass, nodded. "Yeah, it looked as if you two were pretty close. What happened?"

"Man, you really are an investigative journalist, aren't you?"

"Just trying to help," Nic said, turning his head and

looking disturbingly sincere. "She seems like a good person. I don't think you would have walked out on the family business over a woman you didn't love. Did you tell her?"

The word was like a knife to the heart. "She said it wasn't enough," he said, feeling the blade twist in his chest. He was a fantasy. Not real. A vehicle for pleasure, not a man of substance—exactly what he'd always portrayed himself as, so he probably deserved this heartbreak he was suffering, but he couldn't stand it. He didn't know how to live without her. Not anymore.

Nic swore under his breath. "She does not look like the kind of woman who would dice up a man when he laid it out like that."

As Nic's words penetrated, Demitri frowned. Eyed Nic. "No, that was something she said when she was talking about why she never wanted to remarry. I didn't actually tell her…"

He sounded like an idiot even to himself. He'd been so busy trying to protect himself, he'd left her hanging with her own declaration.

"I screwed up, didn't I?" For once not deliberately.

"Kinda sounds like it." Nic scratched under his chin. "Did you propose?"

Demitri winced. Longed for the days when he messed up and didn't care. Didn't feel it like broken glass coursing through his veins.

"Not with a ring. Not properly," he admitted.

A big breath expanded Nic's chest. He blew it out slowly. "I'm no advice columnist, but I've proofed a few," he said drily. "Here's the thing I do know. If you want to win a woman, you have to go all in. Give her everything you've got. Pride. Self-worth. Heart. Soul. All of it. Nothing held back."

"I wish it was that easy," Demitri said, thinking of how

hard it was to get Natalie to accept anything. That last accusation of his, about her always wanting to be responsible for everything, not counting on anyone, had been true. In his experience, women expected men's wallets to be opened on their behalf. He had never understood Natalie's deference and protests and putting of others first.

I set my expectations very low...

He'd heard that differently, thinking she was referring to him, too furious about the fantasy remark to process anything properly, but as he thought about why and how she'd become such a little soldier about responsibility, he saw a girl who'd been pressed into service and neglected in her own way. He wondered how many times she had wanted to go to the movies with friends, or continue her ice dancing, and her mother had had to say no. Not by choice, but because Natalie was needed. She didn't resent it, he knew, but life had cheated her so many times. Even her young-adult years of pursuing her education and making mistakes with boys had only lasted one night. Long enough to get pregnant, grow up and never do anything for herself again.

Except steal a few days in France. Other than that, she probably hadn't had a selfish moment in her life. Even her heart, her love, had been given away without her daring to ask for something in return.

Of course she loved him. Of course the words would mean something to her, if they were said with sincerity. The way she loved her daughter, her dead family, was fierce and enduring. She would love him, Demitri, until the end of time, and he was privileged, honored, to realize she'd come to feel such an emotion toward him.

"Thanks, Nic," he said, slapping his brother on the shoulder as he rose, hardened with purpose. "I know what to do." Throwing a few bills on the bar for the drink, he added, "Don't let her leave with Zoey before I get there."

* * *

Natalie wanted to shrink away and die, but Zoey had misplaced her bunny somewhere in Nic and Rowan's suite and refused to leave without it.

Rowan had urged Natalie to sleep on things last night, but when Natalie had dragged her sorry, unrested body out of bed, the suite had still been empty. Now she just wanted to collect her daughter and head back to Canada on whichever transport her credit card could afford.

But it wasn't happening.

And she was starting to see why Demitri found the Makricosta collective so annoying with their inclusive remarks and their cheery engagement with all the children. Everyone showed up for a brunch that Rowan insisted Natalie share with them. Demitri's absence was explained as "having run out for something," and her daughter was being treated as if she'd been born into their ranks.

Natalie mumbled something about too much champagne to explain her sullen mood and hid behind the challenge of cutting up enough waffle to keep the boys busy with their blunt plastic forks.

All she wanted was to be gone before Demitri showed up—not that she really expected him to turn up here. If he did, he certainly wouldn't be coming to see her.

The door clicked and all the adult voices dried up, telling her that for all their lighthearted banter, they all knew she and Demitri had blown up last night.

Footsteps came toward her, but she stayed seated at the table, frozen with her back to him, begging lightning to strike her.

"Don't look at me like that," Demitri grumbled to someone. "I'm fixing it."

His hand came into her averted field of vision, gently taking the knife out of her hand, then the fork.

She dropped her head into her hands, covering her eyes. Hiding.

"Come on, Natalie," he said, not angry or aggressive. Firm, but tender. His touch on her shoulder was insistent. "We need to talk."

"Mom?" her daughter questioned, becoming aware of adult attention falling on Natalie and Demitri.

"It's okay, gumdrop. I just need to talk to her for a minute. We'll be right back," Demitri said in that voice that almost sounded… No, she wouldn't tell herself it was loving. "Come on," he urged Natalie. "Or do you want to do it here?"

No.

She rose, vaguely aware of Theo handing Demitri something as they left, only realizing after Demitri had guided her down to the end of the hall that it had been a security card. They entered a private lounge, silent and still, that was probably used for weddings and private dinners. It had a wet bar off to the side and a handful of trendy backless sofas sprinkled throughout. Floor-to-ceiling windows offered a view across Central Park to die for, sunlight glancing off it from a low angle that made it sparkle under the glitter of light snow.

"What I said last night…" she managed in a strained voice, hardly able to face him. "I didn't mean it to sound as though being part of your family isn't good enough for me. Of course they're wonderful. Zoey…" Already meshed. She wished…

"I'd say forget my family, but I don't want you to forget them. They're as much a part of what I'm offering you as I am. They already care about you, Natalie. They're your backup plan, and they're never going to let me get away with hurting you. Not that I'll let myself get away with it," he muttered.

"Because you're afraid of their disapproval? That's

what I meant last night!" She clenched her hands, turning to glance warily at him, holding her breath to try to get through this without busting open.

"I've had nothing but their disapproval all my life. I'm used to it. No," he said firmly. "Their approval is the last thing I was trying to get when I asked you to marry me. I want your love, Natalie."

His words wrung her heart like a wet rag. And scared her, because once her heart was involved, she was a pushover. She shook her head, trying to stop him from continuing, but he approached with purpose. Determination.

"You love me." He was a fallen angel, brutally handsome, sweetly attentive as he committed his cruelty with delicate care, ambling forward so he stood directly in front of her. He tilted up her chin so she couldn't avoid his eyes. "That wasn't part of the fantasy. It's real. Your love is mine, Natalie. And I won't let you show it to me, then refuse to give it to me. I want it. I'm taking it."

She caught back a sob, eyes on fire as she searched for a place to look. Her lips quivered and her throat thickened.

"And I'm going to give you my love so you can show me how to make it better and stronger."

She blinked, trying to see him through her swimming eyes, certain she'd misheard.

His hand cupped her cheek, and he wiped the tears brimming her lashes. "You're going to accept my love, Natalie. You're going to let me give you everything you need. And if I miss something, you're going to tell me so I can do it right."

"It's not that easy. Zoey—"

"You'll help me do right by her, too. And any kids we make together."

"But—"

"No, listen. I realize that your mom put Gareth first. I know she had no choice, but what did that teach you? That your needs come second. Don't throw Zoey at me and tell me she trumps your right to be happy. You don't have to settle for a few weeks of fantasy, Natalie. You can have this all the time. You can have me. You can have a man who pays the bills and sends Zoey to expensive schools and tells you to work for my brother if you want to, not because you have to. I'm going to open my firm in Montreal and stick around, whether you want me there or not, because I want *you*. I want to be with you. I love you."

His words caught and rent deep in her chest, where secret dreams like ice dancing and husbands who came home resided. Where every aspect of her life wasn't all on her. It was a joint venture. A loving, laughing partnership that she'd convinced herself she didn't need.

But she wanted.

So badly.

Was this really happening?

Her brow crinkled as he dug a velvet box out of his pocket and offered her its contents. A diamond ring. "Will you marry me?"

Natalie began to tremble all over, but with a kind of joy that made the world look sprinkled in fairy dust.

"You could have anyone. You know that, right?" she managed to stammer.

"Natalie, you are the only woman I have ever loved. The only one I've ever proposed to. *You* could have anyone, and I will never look lightly on the fact that you are willing to take me. Are you? Will you marry me?"

"Yes," she admitted in a whisper, as though she was confiding it to Santa.

He took the ring and threaded it onto her finger. It was incredibly tasteful, of course. The man could be outrageous, but never tacky or ostentatious.

He kissed her knuckles, then her lips. She clung to the connection, trembling, still not quite believing, but the sweetness of his kiss filled her up so no empty spaces were left.

"I do love you," she told him, awed and humbled by the gratitude and thrill she read in his eyes.

"I love you, too," he said against her lips, pulling her close to crush her with careful arms. Heads tilted together, they both smiled so big they could barely kiss, hearts battering against each other.

"Thank you for coming back," she said sheepishly.

"Always," he promised.

"Should we tell them?" she asked him after they'd shared a few more kisses.

"I want to see Zoey's reaction," he admitted with a rueful grin. "I'm crazy about her, you know. She's as easy to love as her mother."

Their faces must have told the story. The minute they appeared, beaming and glued to each other's side, everyone clapped and champagne bottles were popped. Natalie showed Zoey her ring and said, "Demitri and I are getting married. What do you think of that?"

"I like it," Zoey said, as if she'd been asked to judge the ring. "It's pretty. If you get married, does that mean you can have a baby? 'Cause I want a little brother."

EPILOGUE

NATALIE EMERGED TO typical chaos in the back garden of Rosedale, Nic and Rowan's Greek island home. The men were barbecuing and talking politics around watching the children. The women were back and forth to the kitchen, trying to keep everyone sunscreened, fed and hydrated.

Oh, how Natalie loved when they were all together like this. It wasn't easy, but they made the children's birthdays a priority and Evie's was tomorrow.

"Who did you find?" Demitri asked Natalie, coming forward to take their nearly three-year-old nephew, Zephyr, off her hip. He'd been cuddly while he'd still been sleepy, but now he energized as he leaped for his uncle. Demitri gave him a light toss in the air before kissing his grinning cheek. "About time you woke up, champ. Everyone's been asking for you. Zoey," he called across to where the children were taking turns riding down the minislide into the little wading pool. "Look who woke up."

"Jaya's awake, too," Natalie said in answer to Theo's questioning glance. "She'll be out in a minute." They'd all converged here this morning, but jet lag was taking its toll on some more than others.

Demitri handed off Zephyr to Zoey and came to hook his arm around Natalie's waist, always affectionate, but especially so when he was relaxed and happy, as he was when they were around his family.

"Zoey, you don't have to carry him," Jaya said as she

came outside and gravitated to her husband. She still sounded sleepy, and Theo cuddled her into his side, rubbing her back.

"I like to," Zoey said, turning back with Zephyr clinging to her like a rhesus monkey. He was half her seven-year-old height and she was all bones these days, growing like a cornstalk, front teeth missing so she lisped. "I carry my other cousins all the time." She started to turn away, then turned back again. "Mom, you said I'd probably never have cousins from you, only from Daddy. Now I have four."

"I know. We did pretty good, eh?" Natalie said.

"We did," Zoey said with a nod of approval, and bore her cousin away.

"Eh?" Rowan repeated in a light tease. "I used to think that was a joke, but you Canadians really say it. Even Demitri's started."

"How many cousins does she have on the other side?" Nic asked.

"It's not a competition," Natalie chided, sharing an eye-roll with the other wives. Theo was mature enough to abstain from juvenile contests, but the other three were not.

"I'm just saying, if we could assist in any way..." Nic continued innocently.

Rowan tilted her head back in a sultry laugh of enjoyment, hugging her husband. "We've been dying to get you all together and tell you! The agency called us. They have a little boy from the same village as Evie. We can get him next week, and we were hoping one of you would keep Evie while we do."

"Of course," everyone rushed to agree, hugging and kissing and congratulating.

As the hullaballoo died down, Adara said, "Of course, that's only one." She shared a look with her husband, flashed one at Jaya and bit her lip. "We have a bit of news ourselves. You know that we've never wanted to open the can of worms that is Gideon's background, so adoption has never really been available to us. But a friend of Jaya's cousin is pregnant. She's very young, but wants to have the baby and have an open-adoption situation. We've talked with her several times and... Of course, anything could happen, but she seems very certain."

"We offered to help her out so she can keep it, but she wants to finish her education and go into law. She's met Androu," Gideon said, indicating their son. "She feels strongly that we can offer a better upbringing. They both do. The baby's father is in the picture, willing to marry her, but he really doesn't have much. And he's scared out of his mind at the idea of being a father. Doesn't feel he'd make a good parent. He'd rather his child have more stability and opportunity."

"She's due in a month and... Well, as I say, things can change, but I think we're expecting," Adara said with a teary smile.

All the women sighed and hugged her; the men kissed her cheek and shook Gideon's hand. Everyone wished them luck.

"So that's two," Demitri said with a nod of approval. "Of course, my brother the math whiz might say differently. How is your wife's jet lag slash food poisoning, anyway?"

"Okay, it's not food poisoning!" Jaya cried, covering the blush that darkened her cheeks. "And it must be a girl because I was never this sick with Zephyr." As she accepted congratulations from everyone, she said, "I hated keeping it from all of you. It's just that silly rule about—"

"Waiting three months, I know," Demitri said. "Bothers me, too."

Everyone went quiet. They looked at his smirk, transferred their attention to Natalie's flushing cheeks and exasperated glance at her husband. They grinned.

Adara blinked back tears and said, "Oh, Natalie."

"I know," Natalie said, growing teary herself. It wasn't just hormones. She was happy. Really, really happy. They'd been waiting until his business was established, which had happened very quickly, given his skill and connections. She was finishing up a special project she and Jaya had been working on for the hotels and now...

Life was about as perfect as it got.

After accepting everyone's felicitations, she hugged Demitri, reveling in the way he gently crushed her into his side.

"Thank you," she whispered. "For giving me all of this."

"Thank *you*," he said, grazing her lips with his own. "I never imagined myself like this, you know."

"A father? Part of a big family?"

"Happy," he corrected. "Living happily-ever-after."

* * * * *

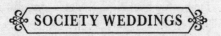

Together with their families

Clio Norwood
and
Stefan Bianco

Invite you to join them as they become

Mr & Mrs

June 2015

The Chatsfield

New York, New York

Reception to follow

...but only if Stefan can claim his unexpected bride!

❧ SOCIETY WEDDINGS ❧

Dedicated bachelors Rocco Mondelli,
Christian Markos, Stefan Bianco and Zayed Al Afzal
met and bonded at university, wreaking havoc amongst
the female population. In the decade since graduating
they've made their mark on the worlds of business
and pleasure, becoming wealthy and powerful.

Marriage has never been something Rocco, Christian,
Stefan or Zayed were ever after… But things change,
and now they'll have to do whatever it takes
to get themselves to the church on time!

Yet nothing is as easy as it seems…
and the women these four have set their sights on
have plans of their own!

**Your embossed invitation is in the mail
and you are cordially invited to:**

The marriage of
Rocco Mondelli and Olivia Fitzgerald
April 2015

The marriage of
Christian Markos and Alessandra Mondelli
May 2015

The marriage of
Stefan Bianco and Clio Norwood
June 2015

The marriage of
Sheikh Zayed Al Afzal and Princess Nadia Amani
July 2015

**So RSVP and get ready to enjoy the pinnacle of luxury
and opulence as the world's sexiest billionaires
finally say 'I do'…**

THE SICILIAN'S
SURPRISE WIFE

BY

TARA PAMMI

MILLS & BOON

Published in Great Britain 2015
by Mills & Boon, an imprint of Harlequin (UK) Limited,
Eton House, 18-24 Paradise Road, Richmond, Surrey, TW9 1SR

© 2015 Harlequin Books SA

Special thanks and acknowledgement are given to Tara Pammi
for her contribution to the *Society Weddings* series.

ISBN: 978-0-263-25066-4

Tara Pammi can't remember a moment when she wasn't lost in a book—especially a romance, which was much more exciting than a mathematics textbook. Years later, Tara's wild imagination and love for the written word revealed what she really wanted to do. Now she pairs Alpha males who think they know everything with strong women who knock that theory *and* them off their feet!

Books by Tara Pammi

Mills & Boon® Modern™ Romance

The Man to Be Reckoned With
A Deal with Demakis

A Dynasty of Sand and Scandal

The Last Prince of Dahaar
The True King of Dahaar

The Sensational Stanton Sisters

A Hint of Scandal
A Touch of Temptation

Visit the author profile page at millsandboon.co.uk for more titles

For the three wonderful ladies who made working on this book such a treat—Andie, Jen and Michelle.

CHAPTER ONE

SHE FELT LIKE GLASS, stretched so tightly that a gentle tap could shatter her forever.

Clutching her wrap tight in her fingers, Clio Norwood looked around for her fiancé, Jackson.

Ashley, his secretary, who had arrived unannounced and interrupted their meeting with a client Jackson was determined to add to his cap, was nowhere to be seen either. Something distasteful hovered in the back of Clio's mind, as if waiting to strike.

With the small get-together of the ultrarich in full swing atop the Empire State Building, Manhattan glittered around them.

Usually, the vibrant, unrelenting pulse of the city that had become home to Clio over the past decade filled her with unending spirit for life. It had kept her going even when she had been struggling after graduation from Columbia University. And had helped her swallow her failures and her naive, broken expectations of making it by herself in the city that never slept.

But tonight, even New York couldn't puncture the bubble of dread that had begun to pervade her of late.

Jackson had returned last night after three weeks from an overseas trip and had been in *a stinker of a mood* as he liked to call it, because he had missed out on some real estate deal.

They had barely exchanged a word all day today as she

had been at work. When she had returned to the posh flat they had been living in for the past year, he had commanded her to get ready for this party tonight.

Commanded and not asked, much less requested. A pattern that was becoming more and more obvious to Clio. Still, she knew the stress of his business, understood the driving need to make one's mark in the world, so she had given in.

Even if she was still bone tired from the out-of-season flu she had had a week ago.

Tonight, Jackson needed her help to convince Mrs. Alcott, an old friend of her parents', to hire him as her personal investment banker. With her estates in Britain and substantial family business, Jane Alcott would be a coup for Jackson's already flourishing career.

But they hadn't even greeted Jane properly before Ashley had approached Jackson with a desperate glint in her eye.

Loath to create a scene, Clio had clenched her teeth and smiled serenely even as she saw the curious looks and stifled whispers among Jackson's clients' wives and girlfriends. Even the utter kindness of Jane's question if everything was all right between Jackson and her had been unbearable.

What was going on with him? What was going on between them?

Because Clio knew with a nauseating clarity that Ashley was just the tip of the iceberg for what was going on between her and Jackson.

Suddenly, it felt blatantly scandalous of Ashley to drag him away with a barely disguised proprietary claim on him.

Squaring her shoulders, Clio let her long stride eat up the space. She hated creating a scene, hated the pitying and speculative glances that had been coming her way far too frequently the past few months, but she had endured it all silently.

Tonight, she had had enough. She stilled as a tall, commanding figure came into her focus.

Clio blinked, the impact of those jade green eyes and generous but scornful mouth instantaneous.

Stefan Bianco.

Her first instinct was to head for the elevator before he could see her, leave the party. Even her parents, with their disapprovingly stifling silence, would have been welcome. She didn't want the man she had known a long time ago, one of her oldest friends, to see her tonight.

Stefan, Christian, Rocco and Zayed made up the Columbia Four—the four young men she had known when they had all been at university together, who had turned into supersuccessful, ultrawealthy, sought-after bachelors for whom the world was a playground and its most beautiful women were playthings.

But before they had all become successful in their own right, she had known them, had seen them every day for four years, and had shared her deepest fears and hopes with them.

And the fact that she wanted to run away from one of the few people who had genuinely known her, had understood her, left a bitter taste in her mouth.

Was she that much of a failure, then? Was she running away from Stefan or was she running away from what she had become?

Stefan Bianco looked around at the glittering cityscape of Manhattan and gritted his jaw tight.

The vibrant pulse of it, the memories from almost a decade ago everywhere he looked, his own sheer naïveté when he had studied at Columbia with his other three friends—the memories rose up around him like a specter that wouldn't let him breathe easy even for a few minutes.

And yet, as the head of a multimillion luxury real estate

company, New York was unavoidable even though he tried to reduce the number of times he came here.

But this time, he had a reason for being at this exact party, on top of the Empire State Building.

It was high time he found a way to stop Jackson Smith.

The memory of his executive assistant Marco's whitened face as he lay against the hospital bed after his suicide attempt, Marco's five-year-old daughter's chubby face wreathed in confusion as she asked Stefan about what had happened to her papa...

The powerlessness he had felt was like acid in his stomach.

Jackson had swindled Marco out of his savings, pushed him to bankruptcy, until his assistant had lost everything, had seen no way out...

The eviscerating self-doubt, the sense of being an utter failure, of letting down everyone that had counted on him—looking into Marco's eyes had been like looking at his own reflection of a few years ago.

Guilt corroded his insides. If only he had found a way to stop Jackson years ago when he had swindled Stefan himself...

It had been the worst time of his life—Serena's betrayal, his guilt driving him to not return to his parents in Sicily and the around-the-clock hours he had worked to secure a deal...

He had lost the little he had made because of Jackson's treachery. He would have been in Marco's place if it hadn't been for his friends Rocco, Christian and Zayed anchoring him, if he hadn't already been woken up to the reality of life by Serena, the woman who had professed to love him.

This time Jackson needed to be stopped, whatever it took.

As though Stefan thinking Jackson's name invoked the very devil himself, the American laughed in a group not two feet from where Stefan stood.

A short blonde, dressed in jeans and a tight T-shirt, dragged Jackson away, interrupting the conversation. His

craggy face tight with tension, Jackson leaned toward another woman in the group, a tall redhead, and whispered
something.

An apology, Stefan assumed. That didn't quite work,
given the way the woman flinched and turned her head away.
More curious than ever, Stefan looked on as the woman's
bare shoulders stiffened, bones jutting out of her shoulders.

Everything about her posture screamed tension and
something more. Jackson let himself be dragged away even
as the tall woman stood ramrod straight, her head held high
and so perfectly still that Stefan wondered if she would
break if someone blew a wisp of breath her way.

Her face wreathed in shadows, there was a quiet dignity
to her. And then he noticed her hair. Even tucked away from
that angular face and scrunched tight into an elaborate knot,
that red hair was as unmistakable as the narrow, upturned
nose and stubborn tilt of the chin.

That face would be perfectly oval and her eyes green,
like glittering emeralds. When she smiled, one corner of
her mouth turned upward in a crooked slant.

Clio Norwood, the one woman he had never tamed.

Every cell inside him went on high alert, as if he had
been infused with a charge of live current. What the hell
was Clio doing with Jackson Smith?

There had been intimacy in the way Jackson had bent
closer to her and whispered something, in the way his open
palm had caressed her bare arm.

Yet Stefan could feel the tension in her as the silence of
the group reverberated against her. Saw the speculative and
intrusively hungry glances cast her way. Noted the way she
retreated into herself as an older woman inquired something.

And knowing Jackson and his perfidious ways, a thousand kinds of thoughts swarmed in on Stefan.

Anything even remotely connected to Jackson, Stefan
didn't touch with a pole. Yet, he found himself moving to-

ward her, his gaze savoring the sight of her. Inch by glorious inch, light bathed that long neck and her face.

He stilled, supremely aware of the insistent beat of his own pulse, of the heightened charge of his own breath.

Clio was just as utterly gorgeous as she had always been, if a little too thin.

His mind cast back to over a decade ago, to his university days with Rocco, Christian and Zayed—who'd become more brothers than friends—to the unparalleled enthusiasm of learning the world and knowing that it could be at their feet, to the glory of discovering women and the pull they held for them, and to Clio Norwood—the woman who had known the Columbia Four as well as they had known each other.

Every inch an aristocrat she no longer wanted to be and used to privileged playboys just like them, she had often laughed at their exploits, seeing their escapades with other women with a decidedly amused resignation and distance. She'd rejected his come-ons that first year, as easily as she had shrugged away the elaborate wealth and standing she had been born into.

Of all the men on the planet, the last man he would have envisioned Clio to be with was Jackson Smith.

In no mood to get into a sparring match with Jackson again, especially when his patience was already dangerously low, Stefan waited. Minutes piled on top of each other. With a graceful tilt of her head, Clio excused herself from the group.

Ignoring the uncharacteristically frantic thrumming of his heart, Stefan cornered her in the next moment. "*Ciao*, Clio."

He wrapped his fingers over her arm to turn her and felt the shiver that went through her. Saw the bracing breath she took before she turned around. A flash of fear, feral and bright, danced in her green eyes.

Until she blinked, those long lashes hiding her expression.

When she looked up again, a flicker of warmth dawned in those green depths. "Stefan…what a surprise…I had no idea you were in New York."

That accent of hers—it had always done strange things to his insides, swept over him with a mix of warmth and heated awareness. But her tone was reserved and artificial; it rattled him.

Granted, they hadn't seen each other in a while, but for four years, Clio had been a part of his life—an integral one and one he remembered without bitterness.

Placing his arm around her toward the railing, he trapped her, shielding her from the rest of the crowd.

"You would have known if you'd kept in touch, wouldn't you, *bella*?"

Tension thrummed in the tight set of her shoulders. "You barely ever set foot in New York whereas this is my home."

"True. But you didn't think it important to even attend Rocco's wedding. Does your new…*life* not allow room for old friends, Clio?"

She didn't flinch as she had done with Jackson, but there was an infinitesimal withdrawal. That shadow of fear again.

Dio, what was her association with Jackson?

"I've always been here, Stefan." A remnant of the old Clio—full of adventure and plans for a new kind of life—flashed in her gaze. "I'm not the one determined to wipe anything related to our life in New York from memory."

"Maybe I realized there wasn't anything of value left for me here in New York. It's not like Rocco, Christian or Zayed live here."

She didn't strike him down with words as she used to, only stared at him with those wide eyes and her mouth pinched. Why didn't she just put him in his place with a cutting remark as she had always done?

Where was this need to land a shot at her coming from?

And why? Just because she had some kind of association with Jackson Smith while she had rejected his cocky advances a lifetime ago?

He didn't need his male ego to be validated by her interest in him.

Women flocked to him with one interested glance from him and he took advantage of it. He liked sex, had a healthy libido and when he was done, he walked away from the woman whether she liked it or not.

He had no place or use for a woman in his life, except in his bed.

Yet he had barely spent two minutes with Clio and suddenly, he was more interested in her thoughts and her actions.

Her chest rose and fell with the calming breath she took, coating his skin with warmth. He saw the mask that fell into place covering up her obvious distress, saw years of breeding and good manners slide into place.

The very thing she had been determined to overcome about herself...

"It was good to see you, Stefan," she said evenly, with a perfectly bland smile. "But you'll have to excuse me. I have things to do."

He clasped her arm. "You didn't answer my question. Why didn't you come to Rocco's wedding?"

Distress marred her gaze, before she composed herself enough to hide it. Her green eyes were huge in her oval face, the pallor of her skin parchment white. "I've been busy with work. Not all of us have turned our dreams into such an amazing reality as you have done with your global real estate company."

"I started with nothing more than you did, Clio. I never took a penny from my parents after they disowned me."

"Christian told me. After Serena, you—" She must have caught the blaze of anger in his gaze because she grimaced and continued, "After everything that happened in the last semester, you never looked back once.

"So stop blaming me alone for a friendship that didn't last. In the first couple of years, Christian kept me abreast of what was happening with you guys. After that, it was hard to miss your success with all four of you hitting young millionaires' lists left and right. But I'm not bitter enough to bemoan your success, Stefan."

"I'm asking now, *bella*. What happened to your dreams, Clio?"

"Reality happened, okay? I discovered how hard it is to actually make it in this world. So kudos to you for doing it." She took another calming breath. "Tell me about Rocco's wedding." It was obvious that she wanted to turn the conversation away from her life, but still, warmth spilled into her green eyes as she said Rocco's name. "It would have been something to see Rocco dance to the tunes of the woman he fell so hard for. Olivia Fitzgerald must be really special."

The wistfulness in her gaze before she looked around herself and covered it up tugged at his curiosity. "Olivia is definitely something, and Rocco is well and truly caught."

He noted the way her gaze kept going to the entrance to the terrace, the same revolving door that Jackson and the blonde had walked through. "It was only a plane ride away, Clio. If it's money for the plane ticket, you could have just asked one of us."

"I'm not destitute, Stefan," she said tiredly, as if she would do anything if he just left her alone. "After Christian paid my rent for a few months that one time, I managed fine."

Shock reverberated through Stefan.

Christian had helped Clio once with the rent? Had it been that bad for her?

But he had no doubt as to why Christian wouldn't have breathed a word. His friend had grown up in poverty on the streets of Athens, was the one who really understood what it meant to make ends meet when you started with nothing.

He understood why it would have been Christian that Clio had gone to. But still, he didn't like that things had been so bad for her and he hadn't even had an inkling of it.

He stared at her anew.

There was no emotion, not even bitterness, in her tone. Only an underlying urgency and fear prompted by what, he had no idea.

It had to be something related to Jackson.

A renewed purpose filled him. He had to help her get out of whatever it was.

"If you ever needed something, you only had to ask."

"I don't want charity. Yours or anyone else's. I paid Christian back when I was able to. I'm fine now."

"Then why did you not come to the wedding? Why did you blanch when you saw me?"

"I told you. I've had too many things going on and—"

"Is it that or is the fact that your new associations and your new way of life don't let you see your old friends anymore?"

She paled. "Whatever it is that you're implying, say it straight to my face, Stefan. It's not like you to worry about someone else's feelings, is it?"

"Jackson Smith."

A stillness came over her and Stefan knew. Whatever it was that robbed all color from her skin, that made a shadow of Clio, it was Jackson. "What…what do you mean?" He saw her throat swallow forcibly.

"Are you not well, *bella*?"

She jerked away from him, her breath coming in sharp bursts. "What. About. Jackson, Stefan?"

"Jackson is a crook. A polished, smooth-talking, self-centered crook. The best thing I can say about him is that he doesn't lack for female company wherever he goes."

Her brittle laughter interrupted him. "I could say the

same or even less about you. A Slavic model and the ripples that she created just a couple of months ago come to mind." A feverish gleam entered her eyes. "What was it? 'Bianco's last name should really be Bastard,'" she finished with a mutinous gleam. "You have been dubbed the One-Date Wonder because you won't even the see the same woman twice."

Her defense of that crook infuriated Stefan. "You have no idea what Jackson could be up to. His business practices are extremely murky. I have been looking for proof for a long time to pin him for it. He's a greedy bastard, a leech who will use anyone to climb the ladder a little more, will use any means, even illegal ones to get what he wants. In straight words, he's scum through and through. Whatever connection you have with him, cut it and walk away, before he brings you down with him."

Every ounce of color fled from her face, leaving a pale, tight mask behind. "I don't believe you. I know that Jackson can be brash and even uncouth sometimes, but he…"

"Then you've also become a fool and are not worth my time or advice."

Fury that she would put him on the same level as Jackson left a bad taste in his mouth. This was not the woman he had known and admired once.

"Or maybe this is the life you lead now, Clio. Maybe walking away from wealth and the status you were born to didn't work out quite like you thought it would. Maybe the facade of status and wealth that Jackson provides you makes being part of his crooked schemes worth it."

Something flittered in her gaze, and against every instinct that warned him to walk away, Stefan stayed. Instead of the anger he expected, hurt wreathed her features. And again, this pale imitation of the old Clio he had known once twisted a knot in his gut.

"You don't think that really."

"A decade is a long time. You might be just as power hungry and itching to be kept like most women I know."

"And you must have really become a cold bastard to be able to say that to me."

Her words fell away like water on rocks. Had he become sentimental about her because he had known her a decade ago?

Clio was no different.

Women with self-respect, women who weren't out for everything they could get could be counted on one hand. Like Rocco's Olivia.

"Touché, *bella*. Maybe we are strangers to each other."

"With nothing more to say to each other."

She looked as if she was caught in a trap with no way out. It would haunt him if he walked away now.

"*Dio*, Clio…are you in some kind of trouble? Just tell me how you know him."

Her chin lifted. As if she was bracing herself for attack.

"I work for him, have done for five years now. He gave me a job when no one would hire me, Stefan, showed me a way to make it in New York when I would have returned home to England with shame on my face. I have to believe that you're mistaken. I have to believe for my own sake that everything you're saying…" As erect and stiff as her shoulders were, she trembled. "Jackson's my fiancé."

"You are…" Gritting his jaw, Stefan curtailed the stinging response that rose to his lips, waited for the shock that was reverberating inside him to abate.

The fact that she had mentioned her engagement to Jackson as a second thought, that she had almost swayed while saying it—nothing could dilute the acidic taste that filled him.

How could Clio, of all the women in the world, be engaged to marry Jackson Smith? Had she changed that much?

Was it all shine and no substance to Clio either?

A memory from a long time ago of a laughing Clio, her lustrous red hair flying behind her, cycling across the campus from one class to the next, challenging him to a race, slammed into him.

Against the backdrop of a lot of ugly memories of New York that persisted in his mind, he could do nothing but let himself be washed in the wake of this one.

"'Two roads diverged in a wood, and I—I took the road less traveled by, and that has made all the difference,'" he said, quoting her favorite line by Frost.

A gasp fell from her mouth, the sheen of tears turning her eyes into glittering emeralds. "I used to think of you as a firestorm, Clio. Vibrant, fierce and so unafraid." His pulse quickened as the scent of her skin teased him. "I used to think you were the strongest woman I had ever met.

"Don't tell me everything is okay in your life, *bella*. Because I can see it's not." He placed his hand on one bony shoulder and squeezed. Felt the tremble that racked her.

She looked up at him, shock and disbelief written all over her face.

"I'll be at the Chatsfield for a couple of days. If you need something, *anything*, come see me.

"We can have a drink and I'll tell you about this girl I met on the first day of university, looking for art class. Her hair the color of molten fire, her smile as big as the ocean…the very joy in every step she took that she was finally free…

"She was a sight to behold.

"Two years later, she bet the champion rowing team of four—" he was smiling now, thinking of himself, Zayed, Rocco and Christian brimming with cocky confidence, amazed at the redhead who dared challenge them while every other woman worshipped the ground they walked on "—that she would walk naked across the university lawn rather than cheer them in the final tournament. Told them their arrogant heads were already full of themselves.

"And the night they did win that match, she ran through the lawn, fully dressed and completely sloshed, like a streak of lightning. Because she thought they would demand that she pay.

"I don't think I remember ever laughing so much as I did that night."

With a hand that was not quite steady, he wiped the one tear that rolled down her cheek. Whispered the motto by which he and the rest of the Columbia Four lived by. Words that had served Rocco, Christian, Zayed and him well, more than once.

"Memento vivere, bella."

CHAPTER TWO

REMEMBER TO LIVE...

Clio leaned against the balcony, her legs trembling beneath her, her heart thumping wildly against her rib cage.

A motto that Rocco, Christian, Zayed and Stefan lived by... She had always laughed at the way they quoted it, at how they used it to conquer the world that had been their playground...

Laughed it away so easily because, of course, she had been a shining example of it...

Had she been that girl once?

Stefan's words swept through her with the force of a tsunami, holding up a picture of the woman she had been so long ago that it was almost like a figment of her imagination.

That Clio had been full of fire and dreams for the future, determined to take on life on her terms.

And yet, here she was today, waiting for the man who had professed to love her. Letting him rule her choice of clothing, her time and even what she did with her life. Waiting for him to look at her again as he had done three years ago. Wishing desperately that he still loved her.

Letting her life pass by with a sigh, her opinions and her words swallowed and locked in her throat.

How had she become this person? Where the hell was Jackson?

Sick of waiting another moment longer, she made her

way into the corridor. The empty space sent her heart thudding in her chest as she took the staircase to the lower floor.

And stilled as a smoky, drawling laugh and the accompanying husky female whisper reached her.

A dreadful suspicion gathered momentum and rushed toward her like a freight train. Every step felt like one toward her own doom. Her skin crawled as a sensual gasp filled the air, and the whispers of clothes and limbs punctured the silence.

"Jackson…oh, baby…I can't do this anymore, Jackson. I love you and I… Tell her it's over, Jackson."

Tears filled Clio's eyes as she stood there, her breath suspended in her throat, her world falling apart around her. Her hands turned into fists by her side, and she shoved one in her mouth to stop the shocked gasp from making itself heard.

She heard more grunts and a soft curse fall from Jackson and instantly, her mind supplied the image required. "Just a few more months, baby. You know how much we need her connections.

"Clio is blue-blooded aristocracy, the likes of whom I won't meet again. Did you see the sheer size and scope of Jane Alcott's estates? A few more clients like that, and we will be set."

"But, Jackson…" Clio could just imagine the pout of Ashley's voluptuous mouth, "I'll be showing by then. Is this how you want our new life to begin? Me hiding in case Ms. Stiff and Proper sees me while you pretend to be her loving fiancé? The thought of you touching her makes me so…"

Ashley is pregnant… It seemed there was no end to the knocks coming her way…

Jackson spoke amidst rattling breaths. "I have no desire to touch her. And you very well know that I have no strength left after one of our afternoon appointments to do so even if I were inclined."

Clio slapped her hands over her ears as she heard Ashley's satisfied laugh.

"Just give me a couple more months." Saccharine warmth dripped from Jackson's voice. "She's still very useful to us. Once I have used up all the connections Clio can provide for us, I'll get rid of her. Until then, appearances are crucial."

"If she backs out before then?"

"Backs out of what? For all her claims of walking away from her family and the man they wanted her to marry, Clio's desperate to be loved, desperate to feel that she's succeeded at something even if it's just scoring a man." There was no hesitation in Jackson's voice. Only the absolute truth as he believed it to be. "The woman she is now, there's no other man who would touch Clio Norwood with a pole, much less want her."

Bile crawled up Clio's throat and she turned away from the door. Pushing the heavy door to the staircase, she only got up one group of stairs before her legs gave out and she collapsed onto the grimy floor.

Desperate to be loved, desperate to feel that she's succeeded at something...

Beating back her head against the wall, Clio closed her eyes, shutting off the tears that threatened to deluge her. Still, a few drops leaked through her tightly shut lids.

How could she have misjudged Jackson so badly? How could she have not seen this coming? How many times did she need to learn this lesson? She had never been valued for anything more than her father's name, had never been valued for herself.

However far she ran, her name and everything it entailed caught up with her. Fury and self-disgust unlike she had ever known slammed into her gut.

For months, she had let Jackson walk over her, she had let Ashley make a mockery of her in front of friends.

There had been too many business dinners to attend,

too many charity galas they needed to be seen at—dressed in designer clothes and sipping champagne, instead of where she preferred to be—behind the scenes getting her hands dirty.

There had been too much of displaying themselves rather than doing anything of substance. Too much of putting herself on parade on Jackson's arm, too much of talking about her parents and her family's aristocratic background and connections.

Too much of being stifled by rules, weighed down by expectations. Too much of being a Norwood, daughter of one of the most powerful aristocratic families in Britain, too much of being the Manhattan elite, power-hungry financier Jackson Smith's fiancée.

Too little of being herself, of just being Clio.

All her life, she had craved her father's approval, even when she hadn't fit right with her family's aristocratic connections. She'd stupidly hoped he would be proud of her if she did as he asked of her.

Had tried to make herself the perfect daughter. Until she found out he had arranged her marriage and choked at the very ropes she had bound around herself.

And she had fallen into the same trap with Jackson.

All the signs had been there and she had been too blind to see them, too desperate to need something in her life to be a success.

She had led herself to the very same place she had left in her home country over a decade ago, into the same life where she couldn't breathe.

Every uncomfortable feeling she had repressed, every doubt she had swallowed so that she didn't mess up another one of his meetings and parties, suddenly balled up in her throat, choking her breath.

Her identity had somehow fractured and attached itself in pieces to Jackson's.

And all for what?

So that he could cheat on her, so that he could impregnate his assistant.

Her love, her fears, hadn't mattered to Jackson at all. And not seeing that truth had all been her fault.

CHAPTER THREE

"I'M SORRY, MA'AM. I can't allow you to go up to Mr. Bianco's suite."

Clio heard the receptionist behind the huge swathe of pristine black marble and looked around herself in confusion. Had she inquired about Stefan? Where had she walked to?

Turning around, she swept her gaze over the quiet and ultraluxurious lounge at the Chatsfield New York. A bank of glass-walled elevators stood to the side.

Utter silence reigned over the marble-floored lounge, the humdrum of quiet efficiency amidst the flowing humanity of Manhattan outside creating a sharp contrast.

The lavish interior of the famous hotel filtered in through her slowly.

"Do you want me to let him know of your arrival, Ms....?"

Blinking, Clio pulled her attention back to the young man. "Clio. Just Clio," she said, working her mouth to make the sound. Just the thought of saying Norwood sent a chill through her. Her entire body felt as if it was operating on some kind of auto mechanism she hadn't known she possessed.

Why else would she come to a man whose power and ambition were ten times those of Jackson? A man who had looked at her as if she had somehow tainted herself just by her association with Jackson?

"Wait, Miss...Ms....Clio, hold on."

Coloring at the curious perusal of the receptionist, Clio wrapped her arms around herself. "I'm sorry for troubling you. I have to leave."

She hadn't even realized how or when she had decided to walk to the Chatsfield, to see Stefan. The enigmatic green gaze and scornful mouth rose in front of her and she shook herself. No, she had no strength to expose herself to his brand of truth and evaluation, didn't have the strength to fare against the memory of a woman she didn't even remember being once.

His disappointment earlier still stung like a slap.

If she went to him the way she was feeling right now, he would lacerate her with his ruthless words, would peel away any remnants of self-respect she still had left.

The thought of telling him what she had heard, the thought of his reaction got her to move as nothing else could.

She took a few steps toward the revolving glass doors when she heard her name called again.

"Ms. Clio, Mr. Bianco authorized a permanent key card for you with us. At all our international branches. He left very specific instructions that we were to provide anything you asked for, anything you needed, should you come."

The receptionist placed the key card on the gleaming counter and pulled his hand back.

As if he knew how close to breaking point she was. As if she were a wild animal he needed to treat with the utmost care. Something in his kind gaze, something in the cajoling tone of his voice shook Clio out of the fog she was functioning in.

Was this what she had become? A woman so lost in life that she had reduced a perfect stranger to pitying her?

She didn't know what she wanted to do, she didn't know how to take the next step in her life. She felt utterly lost, alone.

The fact that all she wanted to do was crawl into the

nearest hole and never emerge scraped her raw. And yet, something in her, some small part of her that refused to whimper like a victim, had brought her here.

Her career, her life, her self-respect and her heart—everything lay in ragged tatters around her feet.

She knew that she needed help. To figure out how to do the one thing that burned inside her while everything else lay in ashes.

She grabbed the key card and palmed the smooth surface. Forced herself to put one foot in front of the other, to take a deep, purging breath. The quiet swish of the lift as it bore her to the fifty-second floor pinged against her tautly stretched nerves.

When the doors finally opened, she stepped out onto an enormous foyer boasting four balconies with glass railings that provided breathtaking views of the one of the world's finest cities.

It was like a castle built amidst the clouds.

Walking past a gold-embossed statue in the middle of the foyer, she reached the lounge. A champagne-and-brown color scheme reigned, with glittering burnished-gold and deep red accessories here and there that matched the white-hot temperament of the man she had once known.

Although the Stefan she had met this evening had been coldly ruthless.

What the hell was she even doing here?

Just as she turned in the direction of the elevator, his silky smooth question rang out.

"You're leaving already?"

Clutching her eyes closed, Clio willed herself to calm down. In a helpless way that made her totally nauseous, she was glad that he had spotted her before she had made a hasty exit.

Because now, she knew Stefan wouldn't let her leave. Now, if she could just find the strength to say what she had come to say without betraying herself…

Every doubt she was harboring ground to a halt as he moved into the lounge with a lithe grace that she followed as if she was mesmerized.

A plush white towel wrapped around his narrow hips contrasted sharply against a tanned chest. Droplets of water clung to chest hair that covered ropes of well-defined muscles. His freshly shaved jawline glinted with that trademark arrogance of his while his olive green gaze pinned her to the spot.

Awareness sliced through Clio like a physical shove to her senses and she swayed where she stood. It was like a deluge of flood over drought-ridden land.

"Clio, is everything all right?" he said, tossing a white towel over his nape that fell onto his chest.

Clio came back to the earth with a thump. Suddenly, asking Stefan for help felt like the most absurd idea she had ever thought of.

Before she could blink, he covered the distance between them. The scent of him, raw and masculine, was like a whiplash that slammed her breath in her throat.

Shaking her head, she pushed her hair back. "I'm fine. Can I have something to drink?"

For a few seconds, he stood there staring at her.

Tall, impossibly wide, six feet three inches of prime Sicilian male, and all his focus was on her. His eyes perused her with a leisurely intensity that made her feel exposed, raw.

Not that she trusted her body's response.

Finally, he moved to the glittering bar that covered one side of the lounge. "What would you like to drink?"

"Just some water, please." There was a false comfort in talking about something so mundane. Maybe because it reminded her that the world did not fall away even through the earthquake in her life. "Alcohol gives me—"

"A migraine, I know. Are they still as bad as they used to be?"

He had remembered. Clio squashed the spurt of warmth

that bloomed in her chest with ruthless will. So one of the youngest millionaires in the world had a good memory. Not a big surprise. "I never found anything to help me. So I don't touch it," she said, shrugging.

The sound of the refrigerator opening, the soft clink of the ice cubes against the glass punctured the silence that swathed them with awkwardness.

She hadn't even told him why she was here. And he hadn't asked.

Yet, it felt as if there was something in the air, an imbalance of power, a swirl of currents eddying around them, caging them together in the cavernous lounge. And she recoiled at adding to it by telling him what had happened tonight.

Would he laugh at her stupidity that she hadn't even seen through Jackson's facade for so long?

She grabbed the glass from him, and took a greedy gulp. All the while, he stood there like a dark specter, watching her, assessing her. And somehow she had a feeling, he found her wanting.

She had fallen in her own eyes. *Did it matter if she did in his?* a rebellious part of her mocked.

The answer had to be no because she didn't have a single feeling to spare for him. There was nothing but cold will to keep her going.

"I'm sorry about intruding on you unannounced," she said, once the cold water brought feeling back into her throat. "I didn't even realize I had started walking toward..."

Catching the gleam of mockery in his green gaze, she faltered.

He took the glass from her shaking fingers. "Clio Norwood—epitome of good manners and decorum, even as she's falling apart."

"I'm not falling apart."

His blunt-tipped fingers landed on her jaw and tilted her face up.

Panic chasing her stringent awareness of him, she caught

his wrist to push it away. The pressure of his fingers increased.

"Then why are you so jumpy?"

There was no sympathy in his voice and for that she was a thousand times grateful. One kind word from him would break the small thread that was holding her together.

Falling apart, in front of him, was not a choice.

"I'm not. I just…" A ball of tears tightened her throat.

"Tell me what's going on, Clio."

The inherent command in his tone somehow grounded her.

Instead of jerking away from his touch, she slowly pushed it back. But the rasp of his hair-roughened wrist, the strong tendons of it, was too much sensation. She dropped his hand, her pulse thudding too loud.

"Have you eaten dinner?"

"No."

"How did you get here?"

She raised her gaze. "What?"

"To the Chatsfield?"

"I walked."

"From where?"

"From the dinner party."

"At the Empire State Building?"

"Yes."

He cursed so vehemently that Clio hugged herself instinctively. "That's almost fifteen blocks from here and it's nine-thirty at night. What the hell is wrong with you that you would walk at night in New York of all places?"

She remained mute, no response rising in the face of his valid point.

He sighed. "Finish that water and then order something from room service. I'll get dressed and be back. And then you can tell me why you look like you—"

Anxiety hit her in waves. If he disappeared, she knew she would lose whatever it was that had brought her this far.

Saving face in front of him would become more important than moving on in her life.

"No, wait. Don't leave. I…"

"Then get rid of that look in your eyes, *bella*," he said. "I can't stand it." A hint of emotion colored that bland statement.

"What look?"

Pushing his tensile body into her space, he folded his hands. The muscles in his biceps curled enticingly and Clio choked back hysteria. Her life was falling apart, and yet it seemed the sight of Stefan half-naked could distract her as nothing else could.

"Like you're terrified of me," he said through gritted teeth. "We might have become strangers to each other but I would never hurt you, *bella*. Whatever Jackson did, you need to shake yourself out of it." His voice fell as if she were a wounded animal he was persuading into his care.

"I'm not a danger to you, Clio."

Oh, but he was, Clio admitted, her pulse skyrocketing.

If Jackson had reduced her to a shadow of herself over the years, Stefan could destroy the small part of her that was still intact. That he knew what she had been once and what she was now, it was a weapon he could wield with ease and without emotion, if he didn't like what she was about to say.

The young man she had known at Columbia had not only been idealistic but also kind, with a rosy view of the world.

This man he was now, he rattled Clio on so many levels.

But she had no intention of ever letting a man define her sense of self. Ever again.

The thought gave her the courage to say what she wanted to. "I decided to take you up on your offer. I need your…I need help, Stefan."

Something infinitesimal flashed in his brooding gaze, gone before she could read it. His defined jaw hardened. He moved to a small side table with delicately carved legs, and pulled out a checkbook.

He flipped it open with a pen poised in his left hand. That familiar sight of him balancing the book on his right forearm brought forth such a strong memory that she almost didn't hear him when he said, "How much do you need?"

Her jaw falling open, Clio stared at him. Acid crawled up her throat and she forced herself to hold his gaze, realizing what his look had meant.

He thought she had come to him for money.

Even as he had reminded her of what she had been, it was clear that Stefan had already written her off as a lost cause.

It rankled just as much as Jackson's treacherous perfidy did; it tore her in half that she had brought this on herself. But it was high time she started fighting for herself, too. High time she started growing a backbone.

"How much, Clio?"

"Will you give me as much as I want, Stefan? How about a million dollars?" Something in her challenged him, pushed to see how far he would go.

He didn't even blink. "A million it will be, *bella*. I will tell my finance guy that this year our charity contribution is going to the Clio Norwood Foundation."

I don't want your charity.

Swallowing back the bile his offhand comment provoked, she reminded herself to not flinch, to not betray the hurt that lanced through her.

She had no idea why she was inflicting this on herself, but she couldn't stop.

"And if I come back for more?"

"I'll give you more." He threw the checkbook on the coffee table between them, the gesture so full of powerful arrogance and a masculine elegance that Clio forgot what had prompted it. Even half-naked as he was, power and ruthlessness emanated from every cell in him.

"You can have as much as you want, Clio. All you would have to do is walk away from that crook. No matter how deep you are in, you can walk away."

"Why? Why would you help me?"

"Once, you were my friend. Once, I used to think the world of you. Seeing you like this…"

Some unnamed emotion flickered in his eyes and Clio stared anew. His face transformed so much when a hint of emotion touched it that it was like seeing a shadow of the old Stefan.

"If I can help you get away from—" he scowled as if he hated even saying Jackson's name again "—I'll save you, even if it has to be from yourself. It's like taking a friend or a family member to a rehabilitation clinic for treatment for addiction."

"Even though you think I'm not worth the ground I'm standing on?"

His dark smile didn't falter for a second. "Your words, *bella*, not mine." A blast of cold solidified in her core and Clio shivered.

It was one thing to think that of herself, another to hear someone confirm it. But with Stefan, there was nothing but honesty. Cutting, lacerating honesty, but honesty all the same.

His gaze swept over her, lingering and intense. "But, yes, even then. I would do the same for Rocco, Christian and Zayed, too."

The Columbia Four's friendship, the inviolate bond they had forged with each other, she had always been envious of it. To be included now as something he had to salvage from the wreck she'd made of herself… "Wow, at least in one regard, I'm in illustrious company, aren't I?"

He moved around the coffee table, and it was like watching a wild animal move. With grace and purpose.

The moment he was within touching distance, everything within Clio retreated inward into a tight ball. But still, the heat of his body incited a trembling in her very bones.

The breadth of his frame swathed her as he bent down.

"Do not ask a question of me if you don't have the constitution for truth, Clio."

Her brain taken over with issuing flight responses, Clio nodded dumbly.

Stefan Bianco was a Sicilian alpha male in his prime.

Physically magnificent, powerful beyond her wildest imagination, ruthlessly rich. A potent combination of masculinity and heat that could probably compel a stone to react if he so intended.

A woman like her, with her very sense of self battered and beaten down, was nothing. She wrapped her hands around herself, as if it could corral his presence and her reaction.

If she wasn't careful, he would overpower her so much that she would get swept away in unraveling that enigmatic disinterest he projected so easily. As so many women did—deluding themselves that they could melt the icy heart beneath the fiery exterior of his Sicilian temperament.

Stefan had buried his heart so deep and so long ago that he didn't even have one anymore, she sensed. Stepping away from him, she shook herself free of his magnetic pull. Met his gaze head-on. "I never want to hear anything but the truth from you, Stefan."

"Deal," he said with an indulgent smile that was more like a threat than a reassuring promise. "Now it's time to put your cards on the table, *bella*. Without fear."

She knew exactly where she stood with him; she would always know.

His brand of friendship—eviscerating and without an ounce of pretension—was what she needed to remake herself, to redefine herself. Stefan was the perfect path for her to walk on toward becoming her own woman again.

"As gratifying as it is to learn I could have millions if I just made myself your charity case, I didn't come here for money. I want nothing from you for free."

"What do you want, then?"

Her chest felt so tight that she had to break his gaze. Had to force herself to speak past the sound of Jackson's and Ashley's combined laughter resonating through her.

Jackson's cheating on her, using her for her connections, reducing her entire identity to the value she provided him in his blasted business, scraped her raw. But that he could be so casually cruel about her feelings, that he would betray every aspect of their lives together, that he would laugh at her fears and insecurities behind her back…it festered inside her like a putrefied wound.

It tainted every aspect of her so much that she was beginning to despise herself.

And she wouldn't be able to move forward, wouldn't be able to look herself in the eye unless she showed him that he couldn't do this to her without realizing the consequences. Unless she proved to him and herself that she was more than what he had called her.

"I want to teach Jackson a lesson he will never forget."

Cold—blanching and eviscerating—dawned in Stefan's gaze and he stepped away as if she was the very plague. His jaw clenched so tight that it was a wonder he spoke through it. "I will not play petty games so that you can make him jealous and win him back. If that's why you came, get out. *Now.* Before I physically restrain you from going back to that leech."

"I don't want to make him jealous. I want to remove Jackson from every part of my life. I don't want even his shadow to touch me anymore."

"That is as simple as walking away, Clio."

"Not without making him realize what he's done to me."

Disbelief shone in his eyes. "Earlier, you wouldn't believe a word I said. How do I know you won't go running back to him the minute he starts whispering words of love again?"

"Earlier, I was a fool who'd have done anything for the man I loved. Now…I feel nothing but disgust and pity for that woman. My skin crawls when I think that I stayed all these years... Does that satisfy you? Or do you want me to prostrate myself before you're ready to believe me?"

His gaze encompassed her from top to toe as though he was enjoying the idea of her prostrating herself. By sheer will, she stood still under that assessing gaze.

"You're angry and emotional right now. Tomorrow, you'll forgive him and crawl back to him—"

"Listen to my proposal first. Then make your decision."

She was so tired of men playing their games with her, controlling her, defining her, owning her joys and her sorrows.

First her father and then Jackson...

So tired of losing herself, again and again. The irony of appealing to another man for help, of letting him see her darkest fears, a man who was a hundred times more powerful and ruthless than Jackson or her father, wasn't lost on her.

But Jackson had been wrong. She still had one avenue left and she was going to throw herself into it.

"Do you want to expose Jackson's reality to the world?"

Something shifted in his expression, a watchful uncoiling of his rigid stance. He was hooked. For the first time in months, Clio felt a surge of positivity fill her.

"Throwing a million dollars at you is easy. What you're suggesting is far more elaborate and requires a great deal of my actual involvement."

"But you'll do it," she said, forcing confidence into her tone.

Heat flared in his gaze at the vehemence of her statement. She braced herself, expecting him to cut her down.

"Why?"

"Because I saw it in your face tonight just as you saw whatever you did in mine.

"When I said he was my fiancé, there was such anger, such distaste in your gaze. I don't know how or what he did to you, but I know that you won't forgive and forget."

His gaze swept over her face with a thoroughly cold appraisal. "I see that there's still a bit of the old Clio in you, *bella*."

"You have found the weak link in Jackson's life. It's me." Her voice wobbled on the last bit, the very venom that Jackson's words caused in her coating her throat.

"I will bring that man down if we start on this path. There will be no half measures, no backing out. No going back to him. Ever."

"I'm not weak, Stefan, not in this. I swallowed the disgust that was roiling through me today, and came to you without his knowledge."

"Tell me what happened."

For a second, Clio could only stare at the authority with which he demanded an answer.

"Does it matter what happened? If I have to face myself in the mirror, if I have to…I'll bring you anything you need about Jackson's business and his hedge fund company. But only if you agree to my proposal."

"What is your proposal, Clio?"

Clio stared at Stefan and willed the words to come, willed herself to put the last part of her plan into words. It had been gathering in the back of her mind like a tsunami, shaking everything in its path, laughing at her weak will, her fears.

She couldn't back out now, as scary as it was to tie her fate to this man even temporarily.

Stefan Bianco, once a cherished friend and now a ruthless stranger, would be the fire through which she would have to walk. And once she emerged from that fire, no man would ever have the power to hurt her again.

No man would even come close.

"I want you to profess undying love to me. In a gesture that captures media attention. I want you to get engaged to me, turn all that brooding arrogance into possessive, fiery love for me. I want you to lend me the might of your status as the ruthless playboy who wouldn't look twice at the same woman much less have a relationship with her.

"And I want all this done in a way that Jackson can't turn his head, can't even blink without our engagement splashed in his face.

"Then, I'll bring you everything you need to expose him."

CHAPTER FOUR

"No."

The word fell from his mouth and boomeranged in the cavernous lounge even before Stefan processed Clio's outrageous proposition. The very thought of tying himself to a woman, any woman, filled his veins with ice.

And to someone like Clio, whom he had liked once...it was unbearable even in thought.

Rubbing his hand over his jaw, he looked up at her.

Desperation and something else danced beneath the steady look she cast him. Her fingers as she settled them over her forearms left pink marks revealing how tightly she was holding on.

Her hair was beginning to fall away from the tight knot at the back of her head. Still dressed in the black sleeveless dress that somehow leached all the color from her face, he knew she had come to him directly from the party.

Had somehow found the strength to come to him.

He shoved away the protectiveness that rose like a storm within him, to be discerned later.

It had been a while since a woman had surprised him with her words or actions.

The fact that it was Clio, a woman he had written off as a lost cause, intensified the surprise.

"As tempting as your proposal is, I have no intention of associating myself with a woman romantically, *bella*. Even for a pretense. Even for a few months. Even for saving a friend. I will never be good to the woman who occupies that role in my life, Clio."

Her chin tilted down, but there was determination in her gaze. "It's just a pretense, Stefan. I won't ask anything of you."

"No."

"Then you get nothing from me about Jackson." Her gaze flashed with determination. "And just so you know what you're saying no to, I'm a board member on his company.

"Of course, I have been nothing but a figurehead all these years but at least it's unrestricted access. To his company's finances, his bank accounts, even his offshore investments."

"Anything shady ever caught your interest?"

She shook her head. "I've never had reason to doubt him."

"The minute the media links my name with you even in a whisper, Jackson will shut you out. You'll be of no use to me. Our antipathy is mutual."

Exhaling slowly, she loosened her fingers, her relief palpable in the way her features relaxed. "Obviously, it's my first time plotting something vicious like this, so you'll have to excuse me if I don't go all *Kill Bill* on you right now, Stefan. I'm thinking on my feet here."

He laughed, glad to see a spot of color in her cheeks again. "Then let's put shopping for a yellow suit and a samurai sword on the agenda, *si*? First stop will be Japan."

An almost smile glimmered around her pink mouth and Stefan had the oddest urge to tease it out completely. The way flashes of the old Clio peeked through the desperation and defeat in her eyes stirred him.

A challenge—that's what she could become to him, if he let her. Because, even a decade ago, he had wanted her, had pursued her doggedly that first year.

But once they had become true friends, he had backed

off, cherishing that friendship more; then he had met and fallen in love with Serena.

His mind was more than eager to wander on the paths they had never gone on, that they could take now.

But there were plenty of uncomplicated, desirable women in the world for his taste. Ones who didn't look as if they were barely holding on.

Clio, for him, clearly needed to be in the Do Not Touch camp.

He couldn't help teasing her, though. "As far as I can see, you're in good shape, so that's good."

Utter silence stretched between them, the moment building and building.

"Since we're counting if I'll be useful to you or not, are you considering my proposal?"

There was a self-deprecation in her tone that masked something beneath. The way she held herself so stiff, the way her fingers clutched her opposite hands—Stefan knew it was fear.

Realizing how close she was to falling apart only made him wonder at the strength of her. But whatever Jackson had done, she was still riding that wave of adrenaline.

Which meant she would crash soon.

And he had no doubt that she would back away, even recoil at the very idea of them joining forces to bring down Jackson.

The young woman he had known at Columbia had possessed the biggest heart he had ever seen, had possessed amazing capacity for love and forgiveness.

That she had come to him like this, that Clio was considering this path, spoke of the damage Jackson must have done to her.

Fury filled Stefan that Jackson's ambition had led to this. If he didn't take care of her, she could end up like Marco. Or worse.

And the thought of anything happening to her at the hands of Jackson drove him wild with panic.

With a control that had taken him years to hone, he forced himself to sound casual. "Your proposal is beneficial to me. So yes, I'm considering it."

"What do I have to do to convince you completely?" she retorted instantly and he found relief in her mutinous gaze.

What he needed now was time with Clio.

Time in which Clio didn't see Jackson and revert back to that pale shadow she had been earlier tonight. Time in which she would crash from whatever was driving her right this minute and consider going back to him again.

Time in which he could keep her close. And even if things didn't work out as per the plan between them, he had no intention of letting her go back to that man.

Even as he had struggled with getting a handle on his intense reaction to seeing her again, he had come to terms with some of it.

He felt responsible for Clio. It didn't matter where it grew from, only that he did.

"I will accept your deal based on one condition."

Clio forced herself to shrug, to affect a casualness that she was far from feeling. She had known the man he was today wouldn't just follow along with her plans.

That he would demand something from her struck fear in her, though. "I have nothing else to give you. My career, my life, even my savings account is tied to Jackson and his company. As of this moment, I don't even have a place to go back to."

"That works out perfectly for what I have in mind, then."

"Was that my miserable life that you were referring to just now?"

A dark smile turned the corners of his serious mouth upward. "If you want to be publicly engaged to me, if you want me to act the part of besotted fiancé, first you have to prove it to me that you have enough guts to see through this whole thing. I won't let you go back on it when it's time for your part."

"I already told you that this is…"

He shook his head. "My way or no way, Clio."

She blew out a long breath, her aristocratic nose flaring with her struggle for control. "Fine. What do I have to do to prove that I'll see this through, that you won't have a hysterical female who's dying to go back to Jackson?"

"You have to come with me to Christian and Alessandra's wedding," he said.

It was the last thing she expected him to say. The last thing she wanted to do in the world.

Coming to see Stefan tonight, she was still amazed at her own strength in managing it. But seeing Rocco, Christian and Zayed, seeing the disbelief and pity that would fill their faces when they saw her, she didn't have the heart for it.

"There's nothing you will gain by dragging me to Christian's wedding."

"That's for me to decide," he said, arrogant implacability in his tone.

"Stefan, listen to me. I'll go back to Jackson tonight and pretend like nothing happened. Even as nauseous as it makes me to do it. For the next week, I'll continue to keep my mouth shut like I did over the last few years and let him think I'm still the same, spineless Clio." Just thinking of it made her skin crawl. "I'll wait until you return from Christian's wedding. That's innumerable chances for me to back out of this thing, by your logic. But I'll be here, waiting. Then you'll know that I'm serious."

"No."

"Why the hell do you care if I go to Christian's wedding or not?"

"If you want to start a new life, *bella*, why not start it with coming back to your old friends?"

"I can't, Stefan. I don't have the…"

"What?"

He reached out to her and pulled her hand into his. Immediately, her fingers stiffened in his but he didn't let go. "Neither of us is going to benefit by lying to each other or by treading carefully, Clio. If this pretense has any chance to work, it has to be anything but between us. *Capisce, bella?*"

"Yes, but I don't see the point in carrying the pretense forward to our friends, too. Will you lie to Rocco, Christian and Zayed, Stefan? Will you be able to?"

"If we want the world to buy into our shock engagement, yes. Leave them to me. You…you will not breathe a word to another soul what's happening between us.

"With Rocco already married and Christian doing the same, the whole world's eyes are already on the Columbia Four. Won't be difficult to get them to buy that I'm following in my friends' footsteps and looking forward to a happily-ever-after with the woman I adore."

"I won't be able to pull it off. Deception and lying have never come easy to me."

"Don't worry, Clio. You'll be just as good or even better at pulling this off as any other woman I've ever known."

"Stop insulting me, Stefan. I'm not one of your—"

"The jury's still out on that one," he cut her off without blinking an eye, without an ounce of emotion. "Think of it this way, *bella*. For us to begin a pretend engagement that the media and the whole world will eat up, we need to lay the groundwork.

"And what better way to start a lifelong love affair that will be the talk of the world than going to an old, mutual friend's wedding? Every way I look at it, this is what we need to start our fairy-tale romance."

A fairy-tale romance with one of the most gorgeous, arrogant, hard-hearted men she had ever met…it was a fate that would have sent Clio running a decade ago.

It had been the fate she had walked away from.

But joining forces with Stefan in this was her choice, she reminded herself.

Meeting his gaze, she nodded. "Fine. Let's go to Christian's wedding. But I have to see Jackson tomorrow."

"No."

"If I have to look through his finances, I can't walk away from him yet."

"Then I will come with you."

"No. I won't fall apart, Stefan. Not tomorrow, not in the coming days."

"Where the hell have you been, Clio? You don't answer your cell, you're not at work…"

Her breath balling in her throat, Clio stilled as she walked into the lounge of the flat she had lived in for more than four years. Jackson swept his gaze over her. Shock pervaded it and something else.

Pushing his laptop onto the sofa, he shot up and walked toward her. And Clio automatically stepped back.

Do not betray yourself, bella.

With Stefan's warning ringing in her ears, she forced herself to not flinch as Jackson neared her. Her gut twisted and she wondered if Stefan had been right. That she was not up to even facing Jackson again.

"Clio?"

At five-nine, she topped him a good couple of inches. His gaze on level with hers, he cupped her cheek. There was no way to curb the shiver that spewed within.

"Is everything all right?"

The false sweetness in his greeting sent nausea rising through her. "Actually, I'm not okay."

There was no need to pretend about her mood. She had not an ounce of belief that she could carry it off even if she tried.

Stepping away from him, she walked to the refrigerator and grabbed a bottle of water.

His gaze was still on her but she let hers drift over the sitting area and the dining room.

Desperate to be loved, desperate to feel she's succeeded at something...

Her chest was so tight that it felt like a miracle that she was breathing. Because everywhere she looked, there was no trace of her in the space she had lived in for four years. It was all either an extension of Jackson's loud personality or the abode of a New York financier. Nothing about the flat reflected her.

How had she not seen this until now? Her fingers shaking on the plastic bottle, she took a sip of the water and forced the knot in her throat down.

"Clio, you left the party yesterday without informing me, you didn't return last night except for that text. Where the hell were you?"

"With an old friend," she replied, finally setting her gaze on him.

Not one strand of his expertly cut blond hair was out of place. He was dressed to impress in a charcoal-gray suit— his ice-blue shirt chosen explicitly to bring out the blue of his eyes by none other than Ashley and picked up at the dry cleaner every week by Clio.

He had screwed his assistant barely half a mile away from her and had the temerity to demand explanation of her. Felt not an ounce of shame or guilt. Not even a shadow of hesitation.

Had she made it that easy for him? Had it been so easy to mock her, to use her?

"Clio… Open that mouth and say something or—"

"Or what, Jackson?" the question burst out of her on a wave of anger. Closing her eyes, she took a deep breath and counted to ten.

The minute Stefan had shown her into the extra bedroom, she had collapsed onto the bed. Yet, sleep had evaded her, the awareness she had tried so hard to shove away descending on her. She pressed her fingers against her temple. "I don't feel good."

Instantly, Jackson's expression fell, like a little boy who was on the verge of a tantrum. "Don't tell me you have another headache coming on. Really, Clio, you would think you would have enough sense to know what triggers one of your episodes… It's damned inconvenient of you to be getting one every time we have something important going on."

Perversely, Jackson's sheer lack of concern filled Clio's throat with tears more than his cheating. "I do not plan them, Jackson."

"Is that why you walked away last night while Jane and I waited? You knew how important that meeting was to me."

"I was ill for two weeks, Jackson. A concept you don't seem to understand because you dragged me there even after I told you so. While you were gallivanting around the world, I was here alone, sick with flu. I had barely recovered when you stormed in here and asked me to get ready for that dinner."

A curse flew from his mouth and he almost shoved the cordless phone in her face. "Fine. Pop some pills. Call Jane Alcott, in the next few minutes. Make another appointment. And then call the Savoy and book a table for tomorrow's lunch, I want this deal with Jane done. Like yesterday. And make sure you sound cheery.

"The old biddy asked me a hundred questions after you left last night. Looked at me as though I was responsible for your headaches. And half the time I can't even understand what the bloody hell she's saying."

"God, show her some respect, Jackson."

He glanced at her with such obvious disbelief that Clio cringed inwardly. Was he so shocked at even the smallest sign of an angry response from her?

"What is wrong with you? You have this crazed look in your eyes. God, you're not pregnant, are you, Clio?"

"How could I be when you haven't touched me in four months?"

The minute she said it, Clio blinked.

Was it any wonder he had walked all over her? The very way she had framed her question meant she had given all her power to him. Every aspect of their relationship had been his to rule.

Something close to shame crossed his face. Would he apologize? Would he make an excuse? Her heart rising to her throat, Clio waited with bated breath. And hated herself a little more for the fact that she did.

"That's not my fault, is it?" he said, his gaze shying away from hers. And something monumental crumbled inside Clio. If there could be a sound for despondence, it would be the sound that she caught in her throat.

"Half the time, you're unhappy with yourself, half the time, you are unhappy with me. And you have a hundred hang-ups about sex. For Christ's sake, Clio, sex is not always about cuddling, and sharing dreams and words of love. Sex should sometimes be just bloody sex. Nothing wrong with letting go in bed. But you can never do that, can you?"

"Do you not care at all about how I feel, Jackson?" The pitiful question left her mouth before Clio knew she was asking it. The desperation in her tone tied with the almost hopeful note made bile rise in her throat.

It was like watching an alternate version of herself talking to Jackson, hoping he would give an answer that would fix everything she had heard last night, as if it could magically erase the ugliness of their relationship.

That infinitesimal sliver of hope was the most pathetic thing she had ever seen in her life.

I don't trust you to not crawl back to him while I'm gone.

Stefan's word pricked her and she turned away from Jackson.

Everything inside her shook, everything inside her

wanted to fall apart and give in to the maelstrom of grief swirling within. But she couldn't. Not yet.

Squaring her shoulders, she turned around and let the years of breeding that she had turned back on slide into place. She had been taught by the best nannies in England about holding her own even when the world around her was in chaos.

"I can't call Jane today. I don't have time."

"Why the hell not?"

"I'm leaving for Athens. I have a hundred things to do before that."

"Athens, Greece?"

A brittle smile curved her mouth. "Yes, Athens, Greece. Christian Markos's wedding won't happen in any other place, I'm thinking."

"Christian Markos? *The* Christian Markos? You're invited to his wedding?" The light that came on in Jackson's face was unlike anything she had ever seen. His suddenly positive energy and the smile that he flashed at her added another layer of ice around her heart.

She meant nothing to him. Even though she had known it, the truth left her shaking.

"Why have you never mentioned that you were acquainted with him?"

"I'm not just acquainted with him. Christian is a very close friend."

"That's even more fantastic." He grabbed the phone and dialed a number, Ashley's she was sure.

Clio grabbed the phone from him just as Ashley said hello and clicked it off. "You're not invited, Jackson."

What had she ever seen in him, Clio wondered. How had she fooled herself so thoroughly when everything about him was so much artifice?

"You will need a plus one. And who else will you bring but me? It's not like you have a whole lot of friends other than mine."

Because she had built her entire life around him.

"I'm bringing no one. Christian and my other friends are—"

"What other friends?"

"Rocco Mondelli, Zayed Al Afzal and—" her throat clenched "—Stefan Bianco. The media is fond of calling them—"

"The Columbia Four," he finished with a hungry gleam in his eyes.

Clio could almost hear his mental gears clicking, could see her pitiful place in his life extend for a few more months while Ashley gave birth to his child.

"Do you know all of them really well? Even that arrogant Sicilian, Bianco?"

"Yes," Clio said, every nerve in her stretched tight. "Stefan is a friend, too." She forced a smile to her lips and crossed her arms. "All four of them are insanely protective of their private lives and I don't want to impose on them."

He ran a blunt-tipped finger over his brow, his gaze assessing her. "It's not the right time for you to be leaving New York, Clio. Cancel this trip. I need you here to finish signing on as Jane's financier and then there's…"

Clio shook her head, her gut twisting at the way he instantly changed tactics. "It's what you said when Rocco got married, too. I let you browbeat me into missing the most important day in the life of one of my oldest friends. I have a life, too, Jackson."

"Do you?"

"Yes," she whispered, not liking the look in his eyes. "One that I have forgotten exists these past years."

"Fine. Go to Athens. Do your socializing and networking. And when you come back, we'll have a little chat about Stefan Bianco. That man's been in a thorn in my side for too long."

The minute Jackson left, Clio's legs gave out from under

her. She sank to the thick carpet, the pristine white walls closing in on her.

Telling herself that she had gotten through the hardest part, she took a deep breath.

She turned on his laptop, then picked herself up and wandered into Jackson's study, looking in his cabinets and drawers. Her heart thudded in her chest but she knew he wouldn't come back tonight.

There was nothing to salvage in her relationship with Jackson. He had trampled her heart and shattered her trust.

Clio shuddered and typed in the password to their company's database, wondering if she would ever be whole again.

CHAPTER FIVE

CLIO LOOKED AROUND the ancient structure of the Parthenon and felt a measure of peace she hadn't felt in a long time.

Christian's wedding last night had been the most beautiful ceremony she had seen in a while.

Deciding to walk the short distance from the luxury hotel to view the ancient ruins up close was the best decision she had made.

The lunch on the terrace this afternoon with Rocco and Olivia, Zayed, Christian and his new bride Alessandra, and Stefan, had begun so well. She had felt like she was among friends.

Olivia had asked so many questions about when the four men and she had been at Columbia together over a decade ago, and Clio had regaled them with stories, glad to fill the brooding silence with chatter.

Until the discussion had turned to Clio's own life.

What had Clio been up to all these years? Was Clio involved with anyone?

They had all been only polite questions from people who were interested in her life. But what did she have to tell them?

Turning around, she clicked a couple more pictures with her digital camera, marveled anew.

Her raised hand stilled as she saw the tall, wide frame of Stefan coming close. June sun shone behind him, leaving his defined face in shadows. His paper-thin white cotton shirt was buffeted against his broad frame, tapering against his waist. Even though he couldn't see her, Clio dragged her gaze away from following down. She didn't need to see his powerful thighs encased in jeans.

The whipcord tightness of his muscles, the tensile strength of his legs, the wide swathe of his shoulders and the way they narrowed down her world to him, she had noticed far too much of him already on their flight to Athens. The sheer luxury and scale of his private jet, which she'd learned was the closest thing to a home for him, had rendered her mute. But it was the man himself who had occupied her mind all through the flight.

All the while she had been packing for the trip, all through the limo ride to the private airstrip where he had been waiting, it had been easy to tell herself that she would see this through.

She still wanted to. Because what Jackson had done had poisoned her so much that she couldn't look at her own reflection in the mirror without wanting to shatter it into a million shards.

It was the man she had gone to, to accomplish her revenge who continually disconcerted her.

Stefan had been nothing but courteous and concerned on the flight, if a bit preoccupied. And yet every time their gazes met or they accidentally touched, the moment arched and stretched, a latent energy pulsed until one of them looked away, or stepped back.

It was the last thing Clio wanted to face.

He came to a halt about a foot from her, watching her.

Feeling compelled to break the intense silence, she waved her hands around. "I can't believe Christian obtained private and uncurtailed access to the Parthenon, of all places. Even I'm impressed by this show of power and status. Does Alessandra mean so much to him, then?"

For once, she was glad that there was no wistful note in her tone. Only open curiosity.

Stefan shrugged, a cold light in his eyes. It was like there was frost all around them even as the sun cast long shadows. "If Alessandra was the kind to be impressed by this, it would make sense. For all the success he has achieved, Christian has a chip on his shoulder about where he started in life.

"He doesn't realize yet that Alessandra is one of those rare women who care nothing about his wealth or status."

Clio blinked. It was her casual comment that a woman would be impressed by the power that clung to the Columbia Four that had made him look so coldly forbidding.

Did he still think of Serena, the woman who had so blithely broken his heart? Did he think all women were like her, that Clio was like her?

Of course he did, Clio realized. And she had only confirmed his view by going to him for help, by suggesting that she wanted to use that very power and status as her shield.

She couldn't begin to care about Stefan's opinion. Not when it was decided already, not when her self-esteem was in such tatters.

"Is he in love with her, do you think?" she said, turning her mind away from what lay ahead.

"I would have said no. But I have changed my opinion about Rocco and Olivia, so who knows?" He tucked his hands into his pockets and took a few more steps. "I didn't realize running away was a habit of yours."

The bland smile falling from her face, Clio looked up. "I don't know what you mean."

"You did it that night at the Empire State Building instead of confronting that jerk. You did it today."

"I did...no such thing."

"Olivia said you looked like you were having an anxiety attack. She was concerned for you, just as I was." There was almost a fond note in his tone for Rocco's wife. "Why did you leave?"

"There seems to be a lot of friction between Christian and Rocco."

"Rocco will need time to forgive Christian for tangling with his little sister. But the fact that he is here shows how much Alessandra means to him."

"I felt like I was intruding."

"Zayed and I were right there."

"You are a part of each other's lives. Rocco and Christian need your support to get through this rough patch. I'm little more than a stranger."

"No. You and I know very well that you were actually a good buffer back there. Those stories you had of the four of us from Columbia made everyone laugh. Everyone took a collective breath."

He reached her and tugged her hand into his. Instant charge crackled around them.

"You said the female students at Columbia used to be supremely envious of you and at the same time sugared you up so that they could get a tidbit about one of us. What did you call yourself?"

She had felt his gaze on her like a physical caress all through the lunch. Now it disconcerted her to know that he remembered every word she had said. The intensity of his attention kept her wondering what about her interested him so. "The Gateway to the Columbia Four."

He smiled at that and warmth filled his gaze. "Rocco has been like a mad bull all this time but even he cracked a smile there. Then you were gone. I thought you had bolted."

"And where would I go? By bringing me here aboard your private jet, you made sure I had nowhere to go except with you. You even had them unpack my stuff and take my passport. Do not manipulate me, Stefan."

Ice coated his words. "I was doing it for your own good."

Clio couldn't back down. If she didn't take a stand now, she never would. Their relationship or the facade of it, was a temporary one. But still, she wanted to set the right tone for it.

Never again would she let her sense of identity be lost in a man.

"Don't presume to know it better than me."

"But isn't that what love-struck fiancés do, *bella*? Cater to your every need and whim? Cosset you in luxuries and act possessive? Know what's good for you better than yourself?"

Clio flinched, the ease with which he used her history to make his point cruelly efficient.

The hardness didn't budge from his expression. "We're supposed to be falling in love even now. You think the world will buy that Stefan Bianco let his almost-intended fly economy on a commercial airline?"

"Maybe the world will think that Stefan Bianco finally met a woman who doesn't fall at his feet?" she retorted, lifting her chin.

He smiled and ran a finger over her chin, a thoughtful expression on his face.

"How come you have no trouble putting me in place, *bella*?" Moving closer, he laid his hands on her bare shoulders and turned her toward the terrace. "Do you know how you looked from the terrace, Clio?"

Not trusting that she could find her voice, Clio shook her head. Even with the sun shining above them, the heat of his body behind her was like a caress.

She should move away, she knew. Stop him from continuing, at least. Cut this line of conversation before it began.

There was no space for personal observations or shared experiences between them. There was nothing but a common, twisted goal. But something in the honeyed tone of his voice locked the words in her throat.

His finger landed on her chin and tilted it up, facing away from the sun.

"Shall I tell you?"

He was taunting her. He knew that she was standing on

the precipice of retreating. He was daring her, even as he was certain of her cowardice.

She had read that the Parthenon had served as a church, a mosque, even a munitions depot during the Turkish occupation of Greece.

Yet there it stood today, majestic, beautiful, a monument to one of the greatest civilizations of the world.

And she, she was afraid of hearing one man's opinion of her. Was afraid of even facing the truth that was in his eyes.

Everything about her life was in ruins just like the Parthenon. But she decided to take the chance. Just for that moment, she would choose to be unafraid. She would pretend she had become the woman she wanted to be when she had set out for Columbia University.

She would pretend that when a man like Stefan Bianco looked at her, there was not resigned concern or eviscerating censure at what she had done to her life. But admiration and respect... The way he had looked at her once.

The base of his palm was hard and unyielding against her lower back. Her skin burned with every ridge and line leaving an imprint on her skin.

Turning toward him, she met his gaze, fighting the urge to pull away and to run far. "Tell me how I looked, Stefan."

The green of his eyes widened just a bit. That she had surprised him, she clutched it to her like a reward for her bravery.

"With that cream dress only covering one shoulder, your hair flying behind you, the sun turning your skin golden, you looked like the goddess Athena herself. For a few seconds, you had me stunned. And it has been a while since I let myself believe in any kind of myth."

Bitter laughter spilled from Clio's mouth and got lost in the vastness around her. "Goddess Athena was supposed to have been fierce and brave. I'm nothing like her, Stefan." Turning away from him, she sighed. "You were right. I ran away from the terrace because I couldn't breathe there."

"Why?"

"Let it go, Stefan."

"No."

"Haven't you seen enough? Won't you leave me with even a facade to hide behind?"

"No, I won't. Better me than the whole world, *bella*, than the corrupt man you left behind. Jackson won't meekly accept our engagement. There's only going to be more—"

"Light on me, yeah? I know."

How pathetic was she that for a minute she'd thought he insisted because he cared. How easily she fell into her own trap of wanting to matter...

She was nothing but a means to an end for Stefan. Just as she had been to Jackson. Only with Stefan, there were no lies, no deception.

"I saw Olivia Fitzgerald, the supermodel. I saw Alessandra Mondelli, world-famous photographer. Every woman who was in there was someone who had made a life for herself in the world, someone who carved a niche for what she exceled in. Then I caught my reflection in the jug. Who'd think a jug could do so much for you, right?"

And both women, while beautiful and successful, had men who respected them and loved them.

"Here I was sitting among some of the most accomplished women on the planet and what did I have to show for a decade of slogging, for a lifetime of walking away from a safe life...

"Nothing.

"I couldn't stay another minute and puncture the happiness of so many people. I couldn't forgive myself if I did that.

"Do you still see the goddess Athena, Stefan?"

His fingers tightened on her bare arms, his face fierce as he looked down at her. "You walked away from him. By your own words, you crawled out from the lowest point of your life and came to me. And you had enough guts to use what you saw in my face that night to your own advantage.

"I know what it takes to move ahead from that moment in which your heart shatters and there's nothing but a hole in your chest.

"All you need to do now is stay the course and carve your life the way you want. And until you can wage your own battle, I'll do it for you."

His words were whispers that reverberated around them in the open space.

Clio nodded slowly.

For all the ruthlessness that had become second skin to him, Stefan was much kinder than a mirror. When she looked in his eyes, her own reflection held promise. Touched by a brave past that she had almost forgotten, it held hope.

He was using her and she was using him. It was the perfect relationship for two people who had been burned by love, who had had their hearts shattered and trodden upon.

A man who would love her unconditionally—she didn't even know what that meant anymore. Maybe she had never deserved it.

But she so much wanted that day when she wouldn't run away in shame, when she wouldn't feel this cavernous emptiness inside at another woman's success.

The day when she wasn't an utter failure in life.

She sketched a bow in front of him, letting hope fill her entire body.

"Then I'm ready for training, Master."

A matching smile curved his mouth and he returned her bow and then stepped back into an elaborate pose that had economic movements and slices through the air that were perfectly synchronous. "Let us begin, Clio."

Shaking her head, Clio laughed. For anyone watching them from the hotel, they would look comical.

"If you tell me you're like a black belt in karate or some such thing, I'll have to knock your teeth in, Bianco. I can only take so much of your all-rounded macho perfection before I start choking on it."

Grooves bracketed his serious mouth as he burst into laughter. With his hair falling onto his forehead, his stunning features bathed in sunlight, he looked like one of those warriors that could have conquered the Parthenon.

"All-rounded macho perfection?" he said, color bleeding into those sculpted cheeks.

Narrowing her eyes, Clio stepped toward him. "Let me look at you," she mumbled, laughter bubbling up inside her. He shielded his face with his forearm and she pulled it down.

"Oh. My. God. You're blushing." She lifted her camera and clicked close-ups of him and he tried to grab it from her. Pushing back at his chest with one hand, which was like an impenetrable wall, she clicked some more.

She swung the camera away from him, still laughing. "There's my fortune. Women of the world are going to be crazy for it. A shot of arrogant Sicilian Stefan Bianco doing something as mundane and human as blushing."

A vein flickered in his temple, his mouth tight with laughter. "Stop it, *bella*."

"Oh, come on. Like you don't know your own appeal. Why do you think that model went nuts over you dumping her?"

"The regular gifts she was ordering for herself from Tiffany's? The champagne and caviar and the trips to Paris and London and Hong Kong aboard my private jet? The modeling contracts she was getting offered by networking through me?"

The camera dangling from her raised hand, Clio went still.

He had become so cynical, she remembered Christian saying a few years after they had left Columbia. But to see that hardness become such an intrinsic part of him that he filtered everything in the world through that, it was such a sharp contrast to the man she had known.

Did he think there was nothing about him, the true him, that would appeal to a genuine woman? Or had he made it true by burying everything that had been so intrinsically good about him?

"You don't believe that of all of them, do you, Stefan?"

"Of course not. Let's not forget my masculine prowess," he added with a wink that in no way belied the cold truth in his eyes.

Clio rolled her eyes and swatted his forearm, hiding the shiver that went through her.

"I'll reduce my *awesomeness* into little doses for you, *si*?" His English favored a stronger accent just then. "I know that you're going all...*fluttery* inside—" he moved his hand in front of himself, encompassing his lean frame "—at the thought of having me all to yourself."

More laughter spilled from her mouth as forgotten memories of him making a play for her at Columbia during that first year rushed forth. His attentions were almost a knee-jerk response to any moderately attractive woman.

Oh, she had had so much fun cutting him down to size every time he had tried it during that first year. Had missed the chance to put him down after he had fallen in love with Serena, though.

"Okay, that's it, Bianco. You need to be pegged down a bit."

His hands on his hips, his lush lower lip jutting out, he stared her down. "And you're the woman for it, Norwood?"

Tingles swept through her at his open challenge, mocking as it was. "Of course I am. If not for me cutting you down to size, you would have grown a second head back when we were at uni."

He grinned. "I do have a second head—"

Blushing and laughing, Clio clapped her hand over his mouth. Sharp teeth dug into the heel of her palm and she squealed.

Her tummy felt tight and achy, and tears ran down her

face as he chased her and she ran, both of them hurling long forgotten challenges at each other.

How long had it been since she had laughed like this?

He had just caught her when they heard the whir of rotor blades.

The sound fractured the moment so effectively that she flinched. Instantly, Stefan pulled her behind him. Shocked at how low the chopper was flying and the long-range camera directed toward the terrace, Clio clutched Stefan's shirt and hid her face in his muscled back.

A pithy curse fell from his mouth.

"Is this all so that they can have a story on Alessandra?" she asked, remembering the scandal that had haunted Rocco's sister.

"Yes. But they won't get anything on her as long as I have something to say about it."

Her heart raced as the muscles of his back tensed under her fingers. "How? Even you can't sprout wings and block the chopper."

His arm shot out and pulled her forward. Tripping against her own feet, she fell onto Stefan. And jerked at the sudden male heat that surrounded her. His arm around her waist was like a muscular rope she couldn't pry off her.

Warmth crawled up all over her body, the scent of him swirling around her, binding her to him.

"No, I can't sprout wings, *bella*." Slumberous heat came alive in his gaze. "But I have a beautiful woman next to me and I can give the hounds a juicier piece of meat first. By the time they're through with us, Christian will have his own security armed and Alessandra protected from the worst of it."

Realizing too late what he intended, Clio pushed away from his chest. "No, Stefan. There has to be another way."

But he was as solid and impenetrable as the walls of the Parthenon. He clasped her face with his palms, and tilted it up toward him.

"Look at me, *bella*. Pretend like you can't get enough of me."

She didn't have to pretend. The errant thought stole through her, inciting a panic. She didn't have to pretend that she was already flailing, falling into the haze he cast over her senses with ease.

She struggled again and their legs tangled, the tensile, hard muscles of his thighs rubbing against hers.

The sound of his jagged exhale settled over her skin, while the whir of the rotor blades of the chopper above felt like a death knell.

Her breath left Clio in a dizzying whoosh, every inch of her thrumming and pulsing. "Wait…I…"

Words melted away from Clio's lips as the pad of his thumb moved over her chin, traced the curve of her lower lip. "It's just one kiss, *bella*. If you flinch every time I lay a finger on you, no one's going to buy it, Clio. Least of all Jackson."

Her breath hitched like a balloon inside her, crushing her chest with a weight she couldn't bear… The last thing she wanted was a kiss and that, too, from the man who could so easily shred the small part of her that was still intact.

But the reminder didn't work quite as well as it should have.

Because when he dipped his head and touched her lips, Clio felt her own walls tremble and quake, her skin burn with need and fire, felt the shudder that racked his wide, solid frame.

His lips were rough and soft, his jaw bristly against her skin, and his thick eyelashes not hiding his shocked expression for once.

"Cristo, bella," he whispered, touching his forehead to hers.

His nose rubbed against hers, a strange intimacy growing around them.

"Stefan," she begged, desperate to flee, but yearning to

feel that rough mouth against hers again. Desperate to be touched again, desperate to feel his muscles tense. "Don't do this."

His fingers crawled over her nape and into her hair, his gaze almost angry. "I can't stop, Clio. Not now."

He slanted his mouth over hers and dragged it across.

Fiery need burst across the seam of her lips and Clio shuddered all over.

With a curse that resounded in the air, Stefan tightened his grip until her scalp prickled. Buried his nose in the crook of her neck and breathed.

"You smell like sunshine and oranges, *bella*. *Dio*, you taste like…"

Clio didn't know what else he said. All the fight left her as he found her mouth again and devoured it with little bites and nips. Stroked and tasted her lips as if she was a feast to be savored.

Kissed her as if there was nothing else he wanted to do, as if nothing but her total surrender would do.

And Clio surrendered. To him and even more, to the desire inside her, both freeing and binding.

Their bodies fused to each other as they crossed a line they shouldn't have.

A kiss they could never undo because it already engulfed them.

A day later, Clio and he were due to leave for New York in a couple of hours and the chasm of need that the kiss had ripped open felt just as raw to Stefan.

He had only meant the kiss as an evasion.

But one taste of her lush, pink, trembling mouth, and he had been knocked in the gut. All of the fantasies he had spun around her as a raging twenty-year-old became intoxicating reality.

Prowling the carpeted interior of his suite, he stared at the video coverage of the kiss that was already being aired on every site that fed on his life, his mood slowly spiraling out of his control.

Just as his libido did by the memories of her warm mouth, the scent of her skin, of the way she had shuddered and moaned when he tangled his tongue with hers.

Watching their kiss shouldn't have been the most erotic experience he had ever had. Exhaling a pent-up breath, he acknowledged it was.

Christian and Alessandra's wedding and reception had gone on without an ugly visit from the media, thanks to his diversionary tactics. But there was a betrayed look in Clio's eyes that pierced him when she met his gaze now.

Like he had crossed an imaginary boundary between them.

And the fact that he could think of nothing but baring her completely to him, of removing the fear and self-doubt that had flashed in her eyes and replacing it with liquid lust, proved her right.

It had been a long time since a kiss had turned him inside out with need.

A long time since anything had touched him.

But he would have preferred if it had been anyone but her.

The short clip was already up on most celebrity gossip websites and spreading like a virus. The rabid speculation had begun.

His features had been distinctive. So the media knew it was him.

What they hadn't figured out yet was her identity. And they were going crazy trying to figure out who the new woman in his life was, angling to find out who else was on the guest list at Christian's wedding.

The press had dubbed her Bianco's Redhead, a name he was sure the redhead in question was going to dislike, if not despise.

He grabbed the remote just as Rocco, wearing the blackest scowl Stefan had ever seen, entered the suite without knocking.

His gaze turned to the plasma screen on the far wall seconds before Stefan turned it off. The silence grew heavy, almost stifling, as Rocco, his oldest friend, studied him.

"Whatever you want to say, don't," Stefan snarled, his hackles rising at his friend's continued silence.

"All four of us have treated the world and the women in it as our playground for years, true," Rocco said, cutting straight to the point, "but I always thought there was still a bit of honor left in all of us. First Christian with Lessie, and now you and Clio… *Dio*, didn't you find anyone else to play with other than our oldest friend, Stefan?"

Stefan had had every intention of telling his friends the utter truth. But now, his friend's well-meaning interference locked the words in his throat. Even as the short clip was sweeping the internet like wildfire for all the world to see, to actually dissect their kiss with Rocco, to reveal Clio's confidence and their deal, felt too private.

Too intimate to be shared.

Which in itself should have rung all his internal alarms like a damn gong.

He ran the heel of his palm against his jaw, striving for a casual tone. One kiss and it was like Mount Etna had erupted.

"I'm not playing with her."

"No? In a decade, I have not seen you make one meaningful connection with another person, much less a woman. And you always had a thing for her. Damn it, you cannot play with and then discard Clio like you—"

"Enough, Rocco," he said through gritted teeth.

Leashing his temper by the skin of his teeth, because no way did he want to betray how much that kiss had affected him, Stefan smiled at Rocco. "Just because you have settled into marital bliss with Olivia doesn't mean you can expect us all to change colors already, *fratello*. Clio…she is safe from me."

Grinning, Rocco clapped him on the back. And once again, Stefan wondered at how well love and Olivia suited Rocco.

He had never seen his friend so happy and at peace.

"You know I had to—"

"Not needed, Rocco," Stefan said.

Rocco looked at him as if he wanted to say something more. Instead, he embraced Stefan and bid him goodbye.

Pouring himself a drink, Stefan went to the balcony.

Olivia and Clio were seated at the outdoor café on the ground floor.

Instantly Stefan shifted to see Clio better. She wasn't laughing like Olivia but a smile curved her mouth. And something loosened in his chest.

He was glad she was smiling again. She had lost that awful pallor, that stricken, lost look she had had when she had come to his suite.

As if she could sense his eyes on her, she looked up.

Across the distance, their gazes held. Stefan raised his glass and she did the same with a nod.

The elegant set of her shoulders, the long fiery locks, the high cheekbones—everything about her drew his attention.

With a ruthless will, he pulled his gaze away from her and went back into his suite.

He couldn't touch her again, couldn't risk any complications. Women and sex were uncomplicated for him. It was the only way he had put himself together, the only way he had moved forward after Serena's betrayal.

Clio, whatever state she was in, deserved a hell of lot more. He had nothing to give her except memories of what she had been, except to be her pretend strength to face a man he abhorred.

The only reason he had agreed to this was because he

needed justice to be served for Marco. He needed her help to see through Jackson's destruction.

Switching his phone on, he made a call to his PR guy and to his head of security, instructing him to leak her name as the woman in the clip.

The sooner they accomplished what they had come together for, the sooner Clio would be out of his life, untouched and unscathed.

CHAPTER SIX

THEY WERE JUST an hour away from landing in a private airstrip in New York. Finally, Clio gathered enough nerve to switch on her tablet and opened a search engine.

More than once, her fingers slipped on the smooth surface. Tension turned her shoulders into stiff rods as she finally typed Stefan's name.

Because he would be at the center of all this, he was the one whose coattails she would be riding through the storm they were unleashing.

Her heart hammered in her throat as the video file played again and she saw Stefan's body enveloping her protectively even as they were lost in each other.

It spoke to the man she had known once.

Closing the video file, she scrolled down and froze at the title.

Bianco's Redhead Is None Other than Clio Norwood, New York Financier Jackson Smith's Fiancée of Three Years.

There was no end to the questions posed, to the number of links to other articles. No end to how the media talked about it as though it was a win on Stefan's part that he had landed her. As though she was a prize and not a woman with feelings and emotions.

How did Stefan Bianco steal Clio Norwood from under the nose of Jackson Smith?

How long has the affair been going on? Is it serious?

Which Man Will Clio Norwood Choose in the End? one

headline read, giving Clio at least the illusion of power over her own choices.

Even having been prepared for it, anger, disbelief and frustration and so many more emotions ran through Clio.

Bianco's Redhead... God!

Clio laughed so hard that her jaw hurt, her eyes pooled. She took the tissue that Stefan patiently extended and wiped her face.

There was a relief in realizing she had seen the worst, and lived to tell it.

Stefan gazed at her with a stunned expression in his eyes. "Clio, why you are smiling?"

Clio pointed to the tablet and shrugged. "Bianco's Blonde has so much more zing, don't you think?" She fingered her hair and pulled it forward. "Maybe I will dye it."

Leaning forward in a movement that jammed the breath in her throat, he caught the thick strands between his fingers, a reverent expression in his gaze. Instant tension wove around them, thick and charged.

"No, *bella*," he said, his words a rough command that would brook no argument.

Wrapping the silky locks around two of his fingers, he turned them around and around, tugging her forward.

There was a feral quality to his gaze as it turned to her, a possessiveness that drenched her in heat. "Do not dare to change a strand of it, Clio. Whatever transformation you think you need, I forbid you to ruin something so glorious."

The sight of his hair-roughened wrists handling her hair sent a tremor through her. As did the inherent command in his tone. There was nothing about him that didn't cause Clio to lose her breath, that didn't make her feel as though she would combust if he didn't touch her.

But if he did, if she let him explore this heat between them, as every tingling inch of her wanted to, there would be nothing left.

And his eviscerating brand of friendship was the only precious thing left to her.

"We can't keep doing this, Stefan," she said, her words hoarse and uneven, completely opposite to how she wanted to sound. "I...can't think straight when you touch me and I need everything I have to deal with Jackson."

The magnitude of her admission hung in the air around them but she would rather face the attraction between them than pretend it wasn't always there.

Slowly, he unwound his fingers around her hair. Disappointment and fury wreathed his features until inch by inch, he pushed them out of his face. "How do you suggest we pretend to be engaged without touching each other, Clio? If you're weak enough to call the thing off because you can't—"

"I don't think it's weak to acknowledge a weakness." She held his gaze steadily. "To pretend in front of the world and even our friends, it's one thing. But I don't want anything else to muddy our relationship."

"It worked perfectly for us this time, but it won't happen again, *sì*."

Rubbing a hand over her tummy, Clio nodded jerkily.

When he met her gaze again, it was impassive, in control. And Clio almost bought it. But now that she had tasted the heat of his kiss, saw him smile and argue with Rocco, she knew it was only a hardened facade.

Stefan still felt as passionately as he had done a decade ago. Only now, all that firestorm of emotion and passion was buried under a coldly ruthless will.

And it twisted her gut that that well of passion, all that love he had to give, would never see the light of day again.

His ready acceptance suddenly threw her even though it was what she wanted. What she needed.

"Anything else, Clio?"

"I won't be made a fool of again, Stefan. Not even in a pretend relationship."

"I do not understand."

Heat crept up her neck and she pointed to the tablet, images of him with other women accompanied with captions like *predatory playboy* in capital letters.

Stefan changed girlfriends like she did her clothes. And their kiss, it had made her feel more alive than she had in years.

Two different facts and both she needed to accept without giving it more weight.

"You are never without a woman."

Something devilish gleamed in his gaze. "You still have me lost, *bella*. Say it in words I can understand, Clio. You forget that English is not my language."

She was not a prude. But thinking of Stefan and sex in the same sentence sent a burst of heat through her belly that she didn't even begin to know how to handle.

He knew how uncomfortable she was talking about this and yet he was goading her.

"What are you going to do for sex, Bianco?" she said, gritting her jaw, daring him to laugh at her now.

He did it anyway, but it was an indulgent smile that cut grooves through his cheeks. Her fingers itched to trace them, to feel the stubble on his cheek.

"Was that so hard?"

"No." She returned his smile, feeling as if they were on equal footing again. "You haven't answered me, though."

"I will not *take up* a woman on the side while all this is going on, *sì*? You have my word, *bella*. And I'm sure a few months of deprivation won't kill me. If I do get desperate, I have two very capable hands," he said, holding them up, his expression deadpan.

Blushing at how quickly her mind supplied an image of him, naked, Clio threw her purse at him. "Too much information, Bianco."

He waggled his brows at her and, shaking her head at that lewd expression, she laughed.

"You have such a beautiful laugh, Clio. You should do it more."

Struck speechless by his abrupt observation, Clio nodded.

"We'll be landing in an hour," he said, tilting his head toward the New York skyline emerging through the clouds and visible through the windows. "Have you started looking at Jackson's documents? Do you require help?"

"No, I can do it myself," Clio replied, just hearing Jackson's name making her feel dirty from the inside. "I have downloaded and printed every document pertaining to his finances and his hedge fund company. There isn't a single number or transaction that I don't have a hard copy of. But I haven't seen anything yet, Stefan. Are you sure—"

"He's dirty? Yes. I'll bet my entire fortune on that."

Leaning back against the seat, he propped one ankle over the other knee. Clasped his hands behind his head, causing his white dress shirt to stretch tight against that wide chest. "Keep looking, *bella*."

"It's fascinating. For example, did you know that when—"

"So you *still* have a thing for numbers," he drawled softly.

"And you're still the only man in the world that can make that sound dirty."

"Now that you have me locked in with no relief in sight, I have to find my pleasure where I can," he said with a twinkle in his eye.

Clio looked away from him, feeling the heat of his gaze like a caress, praying that she didn't fall apart before she had a chance to be whole again.

Because this time there would not even be pieces of her heart and self-respect left.

Leaning forward, he tugged her left hand into his. She barely managed a gasp as the diamond ring slid in smooth and cold against her skin.

Her heart slammed against her rib cage. Instant refusal

rose to her lips. But she held it off as she caught Stefan's expression.

Distaste, and something else, something she didn't even want to know, glimmered in his eyes.

Was he remembering Serena just as she was thinking of Jackson?

That day in the flat, she had removed the heavy, over-the-top diamond that Jackson had bought for her. Had finally felt free after so long.

Eyeing the ring, she willed herself to calm down. This was only a pretense, something she was walking into with her head screwed on right.

At least it was something that was close to her own taste—the most beautifully cut diamond, in a princess setting.

Her gaze flew to Stefan, who watched her with an intensity that arrested her thought process.

"Stefan, thank you...for everything. I—"

"Not required, *bella*. Do not, even for a moment, believe I'm doing you a favor or that there's anything personal to all this. You have your side of the bargain and I have mine to keep up."

While she grappled with his ruthless warning, he leaned forward and unbuckled her belt. "We will see Jackson tonight at a party, Clio. I made sure he can't get to you before the evening. But obviously he will be foaming at the mouth to see you and to challenge me. He will make a scene, *bella*, and if I'm right about Jackson, it's going to get dirty.

"Do you have what it takes to face him, Clio?"

"And if I don't want to?"

"Then I will drag you with me anyway. Jackson needs to be stopped and I won't get an opportunity like this again."

The utter ruthlessness with which he said it stunned Clio. Every time she thought she knew him, he surprised her again. Once again, she wondered why Stefan despised Jackson so much.

But with a self-preservation instinct she should have had long before this, she didn't prod him. For some reason, understanding what drove Stefan was a territory she didn't want to go into. So she reassured him of her own intentions. "I'll never want him back in my life, Stefan. This week has helped me see more than just Jackson's betrayal.

"I'll need you to stand by me tonight, but yes, I'm ready to take Jackson on."

For once, there were no doubts in his gaze as it swept over her face searchingly. And Clio measured her progress in that green gaze, felt a small flicker of hope for herself.

"You have me, *bella*. For as long as you want."

The moment Stefan helped her out of the limo onto the private estate in the Hamptons where the night's party was, Clio heard the exponential rise in the intensity of the charged atmosphere.

Flashes of cameras and microphones were thrust in their faces from behind ropes. Their names seemed like a chant on a hundred lips.

Jackson had always been a media favorite, too.

Handsome, hardworking, successful—the perfect poster boy for America's success stories. Or at least that was the image he had liked to project.

But the crowd that the security team was trying to corral tonight was like nothing Jackson had ever warranted.

Clutching the ring on her finger like a lifeline, Clio fisted and unfisted her hands as security guards ushered them inside the mansion through the throng.

"Mr. Bianco, are you seeing Ms. Norwood now?"

"Ms. Norwood, is it true you and Mr. Bianco were college sweethearts at Columbia?"

"Have you left Jackson Smith for Mr. Bianco? Or is it his bigger and better status and wealth that lured you in?"

She almost slipped until Stefan caught her hand in his and shielded her with his body. There was no end to the relentless questions, no lower depth that they could attribute to her motives.

Gritting her jaw, Clio followed Stefan's lead until one bold reporter shot out a hand and blocked Stefan's path.

"Give us one sentence, Mr. Bianco. Is Ms. Norwood just one of your usual arm candies or is there anything special about her?"

Stefan stilled and took in the crowd around them with a sly smile. Tugging her to his side, he wrapped an arm around her waist until she was plastered to him.

Something glittered in his gaze as he looked at her and a hundred flashes went on again to capture that mesmerizing look.

His gaze was molten fire, his mouth a study in sensuality.

Every inch of Clio gathered into a trembling ball at that heated look. He raised her hand to his face and kissed her knuckles, making sure the diamond on her finger caught the glare of every flash.

He played them so well.

Clio shivered uncontrollably. Gathering her against him, Stefan absorbed the tremors as if his solid, hard body was made for the very purpose of cushioning her and her emotions.

"After all these years, it didn't take us long to realize how perfect we are for each other. Ms. Norwood has done me the honor of agreeing to marry me, yes. And whoever else has been in her life until now, it's me she's walking to the altar with," he announced, possessiveness and pride dripping with each word, a flash of his Sicilian temperament wreathing his face.

It was all an act, Clio reminded herself, *a perfectly orchestrated one by a man who wanted to hit his opponent where it would hurt.*

The crowd went ballistic at the direct cut aimed toward Jackson. Her breath balling in her throat, she clung to Stefan's hard frame to stop from being mobbed with more questions.

She knew she should speak up, she knew that she was remaining calm just as she had done with Jackson. But for the life of her, she couldn't utter a word through the tightness in her chest.

She couldn't help but wish, with a powerless fury, that time would turn back.

Before Stefan had changed and before she had let herself be lost. Before life had woken them up to the gritty reality of it all.

"Mr. Bianco, will you settle down in New York now that your betrothed is here?"

"Will you make New York the base of operations for Bianco Luxury Real Estate?"

For the first time that evening, Clio saw a momentary doubt shadow Stefan's gaze.

His grip over her wrist tightened into a vise and she gasped.

Instantly, it loosened but he didn't break his stride to answer their questions this time.

Clio made it through most of the evening with herself intact. Of course, she had to remind herself more than a few times that what she and Stefan were putting on was an act.

Because it was intoxicating to be in the company of a man who didn't belittle anyone to prove his own worth, a man who could acknowledge the value of a competitor, a man whose confidence and self-belief was so bone deep that it was enthralling to watch for someone like her who had lost all sense of herself.

And because of their genuinely shared history, it was doubly easy to slip into the role of a loving fiancée, to finish each other's sentences, to laugh at a shared joke without having to communicate.

They fit together too well, as he had noted. More than one conservative businessman, some Stefan claimed had never liked him previously, dropped by to congratulate and backslap him.

To tell him in obvious terms that he had made a fantastic choice by finally giving up his playboy ways and turning into a family man.

His brows rose, he laughed as his cell phone continued to chime with calls from his board members from all over the globe.

The worst part of the evening was standing by him without betraying the shiver that went through her when he casually touched her every other minute.

A hand on her waist, a kiss on her cheek, the intimate way he pushed a strand of hair that had slipped from its knot behind her ear, the way his long fingers lingered over her nape, sometimes dipping lower, sometime pressing into the very spot on her shoulders where she was getting stiff.

The chemistry that they had discovered in Athens seemed only to grow exponentially even under the most innocent of touches.

It thrilled her and scared her equally.

Excusing herself, she made her way to the buffet table. Determined to look her best tonight, and at Stefan's urging, which was the nicest way to put his high-handed arranging of her day, Clio had spent most of the day lazing in the ultraluxurious spa at the Chatsfield, nibbling cucumber slices and drinking kale juice that had her looking supersuave in her designer dress—again arranged for her by her arrogant "fiancé"—but that had also left her on edge with hunger.

A migraine was looming, she was sure, and she wanted to stop it before it got worse.

She was about to grab a plate when her nape prickled, and a familiar scent sent her gut twisting into the most painful knot. She cast a look around and realized Jackson had her cornered.

"I didn't think you had it in you to lure someone of Bi-anco's stature. Fool me, huh, Clio?"

Nastiness dripped from every word Jackson uttered. But Clio held off the impulse to instantly scan the crowd for Stefan.

This had begun with Stefan at her side, true, but it was high time she looked after herself. Squaring her shoulders, she turned around.

His mouth curling, Jackson swept his blue gaze over her with such disdain that sweat pooled over her skin.

"Don't make a scene, Jackson."

"Oh, come on, Clio. After that entrance, after that clip of you crawling all over him out there for the world to see... after you jumped into his bed without even telling me we're through, you disgust me."

That he could think all that of her, that he could say it to her face stunned Clio.

"You're the one who's been fooling me for months," she said, unable to curb the words from falling out of her mouth. All the warnings she had given herself about not betraying what she had seen flew out. Her throat felt like there was glass stuck in it and she had to remind herself that it was not her shame.

"God, you had sex with Ashley and you laughed at me with her."

Something like shame filled his gaze, and was gone in a nanosecond, a calculating look emerging in his features. "So that's what this is about? Payback? You think you'll dangle yourself on his arm and make me sorry for what I did? You think I'll come running back to you and beg for forgiveness?"

His gaze took in her designer dress, her upswept hair, the diamond on her finger as if he was cataloging every-thing about her.

Venomous satisfaction filled his gaze. "Of course it is. Why else would a red-blooded Sicilian like *Bianco*, who's known to never date a woman for more than a week, want to marry you of all the women on the planet?"

For the first time since she had heard the sound of him shamelessly shagging his assistant, Clio was filled with molten fury unlike she had ever known.

It was cleansing, it was invigorating and it burned any remaining doubt that somehow, it had been her fault.

She had done nothing wrong except for trusting a deceptive man with not an ounce of honor.

"You have pushed me beyond my limits already but be careful what you say about him. Stefan already doesn't have much of an opinion about you."

"You stupid whore," he spat out, fear and something else shaking his well-muscled frame. "Can't you see he's just using you to get to me?"

They were drawing looks, she was aware of it as if there was another version of her scanning the room. Years of breeding and her own nature cringed at being amidst a spectacle, recoiled at being the center of attention. But she was damned if she let Jackson intimidate her, too, on top of everything else he had done.

"Don't you dare take another step forward, Jackson."

Something in her tone must have registered because he stopped, his mouth still wearing that nasty curl. "The minute he realizes you're of no use to him, just as you weren't to me, he's going to dump your ass.

"He's no more going to marry you than I did in three years. And when he does dump you, when he moves on to brighter and better pastures, I'll still be here to laugh at you, Clio.

"You're nothing but a crutch to be used."

The knowing smile on his lips, the sneering tone of his words, the decided gleam in his eyes that there was nothing valuable about her to any man, the echo of her darkest fear that no man would ever love her for herself and not her name—it unleashed a firestorm in Clio.

She wanted to roar at Jackson, she wanted to raise her hand and slap the sneer off his mouth.

But he didn't even deserve her anger.

Lifting her head high, she gave him an imperious look that cut him to size. "Be prepared to lose, Jackson. Everything," she said loudly, glad that she sounded steady, confident.

She could not let him ruin what was left of her life in the city that she loved so much. She would not let him run her out of New York on a wave of scandal and shame. She could not let him still have so much power over her life, her happiness.

Even if it meant taking the biggest gamble she had ever risked in her life, even if it meant tying her fate to the one man who could help her become whole again, even if he did it by shredding her to pieces.

"You'll be glad that you're the first one to hear this. Stefan and I are going to be married in a week. Here in New York, at the Chatsfield. And you know what, Jackson? You're invited."

Dio, no!

Clio hadn't just said that.

Standing at the back of the crowd that was hungrily lapping up the exchange between Clio and that scum, Jackson, Stefan stood rooted to the spot, a hundred different emotions crashing and derailing him from inside.

It felt eerily like that moment when Serena had callously and without even an ounce of emotion told him that she was done with him, that she had no use for him without his parents' fortune.

In just a minute, he had lost everything—his parents' respect and trust and love, the woman he had given up everything for, and the worst, his belief in his judgment, his emotions, in his self-worth.

His entire world had collapsed.

Her shoulders ramrod straight, her eyes breathing green fire, her small breasts falling and rising, her skin glowing with anger—it was the Clio he had admired and lusted after a decade ago.

She was spectacular to behold, truly an equal to goddess Athena at that moment as she battled the obvious fear that shadowed her gaze.

But even above the fierce pride and admiration he felt on her behalf for finally putting Jackson in his place was the most insidiously ugly and eviscerating thought he had ever faced.

Her boldness in so publicly and irrevocably announcing their wedding in a week…

Had this been her plan all along? Had the distrust and fragility in her eyes, the way she had trembled under his lips, the shadow of the woman that made him want to protect her from everything, had it all been an act?

The minute the thought erupted, Stefan felt acidic distaste flood his mouth. Cursing, he drove his fist into the pillar next to him, attempting to ground himself, struggling to contain his volatile emotions and his mind's poisonous thoughts.

Dio, he didn't want to think along either lines about Clio. And yet the distrust in him was bone deep.

Even as he hated that she was changing his life, even as he couldn't get a handle on his suspicions, he knew how much making a life here meant to her, knew how much she loved this city.

Reminded himself of the desperate courage that had shone in her eyes when she had shown up at his suite.

Running a hand along his brow, he looked back at her.

Jackson was nowhere to be seen and she was surrounded by well-wishers.

A little of the color was back in her cheeks as her gaze swept through the hall, looking for him.

She had more than surprised him, true. But she couldn't

be allowed to indulge in it again, couldn't be allowed to warrant this much emotion from him—whether surprise or fury or this want for her that was becoming a force he couldn't fight.

If she wanted him to marry her, there was only one way that he could do it.

CHAPTER SEVEN

When Clio had moved a decade ago to study at Columbia, New York, the young, handsome playboys she had become friends with had captivated her. Even through the hardest times over the past decade, she had never once considered returning home to England. She had had such spectacular plans for when she would marry, where she would live for the rest of her life.

But she had never meant to make her dream come true this way. Catching back the sigh that wanted to escape, she looked up at Stefan, streetlights and huge ads bathing his face in strips of light.

The hardest New York winter held less frost than Stefan's gaze in the interior of the limo. For the rest of the evening and the drive back to Manhattan, they hadn't exchanged a single word.

Gazing out through the windows, he kept his phone glued to his ear the entire length of the drive. And judging from his conversation, Clio realized he was handling a crisis with his holdings in Asia.

It was a small comfort that he wasn't freezing her out intentionally as she waited on tenterhooks for his reaction.

If he had snarled at her, if he had called her a hundred names, if he had let that fiery temper explode and lashed out at her, Clio would have had some estimate of his reaction.

But this silent chill that he seemed to radiate from every pore, for the first time since she had seen him standing on the terrace of the Empire State Building, arrogance and power emanating from him, left Clio afraid.

Even the ruthless stranger she had come to know this past week would have been welcome.

Feeling a lead weight in her chest, Clio followed him through the gleaming entryway into the soaring luxury hotel steeped in tradition. Every inch of the plush interior screamed over-the-top opulence and extravagance.

Nothing but the best for Stefan Bianco.

But every time she walked in through the doors of the Chatsfield, saw the eager staff greet Stefan, Clio was reminded of the fact that Stefan didn't own a home. Anywhere in the world. He lived aboard his private jet, flying across the globe as his business dictated, without any connection to the world.

And here in New York, of all places, he hadn't even intended to stay past the week.

They had decided they would just leave it as an openended engagement. Scary prospect as it had been, she had even started looking for a new job.

The walls felt like they would cave in on them and trap them in the tension forever as the steel doors of the elevator closed and they were carried to the penthouse suite.

The unobstructed panoramic views of Manhattan from the suite's glass balconies didn't fascinate her as they usually did. The glittering diamond skylights, the floor-to-ceiling windows, the unique artwork alongside stunning artifacts… nothing held her interest tonight.

It was the silent man who did.

Without taking his gaze off of her, he undid his cuffs. Next came the buttons on his dress shirt. Clio held his gaze, even as the shadow of his olive skin under the shirt beckoned.

The column of his throat was a visual feast as were the chiseled angles of his face.

"Damn it, Stefan. Say something."

Not even Jackson's ugly name-calling shredded her composure as Stefan's silence did.

His olive green gaze was hard, flinty even. "I have never been maneuvered into a corner so publicly and so irrevocably, *bella*. I think I have been rendered mute."

Maneuvered? Her stomach tying in knots, Clio blinked. There was no anger in his words, no resentment in his tone. Something else lingered there on a razor's edge, waiting to strike.

"Stefan, I don't know what came over me. I have never lost my temper like that."

His posture screamed careless lounging but Clio knew he noticed every breath she took, every nuance that crossed her face.

"I know it's not something you ask a friend over dinner, but I would owe you..." Shaking her head, Clio caught the words in her mouth. In her wildest dreams, she had never thought she would beg a man to marry her, to ask someone to turn such a big lie into reality.

She reconsidered it in her own head.

If she didn't value herself, no one else would. Not Jackson, not the world and definitely not Stefan.

And she needed Stefan to value her, to respect her. Suddenly, it felt like the most important thing in the world that he did, that she become at least half the person he had known a decade ago.

"I'll bring you everything I can on him, Stefan. This is my city, and my life. I will not let him steal any more from me."

"Think carefully, Clio. You might only be exchanging one awful man for another. Because I'll not change anything in my life for a woman, *cara*. Not even a surprise wife."

Now there was no taunting smile, there was no lazy charm, only utter seriousness in his gaze. Urgency pounding through her, she reached him and grabbed the lapels of his shirt. Thrust her face so close to his that the masculine heat of him swathed her, pinging across her skin, infiltrating every cell and pore. "What do you mean?"

The rhythmic whir of the fax machine in the open study as it cranked out documents filled the cavernous lounge. The sound chafed against her skin as Clio waited for an answer, her breath suspended in her throat.

Grasping her wrists, he pushed her back. Prowled to the fax machine and returned with a sheaf of papers.

He produced a gold-tipped fountain pen from somewhere and nodded toward the sheaf of papers.

"It means the marriage will be only in name, *Clio*, a contractual agreement that we will both sign. It means all you will get from me is a peanut allowance. It means you'll sign a prenuptial contract and a nondisclosure agreement that you won't reveal any of this to another soul or sell the story or write a *memoir* of our life together at a later time.

"It means you won't dictate who occupies my bed after we're both through with Jackson, and you'll not throw allegations of love at me.

"If you accept and then violate any of the above, the consequences will be far-reaching."

Clio gasped for breath, as if someone had kicked her in the gut, as if something icy and vicious had been stuck in her chest. Tears pricked behind her eyelids, her lungs struggling to breathe.

"You think…*you actually think* I planned all this?" she poked him in the chest, hurt splintering into a millions shards. "You think I orchestrated it so that our farcical engagement turns into a real marriage and I can mooch off your millions?"

"The thought crossed my mind, *sì*," he said, without blinking, without a beat, without wondering how much pain he was causing her with his casually elegant shrug.

Clio slapped him so hard that her arm jerked at the impact. Her entire body shuddered but it was still nothing compared to the sharp pain in her chest.

Before she could draw another breath, she was plastered against his hard body, her arms twisted behind her in a firm grip, her breasts crushed against his chest, her lungs filled with the scent of him.

Stefan didn't know what shocked him more. The fact that Clio had actually slapped him, or his outrageous reaction to it.

He had to have truly become a twisted bastard because the sight of her—out of control with anger, her elegance all ruffled, her composure fraying, her lithe body vibrating, turned him on as if a fire had been lit inside his very blood.

That he had driven her to be that old Clio again felt like a win more than anything.

He turned rock hard and she was like heaven in his arms.

He held her hands tight with one hand and shuddered as her breasts rubbed against his chest. The tight tips of her nipples visible against the flimsy silk she had on drew his gaze. The scent of her perfume drenched his pores.

Dio, the woman smelled absolutely divine.

He moved his free hand over his own cheek, and then over hers. She was so silky soft that his mind instantly wandered to other areas. "Corner me into marriage first, then slap me second…no woman has even come close to what you have achieved today, *tesoro*."

She pushed at him again with her hands, not that he budged at her attack. "Don't you dare call me that, whatever the hell it means."

"Then do not push me into retaliating the only way I know, *bella*."

The more she struggled against him, the more aroused he became. He gave himself over to the moment and enjoyed the novelty of his own reaction.

Most of the women he had dated the past few years had been simpering, talking him up, catering to his every need before he even knew it. Until one face blended into another,

until he was nothing but a carefully constructed projection
of himself in their eyes, until there was nothing but emptiness inside him…

No one knew who he was, no woman was herself with
him…

That Clio wouldn't hesitate to be herself with him was
an aphrodisiac unlike anything. It morphed his physical
hunger for her into something else…

"I always wondered about that even temper of yours,
bella. That first year at Columbia I would spend hours wondering if you ever lost it and how you would look if you did,"
he drawled, and tugged at her hair.

Her gorgeous hair tumbled down to her shoulders like
amber fire. Still holding her with one hand, he twisted the
hair around his fingers. Wondered for the millionth time
how she would look wearing nothing.

"I've never in my life even hurt a fly," she muttered, but
it came out husky and uneven.

An atavistic satisfaction filled him. She was just as
turned on as he was, struggling with her want even as she
despised him for doubting her.

"That makes me feel extra special."

"That's because you're an utter bastard."

"Now you're learning, Clio."

He buried his face in her hair and breathed deeply.

There was a freedom that she understood him now. That
she had finally learned he was not the friend she remembered with such fondness. That the man he was now could
distrust her motives and yet still want her with a feral need
that knew no reason.

That she realized he was not doing this for her but because of his desperate need to bring down Jackson.

She would not trust him now, would not expect anything
from him and there was a relief in it.

Suddenly, she sagged against him, as if the fight depleted
out of her. And he relaxed his arms around her.

"Why are you doing this?" she finally said in such a small voice that it shook him more than her slap had.

"Because it's impossible for me to trust your motive, unbearable for me to give a woman place in my life, even temporarily. Isn't that clear enough, *bella*? The fact that I'm even contemplating doing this is because I need that proof, Clio. But make sure you don't up the price any more.

"If you accept, we'll be married next week. Here at the Chatsfield, just as you want. We will show Jackson and New York a wedding they won't forget soon. You'll be the most beautiful bride New York has ever seen."

A shiver racked Clio and instantly his hold on her tightened, his body a deceptively warm fortress around her.

"I will sign wherever you want me to, I will follow every condition of yours. I have...*lost* so much already, I... You'll have your revenge," she said bitterly. "There's definitely something fishy with Jackson's numbers."

"Good," he replied, stepping away from her.

He had shown her his true self and yet, it felt as if he was the one who had been burned.

"Good night, Stefan," Clio whispered, her throat aching, her gut churning in panic.

What had she done? Oh, God, what had she done? How could she have not seen what her enraged, impulsive declaration would turn him into?

Without casting another glance at him, she walked away, her head held high.

For the first time in a decade, Stefan felt the landscape of his life slip from his fingers and all because of a woman. Again.

The only way he knew to protect Clio and himself from this was to set rules, to remove her from his mind, to wipe and forget the taste of her from his thoughts and definitely decouple her from his lust.

To set expectations that neither of them could falter over.

Crushing the overwhelming urge to kiss the hurt away from her mouth, he walked into his office and turned on the huge plasma screens mounted over the far wall.

Walking into the closet, he stripped and dressed in his workout shorts. Cranked up the rowing machine he'd had specially installed in his study and went to work on it.

He was not only seething against the course he had set tonight, but he had sexual frustration added to the mix.

Just the cranking of the machine and the burn of his thigh and arm muscles went a long way toward calming him down.

The news would already be spreading, he knew.

The fact that he—the quintessential third bachelor among the Columbia Four—was finally getting married, and in just a week, so soon after Rocco's and Christian's fairytale weddings, would unleash a storm he couldn't contain.

A picture of him and Clio entering the Chatsfield tonight, immediately followed by a shot of them from a decade ago, lounging on the steps of University Hall at Columbia with wide smiles on their faces, flashed on the screen.

Not everyone trusts a corporation with a predatory playboy at its helm, he had heard his board bemoan more than once when he had questioned why they hadn't made a particular deal.

An evening of being an affianced man—and to Clio— had already changed the business world's perception of him. And stealing Clio from Jackson, as the media was calling it, meant that the focus stayed on his business and him.

It worked for his business and his brand to have a wife, and Clio at that, who was sophisticated and levelheaded and, more important, had no expectations of him. Even if she had, he had made sure he had destroyed them tonight.

It worked every which way he looked at it except for his heart.

Hearing the phrase "Reunited College Sweethearts" stuck in his craw. He was the last man who should have a *fairy-tale love story come true* line attached to his name. He was the last man Clio should have come to for help, he acknowledged now with bitter resignation.

Because, even if he wanted to, he couldn't change himself now. The poison Serena had brought into his life had infused his very blood.

All he cared about now was destroying Jackson and keeping himself and Clio intact until the end of this marriage.

"If you want to leave all this behind, *leave Stefan behind*," Zayed whispered in her ear even as he amiably tucked her bare arm along his under the watchful, hawk-like gaze of Stefan at the end of the vast hall on the other side, "then all you have to do is say so, Clio. I shall signal Rocco and a limousine will appear outside the hotel in a matter of seconds. In a few hours, you can be in Milan, or Hong Kong, or even Gazbiyaa if you don't mind the stark and beautiful desert land of a country on the brink of war."

Blinking, Clio tore her gaze away from Stefan's olive green one. The Chatsfield glittered, and the hungry hush of designer-clad guests, a power list of New York's Who's Who, reached her in stifling waves.

They were all here to witness her union with one of the most sought-after bachelors in the world. Reminding herself to smile like a woman madly in love, she pasted a smile and turned toward Zayed.

And caught the scowl on her fiancé's face in the infinitesimal moment before she turned.

They were standing at the entrance to the Terrace Room, as it was called, just beyond the French doors of the courtyard of the Chatsfield, a room steeped in history and charm.

The room boasted some of the most impressive historical detailing, created in the spirit of the Italian Renaissance. Exquisite crystal chandeliers hung from the ceiling, bathing the vast room in a golden glow.

Swallowing at the hard knot in her throat, she clutched

Zayed's fingers tightly and he returned the pressure. "I thought your loyalty would be to Stefan, Your Highness."

"Not you, too, Clio," Zayed warned her, still a glimmer of the playboy prince in his smile. In just a matter of days, Zayed had gone from second son to the ruler of Gazbiyaa. And Clio couldn't even begin to imagine what must be going on in his head.

"I thought you would warn Stefan away from me, not the opposite."

His deep brown eyes shining with kindness, his mouth set into that diplomatic half smile, Zayed shook his head. Why hadn't she gone to him for help instead of the stubborn Sicilian?

"You forget that Rocco, Christian and I know you as well as Stefan does. And Stefan…he is more than a brother to me, but we have seen him become jaded and more hardened than the rest of us. I wouldn't want my enemy's daughter to be caught in that disdain of his. And *you*…you're a friend, Clio."

Clio hugged the warmth in his tone. "He did not force me into anything, Zayed," she said, wanting to make sure they all understood. Every step of the way, Stefan had only prepared her for what was coming, including his disdain.

"This was my choice." Whether right or wrong, she was glad that it was.

Zayed's expression didn't waver. "None of us want you to be hurt, Clio. He could very possibly do it, and then he won't forgive himself, no?"

Her gut sinking, Clio finally understood their concern, understood the friction she had sensed between Stefan and the three of them the past two days.

Stefan thought they were all protecting her from him.

What he didn't realize was that Rocco, Christian and Zayed were also looking out for him. They were afraid that by hurting her, he was going to irrevocably lose a part of himself.

A tightness emerged in her chest at the very thought and the sinking realization of how complicated the man she was about to marry was.

It's the only way I can do this, Clio, he had said to her when she had signed the contract.

Was it the only way he thought of to protect their fragile relationship from what they were putting it through? And she resolved to not lose him, not to let this mutual need for revenge destroy them.

"I won't let that happen, Zayed."

Whether he believed her or not, Zayed patted her hand. "You have friends, Clio. Always remember that."

Wetness filled her eyes, but Clio smiled through it.

Rocco and Olivia, Christian and Alessandra, and Zayed—all of them had hovered over her the past few days like mother hens.

It had felt incredibly good to know she had so many people who cared about her well-being.

With every detail of the most opulent wedding she had ever dreamed of taken care of, with the grand hotel decorated ornately for what the media were calling the "Fairy-Tale Wedding of the Decade," with people who actually cared about her surrounding her, for a few compelling moments over the past week she could have almost fooled herself into believing it was the wedding she had wanted all her life.

Except for the man in the center of it all who hadn't even looked her in the eye in a week, who had only spoken to her to discuss another blasted clause in the contract he had made her sign.

He had engaged an army of people to oversee every small detail of the wedding. Clio had barely had time to have second thoughts about how big a step she was taking.

Designers and lawyers, makeup artists and wedding planners—there hadn't been a single thing that Clio herself had been responsible for. All she had to do was nod, and maybe use her brain cells to make a choice as to whether she wanted lilies or orchids or another exotic flower she couldn't even remember the name of, whether she wanted chocolate cake or red velvet.

She had blanched when she had discreetly looked up the designer who had been hired to create her wedding gown in a week.

With delicate corded lace on tulle skimming the shoulders and neckline, the fragile gown had a line of buttons sneaking downward between her shoulder blades.

It was the most beautiful dress she had ever seen, and she couldn't swallow the fact that it had been created with her in mind. Diamond bracelets, befitting Stefan Bianco's intended, she had been told when she had argued, had been delivered in a velvet box, along with matching diamond earrings and the most elegantly designed diamond tiara.

She had been stunned at her own reflection, at how perfect the dress was for her slim build, how well it accentuated her almost boyish curves.

The diamonds had glittered and winked in the three full-length mirrors the hotel staff had set up.

And that's when it had hit her.

The money he was spending on the wedding—she had given up adding once she had looked through the hotel's website.

Which meant the cost of the wedding had to be astronomical.

Feeling as dirty as Jackson had called her, she had knocked on his study door one evening.

To find him at the rowing machine, dressed in shorts and bathed in sweat. It was a sight that was burned into her brain, her skin, her very cells.

The sight of his curling biceps, ropes of sweat-slicked muscles in his chest and back, the sleek contours of his torso, dissolved every brain cell into mush.

God, they had been rowing champions at Columbia, the

four of them. And he still looked just as fit as he had been a decade ago, if not better. She had spent several minutes staring at him, heat uncoiling in her lower belly, every inch of her body vibrating with desire.

When she had finally found her voice and expressed her concerns, he had cast her a look that was like a bucket of ice-cold water over her heated senses.

"Don't worry, *bella*," he had said, rising to his feet. His thick hair was curled with sweat. "This doesn't count against you. After all, our whole agreement rests on the pretense that I want to throw the love of my life the wedding of her dreams, *si*?"

Faced with that mocking scorn, Clio had had to fight against the instinct to rush out of there. "I have been going over the seating charts and I didn't see your parents' names," she finally managed.

His expression shut down instantly, as if a light had gone out. "They're not coming."

A warning vibrated in his answer. But instead of heeding it, her mind thought back to them. The rest of the Columbia Four and her included, had all envied Stefan his parents' unconditional love more than anything.

The Biancos were those picture-perfect Sicilian parents for whom family came first and foremost always. And it had been a shock when they had threatened to cut him off if he didn't come back home after graduation.

And Stefan hadn't cared about his inheritance. Only Serena had betrayed him when she realized he wouldn't have the Bianco fortune behind him.

"Stefan, your parents…they forgave you, didn't they? For trusting Serena?"

"I have not asked them for it, *bella*."

Why? "Wait, you haven't… I don't understand."

His gaze unblinking, he opened the door for her, his withdrawal sending the room into subzero temperatures. "They are not on the guest list because I didn't invite them, *cara*. We don't need to involve any more people in our deception, do we?"

"No," Clio had replied, reeling from the frost in his words.

What had he meant by that? Had he not seen his parents all these years? How could he bear to keep them at a distance like that?

In that moment, Clio had realized what an utter stranger he was to her.

His distrust of her motives, his insistence that they do it per his rules, the cold front he presented if she asked anything personal—she finally understood he wasn't just lost to her.

He *had* buried everything good and decent about him. But before she left his life, before he was through with her, she was determined to remind him what he had been once. And she had to begin with bringing his parents back into his life.

Hers would never forgive her, but Stefan...he could have his parents back.

"Clio?"

Coloring, Clio looked at Zayed. "Thank you so much for reminding me that I have friends, Zayed." She blew a long breath out, remembering her mother's unforgiving words, and their blatant refusal to come. Reminded herself that she had friends who would always stick by her. "And for agreeing to give me away."

"You did me an honor when you asked me." Still smiling, he cast a quick look ahead. "I can feel Stefan's gaze drilling holes in my head. Not even my enemy country's politics make me shudder so," he said with a mock shiver. "Are you ready for him, Clio?"

Sucking in a deep breath, Clio turned toward her waiting bridegroom.

Dressed in a black evening suit, his thick hair combed back, he stood out so prominently amidst the rest of the men.

He had promised her he would help her. And that he kept his word—even though a wedding, even of the fake kind, clearly filled him with utter fury—she hugged it to herself.

Whatever else he claimed, Stefan Bianco was a man of honor.

"I'm ready, Zayed," she whispered.

Her hold on the lilies in her hand shaky, she followed Zayed's lead as the music began.

With both her parents and Stefan's not in attendance, she had decided to do without a maid of honor, electing to stick to the traditions only by a bit. Somehow it felt as if it fit them—this wedding among friends who were their true family, in the city that had welcomed them with open arms a decade ago.

Everything about the wedding was perfection itself. Even the weather was a beautiful June day, gorgeous with the sun shining.

It wasn't a real marriage, Clio reminded herself as they reached Stefan and Zayed handed her over. It was all a story they were creating for the media and Jackson.

Her heart zigzagged all over the place as Stefan clasped her fingers tight in his.

But as she met his gaze for the first time in a week and saw the dark, possessive fire flickering to life there, she shivered.

How was she supposed to resist him when the liquid lust in his eyes felt like the only real thing today? How was she supposed to resist him when despite his distrust of her, he made her feel as if she mattered?

CHAPTER EIGHT

HE HAD A WIFE.

One who was dressed in delicate white lace that displayed her alabaster skin in its glory. The row of buttons going all the way to her lower back was all he could think of.

Her flaming hair, combed back into a tight knot at the back, the long line of her jaw and neck were a temptation for his fingers.

Her dress, while lacy, was elegant, sophisticated, as it hugged her lithe frame and small breasts.

She looked as she always did—demure, stylish, perfectly put together. Only he knew what simmered beneath that calm exterior.

He had a wife and he couldn't turn his gaze away from her.

The thought was so disconcerting and disturbing that Stefan kept turning the platinum band on his finger round and round, as if he could make it disappear, as if he could change reality by stubbornly refusing to accept it.

He not only had a wife but one he wanted to kiss more than he needed to drag in his next breath.

And the most shocking fact of them all was that his new wife had almost flinched when he had touched her lips with his.

He, Stefan Bianco, the man who had dated some of the most beautiful, accomplished women in the world, badly wanted to touch and kiss and seduce his wife, the one woman he should never touch or want in any way.

It was how he had felt when he had first eyed Clio across the campus lawn a decade ago—full of raging hormones, and an almost laughable naïveté about the world.

He still wanted her just as badly except now that naïveté was dead and in its place was a voice that kept whispering that he could have Clio if he wanted this time.

Like the rest of the women in the world, Clio Norwood had a price, too. And he had already paid the price.

It was such a disgusting line of thought that nausea filled his throat. And yet he couldn't erase it.

Was this what he had become? Was there nothing honorable left in him?

For the first time in years, Stefan looked inward and cringed, wondered what else he had lost in the name of Serena.

"You'll break the champagne flute if you don't stop glaring at Zayed and Clio, *fratello*," Rocco whispered from behind him.

He couldn't blame his oldest friend for the continual jeering because what Stefan wanted to do was throw the champagne flute on the dance floor so that Clio would stop smiling at Zayed and look back at him.

"She's always been a beautiful dancer, hasn't she?" Christian chimed in, and now the vein in Stefan's temple felt as if it would burst open.

He knew very well what his three friends were up to. He also knew very well that Rocco had eyes for no one but Olivia, and Christian for his pregnant wife, the beautiful Alessandra.

In the rational part of his mind, the increasingly small one, he was also aware that as much as Zayed seemed to be whispering little jokes in Clio's ear and had been flirting with her outrageously for most of the evening, he had never had any interest in Clio.

Even if he hadn't guessed that the fairy tale that Clio and he were projecting to the whole world was just that—a tale of epic proportions.

But knowing it and telling his body and his libido to behave accordingly was another thing.

Because the moment he had slid the gold band onto her trembling finger, the moment he had touched her lips with his own, the moment he saw the despondency in her eyes as she slid the ring onto his finger, Stefan had felt the most possessive, an almost Neanderthal, urge to drag Clio away from the celebration that followed and ravish her.

He wanted to drive the thought of another man from her mind, he wanted to kiss away the hurt from her mouth, he wanted to shred her control as she was so effortlessly shredding his.

He wanted her to smile at him as she did at the whole world, even though he had done everything to wipe it from her face.

He wanted to sink into her wet heat again and again, until the small fancy, which was now growing into a full-blown obsession, was gone from his blood.

He could seduce her, too. He had no doubt about it. Whatever poison that asshole Jackson had spewed into her mind, whatever she believed about her own nature—because there had been plenty of occasions over the past week to figure it out—there was an explosive energy every time they occupied the same space.

Something his all-too-clever and observant friends had remarked over the past week. But if there was one thing Stefan didn't want, it was to see that betrayal in Clio's eyes the next morning. She would never sleep with him and then walk away unscathed. And as fragile as she was right now, he didn't want to be another bad decision she regretted.

He wanted her to be consumed by him as he was by her. Which seemed a far-out fantasy right then.

If he could forget the contract they had signed, he could have almost believed her to be the old Clio, having the time of her life, supremely happy with her life and the world.

Except when she looked at him. Then, the smile fell off her face as if she had eaten something that lived under those gold-lined slippers she was wearing.

Except when it had been their dance. She had been stiff like a board, her features frozen into a mask of icy politeness, so tightly withdrawn that he could break her with a hard grip.

She had hardly touched her dinner but her face had lit up when it had been time for the red-velvet cake they had cut together.

Every time she had lifted the gleaming spoon and licked away the dessert, Stefan smothered a groan himself.

"Come have a drink with us," said Rocco, interrupting Stefan's thoughts as they veered into dangerous territory about how snugly Zayed was holding Clio and how neatly she fit against his tall, wide frame. Tendrils of hair were beginning to come away from her elaborate hairstyle and kiss that delicate jawline.

He heard another laugh fall from those beautiful lips, saw her tilt her head and whisper something and he'd had enough.

He was on the dance floor and cutting in on Zayed and Clio before he knew what he was doing. As though guessing that he was as rational as a charging bull, his friend instantly relinquished Clio, a cunning smile in his eyes.

Among the four of them, Zayed was the diplomat, yet Stefan didn't doubt for a second that he was also the most perceptive. With a slap on his back, Zayed pulled him closer into a hug.

There was no humor in his gaze just then. "Take care, Stefan. Our fate cannot always be controlled by us, my friend."

Stefan didn't smile either. He knew he had become an untenable, mistrusting bastard in the past few years, that he had pushed Rocco to the limit by doubting the wonderful Olivia's intentions toward his friend, but Rocco, Christian and Zayed—they had always stood by him and loved him no matter what.

That was the only relationship, the one good thing Serena hadn't destroyed in his life, an anchor that had held him steady when he had been sinking.

"You think I'm capable of falling in love, Zayed?"

"No, I do not. I don't think you or I will have the fortune that has been bestowed on Rocco and Christian, nor do we want it. But do not destroy the good that has somehow found its way into your life."

With Zayed's advice ringing in his ears, Stefan tugged his new bride toward him. Every muscle in his body tensed when she came into his arms pliantly, wrapped her arms around his neck.

Her small breasts rubbed against his chest, one toned thigh pressing flush against his muscular one. She smelled decadent, her skin soft like the sheerest silk. His pulse thudded heavily in his blood, the delicate crook of her neck and shoulders beckoning for a taste.

Wrapping his fingers around her nape, Stefan tugged her head back and looked into her eyes and received another shock.

"You…need to lighten up, my dear husband," she whispered against his cheek, dragging her mouth over his stubble, toward his jaw. "We're supposed to be madly in love, remember?"

Her touch was possessive, reckless, and it made him want it everywhere, made him forget right and wrong.

Clasping her cheeks, he pushed her chin up to meet his eyes.

His new wife was utterly sloshed.

Something akin to a burn began in his chest as he looked into her eyes, the blacks dilated against the glittering green. Tucking loose tendrils of her hair beneath her ear, Stefan picked her up to rising cheers and comments from the guests.

Clio had never imagined that she would be drunk on her wedding night. She had never thought she would feel like a half terrified, half hopeful Victorian virgin that the pirate would carry aboard his ship and ravish.

In the past couple of years when Jackson had evaded all talk of their wedding with such skilled precision, she hadn't imagined she would ever have a wedding, much less a wedding night.

So with everything that had gone sideways in her life, the fact that she was drunk was the least disconcerting thing about the night.

Not that she had planned it that way.

She had signed the agreement as he wanted her to. She had smiled and gushed like a woman in love so much that her jaw had begun to hurt. She had tried not to flinch and betray the trembling need she felt when he touched his soft, hot mouth to hers.

Not once during the day had she behaved in a wifely manner whatsoever.

So she had no idea what it was that had turned Stefan more and more distant and forbidding. Unless, it was the very sight of her wearing his ring.

With him radiating an icy scorn from every pore at her side wherever she turned or whoever she looked at all evening, she had drunk her first glass of champagne without getting any food first.

Of course, she had devoured her cake—which sadly was the high point of her wedding day, but by then she had already had a buzz. Which made it all too easy to reach for the second one.

It had made her unafraid, as she had been a long time ago. *Unafraid, uncaring and free.*

And because she had loved being that old Clio again, even if it was the alcohol, she had drunk two more glasses. Even the thought of a head-splitting migraine that was sure to arrive first thing tomorrow hadn't stopped her.

She had thoroughly enjoyed dancing with Rocco and Christian, and Zayed flirting with her. He had done it out of pity because her very real husband couldn't even fake a smile, much less pretend to be besotted. Still, she had enjoyed it.

The most disturbing thing about the night, however, was the solid hard muscular chest that she was cradled against with utmost care right now. The scent of his aftershave— lime—teased her nostrils.

But she didn't want to be held like that, she didn't want him to suffer her company as if he was cursed to do it.

Just then, the elevator rocked.

Giving up any effort at a pretense, Clio sighed and clutched him tighter.

Then she felt it more than heard it—the choked-up, almost suppressed laugh that had his chest rumbling beneath her arms. Cracking her eyes open, Clio dared a look at him.

He was laughing.

The beast who had glared at her all evening, who had looked at her as if she was the most untrustworthy woman on the entire planet, no the universe, who had driven her to drink when she generally couldn't stand alcohol, was laughing.

Granted, to see that sensuous, cutting-grooves-in-his-cheeks smile was *almost* worth any price.

Thrusting her hands under the collar of his dress shirt, Clio tucked his chin up until he was staring into her eyes. "What the hell are you laughing about?"

"You, *bella*," he replied.

"What about me?"

"A Victorian virgin aboard a pirate ship that was about to be ravished?"

Heat swarmed her face. God, she had said that out loud?

"I'm drunk," she drawled, loving the *thump-thump* of his heart beneath her ears. He was so solid and warm around her that perversely, she felt safe around him. "Anything I say tonight should be disregarded," she retorted. "And I'm no Victorian virgin that needs to be ravished or for that matter saved."

"Seeing that I'm not the saving-hero kind, that's good." The elevator doors swished open. And he stepped out. "It's almost scary how perfect we are for each other."

"'College Sweethearts Who Found Their Way to Each Other After So Many Years'?" she said, quoting the headlines about them. "'Destiny Brings Old Lovers Together Again!' 'True Love Conquers All.' I wouldn't have wanted a better tagline for Jackson to look at every time he turned his head."

Instantly, the smile slid off his mouth as if she had poisoned the very air around them. There was such a bright ire in his gaze that Clio wondered for a second if he would let her fall to the floor.

But, of course, he didn't.

Stefan would never cause her harm, she knew that. Just as he would never trust her any more than a strange woman he picked up in a club or a party or wherever he picked up women from.

She had thought she had accepted it, but it was beginning to matter more than it should. Even if she had fallen on her face these past few years, didn't he know what kind of a person she was?

He crossed the cavernous lounge and carried her into one of the bedrooms at the back.

He slowly brought her to her feet. Miscalculating the buzz in her head, she swayed and he caught her.

His arms came around her from behind to steady her.

Her body operating on its own, Clio sagged against him. But his arms were like iron vises around her waist, holding her still, stopping her from leaning back.

A devil inside goading her, Clio clutched his forearms and pushed back.

But he didn't loosen them.

"Stay still, Clio," he said in a harsh whisper that had goose bumps rolling over the exposed skin at her neck.

Furious and confused and so many things that she didn't have a name for, Clio pushed again. Her legs tangled with his and she fell back against him.

A shudder racked through her.

He was a cocoon of heat and hard muscle behind her. His fingers, splayed on her hips, burned through the flimsy silk of her dress.

Molten heat drenched her inside out, turning her blood into drugged honey.

He engulfed her every sense and she had never felt more like sinking.

"Do not tease a fire in me that you're in no way equipped to handle, *bella*," he whispered, before he licked the rim of her ear. "I'm not particularly fond of celibacy, especially now that I have every right in front of God and law over the one woman I've wanted so desperately for so long."

Shock waves jolted through her, spreading heat and need to the tip of every finger and toe.

His thighs were concrete columns behind hers, his midriff a steel wall. And his erection grazed her left buttock.

It was enough to jerk Clio out of the buzz.

Mouth dry, Clio jerked to the front. Or at least tried to. With one arm locking her snug against him, the other climbed up her belly, up her breasts and clasped her jaw.

Long fingers traced her lips, and she forgot how to breathe.

Stop it, please, she wanted to say but the words were consumed by the raw need coursing through her.

The blunt tip of his finger traced the cushion of her mouth. "Open that luscious mouth, Clio." She did and he pushed his finger inside.

Closing her mouth around it, Clio sucked it while her tongue laved it. Wet heat rushed between her thighs.

He cursed again, louder, harsher, and his arousal grew against the valley between her buttocks. Left her too tight inside her own skin.

She gasped as his teeth dug into the flesh at her shoulder. Pain and pleasure fused together as he licked the tender spot, his breaths coming on top of each other in a harsh rhythm.

And still, he didn't let her move. Didn't give her anything more than he decided.

He cupped her breast, and heated wetness drenched her sex. Throwing her head back, Clio pushed into his touch.

Just once, she wanted to feel his touch all over. Just once, she wanted to let it be about pleasure and only pleasure. The hardened nipple rasped hungrily against his palm, an answering pull between her thighs.

Mouth buried in her neck, he licked her skin, and Clio moved restlessly. The slide of her garter against her thighs, the rub of her own skin was torturous, her sex aching and throbbing.

With his fingers under her chin, he tipped her face up. Caught by the reflection in the oval, floor-length mirror, Clio flushed. Her eyes were droopy, her mouth trembling.

And he…he could have been cast from marble for all the expression in his eyes.

"Have you had enough, *bella*?"

Something in that mocking tone of his lit a fire in Clio. It was a fantasy to believe that he could feel anything for her—hurt or pain or desire—without allowing himself to do so, a fantasy to think she could affect him in a way he couldn't control.

A fantasy she was becoming more and more invested in, a fantasy that would break her if she didn't kill it now.

That fear sliced through the haze of desire and alcohol. "Have *you* had enough, Stefan?" she said, meeting his gaze in the mirror. She had no idea how she strung the words together, no idea how her brain even cooperated when she was aching everywhere. "Have you proved to yourself that you can have me panting in heat within a few seconds, that I'm the same as every other woman on the planet in this, too? Isn't that the game we are playing, dear husband?"

He turned her around, and still there was not a glimmer of emotion in his face.

Clio would have taken anything, even fury at this point. She wanted to crack that hardened shell he wore like armor; she wanted to shatter it and wound him. And it was the most dangerous thought she had had in her life.

"Why did you drink tonight when you never do, *bella*?"

"Because you're a mistrusting, cynical asshole who hates the very sight of me and who thinks I'm a manipulative bitch out for your millions."

"I never said that."

Clio didn't know why she was so angry, only that it was unbearable that he wasn't even moved. "Your look all evening did it for you. After that first drink, I found it was easy to not give a damn about you and your glaring and your low opinion."

"Or it could be because you know what's been building between us this past week and you're terrified to face it and you wanted an easy out.

"Whatever happened tonight, come morning, you could say, *I was out of it*."

He dissected her emotions, her decisions so easily that she felt raw, out of control, bereft of words.

He undid the golden cuff links and pushed his sleeves

back, arrogant confidence dripping from every pore. "Is the buzz evaporating yet, *cara*?"

Clio pushed him, something hot and achy clamping her throat. "I've had enough of you and your—"

"No, you haven't," he said grabbing her again. This time, she was facing him and there was nowhere to hide. "Stop hiding, Clio. Unless you stop and face it, there'll always be another situation to run from."

"I'm not—"

"You left England when you found out that your father had arranged every day of the rest of your life from what you'll study to who you'll marry. It was an incredibly brave thing to do but it was still running away.

"For all these years, you hid even when you knew Jackson was cheating you—you let him do it. Tonight, you drank because you don't know what to do with me."

He placed his hand over one breast and a gasp fell from her mouth. He covered her mouth with his and sparks cindered at her mouth spreading far and wide, making her hungry and desperate for more. "What you're doing to me, standing here like this, with desire lacing your gaze... Do you have any idea how torturous this is for me?"

And he gave her what she wanted.

He stroked and bit, nipped and laved at her mouth while she clung to him, her body, her will, her mind, all his.

"You drank because you didn't want to be responsible for this, Clio," he whispered against her swollen mouth.

Slowly, he pushed her back, creating distance between their bodies.

"For all the names the media calls me, I will not seduce you tonight and shoulder responsibility for it tomorrow while you call it a drunken mistake."

Disappointment cooled her body as neatly as if he had dumped the champagne bucket full of ice over her head. "No?"

"No. When I take a woman to bed, it's not out of pity or shame or joy or anger. It's pure lust, *bella*."

"So you won't finish what you've started, then?"

"Not unless you speak the words." In an intimate gesture that set fire to her skin, he tugged the delicate neckline with rough fingers. It gave in with a tear and a rasp—thousands of dollars and ripped now. The upper swell of her breast bared to his slumberous gaze. He bent his arrogant head and pressed a hot kiss to the flesh. Nipped it with his teeth.

Need knotted at her nipples, making them achy and tight. Her sex pulsed, wet and aching.

Clio had never known such liquid desire, as if her skin and sinew was all filled with want. Want for him. Want for the one man she shouldn't want.

Want for the man who had given her everything, but really nothing.

"Tell me that you want me to tear that dress off of you completely, *bella*." Anger colored his words. "Tell me to run my hands and mouth over every inch of your skin, tell me to sink into your heat until it is all either of us can feel." Contempt punctured the heat in his words. "Tell me to give us both the relief that we're both so desperately craving.

"Tell me and your every wish will be my command, *bella*."

Utter resignation reverberated in the way he held her loosely against him, in the way he sighed against her willing flesh. And it was that resignation, that shuddering exhale as if he was giving in to the inevitable even as he hated it, that cleared the haze from Clio's head.

Had she known that this moment was coming? Was this the only way she could think of having him, when she could absolve herself of all responsibility? Was this how she had let Jackson walk all over her?

Would she always let life happen to her, rather than take charge of it?

Shame cooled her skin, leaving her shaking. Tugging

the torn lace of her dress upward, she stumbled back. Her breathing out of sync, she tried to collect her aroused senses together.

She wanted to be held and kissed and touched by him so much that it was a cavernous chasm inside her.

But not like this.

No. This was not fair to either of them.

She looked up and met his glittering gaze, every inch of her vibrating with need. "When I look back at this night a decade later, I want to remember something else other than your self-disgust that you want me and my desperate attempt to escape it, as you put it so well."

"Clio—"

"Yes you do, Stefan. You hate that you want me when it isn't your will, don't you?" She blinked, striving for strength. "I want to have one thing that will make me proud about today. I want you to leave. Thank you for saving me from myself once again."

The flesh over the angular bones of his face, already so lean and spare, tightened even further, until he was all jutting angles and brooding arrogance. He went still, inch by inch, ridding himself of that glittering want and desire, ridding himself of any emotion.

That growing stillness in him, that willpower in action—it was the most disconcerting thing she had ever seen.

"As you wish," he said with one lingering look before he turned and left.

She could almost believe that her words had pierced him. Almost.

Roughly tugging at the bodice of a dress that could have probably fed a starving family for a few months, Clio sank to the bed and covered her face.

As caustic as his analysis of her life had been, Stefan had stopped them from making an irrevocable mistake.

She should be glad for it. All she needed was to convince herself of it.

* * *

Standing under the ice-cold shower spray, Stefan shivered. His teeth chattered in his mouth, his skin grew goose bumps. If he looked down, he would probably see that his balls had forever turned blue.

But even the possibility of permanent damage to his manhood couldn't erase the picture of his wife from his mind.

He had never seen a more beautiful woman. Her vulnerability shone in her eyes, her desire too pure and real to be anything but temptation, her struggle to be better than herself a wonder for him to watch.

Neither could he curb the small flicker of warmth in his chest.

Was this what Clio would do for him?

Punish him, torture him and yet push him toward being a better man than he had been this past decade?

That he had resisted her, that he hadn't given in to his need and taken what she had so freely offered, that he had protected her, even from himself, he would count as a win; he would count it as a little bit of honor still left in him.

CHAPTER NINE

WHEN CLIO OPENED her eyes the next morning, there was a hammer and a pointy needle inside her skull, *and* someone had pulled the silky curtains aside to let in reams of sunlight to punish her with.

Or at least, that's how it felt.

Clutching her head, she turned to her side and groaned. Tears prickled behind her eyes at the dull, pounding ache through the top of her head.

Her mouth was dry, and her throat parched. She tried opening her eyes again and was about to sit up when a strong arm pulled her up with infinite gentleness.

A whimper erupted from her throat as a blend of lime and aftershave and masculine musk teased her nostrils. It was like a slap to her senses, at once decadent and eviscerating...

Just like the man was.

She stiffened in his hold but he didn't relent.

Of all the unholy, damnedest things in the world, why did Stefan have to be up before her on the first morning of their ill-conceived marriage? Why couldn't she have started it by setting an unaffected tone, one that she wanted?

"Buon giorno, cara."

The honeyed words boomeranged against her skull as if he had shouted them.

Another moan escaped her and a smile curved that sinful mouth.

Thick wet hair fell onto his forehead. His freshly shaved

jaw glinted, and he smelled clean and nice and as sinful as the red-velvet cake she had devoured last night.

Bastardo, she mouthed the word that she had heard Alessandra use.

His gorgeous green eyes glittered with humor, his smile so beautiful that her chest hurt.

"Go away," she said, hiding her face in the pillow, super-aware of her messy hair, parched mouth and her old Columbia T-shirt that constituted her nightwear.

"Take this," he said, opening his palm to a white pill—her migraine medication—and a glass of water in the other hand.

Too far gone with the ache in her head to even offer a token protest, Clio grabbed the glass and ingested the pill. She lay back down gingerly, any sudden movement piercing her head.

His handsome face filling her vision, Stefan straightened the cotton duvet around her and tucked it to her chin. Tapped her nose with his finger, and pushed her hair back from her temples. "Sleep, *cara*," he whispered.

Sleep and exhaustion hit her in waves and Clio decided the concern she had heard in his voice had to be a side effect of her medication.

The next morning, Stefan awoke in his bed with the smell of coffee teasing him awake. It took him a few seconds to figure out why he had a feeling that he had missed something. He looked at the alarm clock on the nightstand, which said eight in the morning. The red digits burned his brain.

He hadn't checked on Clio in a few hours.

Pushing back the covers, he leaped from the bed and walked through the corridor to her bedroom.

He came to a halt as he found it empty with the bed neatly made up.

The scent of gardenias clung to the air and before he knew it, his lungs were filled with it. Running a hand through his hair, he leaned against the entrance, a wisp of something keeping him in the room.

A hairbrush lay on the dresser opposite the bed, and a pair of jeans and a silk top neatly folded on the bed.

A strange quiver gripped his abdomen to see the bed empty of her tall, athletic form after seeing her there all day yesterday. She had refused to even eat anything, only asking for water again and again. Silently bearing it as if it were her punishment. Looking at him with eyes wide with shock as he checked on her every couple of hours.

Why are you checking on me? she had asked once, her eyes drugged with sleep.

Did she think him so heartless that she was shocked at such a small act of concern? Had he given her a reason to think differently? Why did he care?

Irritated at how scattered his thoughts were, he walked back to the kitchen, following the smell of coffee.

He came to an abrupt halt at the unusual scene in front of him.

Clio stood at the counter, her back to him, unpacking breakfast, he assumed, from the mouthwatering smell.

She was dressed in dark blue jeans that hugged her long legs from ankles to her trim waist and a sleeveless white silk shirt that showed off her tanned arms.

Her hair fell straight to her waist, a river of ambers and reds, glinting where sunlight struck it.

He watched in rising fascination as she slid the lid off one plastic box, grabbed a fork and popped a piece into her mouth.

Pancakes and maple syrup, mouthwatering bacon and coffee—his favorite meal from back when they had been at university. They had all teased him because he would eat it for breakfast, lunch and dinner.

Her face turned toward the French doors, she closed her eyes and let out a long moan as she chewed. A drop of syrup stuck to the side of her mouth and she licked it off with another satisfied little groan. Color suffused her cheeks as she repeated the ritual.

Bemused and turned on, Stefan watched as the pleasure she wrought from the little ritual rendered him stupefied.

The next time she picked up another piece with her fork, it took everything he possessed to not join her and direct her fork to his mouth. Or not to taste the syrup on her lips.

"The suite comes with a butler on call twenty-four hours, Clio," he said, pushing off the wall and walking into the kitchen. "You don't have to arrange our meals, *bella*."

Her fork clanged on the counter, the tinkering sound of it filling the silence.

She turned and watched him with those big eyes, color climbing up her neck.

The silk blouse was so sheer that he could see the outline of her bra, and the dip of her waist. It was so strange how so many small things about her he observed, his fascination arising from the most mundane of moments.

Like the delicate turn of her wrist and the blue veins there, like the crooked slant of her nose, the way she grabbed her hair away from her face with both hands and roughly pulled it back thrusting her breasts up...

Dannazione, the woman was lethal in how quickly she made him think of sex and skin.

Shrugging, she stepped back as he advanced. "I actually wanted to cook breakfast as a thank-you," she muttered. "But this state-of-the-art kitchen doesn't even have sugar and milk. So I walked a bit and grabbed breakfast."

"A thank-you? Why?"

Her expression was straightforward, her shrug a bit too casual. "For looking after me yesterday."

"Do they always last that long?" he said, thinking of how she had held her head. For a couple of hours, he hadn't left her side, a tenderness he had forgotten he had possessed keeping him there instead of ordering the staff to help.

It had been a long time since he had done something so

simple and satisfying as looking after someone. He used to do it all the time.

Another of his innate traits that he had buried deep.

"Kind of, yeah." Another shrug. "This whole week has been very stressful and then I didn't eat anything the whole day of the wedding and then guzzled down that champagne, so it was kind of like inviting the demons to play inside my skull."

"Why was it stressful? Didn't the wedding planner take care of everything?" he said, covering the distance between them.

The closer he moved to her, the heavier his blood flew in his veins. Just the scent of her soap and skin…it set up an instant reaction in him.

Blinking rapidly, she clutched the counter behind her. Which stiffened her posture and thrust her small breasts up.

"You're joking, right?"

"Why were you stressed, *bella*?"

"Because I was getting married under the strangest conditions that I ever dreamed of and the beast I was marrying thought I had trapped him into it," she said, thunder filling her voice.

He grinned. "The beast?"

"Yes. Anyway, I know that our contract doesn't stipulate looking after each other in case of migraines brought on by stupid decisions and showing concern toward each other, so I'm really grateful to you for—"

"Shut up, Clio," he said, staggered at how easily she had him swinging from mood to mood, like a damn monkey being operated by a switch.

Just fifteen minutes into the day, he had felt a strange warmth in his gut at the way she occupied every inch of the suite that had always been free of feminine intrusion, had given him unrivaled morning wood just by standing in his kitchen and now he was annoyed as hell.

At her and at himself.

All he wanted to do right now was tear up the bloody contract, pick her up, carry her to his bedroom, and peel that denim off of her slowly, inch by inch until he could touch her all over.

"Is the migraine gone now?"

"Yes, thank you," she said primly.

Was it his arrogance that rankled at being dismissed so well? Or was it the allure of a woman who didn't immediately fall for him?

Chewing on that errant thought, he picked up one of the coffee cups and took a sip.

The bitter brew on his tongue instantly reminded him of his home, a home he hadn't visited in so long. "You found a Sicilian blend in Manhattan?" he said, surprised.

A flush claimed her cheeks at his pointed question. "I know a Sicilian coffee stand. I go there every once in a while."

"My favorite breakfast *and* coffee. *Grazie*, Clio." Leaning next to her, he tried to corral the various emotions exploding inside. Clearing his throat, he offered her an awkward smile. "Take the day easy. Go to the spa or if you want, I can have the pilot take you to…"

Her face fell. "I have no other machinations behind bringing breakfast for you except to say thank-you, Stefan."

Beneath the caustic tone there was a thread of hurt that struck a chord in him.

Should he be so satisfied that she cared what he thought?

Even as he had stood under the icy jet of his shower on his wedding night, his shredded control an astounding concept in itself, there had been a strange exultation in knowing that he had been the reason she had drunk.

A sadistic streak that he now possessed apparently, in addition to being a mistrusting asshole.

Dio, the woman was turning him inside out.

"I was just surprised, Clio."

"Because I brought you breakfast? Is that really such a

hard thing to grasp that I would want to do something so mundane for you? Are you going to weigh and give a price to every little exchange between us as long as we are stuck with each other?"

Stuck with each other?

That very phrase riled him up to no end.

He had moved so close to her that he could see the green of her eyes darken, could see the pulse in her neck flutter unevenly, could hear the way her breath fell short. "*Dio, bella.* Shut up or I swear—"

"Or what? Will you add another clause to the contract that I can't speak unless you give me permission—"

Grabbing her slender shoulders, Stefan slammed her to him and kissed her. It was the best thing to start the morning with.

With a gasp, she fell against him, anchoring her hands on his chest.

Shaping her head with his fingers, Stefan slanted her mouth and nibbled at it, his desire slowly spiraling out of control.

She tasted of syrup and coffee, sweet and bitter, like fresh desire and old memories all blended together to drive him to distraction. The scent of gardenias entered his bloodstream and teased his senses.

He groaned as she sank her fingers into his hair. Turned into stone as she sank those teeth into his lower lip.

If only he could finish what they started in the kitchen...

He couldn't think of one reason why he couldn't take his wife to bed. Or why kissing her first thing in the morning, in a domestic setting that should have given him hives, felt so natural.

If they continued this way—kissing and nibbling and pressed flush against each other—it wouldn't be long before he had her trapped beneath him and thrusting into her wet heat on that huge bed in his room.

The thought, instead of scaring her to her senses, painted such a vivid, erotic picture that Clio whimpered against Stefan's mouth.

The hands shaping her hips and her bottom with a possessive grip instantly relented, a breath of air blowing over her tingling lips. "*Merda*, Clio. What am I going to do with you?" his ragged whisper snagged onto her senses. "We should have included a clause for this, *bella*."

Somehow, Clio found the sheerest thread of self-preservation and hid her face in his shoulder. His skin was like heated velvet—the muscles beneath tensing.

It had been a flippant thing for her to think the thought about including sex in their contract. But to hear him actually say it, to see that he couldn't think of anything between them as anything but a transaction, it punched her in the gut like a blow she hadn't seen coming.

Did he really think no more of her than any other woman? And if he did, why did she care?

Before he could enslave her with his mouth again, she moved away around the breakfast bar and leaned against the wall.

Her legs trembled, her breath felt as if it would never be normal again, but she had finally put distance between them. And judging by how his eyes glittered, it was no small feat.

"Clio—"

She pushed away the need in her to one corner, the cascading hurt to another.

"I know that the media focus is going to be on us for a little longer, but I still would like to be more than your arm candy and apparently, 'the recipient of scorn and envy of a number of your ex-girlfriends'," she said quoting from one article she had read today.

All she had done was scan the internet for world news as was her habit with coffee. Instead, she had opened the

Pandora's box of Stefan Bianco's exes and their reaction about his wedding.

It was a long list comprising models, actresses and singers that even a pretend wife could get insecure about.

He frowned, looking at her as though she had sprouted another head. *"Mi scusi?"*

It seemed walking away from his embrace cost her every brain cell she possessed. The man kissed like he did everything—with absolute dedication. Her lips still tingled, her breasts felt heavy and her entire body was one pealing mass of sensation.

Marshaling her thoughts, she began again. "I'm beginning Phase One of my reincarnation, beginning a life that's not defined by whose wife or fiancée I am. I have received a couple of callbacks on some jobs I applied to. Hopefully…"

He started shaking his head and her words trailed off. "Not necessary, I—"

"If you make one comment about me *mooching* off of you—"

Thunder danced in his eyes. "Keep that delectable mouth closed, *cara*, or I know of a very enjoyable way now to do it for you. Christian told me just last week that the charity the four of us runs needs a manager. I think you'd be a good fit for it."

Clio blinked and stared. "Are you serious?"

"Dio, bella! Why are you so doubtful about your own abilities? Where is the woman who thought everything in life was a challenge she had to rise to?"

Clio flinched. More at the fact that she had no answer rather than from his tone.

He clasped her cheeks and lifted her chin. His gaze was awash in tenderness. The unexpected gentling of his mouth mocked her doubts. "Yes, I'm serious. I would never tease you about this, Clio.

"Instead of turning your back on all those connections your name brings, instead of turning away from the powerful friends you have, instead of stubbornly refusing your new status as my wife, use them, *bella*.

"Use them to further your career, use them to help someone who's never had the advantages we had, use them to make whatever you want of yourself, Clio.

"You've already conquered the hardest obstacle by staying the course on what we started, by showing Jackson what you're made of."

"But I swore to make something of myself, Stefan. If I—"

"Nothing will come of all the resources and connections of your family and background if you aren't smart enough to channel them properly, Clio."

A lightness filling her, Clio wrapped her arms around her waist. She wanted to hug him so bad. But he wouldn't like it.

"That is, after and *if* you ever find something on Jackson."

"I will," Clio said with utter confidence. "It's just a matter of time."

"Then make that time now, Clio. As long as we carry on this pretense, you already have a full-time job of being my adoring wife."

"*Believe me*, it's not easy to remember the adoring part," she quipped.

With a deft aim, he threw a plastic spoon at her.

The way his eyes lit up, he reminded her of when he had been so carefree and affectionate and open. The memory that smile brought was so strong that she stared at him greedily.

"My board members and their wives are dying to meet you. And my assistant tells me we've been invited to several dinners and charity galas, in and out of New York."

"I should probably charge you for making me into a glorified escort."

"I think escorts provide other services, *bella*." He sent her such a scorching look that Clio should have combusted on the spot. "Are you offering?"

"Do you want to start our fairy-tale marriage with domestic assault, Bianco?"

He grinned and it was like her own personal sun had dawned in the living room, filling her with his warmth inside out. "No, Mrs. Bianco," he countered smoothly. "I'd like to start it with a kiss from my wife."

Robbed of speech, Clio stared back. It shouldn't bother her. It was just a technicality. He was teasing her.

Still, the words clung to her like a physical brand on her skin.

Apparently satisfied that he had shocked her, he forked a piece of pancake into his mouth. The usually scornful curve of his mouth relaxed with a sigh.

"It's not my fault that they all want to meet you. Apparently, you're an asset any sensible man would be lucky to have."

"Of course. Let's not forget how valuable my blue blood and where I come from are. Because there couldn't be any other reason in the world that a man would want me, right?"

"Do not put words in my mouth, *bella*. But I will tell you this because you seem to be forgetting it. It took guts to tie yourself to me, Clio. If you didn't know it before, you know it now, *si*? I will give you nothing but what you have rightfully earned from me.

"Yet you didn't back off. It took guts to start on the path to reclaim yourself. It took guts to take a stand on what matters to you when Jackson used those filthy words for you.

"You're far stronger than you give yourself credit for. Now find something on Jackson during the day while you dazzle the world as my wife at night."

Clio stared at his back, his words ringing in her ears.

He was right. That decision had entirely been hers. But only two days in, she wondered if it was more dangerous than courageous.

Dazzle the world was what they did and they did it so well that even Clio couldn't tell where the pretense ended and where reality began.

Charity galas and dinners with influential, powerful men from all over the world, sometimes in New York, once in Hong Kong and once in London—from visiting art galleries to the charity-sponsored schools and shelters all over the world.

And everywhere they went—big or small—the media followed them.

In just a couple of weeks, Clio and Stefan had been almost around the world aboard his private jet and had become the media's favorite couple to talk about.

Frustrated more than once about hitting a wall with Jackson's financials, Clio had taken to alternately learning as much as she could about the charity that Rocco, Christian, Stefan and Zayed had set up to help underprivileged kids in so many cities complete degrees through scholarships and find jobs.

The range and scope of the charity stole her breath. It made her immensely proud to learn of the continuing resources and time all four of them poured into it and excited her beyond limit that she could be a part of something so fulfilling.

And wherever Stefan and she landed after their marriage, she wanted to be a part of it for the rest of her life, could see herself carve a path through it.

In a weird twist of fate, she was enjoying the pretend life with Stefan more than she had enjoyed her real one with Jackson for three years, even though it was essentially the same kind of life—jet-setting, networking, showing off, making and breaking deals over dinner and drinks.

The man at the center of it, however, made all the difference.

Being around Stefan was like being caught in the orbit of a star—invigorating and exciting. And it made her never want to leave. Everywhere she went, she saw acquaintances—some she had known through Jackson—but it seemed like a foregone conclusion that, of course,

Stefan was the victor in some fight against Jackson, and she the spoils.

She knew she shouldn't feel pleasure at that so much, but as Stefan had said, Clio was going to take every small victory. Because the one time they had run into Jackson, he hadn't dared meet her eyes, much less utter a word.

Only the price she paid for that felt increasingly high.

The most luxurious and spacious suite in one of the finest hotels in New York wasn't big enough for the both of them.

She felt Stefan's restlessness at being caged in the suite like a physical force, sensed a loneliness that had hardened into a shell around his emotions.

The only time there were flashes of the old Stefan was when one of his three friends was present. It was the only time she saw genuine laughter in his face.

And the more she saw of this new Stefan, the more she wanted to shatter that shell.

Despite knowing that it was the last thing she should be doing, she couldn't stop from trying. She had already contacted his parents, was counting the minutes to when they would arrive in New York.

Was desperately praying that he wouldn't throw her out of that suite the moment he saw them.

"Your wife is the most beautiful creature I have ever seen," his fifty-seven-year-old accounts manager gushed and Stefan barely stifled the urge to punch the man's ruddy face. The old lech had already pawed at Clio when Stefan had introduced her.

Smiling at him, which took quite a considerable effect, he turned away from the man, leaving him midsentence.

"Ready to go home?" he whispered, reaching Clio.

Flinching at the palm resting against her lower back, Clio covered up the wariness in her eyes.

Before she could reply, Stefan's cell buzzed and he checked the identity of the caller.

It was the hospital where his assistant, Marco, was still struggling for his life. His gaze fell on Jackson in the crowd just as he switched his phone on.

Two minutes into the conversation, grief knocked the breath out of his throat. Turned his gut into an aching chasm.

Not trusting his temper, he marched into the balcony and pushed his fist into the wall. Even the pain that radiated from his knuckles and up his arm was not enough to blunt the pain of losing Marco.

"Stefan?"

He heard more than saw Clio's hurried steps in the darkness, felt her search for his hand. Distress filled her gaze as she pulled his arm to better see his knuckles.

Her gasp resonated in the lush night. "I have a first-aid kit in the car. Let's go." He had a feeling she was barely keeping the tears away.

"No," Stefan roared, pulling his hand away from her. He had no idea what he would say or do to her. "Leave, Clio. Instruct the chauffeur to drive you home."

The stubborn woman stayed right where she was, a resolute tint to her chin. "I'm not going anywhere. Not until you tell me why you rammed your fist into the wall like a—" a catch in her throat "—Stefan, please. Tell me what's going on."

"My executive assistant, a man who's been there with me for ten years, through every up and down, he was swindled by Jackson."

He saw her disbelief in her stunned look. "This man… he was not just an employee?"

Somehow, she had reached the crux of the matter. "No. Marco…he started out with me when I began investing in real estate. He was so loyal and caring that he became important to me, despite the bastard I became. Strange, huh?"

A small smile curved her mouth. "Not really. How much can you deny your own nature, Stefan?" She looked away for a second. "What happened to Marco?"

"He tried to kill himself and was hospitalized. Today, he died, leaving his little girl without a father. A little girl, *bella*...and that scum is still free to enjoy his caviar out there."

Instantly, she threw her arms around him. But Stefan saw how pale she had turned. Saw the flash of guilt in her eyes as if she was responsible for Jackson's actions. Which was why he hadn't told her so far.

She had enough burden of her own to carry.

"I'm so sorry, Stefan. I...don't know what to say."

Untangling himself from her, Stefan looked away. "He did the same to me years ago, Clio.

"It was a year after Serena left. I had struck gold with a few investment ventures and I realized the luxury real estate market was huge and I wanted a big chunk of it.

"I did extensive research and acquired stock in a small trading company. For months, I slogged round the clock, put everything I had into this one venture.

"In just a matter of minutes, the stock I purchased crashed, all the money I invested in it went down the drain. And I was back at square one.

"It was the lowest point of my life. I had lost everything after Serena left, and to be knocked back like that...it made me question everything.

"If it wasn't for Rocco and Christian and Zayed anchoring me, if it wasn't for the fact that my father had always taught me to stand up after one of life's knocks, that would have been me."

"I'm so sorry for your friend, Stefan. But that would never be you. God, I can't even bear the thought."

"I have to stop him, Clio."

Nodding, she wiped her cheeks roughly. "We will, Stefan. I promise."

Just as his arms relaxed around her, just as he found the knot in his gut loosening, she stepped away from him. "I'll...I will leave you alone. See you later."

"Running away again, *bella*?" he asked with a mocking smile. "For days now, you have avoided meeting my gaze. You touch me, you smile at me, you kiss me when we are in public and the moment it's just us, you…can't wait to run away. How long are we going to continue like this, Clio?"

Her steps faltered and she looked around.

"I won't let you turn sex into a transaction, Stefan. I won't join the leagues of women who have slid into this slot you have for them. And you and me…"

"What about you and me, *cara*?"

"I let one man lock me in a relationship for everything but the right reason. Wanting you, being near you, not touching you, it's a lesson in itself," she said, shocking him with her honesty.

Her gaze glittered with a power he hadn't seen. The way she looked at him—all consuming and without hiding anything—knocked his breath again and in a completely different way. A wave of desire, laced with something else, buckled him.

"But I can't give in, Stefan. I can't just have sex with you and pretend like nothing has changed between us."

Stefan watched in rising fascination and frustration as she walked away without looking back.

Something had changed in her, and something had changed between them.

He didn't know what. Only that he couldn't hide from the truth she had so neatly pointed out.

Turning away, he stared into the dark night. He would never be able to reduce Clio into another nameless woman that satisfied his body.

He hadn't even told the other three how defeated he had felt when he had lost what he had made because of Jackson. How close he had come to giving up and going home in shame to his parents.

Clio made it so easy to depend on her, to confide in her. Even her censure somehow changed him.

He was so desperate to touch her, to brand her, to claim her as his in the most intimate way possible. He couldn't breathe in that cage without seeing her stamp everywhere.

To tangle with his wife would mean relearning himself because Clio wouldn't leave him untouched. And that was a risk he couldn't take.

CHAPTER TEN

THREE WEEKS AFTER their wedding, Stefan had the usual early-morning online meeting with most of his executives around the world. The scent of freshly brewed coffee, which Clio religiously picked up, dragged him into the kitchen as it did every day.

He poured himself a cup, took a sip and watched Clio at the dining table, poring over a bunch of documents and making notes.

A frown tied her brow, her face was rapt, reminding him of the time they had crammed for an exam together years ago.

Suddenly, he felt a burst of warmth in his chest at the sight of her, an almost forgotten sensation.

It had become a ritual—one among numerous others that they had fallen into when they returned to New York between trips around the world.

Sharing a cup of coffee, looking through Jackson's financials, discussing new initiatives for the charity, and the best of them all for him personally—rediscovering all the little offbeat eateries in different corners of New York they had all used to favor back when they had been at university.

He frowned, suddenly seeing the pattern, the determination with which Clio had dragged him against his will the first couple of times. As if she wanted to erase all the bitterness of his love affair with Serena, the bitterness he had let corrupt his memories of New York and the happy years he had spent here, the aversion he had developed to settling down in one place or making meaningful connections with anyone.

As if she wanted to remind him of his true nature, of the parts of himself he had destroyed to move on in life.

That he hadn't recognized her intentions until now showed how deep he was into their farce of a relationship.

He was about to interrupt her when he heard the elevator doors open with a swish at the entrance to the suite, followed by familiar voices. Clio instantly went still, the knuckles of the fingers clutching the pink ballpoint pen becoming white.

Feeling an uncomfortable knot in his gut, Stefan made his way through the corridor into the lounge and stared wordlessly.

Wearing a beaming smile, his mother practically ran toward him. Threw her petite form into his arms, uncaring whether he caught her or not.

As it had been for a decade, shame sideswiped Stefan, robbing his ability to speak.

His father, tall and broad like Stefan, was more remote, watching him silently.

He hadn't seen his father in almost a decade and his mother only a couple of years ago when she had traveled to Villa Mondelli, his friend Rocco's house in Milan, to see Stefan.

Tears flowing over her cheeks, his mother launched into a rapid dialogue just as Clio arrived from the lounge.

His father, a traditional and usually reticent man, moved toward Clio and grasped her hand in his. Studied her with a mixture of curiosity and warmth. "You're as beautiful as you are generous, *bella*."

The familiarity his father showed Clio stunned Stefan, rendering him mute.

Her face suffused with warmth, Clio was shaking her

head. Her hands trembled, her gaze resolutely turned away from Stefan. "It's nothing, Mr. Bianco. I was just doing my duty."

Duty?

"Thank you for inviting us to your home, Clio," his mother said in heavily accented English from the circle of his arms.

"You have to excuse us, it's not a proper home," replied Clio, looking anywhere but at him.

"But home is where your heart is, *sì*?" his mother said, fresh tears filling her eyes again.

His head swapped between Clio and his parents as if he was at a tennis match, shock literally robbing him of coherent speech.

A decade ago, he had tried to convince his parents of the same thing—that he had fallen in love with Serena and that he wanted to stay back in New York.

They had been so against it that they had threatened to cut him off and he, so naive, so desperate to be in love, had told them he was fine with that.

But Serena had wanted nothing to do with him without his parents' fortune.

"We would have loved to come for the wedding but it was not to be," his mother piped up again, glossing over the fact that he had not invited them.

Except for phone calls, he hadn't been able to even meet his father in the eye.

"He's fortunate, to have such a loving wife." This was said to his father.

"Please, come in," Clio finally said, her voice hoarse. "Did you have a safe flight?"

"Yes," his mother replied. "Aboard Stefano's luxury jet means we don't need anything."

Shock shuddering through him, he grasped Clio's wrist and tugged her toward him.

"I have to call the butler and have some food arranged for them," she said, tugging her hand back.

"How long will you run, *bella*?" he whispered before his mother commanded his attention again.

He felt the shiver that racked through her slender frame. The little minx had arranged everything, even commanded his pilot without his knowledge.

All Stefan wanted to do right then was to excuse himself from his parents, drag his wife inside and demand an explanation. Or maybe ravish her first and demand explanations later.

Because his desire for his alluring wife seemed to be the only constant thing in his life these days.

After a dinner of expertly prepared *pasta con le sarde* and *impanata di pesce spada*, swordfish pie, his favorite, which Clio had requested the butler learn and cook for dinner, and lots of colorful conversation—which had been mainly his mother's curious questions about how they had fallen in love, the wedding and when they were planning *bambini*, and Clio's deftly spun tales for answers—the silence in the cavernous lounge jarred on Stefan's nerves.

Every time he had visited New York over the past decade, he had stayed in the same suite at the Chatsfield. Now it was as if a volcano had erupted all over his life and there was no way he could contain the damage being done, couldn't turn it back into the safe, sterile place it had been just a month ago.

His father's hand on his shoulder prodded him out of his thoughts. "You're angry with your wife for inviting us."

Stefan shook his head in automatic denial before he caught a flicker of understanding in his father's eyes. His father had never lied to him, had never done anything but love Stefan.

"You know we would have welcomed you back all these years." Not even a hint of hesitation could be heard in his father's voice. "Why have you not returned to Palermo even once? Why have you stayed at a distance, Stefano?"

The unhidden ache in the question came at Stefan like a sharp punch, ripping through the shell he had built around himself.

Had he known, somewhere, that his father, of all the people in the world, could sense how changed he was from the inside? Had he been afraid that his father could see that there was nothing good left in his son after what Serena had done?

"Was it to punish us for threatening to cut you off all those years ago? Have you become such a cruel man, then?"

"No," the denial waved out of him. His father would accept nothing but truth. For the first time in years, Stefan looked inward.

"What kind of a man keeps away from a mother who dreams of holding her son in her arms again?"

To hear that painful resignation in his father's voice was Stefan's undoing. Words rushed out of him on a wave of guilt and shame and so much more that he had locked up for so many years. "Serena...she took my very belief in myself when she left me. In just one day, I became a stranger to myself. I didn't know myself and I could not face you as a failure. I...was not worthy of you and Mamma after choosing such a woman over you. How could I face you after I had so selfishly shattered all your dreams?"

Understanding dawned in his father's gaze. "And all these years? After you built your empire, after you proved to yourself that you could succeed?"

Stefan shook his head, a lump in his throat. He had no answer for his father.

"Has she taken everything that was good and kind about you, too?"

She hadn't. He'd given it all up willingly. He hadn't wanted anything that could have made him vulnerable like that again. Along with his naïveté, he had also given up his heart.

After everything he had done to wipe her from his life, he had still let her win.

The realization clawed in his gut. He had held on to her rejection, had held on to the poison she had spewed into his life for so long.

Had let her corrupt everything that had been good and pure in his life even though he had been determined to prove her wrong.

He had denied himself and his parents the joy of seeing each other.

Clutching his father's hands, Stefan spoke. "I have let my shame and guilt stop me from visiting you these years…I wanted to prove myself worthy of you again and in the process, I forgot what you taught me…I forgot everything that is important in life."

Nodding, his father patted his back. "Your mother, she does not see things. But I would have been immensely sad to see my son become like this…if it were not for your Clio, Stefano. To see you with a woman like that, it makes my heart easy."

What would his father say if he knew it was nothing but a farce? What was stopping him from making the woman he wanted with an insane hunger his own? The thought erupted on the heels of the first one.

The elevator swished open and his parents left, beaming smiles on their faces.

Instantly, Clio excused herself and Stefan let her run away for now.

The way he felt right now, it was better she stayed away until he was more in control of himself and his emotions.

All day, his parents had commented on how well Clio and he suited each other, had been ecstatic at every small exchange between them.

Hadn't been able to keep their eyes off Clio as they went sightseeing into the city. Had demanded Clio and Stefan show them the Columbia University campus, all the spots that the media had dug up and built their love story around.

His mother had pronounced proudly that Stefan and Clio's marriage would last longer than her own marriage of forty years, that they would continue the tradition of a long, happily married life as the Biancos always did.

His mother's comment opened up a wound he had resolutely patched up long ago, an ache that could consume him if he let it.

Because he could never trust another woman, never reach for that happiness ever again.

And try as he did to ruthlessly remove that small part of him that wanted a fantasy to come true, Clio kept igniting it, kept pushing him toward the path where nothing but pain awaited him.

Even the happiness he had spied in his parents' eyes demanded a high price of him.

Clio had unnecessarily brought his parents into their pretense, cruelly shown him glimpses of a future that could never be his.

And that she made him want it again was unbearable.

Closing the door behind her, Clio entered her bedroom.

Anticipated fear churned through her gut. Her fingers slipping on the keys of her laptop, she typed in her password and looked up her bank account.

Sweat running down her back, she pulled a sheaf of papers she had left on her nightstand.

Jackson's financials...

Her gut folded in on itself as she finally pinpointed the discrepancy she had been trying to find, and the tremendous truth of her financial affairs rammed home.

Jackson had robbed her of every last penny, literally...

This was proof enough for the Securities and Exchange Commission to investigate Jackson. Proof enough to pull everything on him...

Her legs gave out under her and she sagged to the cushioned chair in front of the vanity, her breaths rushing on top of each other. Why it had finally come to her today, at this moment after weeks of trying, she had no idea.

Today when she had seen a real smile curve Stefan's mouth, today when she had seen the flash of pure joy in his eyes...

Today when it seemed like she had made a difference in his life.

This was all Stefan needed from her, why he had agreed to her deal, why he had married her... And once he had it...

Clutching the chocolate-and-gold veneer of the table, she leaned her forehead to it, trying to lock the tears in her throat.

The whole day had been the upward ride of a roller coaster—going higher and higher on the tale she had spun about Stefan and her, the pressure building. Until this moment when she was crashing down.

Rosa Bianco looking fondly at Stefan and her, and weaving dreams for their future life, had been the same as looking at a reality that was even better than the one she had wanted for so long, one that she was living every day, but was still out of her grasp.

Pretending to be the woman Stefan adored was like a drug she never wanted to quit, that could distort her reality and delude her. Still, she didn't want to give him the proof yet.

"You shouldn't have interfered, Clio."

Stefan's voice behind her simmered with anger and emotion.

But she had done what she had intended. She had finally gotten past that shell of his.

She had to face the music now, but for his sake, she would do the same again.

"Turn around and face me. There's nowhere to run tonight."

Warning vibrated in his tone, along with arrogance. And instead of scaring her, it goaded Clio. Someone had to show Stefan what he had become, had to remind him what he used to be.

Still seated, she turned around to face him.

"I didn't interfere, Stefan. Nor do I have any intention of running away."

"No? Because I have a feeling you're taking our vows literally, *bella*. Everything that you have been doing these past two weeks, everything you think I need, you can stop it. You have no *duty* toward me, Clio."

He spat the word as if it was a curse, as if he couldn't stand the idea of her doing anything in the name of it. Her muscles quivering, Clio frowned.

It was as if there were two parts of her within—one wanted to back down, apologize before the tension in the room exploded, one wanted to challenge him about her place in his life, wanted to hurt him as he did her.

For what else was the tightness in her chest?

Uncoiling from the chair, she straightened her spine. "Maybe I have no duty toward you as a wife, Stefan. God knows nothing but that bloody contract defines that between us. But what about as a friend who wants to do something for you, who wants to see you smile again?"

He prowled into the room and into her space. Long fingers wrapped around her nape possessively. "I have three friends—ones who don't interfere in my personal life. I don't need another friend."

"So everything you have done for me then, what—?"

"That's a different matter."

Clio half snorted, half laughed, her temper getting the better of her again. "Can you hear yourself? You gave me the right to interfere in your life when you interfered in mine. Goose and gander, Stefan."

"You've lost me again. But do not repeat this, Clio. Or I

have to forget my own rules, too, and they are already very muddy right now."

"They were over the moon to see you, Stefan. And I know that it meant something to you, too."

Scorn filled his gaze. "Then why didn't you invite yours, *bella*?"

Burying the hurt that instantly swarmed to the surface, Clio shrugged. "I did invite them. I thought a farce it might be, but this is the only wedding I'll have. My mother said, *I hope you fare better with him than you did with the American.* They have no interest in my life, Stefan. Not after I walked away from the one they decided on for me.

"But having seen your parents today, I don't regret what I did. They adore you, Stefan. To not invite them to the wedding…"

His mouth tightened.

"To reject something so good and pure, this is not you."

"I doubted your reasons for wanting to marry me. I made you sign a filthy contract. Have you still not learnt who I am now, Clio?

"The naive, romantic Stefan you remember is long dead. In its place, there's only poison, Clio, poison that will destroy you. I'm warning you, *bella*…leave me alone."

His jaw concrete, he growled a sound of such utter pain that her gut twisted.

"Do you realize what you've done by involving my parents in this? They think the sun rises with you now. What happens when this is all over? How will I face them with another failure in hand? How will I explain your absence in my life, *bella*?"

That he still thought in such rigid terms should have brought Clio down with a thud. That he didn't even indulge the thought of some kind of future together, when it was a path she kept getting pulled into, should have stopped her.

"I don't know how you will. We came together to ruin Jackson. Can your parents' happiness not be the one good thing that comes out of this, Stefan? Does our marriage have to leave only destruction in its wake?"

Because that's how it felt right now.

Stefan had already helped her gain her self-respect, her strength, back but he was also going to steal a part of her. The damage, it seemed, was already done.

How could she stay away from him when he was so gorgeous and kind and honorable? When her heart gave a little leap when she saw him every morning? When her throat ached at the way he shut his emotions off as if he couldn't bear them?

She walked over to him and wrapped her arms around his unforgiving form, hid her face in his shoulder. She felt as if she was standing on the precipice of a cliff, wanted to give in and jump so much that she was feverish from it.

He tensed instantly, his grip on her arms bruising, poised to push her away.

Slowly, Clio settled into his embrace, the hard contours and sharp angles of his body pressing and pushing her own soft curves, until they fit perfectly. Heat and hardness—his maleness made her feel so secure, and wanted.

His arms came around her finally, and her breath left her in a long whoosh. His hands moved and roamed over her back, as though he was testing their fit, too, and then came to rest around her waist. Left scorching heat on her bare flesh between her top and jeans.

Warm air from his exhale coated her skin. "Thank you for bringing them here. For bringing such wonderful smiles to their faces."

Warmth exploded in her chest and she struggled to contain it. Nodding, Clio wrapped herself even tighter around him. "You have to let me in, Stefan. Just a tiny little bit."

"Tiny little bit, *bella*? You're like a stubborn virus." His smile against her temple took the bite out of his words.

She had no name for what was happening. Only that,

after years of unhappiness and misery, she had smiled so much these past few weeks, she was happy with herself.

She felt a sense of power over her own life, over her emotions she hadn't felt in so long. She would tell him about the proof, but for these few minutes, she wanted it to be only about them.

"We have no expectations of each other, which means we won't hurt each other either." His heart thudded under her hands. Out of the mess she had made of her life, it seemed there was still one good thing. "We are safe from each other."

He smiled, baring his teeth like a predator. "Are we, *bella*? Because every minute of every day, I feel like I'm on the edge. You smile at me, you tease me, you rile me, you challenge everything I think of you, of myself, of the world. And now, my dear wife, you're meddling in my life. Safe is the last thing I am with you around."

Bending that arrogant head, he breathed the words into her temple, her scalp prickling at the way his finger tugged her hair.

"And what I do want, *so desperately crave from you*," his free hand moved up her midriff and rested in the valley between her breasts with his hot mouth buried in her neck, "you won't grant me, *bella*." Speech slurring, he licked the fluttering pulse. "It feels like I've waited my entire life to make love to you, Clio."

Her spine melted, liquid fire licking along her nerves. She was sinking in desire and she clutched him with her arms, his body a welcoming cocoon.

"You're seducing me with words, Bianco," she managed huskily with the few brain cells that were still functioning.

"Me seduce you, *bella*?" His solid frame shook with laughter, sending ripples through her. He dug his teeth into the skin at her shoulder and bit.

Wetness drenching her sex, Clio shuddered as pain gave way to pleasure so intense.

With his arm around her, he absorbed the quivers in her body, locking her against him.

"For someone who scowls and argues that I have defined everything between us by that contract, you have me in your thrall, Clio. Quite the power trip for you, no?"

A smile tugged at her mouth and Clio gave in. Desire and joy flooded her, a honeyed combination.

That he didn't resent the desire between them—it was a step forward.

She knew how he wanted to define and restrict their relationship. He was allowed to do anything for her, but she...her every action concerning him, every word to him, he would scrutinize it. Either attach a price tag to it or reject it as unwanted.

But she couldn't not do it, she couldn't stop trying.

Whatever they presented to the world, Clio wanted, *needed* something real between them. And it seemed it could be nothing but this desire, this fire that consumed them.

She reached up within the circle of his arms and vined her arms around his nape. Pressed her mouth to the corner of his and breathed deeply. His skin, rough and stubbly, scratched her soft mouth, heavenly in its contrast. The taste and scent of him exploded on her lips, urging her to press closer and tighter. "I want it clear that this is not a power trip or a transaction or a bloody clause in your contract, Bianco."

His hands kneaded her hips, pulled her closer until his erection, a hard length, pressed boldly against just above her sex. Her mouth dried, her breath lodged in her throat.

"*Sì.*"

"I want it clear that I'm doing this because it's you."

"No gratitude, *bella*. I don't want to be your thank-you f—"

"No," she said, covering his mouth with hers. "It's because you're the most gorgeous man I've ever seen and because…I can't breathe if you stop kissing me."

His eyes glittered. "*Dio, bella.* You'll be the death of me."

Rough fingers kneaded her butt while his tongue licked the pulse at her throat. Sinking her fingers into his hair, Clio tugged hard until he lifted his head and met her gaze, until the vein in his temple throbbed, until the sculpted planes of his face stood out in stark contrast.

"Kiss me, please."

Make me feel like I can do this right. Make me whole again in this, too, she wanted to say, but held back the words, shame and fear locking them deep down.

She kissed his jaw this time. With an urgency and courage she had never known before, she pulled the lapels of his shirt until the buttons popped and flew.

Sank her hands under his shirt. Felt his heated skin and the tensile muscles. Heard the rough exhale fall from his lips. Bent and finally tasted his skin, licked his flat nipple, dragged her teeth over his skin, marking him, tasting him, until his fingers were this short of hurting in her hair, until his hard body was shuddering around her. Until his control was in tatters just as hers was.

Salt and tang and desire, he tasted so good on her lips, and he was all hers.

At least, for tonight.

CHAPTER ELEVEN

SHE LOOKED LIKE a queen, imperial, so poised, and yet she was trembling in his arms. Her pink mouth was already swollen with his kisses, her eyes drugged and hazy.

It was his wildest fantasies come true and it was much better than he had imagined.

Picking her up, Stefan carried her through the lounge.

Her hair flowing behind her, she laughed. "The bed in my room works fine, Stefan."

"*Sì*, it does. But it's not mine, *bella*. I have spent, it seems like countless nights, tossing and turning, and thinking of you on my sheets. Once we're through in my bedroom," he said, "we can go back to your room, Clio. Or that beckoning vanity in the bathroom. Or the chaise longue on the balcony overlooking the glittering skyline of Manhattan. Or the terrace where you can see the sky while I lick my way down your body."

A flush overtaking her, her eyelashes flickering down, she clung to him, trembling.

That she blushed only made his blood heavier in his veins. "*Dio*, Clio. How can you be this sensuality-personified and still blush, *bella*?"

As they stepped over the threshold into his bedroom, he slid her to her feet, her eyes rounded in her oval face.

Her gaze traveled around the room—took in the views of Central Park on one side, over to the king bed on the other side.

Grabbing the remote, Stefan turned on the lights to full. She turned toward him, her neck and cheeks still pink, a sudden shyness in her gaze.

Reaching her, he pulled her to him softly. That Jackson put those shadows in her eyes, his blood boiled just thinking about it.

"Clio, *bella*?"

She swallowed and raised her gaze to him. "Can we turn off the lights, Stefan?"

His first instinct was to refuse, to tell her that he demanded all of her, that she couldn't hide herself from him, that she was his, scars or flaws and all.

He noted the vulnerability in her stance. Suppressed all his macho claims and nodded. Stared at her hungrily until every inch of her was burned in his brain. And turned off the lights.

Cupped her cheeks and brought her mouth to his.

With her expression hidden from him, with her face only visible in strips and flashes of the moonlight, with her curves accessible to him only through touch, every other sense became intense.

The scent of her, the rasp of her breath, the tremble of her chin…he was engulfed by her, ensnared.

He kissed and stroked her lips, tangled with her tongue until the roar of his own blood was the only thing he could hear.

The hot drag of her lips over his, the hesitant slide of her tongue against his, the honeyed taste of hers, it was a feast he couldn't get enough of.

Kissing a woman until now had never been more than a forerunner to release, never more than foreplay. And yet, he could kiss Clio for hours, hear the soft mews and moans that fell from her mouth for days. Could lose himself in her soft mouth for aeons.

He would never have enough of this fantasy-turned-reality that shredded his control. He would never have enough of *her*, something warned him. He would never be satisfied with possessing her, yelled the cavernous chasm inside him.

He could never keep her from pervading his life, his days, his every moment, his every breath.

She was already everywhere, making him ache, making him want, pushing him toward the man he vowed he'd never be again. Shattering through the shell he had grown and reaching the most vulnerable part of him.

Soon, she would know all of him, she would know his darkest fear.

She would know how he had turned against his own nature and buried his heart and his deepest desires so that he could move on in life. She would know how much he envied Rocco for finding the woman who adored him for who he was in Olivia, and Christian for the family he would have with the lovely Alessandra...

How in the process of putting himself together after Serena's betrayal, he'd lost something fundamentally good in himself, how he didn't even know how undeserving and out of control he felt as he had watched Clio struggle with her fears and insecurities and emerge victorious.

How she made him wish he could be that old Stefan again.

But even through the aching vulnerability that he despised so much, he couldn't walk away.

Instead, it fused with desire, pumping powerlessness through him.

Her soft gasp when he dug his teeth into her lip sharply dragged him from the edge of his own desire, remonstrated his lack of control.

He had bedded numerous women over the decade, and yet nothing like this need today had even touched him. He craved so much more with Clio.

Of her scent, of her skin, of her aroused gasps. She was

vined around him, her slender body arching and pressing, as he devoured her mouth again.

One hand sank into her hair to hold her immobile for him, while the other snaked around her hip, pressing her into his erection.

Whatever he did to arouse her, to drive her out of her mind, he was the one who felt owned by her, consumed by his need for her. And it was a feeling he couldn't shrug off.

All he seemed capable of was drowning and that's what he did. But if he was going to sink, she would, too.

His mouth was so hard and perfect over hers. And so desperate and urgent. Her lower lip still stung, radiating waves of pain and pleasure all over, awakening a million nerve cells that had been dormant in her until now.

At least, that's how it felt.

He was hers. Clio couldn't stop the thought from resonating like a drum inside her head.

He was hers like he had never been anyone's, she knew it from the increasingly erotic strokes of his tongue.

His mouth was an erotic lesson, a blast of heat to every inch of her, a fire that spread to every tip.

"*Dio, bella.* I knew not being able to see you would be a punishment. But not in this way," he said angrily.

But Clio didn't care why or how. All she cared was that he sounded on edge. Winding her arms tighter around his nape, she pressed herself closer, tighter, relishing the hard give of his muscles. Rubbed herself against him until her breasts were crushed and her breath a chore.

He growled in response, dug his fingers into her hips in a bruising grip and swept her up into his arms.

Settling her on the high bed, he moved between her legs. Grabbed the edges of her silk blouse and pulled.

The pearl buttons flew in all directions.

The urgency in him, instead of scaring her, filled her with power. That she could send his muscled body to shudder, that she could send him to desperate need, it was a balm over wounds Jackson had inflicted so cruelly.

She looked down the same time as he did.

Her flesh was milky white in the moonlight, her nipples tight points of need against her silky bra.

His pithy curse as he traced a long finger against the seam of her bra was a song to her ears.

But instead of touching her as she ached to be, he pulled her to her knees and unzipped her jeans. Tugged them down past her thighs, and feet. Threw them across the room and settled her on the bed again.

Until she sat in front of him in a thong and bra, her bare legs stretched indecently to make space for his broad frame, exposing the heart of her.

But she sat still, the dark of the night giving her a courage she wouldn't have had if his hungry gaze settled on her. She hated that Jackson was still there in her fears when he shouldn't be, she hated that she had let him break her confidence.

"Stefan?" she called out to him, only now sensing his stillness.

Grasping her ankles, he pushed her onto the bed. And she slid soundlessly on the luxurious goose down sheets.

In the next blink, the lights came on and he leaned over her lower body in a movement of such sheer perfection that Clio forgot the glare of lights.

His gaze swept over her like a white-hot flame, inciting little sparks wherever it touched. With a gasp, she moved to cover her sex but he grabbed her hands, held them over her head, liquid lust and resolve dancing in his green gaze.

"I won't let him take away even a single part of you that should be mine today, *bella*." He sounded ravaged and angry and determined, all at the same time. "I won't let that bastard be a silent specter in this room between us."

Her heart slammed so violently against her rib cage that Clio shivered. That he could read her fears so well made her feel more exposed than her most intimate parts on display for him.

He ran a reverent finger over her rib cage to the hairline over her sex. And Clio caught the moan that wanted to hurtle out. "I can't bear it if you—"

"You're so breathtakingly beautiful, Clio, more so than my imagination could do justice. *Dio*, why would you hide yourself from me? Why would you deny me the pleasure of seeing you when you know how much I want you?"

Clio tucked her face away from his, shameful tears filling hers.

He trailed hot kisses along the seam of her bra, kissed the curve of one breast, and she shifted restlessly. She needed his hands on her breasts, needed to feel his mouth over the tight, aching points.

But, of course, he wouldn't give her what she wanted unless she stripped herself bare of that last layer. Until she was completely exposed to him.

Until she was all his.

His hand caressed the flesh of her hips, tugging her close, until he was leaning over her and she was looking up at him. "Tell me."

"I was not hiding myself. I was hoping to not see your reaction, Stefan."

With a hard grip, he turned her to face him. "Explain."

"No."

"Yes."

Being naked in front of him should have made her awkward. But the maddening circles he drew over her hips, the protective circle of his arms, freed Clio from that last fear. "He…I have been unhappy for a while. With myself, my career and, of course, my relationship with Jackson. I…somehow found myself without friends even. And it affected everything I did. How I dressed, how I ate, how I interacted with others. Even…"

"Sex?" He gritted out the word as though the very thought of Jackson and her set his teeth on edge.

"Yes. It became such a chore that one night he said the Hudson River in winter would be more warm and receptive. After that, I kept finding excuses to not do it. That he cheated on me so blatantly and for so long is unforgivable but I can't help thinking I pushed him to it. That it was something in me.

"I don't want to see the same disappointment in your face, Stefan. If the lights were off, I could still lie to myself about…"

To bare this last fear of hers felt so excruciating that her words died on her lips. Clutching her eyes closed, she waited with her breath hinging unevenly in her throat.

Seconds piled on top of each other but he said nothing.

Until Clio felt his fingers crawl up her thighs, and part the folds of her sex.

Invasive, arousing and utterly addictive, he pressed the bundle of nerves that had been aching for his attention with his thumb. Drew on it in mind-numbing strokes.

Her spine arched, her breath flew out of her in a wave. A lick of heat swept through her as he kissed the sensitive skin of her thigh, as she felt the warmth of his breath.

"You smell so divine, *bella*." In one smooth move, he pushed two fingers inside and Clio gasped at the avalanche of sensation. "And, *dannazione*, you're so wet for me."

Turning toward him, Clio met his gaze, heat pooling under her skin in a rush, blasting through every tip.

Bending over, he tasted her mouth. Palmed the engorged and needy tip of one breast.

Clio moaned into his mouth.

"I was not joking, Clio. I have always wanted you, even back then."

Surprise glinted in her face. "Hitting on every woman you met was your knee-jerk response."

"I have always wanted you. And now, the reality of having you in my bed…you have no idea how crazy you drive me, Clio."

While Clio grappled with that information, he bent his dark head and sucked her nipple.

Raw sensation zigzagging over her, Clio sank her hands into his hair and arched into him, needing more.

With a smile, he continued the rhythmic pull of his mouth, driving her out of her skin, while his other hand delved between her curls down below and started a fire again.

He stroked and palmed her heat while suckling at her nipple. The relentless caresses even as he whispered the wickedest words in her ear started Clio on a chase that knocked the breath out of her lungs.

There was nothing but sensation and pleasure, beating at her from every side. There was nothing but Stefan—his kisses, his touches, his body's warmth and the best of all, his words.

And Clio forgot all her fears, all her doubts as her climax hit her in wave after wave, throwing her out of her body. She felt like she had been shattered and then remade.

Tears seeped out of her eyes.

Feeling his gaze on her, she opened them and saw his raptured look. Gasped when he pulled her onto his lap and took her mouth in a bruising kiss.

But she wanted more, she wanted to be utterly possessed by him.

She ran her hands over his chest, traced the ridges of his ribs, learned his skin to her heart's content. Reveled in his short breaths, the flexing of his muscles to the slightest of her touches.

Reaching down, she unbuckled his belt and pulled it out. Unfastened his trousers and sneaked her hand in.

Felt the already engorged length of him grow harder and longer in her palm.

Rubbed her thighs together as the heat that rushed through her at the rigid weight in her hand.

Coming to a kneeling position, she vined her arms around him, and licked the rim of his ear. "What else did I do in this fantasy?"

His muscled frame racked in her arms, and she felt like the most powerful woman on earth.

"Some other time, *bella*," he whispered back, his abrasive palms roaming restlessly over her back.

"Now, Bianco," she commanded, and bent down to lick his flat nipple.

His hands tightened in her hair, whether to hold her there or push her, she had no idea. Kissing the ropes of muscle that had fascinated her for so many weeks, she looked up and caught the flush in his cheeks.

Saw the truth shining in his hungry gaze.

Grinning, she trailed wet kisses down his rock-hard frame. The muscles tensed harder and harder as she moved downward.

The tip of his erection lay against his taut belly.

Clamping her thighs together at the thrill in her own blood, Clio licked the soft head.

His harsh groan fell on her ears, a thunderous roar that goaded her on.

On the next breath, Clio fisted her hand at the base and took him in her mouth.

Tasted the hard length of him in a long suck that sent little tremors to her own sex. She continued as he shuddered beneath her caresses, as he cursed and groaned.

"Now this feels like quite the power trip, Bianco," she whispered, and before she could breathe again, she was on her stomach on the bed.

"We will see who has the power, *bella*," he threw at her, before he pulled her onto all fours.

On the next breath, he held her hips still, and thrust into her wet heat.

Closing her eyes, she made a ragged sound that ripped from her. His hand snaked out under her, and kneaded a heavy breast as he set a rhythm that left her with no thoughts of power.

Only sensation remained. Only he and she remained, joined together in the most intimate of bonds.

And as he pushed her onto her release and found his own, only pleasure remained.

Not contracts, not shadows of old fears, nothing but the man who was a perfect fit for her. Nothing but the man who had awakened every part of her.

"I found the proof today, Stefan," Clio whispered, as she lay supine in Stefan's arms. Maybe it was the fact that after a long time, she felt completely at peace. That she felt secure about herself, about the direction her life was heading in.

Even if the future was still an enigma.

Maybe it was just the fact that the man who held her to him so tightly with his arms around her, as if he couldn't let go, had made love to her so well that the postcoital haze had lent her false courage.

The thing she knew for sure was that she wanted to tell him. She couldn't remove his pain about losing a friend of so many years, but she could at least give him the satisfaction of bringing Jackson to justice at last.

Stefan stilled behind her. It was so complete that she wondered if he breathed anymore. Suddenly, his arm around her felt like a lead weight.

"I have lost every penny I had." The words rushed out of her haphazardly, the weight of saying them out loud stunning her anew.

"What, *bella*?"

The sheets rustling around her, Clio lifted his arm and turned around. Caught the resigned look in his eyes just as he blinked and chased it away.

With the gears in her head running finally, understanding dawned in her.

She swallowed the knot of hurt in her throat that felt like glass. He had thought she was commenting on the state of her funds, asking for a handout in a roundabout way.

Kicking into a sitting position, he pulled her up, until she was sitting by his side on the enormous bed. When he looked at her again, there was nothing but curiosity. "What are you talking about, Clio? If you need money, all you have to—"

Clio stopped his words with her palm over his mouth, before he could deal her more than a surface scratch. It was his automatic reaction to any question, from any woman regarding money, she pacified herself.

He had made a conscious decision to ask her politely about it instead of seething with distrust and contempt.

It was a step forward in their fragile relationship.

That was the best she was going to get from him.

Pulling her hand into his, he laced their fingers together and kissed the back of her palm. "Clio?"

Shaking her head to chase away her stupid misgivings, Clio offered him a small smile.

"I'm sorry. It hadn't quite sunk in and saying it out loud finally did."

With his finger under her chin, he tilted her face up. "Clio, I want honesty between us, *bella*. Above everything else. That's how this began," his knuckles tapped her chin, "and that's how I would like us to continue."

Her stupid, grasping, desperately greedy mind latched onto the fact that he wanted this, *whatever this was*, to continue.

She was on a slippery slope in this relationship they had now, and yet, she wasn't scared or afraid.

All she cared about right now was that he wanted her, in his life, in whatever capacity it was. Her heart thudded so loud it was a wonder he didn't hear it. "Of course. Do you remember I told all you guys about my aunt Grace once?"

"The one who hated your parents and vice versa?"

Smiling, Clio nodded. "She had always been sweet to me when I was growing up. She died a couple of years after I came to Columbia. I went to her funeral and found out that she had bequeathed me a bit of money. I think it was her way of high-fiving me for walking away from everything that my parents had wanted for me."

Stefan grinned. "Sounds like a sweet lady."

"She was. You should have heard her swearing. She did it like a sailor. Anyway, it took a few years for the legalities to go through and I received the money a year after we graduated. About twenty-five thousand pounds."

Pushing back from her, Stefan stared at her. "But if you had that much cash in hand, why did you have to borrow from Christian? Why not use it to secure your rent or to pay off your school debts?"

"Because my parents knew that Aunt Grace had bequeathed me that money. My mother even commented that for all the claims I had made, I was happily taking handouts. So I locked it up in a secured bond, determined to make it in New York through my way.

"And when I was broke, it was better being obligated to Christian than letting them learn that I needed help."

"You are a stubborn woman, *bella*. Isn't it enough you turned your back on such a prestigious family and started a new life halfway across the world?"

"Why didn't you go back to your parents after Serena left? Why start from scratch, Stefan?"

Thunder dawned in his gaze. "I don't want to talk about her."

"We're talking about what made us who we are today." Kneeling in front of him, she clasped his cheeks when he would have moved away. "We're talking about you and me, no one else."

Tension seethed in his shoulders but Clio held on to him. "Serena walked away from me because I was nothing without my parents' fortune. She made me question my very belief in myself. I was determined to prove her wrong, determined to make the fortune she wanted all on my own. Pride and shame, *bella*, I was drowning in them so much that I hurt my parents for so many years."

The flash of pain that wreathed his features pierced through her. That it could still affect him so much…

"After all these years, do you not still realize it is her loss, Stefan? To walk away from you because your parents disowned you, to leave a man like you behind…"

God, he had loved that undeserving woman so much, with all of his heart. To have a man like Stefan love her unconditionally like that… Clio couldn't imagine what it could even be like. The very thought had such a mesmeric, compelling quality to it that her entire being resonated with it.

She kissed his mouth, heat and tenderness and affection and a hundred other things rushing out of her on a wave she couldn't curtail. "That woman was a first-class moron, if I may say so."

A smile curved his mouth. "Wow… Are you sure you don't need to wash out your mouth?"

"Oh, don't encourage me, Bianco. It could get a lot dirtier, believe me. The reason I liked Aunt Grace so much was because she had no problem cursing in front of kids either."

"I can't wait, *bella*."

Clio laughed against his mouth, a river of joy flooding her.

As if it was as natural as drawing breath, he captured her mouth with his. Molten heat uncoiled in every nerve, every muscle. It was as if her body knew what he could give, and craved it.

Tongues dueling, lips scraping against teeth, in a matter of seconds, they were both breathing hard.

Somehow, Clio had climbed into his lap and was straddling his erection. With a moan, she moved, the crease of her sex rubbing against his, sending erotic tingles through her lower belly.

Cursing, Stefan locked her hips before she could do it again. Color bled into his cheekbones, his nostrils flaring. "As much as I would love nothing but to be inside your wet heat, *bella*, I want to hear your story more."

Sighing dramatically, Clio smiled. "Oh, to be denied sex for a story… Your libido and prowess has been overestimated by the media, Bianco."

He bit her lower lip as punishment and a hundred nerves jangled within Clio. "The sooner you tell me, the sooner you can have me, Mrs. Bianco." His grin was so natural, so filled with that openness he had possessed so long ago that her breath caught in her throat. "Any way you want."

"Fine. But don't forget your promise."

It was the first time he had actually smiled after a conversation about Serena and the poison she had spewed in his life. For that smile, she could give up all the money in the world.

Clio hugged the fact to herself like a proud accomplishment.

"What about the money your aunt Grace bequeathed you, *bella*?"

Knowing that his mood was going to worsen, Clio slipped off him and got to her feet. "I met Jackson a few years later. Until then I put Aunt Grace's money in a CD that I couldn't break for five years. It had matured a year after I met him. And he talked me into investing it in his hedge fund company."

The room went from warm to ice-cold in a matter of seconds.

Uncoiling his huge frame from the bed, Stefan reached her. "And?"

"I have known it for a while at the back of my mind from the bits and pieces I have heard him mutter about over the last year. And I have seen proof of it now. He lost most of the investors' money."

"That's a risk you take with hedge funds, *bella*." Pulling her to him, he wrapped his arms around her. "I'm so sorry you lost the money she gave you, Clio. I'm sorry he deceived you in so many ways."

Clio went into his embrace as if it was the most natural thing in the world to do. And the fact that he had done something nonsexual and intimate without reservation, it blunted the shock of realizing another level to Jackson's deception.

That something her aunt had given her out of love was now lost to her hurt more than the fact that she was basically penniless. Again.

"That's not it. From all the claims he made, and the returns he's been showing in his statements, my investment should have grown by leaps and bounds."

She went back to her bedroom and grabbed the files. He was heading into the kitchen, so she laid them on the table. After a few seconds of rifling through it, he stared at her with icy fury in his eyes.

"These records show your investment had nearly fifty percent returns. But the actuality is that he's lost it all? He's fronting the funds from somewhere else?"

"Looks like it," Clio whispered.

Instantly, she was lifted off the ground in a bear hug. "You did it, *bella*. You found it." Putting her down, he cradled her face in his palms. "That's all we need to expose him, *bella*. Jackson won't recover from this."

"It doesn't feel like an achievement, Stefan. I have a sick feeling in my gut. Everything he did, everything he ever said to me, it was all such a big lie. How can I ever—"

She was more than surprised when he pulled out a dining chair and pulled her onto his lap. His long fingers tracing the angles of her face, he pressed a kiss to her temple. Held her within the cocoon of his embrace. "Shh… It's all his shame, Clio. Not yours."

It was a place Clio never wanted to leave, and the want was so visceral that she shivered.

* * *

Holding Clio in his arms as she trembled, seeing the pain in her beautiful gaze abate as he kissed the lush curve of her mouth, Stefan finally felt at peace after a long time.

Strange since seeing his parents after so long, unburdening his shame and guilt with his father, and making love to Clio, the day should have been an emotional roller coaster.

Yet the facts that Clio had uncovered about Jackson, that he finally had a chance to bring him to justice for all the wrongs he had done to so many people, freed something inside him.

He couldn't find it in him to be angry with Clio anymore for interfering. Instead, he felt grateful.

With her actions, she had only shown him how much power he had given Serena's rejection over his very life. And yet here she was, struggling to find herself again after Jackson had stolen so much from her.

In the face of her strength, Stefan felt some of his own bitterness melt. He lifted her and carried her back to her bedroom, drenched in the realization that a small part of him could trust a woman again.

However their marriage had started, it seemed he had a wife who bore his name with care and honor and duty.

CHAPTER TWELVE

TWO WEEKS LATER, Stefan and Clio arrived in Gazbiyaa, Zayed's desert kingdom, the evening before Zayed's wedding was to take place. The desert palace glittered in the setting sun, breathtakingly beautiful, a haven of luxury amidst the stark landscape of the desert.

Stefan and she had been shown to a suite in the wing of the palace that was away from the festivities of the wedding and provided privacy, just as Rocco and Olivia, and Christian and Alessandra had been.

With Stefan catching up with Rocco and Christian, and feeling a bit fragile to face the other women yet, Clio toured the Gazbiyan palace with a bevy of maids—at least the portions that she was allowed to without infringing on the customs of a kingdom that clung to its traditional roots. A kingdom that Zayed was determined to pull away from the brink of war with its neighboring nation.

Everywhere she looked, there were festivities going on with a pulse of joy beneath them.

The next evening, reunited with Rocco's wife, Olivia—they had bonded over her and Stefan's kissing scandal at Christian's wedding—and Alessandra, who was beginning to show a growing baby bump, she visited Nadia, Zayed's intended.

Even as Stefan and she were taking part in Zayed's extravagant wedding, back home in New York, Jackson was under investigation by the SEC. The guilt she had initially felt had eased as more and more of Jackson's illegal business practices began to come into light.

Driven by greed, he had fleeced so many people.

Under Stefan's expert guidance on all things related to the charity and its finances, she had hit the ground running in terms of her work. When he looked at her now, there was nothing but admiration and respect in his gaze.

She had achieved everything she had set out to do when she had stumbled into his suite at the Chatsfield with her life in tatters.

As much as she had feared ruining their fragile relationship, making love with Stefan was the most natural path they could have taken.

More than a week went by where they lost themselves in learning, exploring each other, where Stefan, as if determined to be the only man in her thoughts, seduced her so thoroughly that Clio felt like a new woman in her own skin, free to embrace her wants and desires.

And the more she let herself go with Stefan, the tighter he bound her to him with his own desires. Sometimes he would wake her up with kisses, make love to her so slowly, with such thorough care that she thought her heart would burst out from his tenderness.

Other times, his desire was touched by a desperate passion that shredded his control, that had once had him taking her against the wall in the lounge, seconds after he had returned from burying Marco.

I needed you so desperately, bella, *that a week has never felt more like a lifetime.*

At those times, she felt like she wouldn't be able to breathe if he stopped.

The different depths to his desire left Clio addicted and just as desperate as him. And terrified that he was slowly, but irrevocably stealing a part of her soul.

Because as demanding and giving as he was when it came to sex, he didn't say a word to her out of that context.

She had begged to go accompany him to Marco's funeral, wanted to share the ache of that moment with him. But he had stubbornly denied her.

It was as if he could communicate with her only through sex.

Now, as she dressed for Zayed's wedding, Clio trembled when the gold silk caftan slid over her skin with a whispered caress, imagining Stefan taking it off her. She remembered the heat of his erotic promises, the addictive strokes of his tongue at her core, the sinuously abrasive texture of his skin, the whipcord strength of his thighs...

It was as if he was spreading through her every cell, every thought until he was a permanent part of her.

Grabbing her hairbrush, Clio ran it through her hair and met her reflection.

He deftly alleviated her concerns and yet didn't give anything of himself that he didn't want to.

The default pattern of their relationship.

As they stood witness to Zayed's own wedding, amidst the noise, extravagant pomp and celebration, amidst the acres of garden and incredible feasts unlike anything she had ever seen, Clio finally pinpointed the root of the growing panic within her.

It was the uncertainty of what tomorrow with Stefan would bring.

And yet, she didn't dare ask him where they were headed or what he wanted. Couldn't bear to hear him say they were done with each other. Not yet.

As usual, every small thing she required, from the elaborate, long-sleeved designer dress to the jewelry that would go with it; from the gold-colored sandals to her bangles; everything had been arranged as it suited to Mrs. Bianco's status.

He would give her everything but would he give her even a little piece of his heart? How long was she willing to let this uncertainty hang over her?

And how had she, *again*, found herself in that very spot where her happiness, her entire sense of self hung precariously on the whims of a man, and one who had ruthlessly warned her that he had nothing to give her?

Stefan pocketed the sheaf of papers that he had collected from the printer in Zayed's office and stepped out into the enormous gardens in front of the majestic Gazbiyan palace.

The most extraordinary stunts were being performed in honor of Zayed's wedding and yet the flutter of excitement in his gut felt stranger than anything he had seen.

For the first time in years, he felt as if he could have a different kind of life, felt as if Clio could fill the void he had been determined to ignore.

Burying Marco who had had such a long and wonderful future ahead had made him think hard about his own life.

He could never love Clio, never be the man who believed in it. But he wanted a future with her. And just the prospect of taking his wife home and making love to her in their bed…it was the best thing he had looked forward to in a long time.

Spotting her, Stefan laced his fingers through hers.

"Boys' club dispatched for the night?" she said with a smile.

He nodded, without bothering to clarify that he hadn't been with Rocco or Christian. Or that he had been cooped up all day in the office that Zayed had lent him, on a phone call with his lawyer. Or that he hadn't slept a wink in over a week deciding what to do.

Pulling her close to his side, he let his hand wander over her hip just as the sky burst into a million colors.

A chorus of laughter and shouts erupted from the crowd.

"You were hard to find after the wedding ceremony, *bella*," he whispered at her ear. "Almost as if you were avoiding me."

Slowly, the tension in her lithe frame dissolved. Reaching a hand up, she pushed a lock of hair away from his forehead. The intimate gesture pierced through Stefan, finding a vulnerable spot.

Her mouth tightened and then relaxed. Slowly, she pulled herself back and looked around. "I just wanted some time to think."

Stefan hooked their arms and tugged her away from the festivities.

When she didn't budge, he turned around.

There was a wariness in her eyes that he didn't like. Knew it was there because of him, because he had kept her at a distance the past couple of weeks.

"I want to stay back for a little while more."

Fighting the first urge to let her be, because there was something in her tone, in the look in her eyes that prickled his skin, he clasped her face. "I told a guard I was looking for a woman with hair the color of fire, and eyes like emeralds and skin like the softest rose. Told him that she was the most poised, the most breathtaking woman dressed in a gold dress that floated with every step she took and that she looked like a queen."

Shaking her head, Clio laughed. "Flattery will get you nowhere with me, Bianco." She was laughing and yet it had a forced quality to it. "And it's Nadia that's the Sheikha among us. I'm the pauper, remember."

"The guard reminded me of that, the part about Nadia at least. But said he could also understand why I would come to that erroneous conclusion. And then pointed me toward you."

As they reached one of the tents that were erected away from the celebration, she dug her heels in.

"Come on, *bella*. I want to show you something." He sounded eager, like a schoolboy, yet he couldn't control it.

It had been so long since he had looked forward to anything so much, so long since he had wanted something in life beyond another business deal.

"I have already seen it, Bianco. And as much as I agree that it's spectacular, I don't think a tent amidst a crowd of festive and raucous Gazbiyans is the place or the time to get it on."

Laughter poured out of him, shaking his chest, loosening every muscle. When she argued further, he lifted her and brought her into the tent.

When Stefan finally put her down, Clio looked around the soaring, tented structure with her eyes wide.

The interior walls were decorated with lush Persian rugs and priceless silks. Low-slung divans with a number of pillows in vibrant colors with golden tassels sat on three sides. On the fourth was a four-poster bed with a sheer veil resting around it.

An image of Stefan and her on the bed instantly flashed in front of her eyes, an insistent pull of desire between her legs. And yet something in her also recoiled at it.

She had laughed about it outside, but inside she was trembling with anger and a powerlessness that she loathed.

Only realizing how silent he was being, she turned around and found Stefan's gaze on her. The molten desire instantly heated her skin.

When he pulled her into his arms, excitement flared, her body automatically craving more. When he buried his mouth in the crook at her neck, at the spot that drove her crazy, snuggled into her behind so tightly that his arousal pressed into her, branding her, she pushed back into his touch, needing more.

Yet, another warring emotion emerged, polluting the want. God, she had tried so hard to not ask anything of him. To hold herself aloof, to not define their relationship in any way.

Self-disgust roiled through her and she pushed away from his touch.

His head recoiled, hurt flashing in his gaze. "Clio, is something wrong?"

"No. Yes. I hate what you're doing to me. *I hate what I'm letting you do.* I hate that I can't say no when you touch me."

His mouth tight, he rolled his shoulders. "You're doing just fine now, *bella.*"

"I can't become that shadow of myself again, Stefan. You either want this thing between us, or you don't."

"That's all I have been thinking about these past weeks, Clio."

A sheaf of papers materialized in his hand, and Clio's heart sank to her gut.

It was a contract, she knew without looking at it. Another piece of paper that would define her exit from his life.

And just the thought of walking out of his life, the thought of not sharing that suite with him, the thought of not laughing with him and not loving him again sent her into a spiral of pain so acute that she shivered all over.

Oh, God, how she had fallen in love? Where was this unbearable avalanche of emotion coming from?

How was it even possible that she still possessed this much capacity to feel? What did it say about her that after everything she had been through with Jackson, she had so easily surrendered her heart to a man even more ruthless?

How was she to survive now?

She sank to one of the divans, her legs refusing to hold her up, a hollow emerging in her chest.

When Stefan joined her on the divan, she flinched. "Just spell it out for me, Stefan," she managed somehow.

"Look at me, *bella.*"

"No." She clutched her eyes closed, desperate to keep herself together. From the beginning, he had seen her at her lowest, her weakest. Now, she couldn't bear to betray herself, couldn't bear to have him look at her with pity.

Couldn't bear for him to know how irrevocably lost her heart was.

When his fingers landed on her chin, she swatted him away. "Tell me where you want me to sign, Stefan."

But he didn't let her leave. Locking her arms, he knelt on the rug before her. "Look at me, Clio. It's not what you think."

Shock pinging across every inch of her, Clio looked down at him. His face was so gorgeous that it hurt to look at him. His gaze touched her with such naked, honest desire that her heart ached.

It hurt to look at him, to touch him, to feel his heart and to know that he would never be hers.

"What do you mean?"

"I want us to start fresh, *bella*. I want to try this marriage for real."

Her heart thudded so fast that it was a wonder she didn't have a heart attack. Throat aching, she forced the words to form. "What's the catch? What are those documents?" she said, so terrified of the answer, and yet so hopeful that he would say there wasn't one.

That all he needed was her acceptance.

That all they needed was time with each other.

Her hope would cripple her if not kill her.

And Stefan crushed it under his Italian loafer when he said, "You get five hundred million dollars when you sign it."

"Five hundred million dollars? I don't understand."

"No matter what happens in the future, I want you to have security. I want you to—"

"So you don't expect us to last, then?"

"Nothing in life has guarantees, *bella*."

Nausea bubbling up her throat, Clio searched his face, wondering if he was joking. Praying that it was a nightmare she would wake up from. Hoping it was one of her migraines playing a trick on her.

Because this couldn't be happening, could it? Another

man wasn't measuring her worth, equating her love with money, was he?

"I don't get it, Stefan. You're paying me so that you can buy the trust you apparently can't show in me? Like all the celebrity couples who first draw prenups to protect their assets from each other?"

"You do not have any assets."

"Exactly. So are you protecting yourself?"

He cursed so long and loud that Clio had goose bumps on her skin. "You're completely misunderstanding this. I tore up the old contract. I hate how Jackson cheated you. I want you to never have to worry about…"

"Really? After a decade of knowing me, you think all I want is a free ride through life?"

"No. This is something I want you to have, something for my own peace of mind."

Clio shook her head, understanding dawning. She shot up from the divan, furious energy burning through her, looking for an outlet, even as a deluge of pain broke her within.

It was so easy to think it was her fault, so easy to think he was doing this because she didn't have any money, to think it was because he lacked trust in her motives, in her.

It wasn't.

It wasn't about her at all.

Stefan knew her better than any other person in the entire world. But the freeing thought only gave way to another gut-wrenching truth.

"Five hundred million dollars—is that my price tag, Bianco?" she said gasping for breath. "Because I'm sure if you have a chat with your buddy Jackson, he will tell you that I should come in a lot cheaper."

The most unholy fury dawned in his gaze. He grabbed her arms in a viselike grip, a vein throbbing in his temple. "Don't you dare talk as if Jackson and I are the same kind of man, *bella*. Don't you dare cheapen yourself."

"So the man does bleed," Clio threw at him, agonizing fury coming to her rescue.

"Stop twisting my words."

She grabbed the contract and threw it on the ground, tears falling over her cheeks. "God, you still don't get it, do you, Stefan?

"This is the price for everything we share, Stefan. This is the price for our happiness, our life together that you're talking about. You're buying me, my affection, tainting every word I would say to you, attaching a price tag to even the sex we have."

"Enough, Clio! You're reading this all wrong."

Shaking her head, she ran a hand over her cheeks. "The sad part is you don't even realize it. You're giving me money because that way anything I offer you, you already have a reason for it. Because you don't have to accept anything I give you."

"No, *bella*." His olive green gaze turned hard, untouched. "You told me you didn't want anything from me. And I told you I don't want anything from you."

"All I wanted was one sentence that you wanted this to be real between us, that you wanted to at least try. That you want to see where we could go from here."

"It is what I want, too."

"With a caveat, yes. The awful thing is I'm so anxious in here—" she rubbed her chest, as if she could relieve the tightness there "—so tempted to just sign the damn papers, to accept the little crumbs you will throw me. So in...so in love with you that I'm prepared to just take whatever little you give me. How pathetic is that?"

Stepping back from her, he looked as though she had struck him again. As though he couldn't bear to hear the weight of her confession.

As though he never wanted to set eyes on her.

As though she had stuck a knife in his back while smiling to his face.

And it was the haunted expression in his gaze, the horrified look that sealed her fate for Clio, that ripped her last thread of hope into pieces.

He would never accept her love. He would never give her his trust.

"You're not in love with me. You're deluding yourself like every other woman that has come into my bed before you. I warned you about that, *bella*."

The nasty barb landed where he intended, lacerating her, carving a nice little slice in her breastbone.

That he would throw his own past in her face, that he would dirty him and her and what they shared, only showed how much her declaration rattled him, how deeply buried his heart was.

She wished she could be furious with him, she wished she could hate him for it.

But all she felt was a keening gnawing that ate through her gut.

"I didn't think I would ever feel like this again, that I would ever want to place my happiness in another man's hands. But it's not my fault. Even with the block of ice you have for a heart, even with the poison you have held on to all these years, you're kind and funny and you're the most honorable man I've ever met."

He recoiled as though she had struck him again. "That is proof enough that you're still lost, Clio." He sounded so far away.

"No. Finally I know myself, Stefan."

"How can you forget the pain Jackson caused you? How do you even know what you…what you claim is real?"

"By putting a value on you and me, our happiness together, you have showed me how priceless I am, how all consuming and incredible my love for you is. And how little it will always mean to you, how we could do this—" she moved her hands between them "—for the next decade and you will still never give me what I want, what I deserve.

"You're my knight, Bianco, once again saving me from my own desperation. You're the best friend a girl could ask for, the best lover for a woman with tattered self-esteem. But to spend a lifetime with you...it will destroy me."

His gaze darkened, inch by inch of his face hardening as if he was willingly shutting himself down.

"Don't do this, Clio," he said, grabbing her. His mouth branded her in a fiery kiss that almost broke her resolve. Her knees melted and she clung to him as he seduced her with tenderness and passion. "We can have a good life together."

Clasping his cheeks, she pushed him back, stared at the storm gathering in his gaze. He wasn't untouched by this. But it wasn't enough. Nowhere near enough.

She was greedy, she wanted all of him.

"No."

"Stay, *bella*." Even now, he only commanded with that hard look in his eyes, even now, he held his heart locked away from her.

Even now, he scowled at her because she had dared to fall in love with him.

Smiling through the tears in her eyes, Clio shook her head. "I would have, a few hours ago. I would have danced with joy, thrown myself at you. But I can't now. I don't want your money, and I don't want the little you offer of yourself. Have a nice life, Stefan. And thank you for teaching me my own worth."

Without looking back, Clio stepped out of the tent and into the open grounds.

A thousand sounds and scents greeted her, but nothing could touch her past the audacious hope ringing through her that he would chase after her, that he would kiss her and hold her and tell her that everything would be fine. Tell her that he had made a colossal mistake and that he wanted her in his life.

That he wanted to be loved by her.

But he didn't.

And the emptiness around her only made her realize what she wanted that much harder.

She wanted the Stefan who had admitted to having a wild, reckless thing for her.

She wanted the Stefan who admired her and respected her.

She wanted the Stefan who had been one of the warmest, most openhearted men she had ever met.

She wanted to lose herself in his arms and be the woman he lost his control over.

She wanted to be the woman that made him smile, laugh and she wanted to do it for years to come.

She wanted them to be friends, lovers and so much more. She wanted the contract ripped and burned, she wanted his millions and her penury to never come into the equation between them, in any form.

She wanted it to be just her and him and their love for each other.

Clio wanted all of him, every breath and every cell, every thought and every sigh, every kiss and every touch.

And the want was so deep, so raw that it was a physical ache in her gut. That want was so desperate that she shook all over, waves of pain splintering inside her.

But this time, she would not settle. She would not let a man, even the one who she loved with every breath, define what she was worthy of.

Because she deserved all of him.

Stefan sank to the divan, reeling under Clio's angry accusations, reeling under the weight of her confession.

So in love with you...

Those words pierced him even as he recoiled at the fury that had been shining in her glittering gaze, even as he couldn't believe the truth of it.

How could she love him? How could he begin to believe

her when there was nothing to love, when he had given her nothing but pain?

How could she ruin everything by bringing that word between them?

He had no use for her love. He had nothing to give her back. And the one thing that he had wanted to give, the one gesture he had made because he cared about her, she had thrown in his face.

How could she let her claim destroy what they had?

He wanted to call it a dent to her pride, a tantrum she was throwing because he had hurt her with offering her money.

But Clio never threw tantrums and Clio didn't have any fascination with his wealth.

Clio didn't drop hints for gifts, Clio didn't ask to be introduced to his powerful friends. Clio didn't flirt with other men to make him jealous.

Clio didn't dangle sex as a bargaining chip.

In only a few weeks, Clio had made him laugh more than he had in a decade. He had lived more and for the first time in years, he had made love to a woman instead of seeking physical release.

Clio was the farthest from what Serena had been.

Clio was Clio—generous, kind and vibrant. Clio was the first woman, other than his own mother, who cared about his happiness, who cared that he smiled.

Clio had walked through the fire of his distrust and Jackson's treachery and emerged whole.

And he… *Dio*, he had treated her worse than he had treated any other woman in his life from the moment she had set foot in it. Had punished her for his own demons, put her through so much because of his own insecurities.

Because somehow, through her struggle with Jackson, through her struggles with herself, through her determination to remind him of what he had been once, Clio had become a mirror in which he saw what he had become.

The picture he saw of himself over the past few weeks, he despised it.

But it was too late.

He buried his head in hands and growled, a chasm of pain opening up in his gut. The tent reverberated with her words, her pain, with the rawness and purity of her emotions. With the darkness of his own poison, with his loneliness, with his utter desolation.

He had done just as Zayed as predicted. He had ruined the most wonderful thing that had come into his life, shattered any chance of happiness with his own hands.

All I wanted was one sentence that you wanted this to be real between us.

But he hadn't been able to ask that small thing. He hadn't been able to give her even a small part of him. He hadn't been able to take the warmth and generosity and the wonder that was Clio.

He still couldn't. He couldn't take that step and open himself to pain and agony again.

Wasn't that why he had offered her that settlement instead, even if he had realized it too late?

Even after all these years, even as he had found the perfect woman, the woman he had dreamed about his entire teenage years, the woman whom he would have loved for the rest of his life, he still couldn't take that final step, couldn't find the courage to be the man who laid out his heart.

CHAPTER THIRTEEN

ALMOST TWO MONTHS LATER, Stefan was in the midst of a meeting in his Hong Kong office when his laptop pinged. Still listening to his main accountant drone on and on about their Asian holdings, he looked at the screen and stilled.

The email was from Zayed's wife, the Sheikha of Gazbiyaa. Wondering what it was that Nadia, the deceptively strong woman his friend had married, would send him, Stefan clicked on it.

His heart pounding so hard in his chest as he viewed the thumbnail, he clicked the attachment open.

It was a shot of him and Clio the morning of Zayed's wedding that someone must have clicked unknown to them.

They were standing at one of the turreted balconies in the Gazbiyan palace, the morning sun behind them. He remembered the moment instantly.

Rocco and Olivia, Christian and Alessandra, he and Clio, and Zayed had just finished breakfast. Clio had wandered to the balcony, and as if pulled forward like a string, he had instantly joined her there.

Had covered her bare arms with his and shuddered as the scent and warmth of her had stolen into him. Had pushed the thick fall of her hair away so that he could see the delicate crook of her neck. Had loved tracing her slender hips with his hands, had loved how naturally she had fit against him.

An instant surge of yawningly desperate need claimed him and he closed his eyes.

Dio, how she would respond when he pressed his mouth at that crook…how her long fingers would rake over his skin, marking him, owning him as he pushed into her, how boldly she had looked at him that last time, binding him to her… Drenched in the memories of her, which were at the same time so vivid and yet so distant, Stefan almost reached out for her.

She hadn't flinched or pulled back that morning. Burrowing into his body, she had looked up at him and smiled.

He opened his eyes and stared greedily at the shot again.

And the shot had captured that smile.

There had been no hesitation, no artifice, no shadows in it. Everything she felt for him—it was in that smile.

It spoke of love, courage and the thing that stuck in his chest like an ice pick, open joy. It said so much about their intimacy, about how gloriously perfect that moment had been in his life.

Life with Clio would be full of such indescribable moments—of love and happiness.

In that stunning moment between powerlessness and need, it struck him how much he loved her. How he would do anything if it ensured she would always smile like that.

It was like a lightning bolt, washing away the poison that had festered in him for so long, opening the hurt inside him like an avalanche.

And that smile, that love that shone so beautifully in her eyes, that was what he had gambled away.

The voices around him sounded as if they were coming from far off. The view from the fortieth floor faded as he struggled to breathe past the tightness in his chest.

The ache in his heart, the fear in his gut, was so visceral that he rose to his feet jerkily. That moment brought all the yawning emptiness he'd felt over the past couple of months to the fore.

She had banished him from her life with such ruthless will that even he was impressed. In two months, he had

had only heard from her once—one paltry email that had stripped him of even hope.

Do not come back to New York, please. This is my home. If you ever valued me for even a minute, leave this city for me. Leave me be, Stefan.

And so he had. Against his very nature, he had left her to face the media. Left their marriage in a limbo.

Because his business empire was spread out all over the world, it had been easy to stay away.

He didn't know if she wanted a divorce. He didn't care.

He had snarled at Christian when the latter had visited him in Hong Kong, told Zayed to leave him the hell alone and had thrown himself into work. Nothing could fill the increasing chasm of his lonely days blending into endless nights, nothing could touch him past the morass of his guilt and grief and emptiness.

He had spent fifty-six days in a hell of his own making, dying to hear her voice, craving her smile, wondering if he would ever kiss her mouth again, listening to little tidbits about her from Olivia, who, he had a feeling, would love to see if he would bleed.

She was flourishing in her new position at the charity.

She had been called in connection to the SEC's case against Jackson.

She was looking good.

Every day, he broke a little more inside until there was nothing. But he couldn't be this coward anymore, he couldn't bear another day without seeing her, without holding her in his arms.

How lost had he been to slap a price on his heart?

She had been right about everything.

He had given her everything except himself.

And the woman she had grown into these past couple of months, she would settle for nothing less than all of him.

He must have said something because suddenly the conference room was empty around him.

Picking up his cell, he made a call, his heart in his throat.

His voice muddled in sleep, Rocco answered. "Stefan?"

"Where is she, Rocco?" he said without preamble

His oldest friend understood immediately. "In New York."

"I know that. But not where. I know that Olivia knows. I know that Clio went to her. I need to see her, Rocco. *Now*."

After what seemed like an eternity, Rocco sighed. "I'm sorry, Stefan. Believe it or not, my stubborn wife hasn't told even me where Clio is."

"She is your damn wife, why the hell not?"

"Because she takes standing by her friends seriously. If you want to know where Clio is, you have to ask Liv. Stefan… take care, *fratello*."

Stefan barely heard Rocco's warning. In two minutes he instructed his pilot to fuel the jet, ordered his secretary to cancel everything indefinitely.

Nothing in his life had any meaning without her.

He needed his wife, his friend, his lover back. He needed the woman who had made him live again, smile again, made him feel so much again that he couldn't breathe for the ache of it. And he would beg if that's what it took to bring her back into his life.

As Clio stared at Stefan, standing at Olivia's friend's doorstep, his face haggard and covered in stubble, his thick hair rumpled, his collar askew, her entire world tilted and shook. Her gut folded on itself, her breath balling up in her throat.

She pulled the edges of the threadbare cardigan together defensively as his perusal, hungry and invasive, continued.

Without a word, he entered the flat and closed the door

with an arrogant kick of his handmade Italian shoe. Wandered soundlessly through the small flat.

Every inch of her stilled in panic as he picked up the cardboard box she had discarded carelessly on one of the sofas.

Anger flashed in his green gaze and then cycled to fury and then to utter powerlessness. He turned the box around and around with those long fingers.

Her breath quivered in her throat noisily as she stared at the expression she thought she never would see. The box was crushed in his hand, his knuckles showing white.

"When did you take the test?" he finally said, something so desperately painful in his tone that she just stared at him.

"Clio?"

Recovering, she fought the urge to go to him. "Yesterday morning."

Another silence ensued, stretching her nerves so tight that a breath of wind could tear them apart.

"Yesterday morning…"

A quiet sound fell from his lips, shock marring his features. "And?"

The tiny room reverberated with the sound of his question, all the more unnerving for the whispered entreaty that it was.

Clio swallowed and instinctively wrapped her arms around her still-flat tummy. She had expected him to give her a display of that fierce Sicilian temper. This silently obvious conflict rattled her on so many levels. "It was positive. I made an appointment to see a doctor in two days to have it confirmed, but I…I'm pregnant."

"And you didn't think to tell me?" came the instant retort. He pushed his fingers through his hair, paced the small room. Let out a string of angry curses. Came to a standstill within touching distance, his features wreathed in torturous agony. "*Dio*, Clio… Would you have hid this from me if I hadn't come today? Would you have…"

Hands tucked in the pockets of his trousers, he turned away from her abruptly. As if he couldn't bear the sight of her. The tension in his vibrating frame sent her into a panic.

She knew that final thread of his control had unraveled, the last piece of his armor was broken. Knew that he was hurting and that he would attack at any moment. Knew what families and children and the bonds of kin would mean to his Sicilian blood.

Knew that his vulnerability, beneath the hard shell he had acquired all these years, lay in the depth and intensity with which he had once wanted love and family and laughter in his life.

Knew that he was made for it, that he would make a fantastic father. Knew that she was weakening already after facing the truth about the pregnancy, and seeing him so close by, remembering how good it had felt to give herself over to him…

He was the man she adored with every breath in her. He was the man who showed her to be strong, who showed her what she was made of.

He would fight for custody, she knew. He would do what he deemed to be right by their child. He would tie her up in clauses and contracts, he would use the fact that she hadn't instantly told him to tie her to him.

To achieve what he had wanted two months ago.

Even as every inch of her thrummed with pain, even as every inch of her recoiled at subjecting her coming child to separate parents living across the globe, Clio made her decision as the woman he had helped her become.

It was better her child had two parents who loved him, rather than a mother who would forever be in agony, living with the man who would never love her back, a mother who would so easily become a shadow of herself.

She straightened her spine and faced him. Waited for the hardest battle of her life to commence. "No. I wouldn't have hid it from you. But I…" she swallowed the tears in her throat, "I would have given myself a few weeks to prepare first."

"Prepare for what?" Stefan threw back at Clio, finding it unbearable to meet her eyes. How deep and sharp her words cut, how easily she had turned him into this mass of ache and love…

Her denial didn't bring him even infinitesimal relief. His gut still ached, his breath rushed out of him unevenly.

She would have taken a few weeks to prepare herself… that he had driven her to this, it traveled through him like a missile launched specifically to torture him.

He turned, not sure what he would say, and stilled.

With her palm splayed against her stomach, her green eyes shining with tenderness and determination, she faced him. The wide curve of her mouth trembled. It was the most beautiful sight he had ever seen and it only brought home again how much he loved this woman. How fortunate that she would mother his child…

"Please answer me, Clio. Preparing for what?" he asked again, fisting his hands at his sides, stifling the urge to take her in his arms.

She shrugged, but the casualness she was going for didn't come through. There was a wariness in her eyes that he decided he would never be the cause of again.

"I knew that if I had told you immediately, you would come armed to the teeth with clauses and contracts. That you would want this child and me and the whole family thing. That you would seduce your way into my life and convince me this was for the best. As sad as it sounds, I need to shore up my defenses against you."

"You think I will bind you to me in the name of our child? You think me that heartless, Clio?"

Tears ran over her cheeks and she swayed. Cursing himself over and over, Stefan caught her.

"What am I supposed to think, Stefan? Two months have gone by and you didn't call me once. Two months in which I wondered if I would ever see you again. Two months in which every minute felt like an eternity. Two months in which I battled the urge to come to you, to beg you to take me back any way you wanted."

He grabbed her hands, willing her to understand him. "I hurt you so much that day. I couldn't face myself in the mirror thinking of what I had ruined. The minute you had walked out, I realized what I had done, how wrong I was.

"I have been cursing myself, wondering if I could ever take back what I had done. I was terrified that I would hurt you even more after everything you have been through, Clio. I'm terrified that I might never be worthy of you, *bella*."

He knelt in front of her, wrapped his arms around her. Bent his head, burrowed into her warmth, the love he felt for her unmanning him.

And even as he trembled at the thought that he might have lost her, he could feel the rightness of this, feel everything in him slide into place. Striving for control that was out of his reach, he pulled her fingers in his hand and kissed her.

"Stefan?" she whispered. There was so much pain and hope in it that he ached.

He raised his head and met her beautiful gaze, poured the emotions flowing through him into words. "I'm desperately in love with you. With every breath in my body. With every cell in my being. I come to you today with nothing but my heart in my hands, Clio.

"All I want is to be part of your life, a chance to show you how much I adore you. Every moment of my life, every decision I have ever taken, it…it has made me into this. But it also brought me to you, *bella*.

"The bastard that I am today, I'm still all yours to do with, Clio."

Sinking to her knees, she clutched him. "Oh, Stefan…"

And just when Stefan thought he couldn't fragment anymore, that he could feel no more, the sound of her pain pierced him again.

Wrapping his arms around her gingerly, he pulled her onto his lap. Buried his face in her hair and breathed in a lungful of her scent. Pushed himself to be the man that was worthy of the generous, brave woman that his beautiful wife was.

"Please, Clio. Do not cry, *cara*. I will not challenge you over our child. I will walk out, I will sign any paper you want me to sign. All I want is your happiness, even if it will kill me to be away from you."

Meeting his gaze, she rested her forehead against his. "You really want me? Me and not just the mother of your child?"

Hating that she doubted him, hating that he had given her cause to, he hugged her to him.

"I came today because I couldn't bear to be apart from you anymore, Clio. I couldn't breathe for the thought of never seeing you smile again." His hand moved over her stomach, and his breath caught in his throat. "That you… that you carry a part of me inside you…it's more than I wished for in my wildest dreams, *bella*. Will you truly be my wife, Clio? Will you help me be the man you deserve again?"

"You're already everything I could have ever hoped for, Stefan. You know me better than anyone else in the world. And you take care of me, you enable me, you…you love me more than anyone else ever has, even as you shred me to pieces. Loving you—" tears pooled in her eyes and overflowed "—somehow, it has only made me stronger."

His heart thudded fast in his chest, the back of his eyes prickling with warmth. "I love you so much, *bella*...I have missed you so much...it felt like a part of me was forever gone. Promise you will never walk away from me, Clio. Even if I make a mistake, promise me you will fight for me."

Shaking her head, she covered his mouth with her hand. Sank her hands into his hair and tugged him up. Pressed her mouth to his and kissed him so hard and for so long that he came undone.

"All I want is my friend, my lover, my husband back, Stefan. All I want is the man who made me the best I could be. And if we make a mistake, we'll rail and rage at other, but we will always find our way to each other again."

Reaching for her mouth, Stefan breathed in her scent, clutched her to him. With Clio by his side, there would be nothing but happiness and joy in the coming days.

Combing his fingers through her hair, he kissed her forehead, a smile curving his mouth. "I want a little girl with hair the color of fire."

Turning around, Clio tucked her face under his chin, her arms tightly vined around his midriff. "Do you think we will be good parents?"

The thread of anxiety in her tone, that she would show him her fears, made his chest fill up. "We will be the best parents in the world, *bella*. If we do make any mistakes, he or she will have grandparents and a host of aunts and uncles to complain to," he said, thinking of Rocco and Christian and Zayed and the wonderful women they had married.

His heart seemed as if it was bursting to the full. Their friends would be over the moon for him, would find so much happiness in his.

"New York or Sicily?" he said, his hands roving restlessly over her lithe curves. With a moan that curled around his senses, she pushed herself into his touch.

Found his mouth with hers and demanded everything. Nipped his lower lip with her teeth until he was rock-hard under her. Splaying her legs wide around him, she rubbed herself over his erection, and let out another long moan.

"New York and Sicily, with regular stops at Milan, Athens and Gazbiyaa," she breathed, her fingers busy over his belt buckle.

The moment her fingers danced over his rigid shift, Stefan pushed her down to the carpet and covered her with his body.

This time, they both groaned, and joy filled his heart. "That should work, *bella*," he finished and kissed his wife's luscious mouth.

* * * * *

Look out for the next installment of
SOCIETY WEDDINGS:
THE SHEIKH'S WEDDING CONTRACT
by Andie Brock
Coming next month!

Read on for a SOCIETY WEDDINGS *exclusive!*

DELETED SCENE

"WHERE IS SHE, OLIVIA?"

Olivia Mondelli stared with increasing shock at the man standing on the doorstep of her Manhattan apartment, his face wearing the most unexpected expression she had ever seen.

Stefan Bianco...

That expression was a combination of fear and something she thought she would never see on one of the hardest men she had ever met.

Oh, she had seen the best of them during her career as one of the top models in New York. Playboys, charmers and models alike, but no one quite like Stefan.

The hard shell that the man had beneath that sophisticated arrogance, it was bone deep.

And yet, Liv had seen that shell rattle over the past few months as Clio had come back into his life.

Had watched in fascination as the fiercely protective side of him emerged as, to even Rocco's shock, Stefan had married Clio in a wedding that was nothing short of a fairy tale. Had seen Clio change from the pale shadow she had been at Christian's wedding into one of the strongest women Liv had ever seen.

Even more of a shocker was the genuinely contented laughter she had seen in Stefan's eyes at Zayed's wedding.

She had even held her breath for them as she had seen the obvious truth of how deeply Clio had fallen for him.

She had bet Rocco that they would make it, had believed that if anyone could shatter the hard shell that Stefan carried around, it had to be Clio.

Clio, who had become as close to her as the sister she had never had.

But, of course, Rocco had known his friend better, and had waited on tenterhooks almost for the crash that had eventually come at Zayed's wedding.

Only a few hours after the wedding, Clio had come to her, pale and trembling and yet somehow, stronger than she had ever seen before, begging to leave Gazbiyaa with Liv and Rocco, and return to New York.

That was almost two months ago.

Two months in which Clio had stayed in New York and Stefan, to Olivia's shock, had disappeared. She had seen him a couple of times traveling with Rocco and both times, he had been hungry, almost desperate for information about Clio.

Yet, he hadn't inquired once after Clio.

Today, Rocco, who was in Milan, had called her exactly two hours ago, warning her that Stefan was coming back to New York.

And here he was, glaring at her, as if it was his God-given right.

Olivia would have despised his arrogance and his irrational dislike of her when they had first met if she hadn't seen firsthand how fiercely devoted he was to Rocco and Christian and Zayed.

"Hello to you, too, Stefan," she said cheerily, opening the door wider. "It's a gorgeous New York morning, isn't it?"

He didn't even blink at her saccharine tone. Prowled inside casually with his long-limbed stride and yet, Liv could sense something restless in his calm movements, something strange.

For the first time in two months, Liv felt a flutter of hope for Clio.

"I want to see Clio, Olivia. Where is she?"

The smile disappeared from her face, an image of Clio with tears in her eyes flashing in front of her eyes.

"Does Clio know you're here, Stefan?"

The facade of politeness crumbled from his face and Olivia caught her gasp from escaping.

Vulnerability and Stefan Bianco weren't words she would have thought of in the same sentence even.

"How the hell does it matter if she knows or not, Liv?"

"Because I remember her telling me that she didn't want to see you, Stefan."

"Damn it, Liv, she's my wife, and I would like to see her. When the hell did you become her gatekeeper?"

"When I saw how broken she was after Zayed's wedding. That's when. I let down a friend once and I won't let anything to happen to her. Even though you don't realize it, Clio is—"

"*Dio*, Olivia. Clio is precious, don't you think I know that?" While Olivia stared stunned, he ran a hand over his eyes. And Liv saw past her own prejudice and noticed how tired he looked. He cleared his throat as though choosing his words carefully. "I'm so glad that you're looking out for her. But I need to see her. I need to…"

"You need to what, Stefan?"

A glimmer of a smile curved his mouth, transforming his entire face. "This wouldn't be revenge, would it, Liv? For my doubting you when you and Rocco were beginning? Because, really, you couldn't have chosen a better way to torture me."

Such warmth radiated from his green gaze that Liv felt her heart contract. This was the best friend her husband cherished so much. Finally, she saw why Rocco worried so much for Stefan, especially after Rocco and she had found each other.

This was what he and Stefan and Christian and Zayed did for each other.

Swallowing the lump in her throat, Liv smiled at him. "No. As enticing as it sounds, this is not revenge, Stefan. Clio is my friend now."

Liv met his gaze and waited. And his confession, when it came, was so hoarse and uneven.

"I love her, Olivia. I…I have insulted her, and bullied her and I…hurt her. I can't…I can't live without seeing her smile…but I have nothing to offer her."

Olivia had goose bumps on her skin, tears in her eyes. "Remember what you told me that day, Stefan?" Grabbing his hand, Liv squeezed it, dying to call Rocco and tell him.

"Those three words…that's all it takes, Stefan."

STOP THE PRESS
NEWS ARTICLE

Stefan Bianco and Clio Norwood—A Fairy Tale Too Good to Believe or a True Love Story?

In a shocking move that has left New York's finance society dropping their jaws, luxury real estate mogul Stefan Bianco, one of New York's very own illustrious Columbia Four, the man who has been dubbed One-Date Wonder by more than one scorned lover in the past, really tied the knot with Clio Norwood, the society hostess who turned her back on her illustrious family a decade ago.

The old college friends from Columbia made it official at the prestigious Chatsfield, surrounded by their close friends and the glitterati from New York's high society.

The redheaded bride shone in a designer tulle and diamonds while the groom, who had stolen her from under the nose of financier Jackson Smith, looked splendid in a black-and-white tuxedo.

"After knowing each other for more than a decade, it's so obvious that they have always belonged with each other," a friend close to the gorgeous couple shared.

Well, here's hoping that Mrs. Bianco can hold on to her title *and* the man this time.